A one-time legal secretary [...] charitable foundation, **Sus**[...] bliss when she became a f[...] Mills & Boon. She's visited ski lodges and candy factories for 'research', and works in her pyjamas. But the real joy of her job is creating stories about women for women. With over eighty published novels, she's tackled issues like infertility, losing a child and becoming widowed, and worked through them with her characters.

Kate Hardy has been a bookworm since she was a toddler. When she isn't writing Kate enjoys reading, theatre, live music, ballet and the gym. She lives with her husband, student children and their spaniel in Norwich, England. You can contact her via her website: katehardy.com.

FLING WITH
THE RECLUSIVE
BILLIONAIRE

SUSAN MEIER

WEDDING DEAL
WITH HER RIVAL

KATE HARDY

MILLS & BOON

First published in Great Britain 2023
by Mills & Boon, an imprint of HarperCollins*Publishers* Ltd,
1 London Bridge Street, London, SE1 9GF

www.harpercollins.co.uk

HarperCollins*Publishers*, Macken House, 39/40 Mayor Street Upper, Dublin 1, D01 C9W8, Ireland

ISBN: 978-0-263-30658-3

12/23

This book is produced from independently certified FSC™ paper to ensure responsible forest management.
For more information visit: www.harpercollins.co.uk/green.

Printed and Bound in the UK using 100% Renewable Electricity at CPI Group (UK) Ltd, Croydon, CR0 4YY

FLING WITH THE RECLUSIVE BILLIONAIRE

SUSAN MEIER

MILLS & BOON

CHAPTER ONE

LOLA EVANS SAT on the bench seat at the back of a neat-as-a-pin sea cruiser while an employee of tech billionaire Grant Laningham steered the sleek boat. The mist from the wake would have ruined her thick dark hair, except she'd prepared for every kind of weather imaginable with her raincoat, umbrella, and hair in a ponytail. She hadn't needed the raincoat or umbrella, both were hooked over her arm. But her mom had always told her to prepare for every contingency, so she did.

The cruiser slowed. The captain expertly eased it to the dock and secured it. She rose and gave her head a shake, shifting her damp ponytail back and forth. With the heat of the South Carolina sun in June, even her thick hair would be dry in ten minutes.

Standing on the dock, the captain offered his hand to help her out of the boat. She took it with a smile. "Thank you."

Before she could add, "And thank you for coming to get me," Grant Laningham strode up the gray boards of the weather-beaten dock, a yellow Lab on his heels. Tall and lean, with piercing black eyes and dark hair covered by a white Laningham Lions baseball cap, he said simply, "Lola?"

"Yes." She extended her hand to shake his. The power of his presence nearly overwhelmed her. His face was perfect. Symmetrical angles and planes and full lips. His oversize

T-shirt couldn't hide broad shoulders and thick biceps. His hips were trim, his legs long.

He was tall, gorgeous and a genius.

With his yellow Lab sitting quietly at his side, Grant shook her hand. "It's a pleasure to meet you."

Though the urge to swoon or gush was strong, she kept her composure. She wasn't here for fun. She'd been hired to ghostwrite his autobiography.

Four years ago, Grant had been ousted from the board of directors of the company he'd founded, his wife had divorced him, and he had almost died after being hit by a car. All in the space of two weeks. He hadn't been interviewed by anyone since then. Actually, he hadn't been seen off this island since he moved here to recover and do physical therapy.

Now that he was ready to return to work, a former employee had penned an unauthorized biography that portrayed him as a narcissistic workaholic who fired people at will, ruining careers. The tentative title was *Laningham the Destroyer*. The book was in the final stages, to be released in six months.

Giovanni Salvaggio, Grant's publicist, had decided the best way to combat it would be to release an *autobiography* first. The hope was people would want to hear Grant's story from Grant, and that even after the unauthorized biography came out, Grant's story would carry more weight.

But all that meant they had approximately six weeks to get a draft to his publisher.

No time for gushing or being a fan. They had to get to work.

"It's a pleasure to meet you, too."

Despite her best efforts to be objective, a swarm of butterflies took flight in her stomach. He was just so damned good-looking. Even better looking in person than in pictures.

But he was a perfectionist genius with a hot temper. Which

was why his board ousted him. When his development team couldn't fix a glitch, he'd fired someone every day for a month. Every day every employee went to work not knowing if they'd have a job at the end of the day.

In an interview a week later, he'd unrepentantly told a reporter he'd done it to keep everyone on their toes—to motivate them. That had been the straw that broke the camel's back for his board, and he'd been fired himself.

Gorgeous or not, he was not someone a smart woman got involved with. Especially not a woman who desperately needed this job.

She glanced around. Thick trees, some pine, some leafy deciduous, hid most of the private island. "Your home is amazing."

"Yes. It is. You can see why I chose to recover here after my accident."

She definitely could.

She brought her gaze back to his striking eyes. Once again, the power of his personality hit her like a sucker punch. That magnetic energy had bulldozed him through a lot of his life. She couldn't imagine him unable to walk, unable to work, virtually alone on an island he'd bought so no one would see him weak or suffering.

Grant motioned toward the path beyond the dock. "After you."

As she turned, the captain jumped on the boat and grabbed her luggage. Rather than give the bags to Lola, he carried them past her and Grant, heading toward a black wrought-iron fence. He didn't say goodbye. She didn't get a chance to thank him. Once he was through the gate, he disappeared into the thick foliage that arched over the stone path.

Grant didn't even acknowledge him.

But that was Grant Laningham: a brilliant man so focused that he barely noticed the people around him—

Which was why Giovanni feared the unauthorized biography. Despite how polite Grant was being with her, his business style and his behavior weren't for the faint of heart. Worse, since his accident, loss of control of his company and his contentious divorce, Grant had become even more difficult. Giovanni had warned her he would be sullen, moody and uncommunicative. But she was supposed to push past that. Get to the heart of who he was to make sense of his business style and clear his name. Should be a piece of cake to a woman who'd made her living as a journalist for nearly eight years before she bought a ranch and moved off the grid—just as Grant had.

Which was why she was more qualified to share his story than most people. As a recluse herself, she probably understood him in a way others couldn't.

The sound of an approaching boat filled the air. Lola glanced behind them to see another cruiser speeding toward Grant's dock. Apparently accustomed to water traffic, Grant seemed unfazed.

The noise got louder. Lola looked behind them again. This time Grant looked too. The cruiser slowed and pulled into the spot across from the boat Lola had ridden in on.

Cursing, Grant stormed back to the dock and strode to the cruiser.

She raced after him. She had absolutely no idea who was in that boat, but Grant Laningham didn't need any more enemies. Giovanni hadn't told her it was her job to keep him in line, but she was the one charged with writing a story that cleared his name. She didn't want to have to refute new allegations of bad behavior.

A short guy in a suit and round glasses hopped onto the dock, then he turned and helped a little blond boy of eight or ten up the few steps. The kid held a small stack of books, some of them chapter books, some of them coloring books.

Confused, Lola stopped.

Someone inside the boat slid two small suitcases and a backpack beside the little boy. The guy in the suit looked frazzled. The little boy never looked up.

"Who are you and what the hell are you doing here?"

The frazzled guy sighed heavily. "Grant Laningham?"

"Yes, I'm Grant Laningham! And you're on my island. *Private* property. Get back on your boat and be on your way."

"Is there somewhere we can talk?"

"No! How many ways do I have to say get off my island?"

In fairness this *was* a private island, but Grant was supposed to be fixing his reputation, not making it worse.

She stepped forward to try to smooth things over, but the man in the suit said, "All right. We'll talk here. I'm Oliver Fletcher. I'm an attorney in New York City. I have in my possession the Last Will and Testament of Samantha Baxter. This young man is Max Baxter, Samantha's son." He paused to catch Grant's gaze. "Your son."

Lola's mouth fell open, as a look of absolute shock came to Grant's face. He didn't move. He didn't speak. It seemed like he couldn't.

She raced over to the small group. "You have Samantha's Last Will and Testament?"

"Yes." Fletcher passed it to Lola. "It explains why we're here." He pulled an envelope from his jacket pocket. "This explains everything else."

He handed the letter to Grant who took it slowly, his eyes never leaving the little boy.

Knowing Laningham the Destroyer would be denying this to high heaven if there wasn't a legitimate chance this child could be his son, Lola eased over to the little boy. "Max, right?"

He nodded, still looking at the ground.

Sympathy for Max swelled in her. He'd obviously lost his

mother. If he was being brought to Grant by an attorney, Lola guessed that meant he was alone—as she had been when her parents died.

Her heart splintered. Especially when she realized he was being left with a stranger, someone Giovanni had warned her would be sullen and moody.

She slid her arm across Max's shoulders. "I guess you've been traveling a while."

The little boy nodded.

"Are you hungry?"

He pursed his lips and nodded again.

"We can take care of that." She turned Max toward the house. "I'm sure this house has a kitchen. Let's find it."

As she walked away, the lawyer continued speaking with Grant. "You have the will and the letter. I delivered Max, per Samantha's instructions. My responsibilities are now ended."

Grant ran his hand down his face. "Okay."

His easy acquiescence all but confirmed Lola's suspicions. He either had reason to believe this could be his child or he *knew* this was his child.

When he said nothing else, Lola stopped walking and turned to address the lawyer. "We're fine. We'll handle things from here. Thank you for bringing Max to us."

Fletcher smiled stiffly and got into his boat.

As the lawyer disappeared below deck, Grant Laningham rounded on her. "You do not speak for me!"

This was the real Grant Laningham. Not the extremely good-looking, polite guy who met her when she arrived. But the guy who fired people. The perfectionist who wanted everything his way.

She'd interviewed terrorists in Afghanistan. She was not afraid of a computer nerd. No matter how tall he was.

"I didn't speak for you. I gave Mr. Fletcher the go-ahead to leave when you seemed too stunned to do it. Besides, you should be thanking me. I kept you from saying something you might regret. Especially right before you put out an autobiography trying to convince people you're a nice guy."

"I don't want to convince people I'm a nice guy!"

Oh, the narcissist was definitely back. "How else do you expect to combat the unauthorized biography?"

"With strongly wielded truth?"

She shook her head. "People will love to see you prove you are an angry, cantankerous man when you put out an angry, cantankerous autobiography. You'll just give credence to the other guy's book."

She eased Max toward the house again. "Grab his bags and I'll get him something to eat."

She heard Grant muttering but when she turned her head a fraction of an inch, she saw him pick up Max's suitcases and backpack. She and Max went to the kitchen and found a short, well-padded older woman.

"Well, good morning!" she said as Lola and Max entered.

"Hi, I'm Lola Evans. I'm going to be working with Mr. Laningham for the next few weeks," she said, introducing herself. "This is Max," she continued, giving the woman a look that told her not to question things. "He's here to stay with Mr. Laningham too. He's also hungry."

"I'm Caroline, Mr. Laningham's house manager. The cook has gone home for an hour or so before she has to start dinner, but I love to make breakfast for lunch." She smiled at Max. "Do you like pancakes?"

Max nodded eagerly.

As Lola set her raincoat and umbrella on an empty chair at a small table in the corner, Caroline guided Max to sit on one of the stools in front of the large center island of the huge kitchen. Restaurant-sized stainless-steel appliances sat among white shaker cabinets. A blue subway tile backsplash complemented the gray-veined marble countertops.

Heading to the stove, Caroline said, "What's your pleasure? Blueberry? Strawberry? Chocolate chip?"

"Chocolate chip."

Those were the first words Max had spoken and the sound of fear in his voice nearly did Lola in. It had been difficult enough as an adult to realize she was alone when her parents died. She couldn't imagine how terrifying it would be for a child.

Grant walked into the kitchen, addressing Caroline. "I left Max's suitcases at the bottom of the steps. I need to know which room to put him in."

Caroline glanced at Lola and said, "How about we put Max and Ms. Evans in rooms next to each other?"

Lola saw what she was doing. A scared kid in a strange house should be near someone kind and understanding. She might not be a part of Grant's personal drama, but she empathized with this little boy. For as long as she was here, she would try to make his transition easier.

"Okay. Sounds good."

The room grew quiet. Caroline retrieved a bowl and the ingredients for pancakes from the cupboards near the stove. "So, we landed on chocolate chip pancakes?"

Max nodded.

Grant looked at Lola. "Caroline is making him pancakes?"

"Yes."

"I haven't eaten lunch either Caroline. I'll have a few pancakes too."

"Absolutely." She caught Lola's gaze. "A pancake for you?"

"Sure." She'd hoped to have a minute or two alone with Max to help him acclimate, but she couldn't very well tell Grant to leave his own kitchen.

The room grew silent. Lola said, "I see you have books?"

Max nodded.

"What grade are you in?"

"Third."

"That's a fun grade. It was my favorite year of school. I had a really nice teacher."

Grant frowned at Max. "Shouldn't you be in school now?"

"It's June," Lola reminded him pleasantly. "Schools are out for the summer."

"Oh. So, you'll be in fourth grade in the fall?"

Max nodded.

There were a million questions she wanted to ask. Had his mother been sick? Had she been killed suddenly? What had this poor child gone through over the past few weeks?

She didn't want to put him through anything else or say something that might upset him. But she needed to get answers so neither she nor Grant inadvertently hurt him.

She took out her phone and typed in Samantha Baxter, Manhattan. Hundreds of entries popped up. She clicked on the obituary and discovered that Samantha had died and been cremated only two days before. Apparently, she'd been in an accident. Which meant Max hadn't suffered watching his mother die, but he had lost her suddenly.

And only two days ago. He hadn't even had time to grieve.

"Here you go," Caroline said, setting a platter of pancakes on the counter.

Lola noticed that dishes had magically appeared while she was searching Max's mom. She took a plate and served him a pancake, then handed the syrup to him.

"Thanks."

"You're welcome, sweetie." Lola's eyes filled with tears.

This poor child. His mom was gone, and he was stuck with a guy who wanted to write a biography that made people dislike him even more than they already did.

This was not going to go well.

CHAPTER TWO

AFTER THEY ATE, Lola suggested she and Max swim. Caroline led them upstairs to their rooms so they could change into swimsuits. Grant headed to his office.

Pulling the explanation letter out of his back pocket, he sat on his big office chair. He leaned back and took the thin sheet of paper out of the envelope.

Dearest Grant,
I prepared this letter in the event that something should happen to me. If you're reading it, I'm either hospitalized or gone. I hope I'm not gone.

His eyes unexpectedly filled with tears. He could hear Samantha's voice as he read her words, remember her sense of humor and her zest for life. If he hadn't met his wife a few days after the business trip in New York when he and Samantha had worked together, he would have continued seeing her.

And his life would have been so much different. He and Samantha might have stayed together. He would have known Max from infancy. He wouldn't have married his ex. The decisions he'd made that got him kicked off his own board might not have been made. Hell, he might not have walked out in front of that car—

He took a breath. Speculation and second-guessing never helped anyone.

You'd already met your wife by the time I discovered I was pregnant. Both of our lives were complicated enough. I believed I had done the right thing by keeping Max to myself. I hope you understand.

He did. Sort of. Samantha had been extremely levelheaded. Not just smart but filled with common sense. If she'd chosen to raise Max on her own, it had been with thought and good intentions.

I have relatives in France, a cousin and her husband. Max and I have visited them for most holidays. He knows them.

The words stopped.

He flipped the page over. Nothing.

That was it? A mention of some relatives?

He couldn't tell if Samantha didn't know how to end the letter or if this had been a draft she'd planned to finish later.

It made the most sense to assume she'd put this draft with her will, intending to complete it later. She'd probably thought she'd had all the time in the world, as he had the day that he'd nearly been killed by the car that hit him.

Obviously, she'd died suddenly, or she would have finished it.

Lola Evans would know.

Not only had Fletcher given the will to her, but also Grant had seen her on her phone while Caroline was making their pancakes. She'd probably searched Samantha's name.

Overwhelmed, he ran his fingers through his hair. He could not believe he was a father, but the timing was right. If Max was his child, he would be nine years old. That corresponded with the two weeks he'd spent with Samantha.

And he knew Samantha wouldn't lie.

He left his office and went out to the pool area. His yellow Lab, Benjamin Franklin, had joined Max in the pool. The dog loved to swim, and Max seemed to be totally smitten with the dog. If nothing else Ben was a good diversion while he talked to Lola.

He saw her sitting on a chaise, her eyes glued to the little boy and the dog. Her blue one-piece swimsuit accented every soft curve of her body, and he swore his mouth watered. With her bountiful black hair and beautiful face, she was stunning enough to make him stutter or trip over his own feet.

Which was incredibly bad timing. Not only was it inappropriate to be attracted to an employee—he'd learned that the hard way with his ex-wife—but the situation with Max had to take precedence.

He sat on the chaise beside Lola's. "What did you find out when you searched Samantha?"

"She died two days ago."

He groaned. "Two days ago?"

"After Max got in the pool, I dug a little deeper and found the report of an accident in the paper. She was walking past a construction site, and something fell."

"Oh. God." He took a long, slow breath as he absorbed that. "She was a really great person. But I met my wife a few days after I returned from the trip where I'd met Samantha. We'd spent two weeks together, but once I met my ex, I was…occupied."

She shook her head. "Unless you want this going into your autobiography don't paint a picture."

He snorted. "Yeah, well, the fun didn't last."

"So I've heard."

He grimaced. The whole damned world had heard. "Anyway, I read Samantha's letter. It's fairly straightforward. She doesn't go into detail or even make an argument about why Max is mine. She simply explained that I'd met my wife by the time she realized she was pregnant, and both of our lives were too complicated for her to tell me."

"What you're saying is you believe her."

"Yes."

"You'd still be wise to have DNA verification."

He agreed, but the realization of being a father suddenly overwhelmed him again. "I had the worst parents in the world. I have no clue how to be a dad. My sister and I basically raised ourselves and if the rumors are true about me being a crappy human being, it looks like I didn't do such a great job."

"I don't know how to tell you this, but you don't have any options. You can't abandon this child."

"I know...but Samantha's letter mentioned that she had relatives in France, people Max knows. I think we should pay them a visit."

She gaped at him. "You also can't dump that little boy off on distant relatives in a strange country."

"They aren't distant relatives. They are cousins—Max knows them. Samantha said they had spent holidays with them. Max may actually prefer living with them. I'm the stranger here."

She sighed, as if seeing his point. "Maybe."

"Look. Samantha wasn't a gold digger or opportunist. She was a highly paid lawyer in Manhattan. She didn't say things lightly. The letter must have been a draft because it ends abruptly. And the paragraphs are sort of disjointed, as if she was trying to figure out what to say. I'm guessing it was in her estate planning file, and it had enough information that Fletcher brought it with the will."

"Okay."

He took a breath. "With the letter unfinished, the mention of distant relatives might mean something. She might have wanted to suggest I let them raise Max. She knew how busy I was. She knew my life was complicated…and public." Suddenly realizing Samantha's reasoning, he groaned. "*Ridiculously public.* When I'm out and about, I'm hounded by paparazzi. My best guess is that she didn't want her son raised by me at all but hadn't gotten around to putting those wishes on paper. Did you read the will?"

"It's all standard stuff. Liquidate her assets. Pay her expenses. Everything that's left goes into a trust for Max."

"She didn't say she wanted him to be raised by me?"

"No. But she also didn't say she wanted him to be raised by the cousins in France."

"That might have been part of how she intended to hide him from the publicity that surrounds me. Wills get filed. Private letters do not. If she named those cousins in the will, everybody would have known who they were—and would have known where Max was."

"That's true."

"There has to be a reason she put them in that letter."

"Maybe she just didn't want him to lose touch with his extended family?"

"Maybe." He sighed. "I can't help thinking she knew me well enough to realize I wouldn't be a good dad."

Convinced that was her motivation for telling him about the cousins in France, he pulled out his phone and called Giovanni, putting it on speaker so Lola could hear.

"Hey…what's up?"

"Lola and I are going to be taking a quick trip to France."

"Oh, no! No. No. No. Look Grant, I know she's pretty but—"

"It's not like that." His brain stalled. She was pretty enough, subtly sensual with her dark hair and nice curves, that he wished it *could* be like that. But she was an employee. His ex had bowled him over the same way. He knew better now than to act on those feelings.

"I have some unexpected personal business in France. We need to handle it."

Lola's sapphire blue eyes widened to the size of small cookies. She shook her head at him and mouthed, "I am not going with you," as Giovanni said, "You can't go to France."

"Look, Gio, I don't have a choice."

"Yeah, well, the publisher putting out the unauthorized biography got wind that you're writing your own version to contradict it, and they've upped their pub date. If you want to beat that book to stores, there is no wiggle room. There's no time for a draft. We're lucky Lola's a professional, meaning editing should be minimal."

Lola mouthed, "No draft?"

Grant said, "No draft?"

"No draft. Whatever you turn in gets edited, you and Lola get approval after that to make sure nothing got messed up in editing, then we go to print."

"What happens if I don't beat him, and we put out my book a few weeks after his?"

"Then your autobiography looks like a desperate attempt to answer everything in his book. It won't look authentic or like you're penning your story. It will stink of desperation."

"Damn it!"

Lola motioned to Max and shook her head.

Grant groaned. "I only said damn it. Not anything earth-shattering. I'm sure he's heard it before."

Giovanni said, "Who's heard what before?"

"The dog has heard the word damn before. He's in the pool but Lola thinks he heard me."

Lola's eyes widened again at the way he evaded the truth. But he wasn't ready for anyone to know about Max. Hell, he hadn't adjusted yet. He needed time as much as Max did.

Gio sighed. "Look, Grant. I don't know what you and Lola are doing, but you've gotta get that book out. Six weeks might be tight, but if you two actually worked you could get it done."

Grant stopped a genuine curse. With so much riding on this, he saw Giovonni's side, albeit reluctantly. "All right. Fine. I hear you."

"You're the one who wants to go back to work."

He did. For the past year, his brain had been coming up with ideas that couldn't wait. New technology could never wait. But having to mend his reputation had taken on an entirely new meaning. Even if he didn't have to raise Max, he had to protect him. He had the kind of life that the paparazzi lived for. They followed him, took pictures from boats only a few hundred feet off the beach, trying to get shots of him limping or struggling with a walker—which was why he had so many plants around the house, especially the pool. If they discovered he had a son, a son he hadn't known about, and that poor Max's mom had died, Max's life would be fodder for the press.

Giovonni's voice brought him back to the present. "You put your book out first. Don't make yourself a saint, but don't make yourself a jerk either. Be honest. No hiding things. Set the record straight on why you fired so many people that your board ousted you. Talk about your wife's affairs. Admit you were an arrogant workaholic and let's get this ball rolling!"

With that he hung up and Grant sat staring at the phone.

"He wants you to admit you were an arrogant workaholic?"

He peeked up at her. "My board ousted me. My wife had numerous affairs. I *was* a workaholic. Responsible for my board's decision and maybe my wife's infidelity."

"This is going to be some book."

Sure. Right. He would be dictating all his secrets to one of the prettiest women he'd ever met. Someone smart enough and kind enough to be good to Max—

That should not bother him. He'd made his decisions about his ghostwriter. She was off-limits.

So why did he feel like scowling? Lola might be beautiful and sweet, but she was an employee. Plus, he knew relationships were a disappointing trap. He should just ignore her.

And he really did need help with Max.

"You didn't want to hire me, did you?"

Her question surprised him into looking over at her. She wore the expression interviewers wore when they wanted to catch someone in a lie.

"Honestly, Lola—" The feeling of her name on his tongue sent the weirdest feeling skittering through him. He shook his head to clear it. "I told Giovanni I wanted a bulldog. I wanted someone to put enough punch in this thing that I didn't look like a wimp. I don't want to look like the jerk my former employee is trying to make me out to be. But I also don't want to look like I've got my tail between my legs. I'm edging myself into a business world that's moved on without me. I have to show people I'm still strong. I want this book to have some teeth."

Her chin lifted. "I can make it bite back."

"You better because it sounds like I don't have time to hire someone else."

He rose from the chaise and turned to leave.

"Where are you going?"

"Inside. To work."

"You can't leave Max out here by himself."

"You're here."

She shook her head. "Nope. Don't go there. Like I'm a woman so I automatically get kid duty. I'm happy to help you while I'm here. But my end of this book will require twice the time your part of it does. Plus, he is *your* son. Lesson one in parenting is that you are bottom-line responsible. And whether you like it or not he needs you."

"Okay. So, what does our schedule look like then? How are we going to write this thing?"

"After hours in a pool, kids sometimes take naps. They like to play on their own sometimes. Especially video games. Plus, it looks like he's making friends with your dog. We'll work when he's on his own. Then you play with him when he wants company and I'll start writing from whatever notes we make in the morning."

He raised his eyes to heaven.

She rose from the chaise. "You know, an interesting angle for your autobiography might be to write it around the fact that you got custody of a child you didn't know you had and how it changed you."

The very thought horrified him. "First, I won't be putting Max into the book. While I'm growing accustomed to being a dad, he's also getting accustomed to a really bad situation. I don't want to make that worse. Second, he might *choose* the Paris relatives over me and then if people know about him but don't know the whole story, I'll look like a guy who dumped his son on relatives. Third, not putting him into the book is the best way to protect him."

She laughed. "Look at you. You do have some parental instincts."

He gaped at her. "Was that a test?"

She ambled up to him and smiled. All his male hormones woke up. Along with a yearning for something he couldn't have. He told himself that was the truth of it. His interest piqued because she was an employee, off-limits the way his ex should have been. But he'd also been on this island for four long years. He'd had a few visits from friends and lovers and women his friends brought to spend time as a group, having fun.

But none of that felt like this. Fresh. Unique. Full of potential.

"No test. The biggest part of my job is to figure out the

angle for this story. I'll be questioning the life out of you and running ideas past you for the next four weeks."

He took a breath to settle his hormones. "We have *six* weeks."

"And I'll need the last two to edit what we put together in the first four weeks. I told you. I'm going to be busy." She glanced around at the pretty day. "Sunny or not, it looks like I'd better set up the office area in my suite today."

She walked away and he scowled at her, then the scowl turned into a frown.

She was not going to let him walk all over her.

Maybe she was a bulldog after all?

The thought pleased him a little too much. His wayward brain pictured all kinds of ways she would be fun to have around, fun to tease and flirt with—

Benjamin Franklin hopped out of the pool and shook himself spraying Grant with cold water, as if he knew it was his job to bring Grant back to reality.

Max looked at him with big, frightened eyes.

"Hey, it's okay. People who stand by pools have to accept the fact that they might get wet."

Max nodded and Grant forgot all about his pretty ghost-writer. His chest filled with pain for the scared kid in his pool. How was he ever going to help this child?

CHAPTER THREE

LOLA SET UP her laptop in her suite on the third floor and pulled assorted files on Grant's life out of her suitcase. She could have stayed in her room another hour. Given that she'd traveled from Montana to South Carolina that day—having to rise at three o'clock to make her flights because of the difference in time zones—what she really needed was a nap. But she couldn't abandon Grant.

Or Max.

Max was the one who really needed her. Grant was the one who scared her.

Not because he was grumpy. Because he was interesting. Sexy. Smart. Overconfident. He would be tremendously fun to tease. But teasing a client was all wrong. Being attracted to him was even worse. She would control both because this job would stave off bankruptcy for a few months—maybe even a year. Her ranch wasn't supporting itself and she had to earn big chunks of cash to keep herself from losing everything she had.

Also, Max needed a levelheaded person to steer Grant in the right direction. If she believed in fate or destiny, she would assume she'd been sent here to help Grant with Max. Not to flirt. And certainly not because of some starry-eyed wish that Grant was her Prince Charming. She didn't believe in a glitzy, fancy, famous Prince Charming. She wanted a nice, normal guy who would settle her life not fill it with controversy.

With her work area assembled, she returned to the pool. "If there's anything you need to do, I'll watch him."

Grant rose from his chaise lounge. "Actually, I do need to make some arrangements with Caroline."

He glanced at Max, looking like a guy who didn't want to leave, and her heart tugged. He might have had bad parents, but he definitely had good instincts.

"I also think we need to do the DNA sooner rather than later."

She agreed. "If there's a mistake of some kind, it's best to find out now."

He nodded, then went into the house.

She slipped out of her bathing suit cover-up and jumped into the pool. "What's the dog's name?" she called to Max.

He laughed. His short yellow hair had spiked from being wet. His blue eyes were filled with little-boy excitement.

Never underestimate the power of a dog with a child.

"Benjamin Franklin."

"I don't think your dad knows how to name a pet. Maybe we could think of a cool nickname?"

Max shrugged.

"No hurry. I'm sure a name will come to us. Let's play a game." She found a Frisbee and tossed it. Unfortunately, a breeze caught the red disc, and it landed on the sidewalk on the other side of the pool. Benjamin Franklin leaped out of the water to retrieve it and brought it back to Max.

The dog really seemed to like the child. Max liked the dog; the dog liked Max. This was the bridge they needed to help Max adjust.

She called, "Throw it again. We'll see what he does."

Max nodded and tossed it to the deep water near the diving board. Benjamin Franklin swam after it.

They spent the rest of the afternoon that way and Lola

was glad. When Max came downstairs for dinner, he seemed tired enough that he probably wouldn't have trouble sleeping.

They ate mashed potatoes, chicken and broccoli, followed by cherry pie. By the time they were done, Max's eyes were drooping. They took him upstairs and found pajamas in one of his bags.

He quietly said, "My toothbrush is in the backpack."

Grant unzipped it. "Got it."

Pajamas and toothbrush in hand, Max went into the bathroom. Two minutes later, he came out in PJs decorated with characters from a popular video game.

Lola tucked him in. "You know, if there's anything you want to talk about, we're here for you."

He nodded. His eyes filled with pain that made her heart stumble.

Grant said, "Yes. We're here."

Still tucking the blankets around him, Lola softly said, "I'm very sorry about your mom."

Max blinked back tears but said nothing. Lola could only imagine his confusion. Two days ago, he had a mom and probably lived a totally different kind of life in Manhattan. Now he had a dad he didn't know, a swimming pool and a dog.

Grant walked around to the other side of the bed and sat beside Max. "I really liked your mom. She was a great person."

Surprised, Lola peeked at him.

"If there's anything you want to talk about, even if it's only to tell stories about her, I'm here. So is Lola." He paused a second. When Max didn't say anything, he added, "Lola and I are going to be working on a project together, but we'll both be spending time with you."

Max nodded. His voice shook just the slightest bit when he said, "Okay."

"Do you know anything about me?"

"My mom said you were smart, and I'll probably be good at math."

Lola bit back a laugh, but Grant chuckled. "Your mom was very smart too. Nine chances out of ten, you're going to be downright brilliant."

Max smiled.

Lola's eyes filled with tears. Not from compassion for Max, but because Laningham the Destroyer was trying to be good to Max in a simple way that ended up being profound.

Grant rose. "Okay. You get some sleep."

Lola said, "Good night."

Max said, "Good night."

They stepped out into the hall and Lola just stared at Grant. "You have parental instincts like nobody I've ever seen."

He led her to the steps. "I told you I raised myself."

And had really bad parents. In her research, she'd discovered they were both doctors, both retired now in the Florida Keys. Both had won commendations. Both had chaired hospital committees and been department heads. She could see where they wouldn't have had time for parenting. She could also see this was a huge part of Grant's story. She simply wasn't sure how yet. Especially if she wasn't permitted to mention Max in the book.

They started down the stairs. Grant said, "I'm going for a short walk on the beach."

Eager to ask him questions while he seemed to have his guard down, Lola said, "I'll come too."

"You think Max will be okay alone?"

"Maybe we shouldn't walk on the beach. Maybe we could just grab a couple of beers and sit by the pool. Tomorrow we'll get a monitor for his room, so we can make sure he's okay if we want a walk."

Grant took a breath. "You're going to interview me, aren't you?"

"Yeah, but in case you haven't figured it out, I've been observing you all day. My work started the minute I stepped onto your dock."

"Great. You witnessed the most unexpected event in my life—discovering I have a child. In one odd day, you know more about my personal life than most people ever will."

"Not after your autobiography is released."

He groaned.

She slid her arm under his and led him toward the pool area. "Let's go get that beer."

He desperately wanted to say something snarky, at the very least swear her to secrecy. But the way she slid her arm around his sent electricity sizzling through him, forcing him to raise his guard again. She was a reporter, trying to establish a rapport so he'd open up to her. Nothing more. He was the one with the attraction problem.

He walked her to the patio. Lights from the pool dimly lit the area, making it a peaceful, private oasis.

"Have a seat. I'll get the beer. Do you have a preference?"

"Whatever you have is good."

He laughed. "I have everything. My college roommates like to pop in uninvited. I'm always prepared."

She named a brand of light beer. He pulled two bottles from the fridge in the outdoor kitchen.

Sitting on the chair beside hers at the round patio table, he handed one to her.

"Thanks." She nodded toward the darkness. He'd left one six-foot swatch of land clear of plants so they could see down the beach, but the ocean was absorbed into the black night. The sound of the waves was the only indicator there was water beyond the sand. "This is beautiful. So peaceful."

"Who says money doesn't buy happiness?"

She laughed. "Probably you, since I get the feeling you haven't been happy a lot."

He grunted. "Who is?"

"Good point." She took a drink of her beer. "Why don't we start at the beginning? Tell me about your parents."

It was the last thing he wanted to talk about. He couldn't think of his parents without thinking of his sister and he refused to go down that ugly road. That was one secret that would never see the light of day. He intended to keep his family out of his autobiography. Especially since he didn't see them as part of his story. His life had begun when he finally finished his degree, got his first job and left his parents' house for good. No reason to mention them.

"I thought you would have researched them."

"Of course, I did. But I want to hear the story from you."

"It's going to be short because there's not much to tell. My parents were successful physicians who constantly told my sister and me that *this* was what success looked like."

"This?"

"Their lifestyle. Work all day, then chair committees and fundraise all night."

"Leaving you and your sister alone?"

"No. We had babysitters. But one night when the babysitter was on the phone with her friends, I looked around and I thought *this* is boring. And *this life* doesn't feel like success. I'm not doing *this*."

"But you did do that. Actually, you surpassed your parents' accomplishments."

He grinned. "Yeah, but I'm not a doctor. That's what they wanted me to be. To follow in their footsteps. To keep the family legacy alive."

She laughed. "You might not be a doctor, but you *are* successful."

"In my way and on my own terms."

She thought for a moment, then she said, "What terms are those?"

"I work for myself, not a hospital or a charity. And I don't do what I do for applause or admiration. I work to change the world."

"And that makes you happy?"

"Not in the way you mean. Everybody gets bursts or moments of happiness, but I think the best a person can be is content and using my intelligence makes me content, fulfilled."

She said nothing, apparently thinking that through. Lights shimmering off the pool glistened around her. With her hair out of the ponytail, falling around her face to her shoulders, accenting her pretty blue eyes, she looked ethereal. Like a goddess.

Attraction rose again. Her interview style was more like a conversation than a reporter digging into his life. In the dim lights, with the world around them a silent place, he was comfortable—the very last thing he expected to be when talking about details that would form his autobiography.

Except he didn't feel like he was giving details. He felt like he was talking with a friend.

"What about you? What's your life like?" The question popped out before he could stop it, but now that it had, he was glad. He'd researched her enough to know she'd been on her way to the top at a network news outlet, then her parents had been murdered and she'd dropped off the face of the earth. Giovanni had had the devil's time finding her.

His curiosity about her knew no bounds, and when he got curious about something he couldn't stop his brain. Given that they were working together he could also make asking about her life sound legitimate. Not like attraction-driven curiosity—though most of it was. "If I have to trust you with intimate details of my life, I should at least know who you are."

"I'm sure you know the important things."

"Like your parents were murdered? Or that you left your job?"

"Either or. That's about the extent of the items of interest in my story. Both were reported on network news because back then I was a celebrity of sorts."

"I also read that you bought a ranch."

"That was long enough after I quit my job that it didn't make the network news." She took a swig of beer. "Meaning, you investigated me."

"I'm trusting you. I had to be sure I could."

"Then you know my ranch is on the brink of bankruptcy."

"It's a tough time for that business."

She looked at him skeptically. "You know about ranching?"

"I know about the stock market, price indexes and real estate. The rest is normal deductive reasoning."

She shook her head. "I suppose now you're going to tell me you know a little bit about everything?"

He laughed and sat back. "Pretty much." He drank some beer then said, "My mind has a thing for details. It loves them. It's how I can think down the board for an answer while everybody else is still stuck in the problem. The more intricate the subject, the more clues my brain can find to improve either a product, a strategy, or a system."

"Makes sense."

"What about you?"

She glanced up at him again. "What about me?"

"What are you good at?"

She held his gaze. "Reading people."

Challenge sizzled through him. But not in the way it did when he got an idea to best a business opponent. This was sharp, sexual, and definitely wrong. But so delicious he couldn't help indulging just a bit. Flirting. Egging her on.

He smiled. "I made a living out of keeping my thoughts to myself."

"With a bunch of amateurs maybe. I'm a pro. I've interviewed bigger, badder, scarier people than you. I'll see right through a lot of your crap."

He laughed. This could be so much fun if he actually had time to make her work for every tidbit that he had to tell her. But they didn't have time and he had a child to attend do.

Still, the urge to flirt wouldn't be denied. He held out his beer bottle to tap hers in a toast. "Here's to you trying to get my secrets. And failing."

Rather than scowl, she laughed. Really laughed. As if the sea breeze filled her with joy.

In less than twelve hours he more than liked her. She held her own with him. She made him think. She made him *laugh*. Even bogged down by the fact that he had to counteract the lies in an illicit telling of his life, compounded by discovering he was a father, she made him relax.

She was also oh, so pretty. Pretty enough that he wished they were walking on the beach, and he was sweet-talking her. Pretty enough and interesting enough that he knew a fling with her would be the most memorable of his life.

Except he needed her. Not only did he want her to write a strong autobiography, but also, she was good with Max. Sympathetic without being condescending. Max needed her.

Which was why he'd already decided she had to be off-limits.

Now he would have to figure out how to be as close with her, as intimate about his life as he'd have to be to pen an autobiography, without all that closeness tipping over into something more.

She finished her beer. "It's been a long day for me. I'm going to turn in."

"Okay." He rose from the table. "I'm heading inside too. Maybe I can find a Laningham Lions baseball game on TV."

"You don't know when your own team plays?"

He shrugged. "Bought the team as an investment. Then I started liking baseball." He shrugged again. "But it's not an obsession."

He followed her as she walked to the door and into the ground-floor family room filled with thick couches, three televisions and a pool table.

Inside, she paused and turned to him. "Good night."

Standing six inches away from her, he let himself enjoy her smile, her pretty eyes. The moment froze in time. It would have been the most natural thing to kiss her good night. He wanted to. Every fiber of his being felt drawn to move in the few inches between them and press his lips to hers. He knew they'd be good together—

The reminder that the last time he'd felt like this had been with his ex-wife filled his brain. She'd burst into his life, the new receptionist at his company, and what had sparked between them was just like this. Happily sexual. They'd laughed as much as they'd made love. From the minute he'd seen her, he hadn't been able to keep himself from flirting. He'd had the unquestionable sense that they'd be great in bed. There'd been a pull so strong he'd forgotten that sleeping with an employee was a bad idea.

Was this Jenny all over again?

Lord, he would not let that happen.

He took a step back. "Good night."

She smiled one more time, then turned away, off to her bedroom on the third floor, the one right beside his son.

His son.

Crazy feelings fluttered through him. Fear mostly.

He picked up the remote for one of the TVs but dropped it again and walked to his office. He found the number for the private investigator whom his best friend and lawyer Brad had hired to combat his wife's allegations when she'd filed for divorce.

The investigator answered after three rings. "Hello."

"Charlie?"

"Well, as I live and breathe. Grant Laningham. Somebody told me you were dead."

"You should have investigated further. I'm not even hiding."

"You don't call being on an island by yourself hiding?"

Grant laughed. "So, you do keep tabs on me."

"I wouldn't say that I keep tabs. I just like to know where all my people are. What's up?"

"The usual confidentiality applies?"

"Absolutely. I still have that non-disclosure agreement we signed."

"I have a son."

Charlie's voice filled with concern. "Oh."

"His mom died."

Charlie groaned. "Nothing is ever normal with you, is it, Laningham? Seems like when it rains in your life, it pours."

"That's it exactly. But at least this time I'm not having trouble in threes."

"How did you find out about the child?"

"A lawyer brought Max here today along with a copy of his mom's Last Will and Testament and a letter she'd begun writing to explain things. She didn't finish it. But what she'd written ends with her talking about relatives in France, people my son knows."

"You don't have their names?"

"Nope. Don't have their names." He picked up Samantha's letter, glanced at it one more time to be sure he hadn't missed something. "Max's mother is Samantha Baxter. She was a lawyer in Manhattan." He rattled off the name of her law firm. "She should be easy to find. I assume you can locate her relatives once you research her family tree."

Charlie snorted. "Probably. If not, I have my ways. I'll get back to you."

Grant expected to be relieved when he hung up the phone, but he wasn't. He knew he was a little more attracted than he should to his ghostwriter, a woman who out of necessity had to be off-limits because his autobiography had to be above reproach. Now, he was also worried about Max. His son deserved so much better than a workaholic genius for his only family.

He hoped Charlie could quickly find Samantha's cousins.

CHAPTER FOUR

THE NEXT MORNING, Lola made her way downstairs to the front foyer, following the scent of bacon to the dining room where breakfast was already in progress. Grant sat at the head of the eight-person table where they'd had dinner the night before. Max sat on the seat to his right.

"Hey, sleepyhead," Grant said, and Max smiled sheepishly.

The sight of Max smiling mixed with the silly way Grant had greeted her, and Lola had to stop to take it all in. First, Max was here, in the dining room. Grant had to have brought him downstairs. Had he gone to his room to check on him? If he had, that was an extremely responsible thing to do.

Second, the little boy was dressed in shorts and a T-shirt.

Third, Max was smiling. Maybe not full-on grinning. But some of the fear had disappeared from his eyes.

A lump formed in her throat. After the undoubtedly scary time Max had had the day before, the sight of him adjusting almost made her weep.

Grant said, "We had pancakes yesterday so we're having oatmeal and bacon today."

She walked to the empty chair beside Grant. "I like oatmeal."

"We also discovered that Caroline has a grandson Max's age."

"Oh?"

"Yes. She went home to get him so he and Max can swim together this morning, while you and I work."

Words failed her. Then she wondered why. Grant Laningham was one of the smartest people on the planet. He was also a problem solver. He hadn't lost his skills or abilities because the monkey wrench in his plans was a small child not a line of computer code. He did what he did best. He figured things out.

And in such a way that Max wasn't afraid anymore.

That's what surprised her. Not that Grant had solved a problem, but that this man who was usually a bull in a china shop was so sensitive to Max.

Feelings she'd had for him the night before resurrected. The moonlight had combined with the simple, easy way he'd begun relating his story to her and she'd felt she was talking to the real Grant. The guy who lived deep down inside him. The guy Giovanni knew well enough to decide that the truth of his life would save him from accusations made in his former employee's book.

The real Grant was a nice guy with an unhappy childhood. He was someone who'd made something of himself with hard work and determination. He'd spoken kindly to Max. And was being even nicer to him now.

That was the Grant she had to show in his autobiography.

A woman in a pink uniform brought Lola a bowl of oatmeal. "Thank you."

"This is Denise. She's the cook," Grant said. "Denise, this is Lola. She'll be here six weeks while we work on a project together."

Denise said, "It's nice to meet you."

Lola smiled. "It's nice to meet you too."

"After breakfast Max and I are going to take a walk down the beach, looking for seashells. By the time we return, Caroline should be back. She's going to watch the boys swim, then you and I can get down to business."

She nodded her agreement, no longer surprised but absolutely impressed by his managerial skills. If he kept up this openness and kindness, writing his autobiography would be a breeze.

Sort of.

He didn't want Max to be mentioned in the book.

He also had a history of ending careers.

She herself had witnessed a bit of his temper.

Somehow, she would have to find that thread of goodness inside him and tug on it until she could connect all the things in his life in such a way that they made sense of his actions.

As she added sugar and cinnamon to her oatmeal, Grant said, "I know last night's interview was informal, but shouldn't you be taking notes or maybe recording our sessions?"

She nodded then took a bite of her oatmeal. "Oh, God, that's good."

"Denise is a world-class chef. She hated the cutthroat nature of Michelin starred restaurants. So, I scooped her up. She and her family love South Carolina and she only works three days a week."

"What do you eat the rest of the time?"

"Believe it or not, I'm good on the grill. Plus, some days are sandwich days."

Max gazed at Grant with a combination of curiosity and awe, and she couldn't imagine what would go through a little boy's head as he interacted so casually with a father he hadn't met until the day before.

When Max said, "And some days are takeout days," Lola laughed. She imagined a busy attorney in Manhattan had served takeout a lot. Max was connecting his past life to his new life.

That was a good sign.

Grant said, "Exactly. Though getting takeout on an island is a little more complicated than it is in Manhattan."

Max studied him for a second. "Do you live at the beach all the time?"

"I have for the past four years. But I may decide to move sometime soon...like in the next couple of months."

Because he was re-entering the business world.

"Where to?" Max asked.

"Well, if I leave here, it will be to go to work. Finding sufficient qualified employees has to factor into the place I choose."

Max nodded.

Grant waited a beat, probably to be sure Max's questions were done, then he addressed Lola again. "So, are we recording our sessions, or do you just take notes?"

"I record *and* take notes. The recording is a backup in case I feel my notes are too loose. But I also use the recordings to verify everything I write."

"What happens to the recordings after we're done?"

"Once you approve the book, you will sign a statement that you said everything that's in the book, and you won't publicly contradict it or sue me because you changed your mind about something. After that, you get the recordings. Destroy them if you like. Or keep them in case something comes up. Most people destroy them."

"Makes sense."

"This isn't my first rodeo. I know how to protect us both."

"Okay."

Caroline entered the room with a little boy whose dark hair looked like someone had put a bowl on his head and cut around it.

"We're back," Caroline said. "This is Jeremy. Jeremy, that's Max."

Max said, "Hi."

Jeremy grinned. "Grammy says you have a dog."

"Benjamin Franklin," Max replied before Grant could. His beach walk with his dad forgotten, he got off his chair. "I'm going to put my bathing suit on."

Jeremy said, "I'll come with you."

The two little boys scrambled out of the room.

Grant chuckled. "Apparently, a love of swimming has already bonded them."

Caroline displayed a bottle of sunblock. "I brought this too. Max is a little fair."

"Good. Maybe you could make a list of things I should have around the house for a little boy?"

"I'll do that while they're swimming." She headed for the door in the back of the dining room. "You two have fun working while I sit by the pool." Her laughter followed her out of the room.

"Watching two kids play would not be a day off for me," Grant said, rising from the table. "But Caroline was thrilled with the idea."

"Grandmothers really love their grandkids."

"That's what it seems." He pushed his chair under the table. "I'll see you in the office in about twenty minutes?"

Lola nodded. "Okay."

As he left, the strangest feeling rumbled through her. She really liked him. She wanted to believe that this was the real Grant Laningham. But she couldn't be fooled. She had to work with him. No, she had to write an accurate depiction of his life. This nice guy had shown up for Max. And only Max.

The real Grant Laningham had almost kissed her the night before.

And she would have let him. There was no denying there was a spark of something between them. Plus, the night had been beautiful. Their conversation had been fun. For a few seconds, she'd wished she wasn't working for him. But that notion fled quickly. A fling might be exciting, but they'd never have anything permanent. He was not the kind of guy that she wanted permanently. Now that her parents had been gone four years, her grief had morphed into loneliness. It was time to rebuild her life. A fling with a crazy narcissist was not the way to do that. Especially if their attraction ruined their ability to work together.

That was what she had to remember when tempted to follow the feelings she had around him. Not only would a relationship between them be unprofessional and risky, but a relationship—even a friendship—with the man she was writing about could skew her perspective.

This was the highest paying job she'd had to date. She had to do it right.

She also had to protect her heart. She had to acknowledge that self-absorbed Grant Laningham could hurt her. Affairs might be a part of normal people's lives, but vulnerable people fell in love too hard, too fast. Even when they knew their partner was all wrong for them. She had enough trouble, loneliness and emptiness. She couldn't risk making all that worse when she was finally at a point where she might be able to let go of her grief and rebuild her life.

Grant strode to his office shaking his head. Lola had dressed appropriately for an island in shorts and a T-shirt but seeing her so casual and comfortable at his dining table had brought back all those wonderful feelings from the night before.

Which was ridiculous. She was a professional here to ghostwrite his autobiography. He had a son, whose life he had to sort out at some point. He couldn't keep Max here if the little boy was supposed to be in Paris, being raised by relatives who knew and loved him. He also had to work on the book, approve everything Lola wrote, guide the process so he accomplished his goals in putting out the story of his life.

He didn't have time to be attracted to her.

They didn't have time for a fling.

He entered his office, walked to the window behind the desk and opened the drapes to expose the amazing view of the ocean. As he was pulling a notebook from his big, mahogany desk, Lola arrived.

She waved a small device at him—probably her recorder. "Ready?"

"Ready." This was exactly what they needed. No more conversations in the moonlight that made him feel like he was talking to a friend. It was time for structure. Recorders. Tablets for taking notes. Conversations about facts.

He *was* ready. More ready than she would ever know.

She sat, placing her notebook and recorder on the desk. "Don't let the recorder intimidate you. I want you to talk the way you did last night. Open. Honest. Casual."

There was no way in hell he would do that. Open, honest, casual had led to inappropriate feelings. Today was the day he took control. He was stronger than any attraction. But he was also smart enough to figure out that part of the lure of her was the simple, easy way she communicated. Today he would do most of the talking. He would direct the conversation.

"I think we should start with my last year at university."

She nodded and motioned for him to begin talking as she pressed the button on her recorder.

He took a breath. "My last year of university I knew I wanted to work for the biggest software developer in the world—"

He went on to describe his friends, their majors and goals, the brainstorming sessions and wishful thinking sessions where he admitted he wanted to best everybody currently working in the tech industry. His friends had laughed and talked about working for him—

"But none of your friends ever worked for you."

"No. They found niches that they liked. For them 'purpose' had a different meaning than it had for me. While I wanted to be the one running the show, they found fulfillment other ways."

Somehow or another that segued into him telling Lola stories of his friends coming to the island for fishing trips. Brad and Matthew, his two best friends, had helped him buy the island when he was still in the hospital after his accident four years ago. They'd taken off work to set up the house and bring the physical therapists in. Brad, a lawyer, had slapped a defamation suit on his wife who had filed for divorce the week before he was hit by the car. The divorce had been inevitable. But he'd objected to letting the end of their marriage play out in the press.

The defamation suit had stopped all her interviews and resulted in a much smaller settlement than he'd thought he'd be handing over to her.

"Interesting."

Jarred out of his reminiscence, he said, "What?"

"You almost died, and she still crucified you in the press."

"Until Brad sued her." He shook his head. "You know what's funny? She'd filed for divorce only days before my accident. Had she waited one week, and I'd been killed, she'd have gotten everything."

"That's morbid."

"No. That's what happens when you get divorced. The good things about our marriage were over after eighteen months. She started traveling. Never being around." He shook his head. "She spent six months in Italy once. I surprised her with a visit and found her lover living in my villa with her."

She grimaced. "And that didn't end your marriage?"

He tilted his head as he thought about how to explain that. "I could give you the easy answer—I was busy creating a new software platform and didn't have time to deal with personal things. And that would be the truth. Except there was a part of me that didn't *want* to deal with it."

"You thought you could fix your marriage?"

"No. Honestly? I believed that's what marriage was. Two people who stuck together even though they didn't like each other anymore."

She stared at him. "See, right now…as an interviewer… I'm wondering if your parents' marriage taught you that."

"It did. Why do you think they spent so much time apart?"

"They were extremely busy people?"

"With more than just work and altruism."

He watched her face as she made sense of what he'd said. "Your parents had affairs?"

"Yes."

"So, you didn't see your wife's affairs as being unusual?"

"Money gives people options and opportunities."

"Okay."

He snorted. "I suppose you're going to tell me your parents never strayed."

"They didn't."

"And you would know?"

"Yes. They were hopelessly in love. But also, we lived in a small town. Secrets didn't stay secrets long. Plus, my parents were sort of broke. Not penniless, but—you know— they only had enough money to pay the bills and save a bit here and there."

"You're saying they didn't have the cash for a no-tell motel."

She laughed. "No options. No opportunities. But don't dismiss the fact that they were crazy about each other. They would slow dance in the kitchen while their chicken and dumpling soup cooked."

"And you think *that's* normal?"

She sighed. "Yes and no."

"You're a dreamer."

"Don't say that like it's a sin!"

"It's not a sin. It just makes life harder."

"Says the guy who admittedly planned his future with his friends long before he even graduated university."

"That was different. I was dealing with facts. I was smart. I was imaginative. I was getting an education. I knew that when I got out into the world there would be no stopping me."

She studied him. "Interesting."

He sighed. "What is *interesting* now?"

"You split hairs. My parents' happy marriage is wishful thinking to you but you *changing the entire world* was just par for the course."

"I had variables that added up. Intelligence, imagination, education," he said, counting off on his fingers. "I was a good pony to put your money on. What did they have? An unreliable emotion?"

"Yes. Except—"

"No *except*. That's all they had."

She frowned and he knew she wanted to argue. Instead, she guided him back to talking about graduating, getting his first job, looking for his place in the industry he wanted to rule.

They paused once when Denise brought a pot of coffee into the office. After that he talked until Denise came in at one o'clock, asking what they wanted for lunch.

He suggested that he grill hot dogs since he had two hungry boys to fill, and Denise left to get everything ready.

Lola turned off her recorder and closed her notebook. "You just spent hours talking virtually nonstop. That's a lot for me to process. I'll be spending the afternoon making notes that will ultimately become an outline."

"I'm not sure what to do with Max this afternoon."

"After a morning of playing in a pool, he might need a nap."

"I'll give him that option. If he declines, I'll probably take him out on the boat for a while."

She gasped. "I'll bet he'll love that."

"One of these days, I want to take him fishing."

"He'll love that too."

Organizing papers on his desk, he casually said, "We need to get that in because I don't know how long he'll be here."

"Excuse me?"

"He's got other family. What if they come looking for him? What if his cousins pop in one day and he's thrilled to see them? He might not want me anymore."

He could see from her expression that she hadn't thought of that, and the idea did not please her.

"We have to have an open mind, Lola. I won't keep him from people who love him and whom he loves."

"You shouldn't. But you should still have a relationship with him."

"I own three jets. A trip to Paris once a month would not be a hardship."

"If he stays here long enough, it won't be that easy for you to give him up."

He sighed. "He is my son. I will never give him up. But I am a realist about my life. He might not fit. He might not *want* to fit."

CHAPTER FIVE

LOLA DECLINED LUNCH. Not only was she not hungry, but she had to get to work. She needed to process everything that had happened that morning.

She'd been worried that she found Grant too attractive and that the good side he was showing might skew her perspective, until he'd started talking about his parents.

She knew people had affairs. She also knew ambition blinded people, so they didn't think what they were doing was wrong. And maybe it wasn't. It sounded like his mom and dad were equal opportunity cheaters. They might have even had an open marriage.

But she'd never thought about how that lifestyle could affect a child. Grant had grown up in a very different world than she had. He saw marriage as something so bleak she wasn't even sure he could define what he thought marriage was.

In a way, she felt sorry for him. She knew the world ran on emotion and connections. Since her parents' deaths she'd seen just how important those things were. Celebrating holidays. Having people to confide in. Knowing people had your back—

She supposed he had those things with his two best friends. Before she'd moved to Montana, she'd had those things with friends, too, but she wanted family. No. She longed for family. For those wonderful ties that had been snatched from her when she'd lost her parents.

With his thoughts on relationships abundantly clear, she no longer had to worry about being attracted to him.

And she had work to do.

She took her notes from that morning's session to the deck outside the bifold panel doors of her bedroom. The thing stretched the length of the house and was filled with Adirondack chairs, chaise lounges, a table and chairs and a hammock. It also had a view of the ocean that took her breath away.

Setting her notes on the table, along with her laptop, she made herself comfortable on one of the chairs.

The scent of grilling hot dogs wafted to her and then evaporated as she read her notes again and again, unable to come up with a theme or a structure for how to showcase Grant's life. The obvious course of the story would be to demonstrate how Max had changed him. But Grant didn't want that. He also might lose Max to Samantha Baxter's extended family. Which was too complicated to sort out in a way that didn't bring his motives into question.

She had to think fresh, think outside the box, figure out how to tell this story.

She toyed with the idea of highlighting the idealistic kid he'd been at university, but lots of people were idealistic before they got into the real world. God knows she had been. Plus, his assessment that he had intelligence, imagination, and an education could come off as vain. Vanity was one of those attitudes they were steering clear of.

No more ideas came. Eventually, she found herself staring at the ocean, thinking again about how different her childhood and Grant's had been.

Her parents had taken her everywhere. Movies. Museums. Theme parks. Zoos. Even to Virginia Beach for vacations. Grant never mentioned a vacation, trip to the zoo, or even a movie.

She didn't want to make his parents out to be negligent, neglectful or even simply bad. Not to protect them, but because that wasn't the tone they wanted to set. Grant was self-made, true. But ruining his parents to demonstrate why he was self-made fed into the he-only-thinks-of-himself attitude most people already had of him, an assumption his book needed to change.

She thought again of her parents. How fun they had been. How easy it had been to return home after trips to war zones or anywhere the global stories were happening.

As if the memories were falling dominoes, she saw the places she'd been, her trips home, and flying off again to cover something significant happening in a distant land. She had been in Kuwait the day she'd gotten the call from her boss to return to New York because her mom and dad had been murdered. Mary Louise Torino, the show's executive producer, had wanted to go to Pennsylvania with her, but Lola had flown into Pittsburgh airport, not JFK. She'd driven to her hometown. Gone to the police station. And crumbled.

The sound of someone knocking on her door came through the opening that led from her suite to the deck. She rose and went back inside to answer the door.

Grant stood in the hall, wincing. "I hate to bother you, but Max is spending some quiet time in his room. If we want to get a little more work done today, we could."

Rather than continue to try to decipher notes that weren't coughing up a theme, time with Grant to get more information might be a better use of the afternoon. "I'll be right down."

He peered into her face. "Are you okay?"

She batted her hand. "Sure. I'm fine. I was just organizing my notes on the deck, and I lost track of time."

"Okay."

She smiled. "Okay."

Closing her suite door, she decided it had to be the smell of the ocean, the reminder of those summer vacations in her teen years that had brought her parents so vividly to her mind. Then she grabbed her notebook and her recorder and returned to Grant's office.

As she sat on the chair across the desk from him, he asked, "So where were we?"

"You'd been talking about school and your friends. But I'm having trouble drilling down to the theme we want for your story or the big picture we want to convey. I thought maybe if we talked in broad strokes for a bit, I could get more of a general idea of who you are. Basically, what I want to be able to do is write an outline that focuses on sections of your life. For instance, school will segue into your first job which will segue into you leaving that company and starting your own company, etc. etc. And from those broad strokes maybe a theme will appear."

"Okay."

He spent the next hour basically outlining his life.

School.
First job.
Left to create apps.
Market too crowded.
Developed new office admin software.
Sales shot to the moon.
Got married.
Sued by the first company he worked at—won the suit because his software was not at all like theirs.
Their suit actually advertised why his product was better. Sales went through the roof again.
Initial public offering of stock in his company made him richer than he'd ever imagined possible.

*Created all kinds of products that made his sharehold-
ers rich.*
Wife had affairs.
His board wanted to play it safe.
He was frustrated.
Angry.
He fired thirty people in thirty days.
Board ousts him.
Wife files for divorce.
Car almost kills him.

"And here we are."

"You don't want to talk about rehab?"

"I told you my friends helped me find this island. I bought it. I did my rehab here."

"Was it difficult?"

He stared at her. "Of course, it was difficult! And painful."

"Yet you did it because…"

"Because that's how a body heals."

She paused for a second, processing everything. "Looking at the broad strokes, I'd say the theme of your life is that you did what you had to do."

"Always." An odd relief filled his voice. "I always just take the next logical step."

Suspicion fluttered through her. The reporter in her knew he was either hiding something or he felt a little guilty because all the kindness he was showing Max was simply the next step for him. He had no feelings. No love. No empathy for his son. He was merely taking the next step.

Was that why he didn't seem fazed that he might lose his son?

She shook her head to clear it. It didn't matter. He would either raise Max or Max would be raised in France. It would work out.

And Grant would adjust.

His dealings with Max were none of her business—

A thought struck her and she almost gasped. Even if she took Max out of the equation, Grant's life was still changing. He was leaving his island and returning to work. Whether he knew it or not, to ease his way back into the business world, he would have to be a better person.

She suspected Giovanni knew that. Gio might have insisted on this autobiography to help Grant see that he couldn't hire an office full of staff and fire half of them the way he had the former employees who hated him.

He had to change.

And the universe had sent him Max.

She'd already seen a kinder, nicer side of Grant because of Max.

She might not be able to put Max into the biography, but she couldn't help noticing that Grant was changing.

Taking the next step, the way he always did.

She returned to her suite to input the broad strokes of his life into her computer, almost as an outline. The theme of change, Grant changing, really grew on her. She could set up his life, show where he had gone wrong, demonstrate that he knew he had to change to go back to work with a new company, a new staff, new investors and a new board.

And maybe even end it on a cliffhanger: a *Will he change? Will he make it?* ending.

It wasn't the perfect idea yet, but something about it felt like she was on the right track. She knew from experience that stories frequently twisted and turned. Themes morphed.

But for now, she had a vision of a sort, something that could guide her into asking the right questions.

She felt so good about it that she showered and dressed for dinner in a sundress and flip-flops. She let her humidity-curly hair go wild and crazy and went downstairs to the patio by the pool where Grant was again grilling.

When she saw only Max lounging on a chaise with one of his chapter books, and Grant manning the grill, she stopped. "Did Jeremy go home?"

"After lunch, remember?"

That was right. He'd gone home after the hot dogs, when Max had gone upstairs, maybe not to nap, but to rest a bit. The second work session that afternoon had made it feel like two days instead of one. That's why she'd gotten confused.

Max pulled his sunglasses down his nose so he could look at her. "He's coming back tomorrow."

She didn't know where Max had gotten sunglasses, but he was clearly enjoying the beach lifestyle.

"That's cool."

Grant agreed. "He'll be back tomorrow morning for swimming and palling around while we work." Grant snorted. "Getting to kid-watch by the pool has Caroline acting like she's died and has gone to heaven."

Lola laughed.

"Then while you assemble your notes in the afternoon, I'm taking the boys out on the boat."

She glanced at Max. "Wow. That sounds fun."

Max nodded. "It's going to be awesome."

She looked for signs that Max was upset and saw none. Whatever Grant was telling him behind closed doors, it was helping him to cope.

As she walked over to the grill, Grant gave her a quick once-over. "You look nice."

His unexpected compliment sent a ripple of pleasure through her. "Yeah. The book's starting to come together in my head, so I thought I'd dress up to celebrate." She glanced at the steaks on the grill. "Anything I can do to help?"

Grant leaned against the sideboard and crossed his arms

on his chest. "No. Just got to wait for everything to cook. We're good." He nodded toward the table. "Max and I even set the table."

She smiled approvingly as she glanced at it. Grant was absolutely changing. She wouldn't mention it and mess it up, but right now the theme of Grant changing seemed to be right on the money.

Max said, "I used to set the table all the time."

"We also talked about his mom a bit more," Grant said, giving her a significant look.

Realizing she was correct, Grant was talking to Max, helping him to deal with the loss of his mother when they were alone, she glanced at the little boy who had gone back to reading.

"Yeah. They didn't have a memorial service. So, I called Fletcher. We're going to have one."

She peeked at Max again. He was still fine. "Here?"

"We decided on Manhattan. You know...a day trip on a private jet. That way we can sort of... Wrap it all up."

He was talking about giving Max closure. Those conversations he was having with his son weren't a one-way street. Grant really was listening to Max, thinking things through, doing what Max needed. It was simultaneously smart and sweet. Max wasn't just a logical next step. Grant was being a father to him.

Her heart warmed as she said, "Okay. I can use the day you're gone to work on the book."

"You're on the guest list."

She blinked. "There's a guest list?"

"Yes. Fletcher gave me some names. I have a private detective looking for Samantha's cousins so they can be invited too. It'll be small. Late Friday morning." He flipped the steaks. "I thought we'd need a break from the book anyway. Plus, there are still things belonging to Max in Samantha's condo. We need to get them out before it's handed over to a real estate agent."

She nodded, once again peeking over at Max. If he was paying attention to their conversation, he was okay with it. Probably because Grant had already talked all this through with him.

They ate their steaks with salads and finished the cherry pie Denise had made the day before. After dinner, Max sat with his feet in the pool, with Benjamin Franklin at his side. The whole evening had been subdued. Grant might be helping Max, but the little boy still silently grieved. Even the dog appeared to be making sure Max was okay.

She let Grant put Max to bed on his own and was just about to leave the pool patio and go to her room when he returned. "He has a million questions."

"I'll bet."

He retrieved two beers from the outdoor kitchen refrigerator. "Luckily, I had read a few articles on children grieving."

She took the beer he handed her. "When did you have time?"

"After lunch before I came to your room to get you, I searched the internet."

"And?"

"And it appears that when talking to a child about death, honesty is the best policy."

"It usually is."

"When he came downstairs, I asked him if he had any questions, and he did."

"And you helped him?"

"You say that as if it astounds you."

"No. It's all good." It was better than good. He didn't merely have instincts; he had worked Max into his life. He made concessions. He gave Max the kind of priority Lola would bet he never gave anyone else.

Even though she was seeing it, it still amazed her. She

couldn't forget this was the guy who'd fired someone every day for a month. After he told a reporter he'd done it to motivate them, most people believed he couldn't possibly have any empathy to indiscriminately fire thirty people with families and mortgages.

But after his accident and with his son, Grant seemed to be behaving like an entirely different person. The theme of Grant changing solidified in her brain.

Grant said, "What fell together for you today about the book?"

"The idea that you're a guy who takes the next logical step," she said, careful to keep the word *change* out of her answer for two reasons. First, she didn't want to influence him. If the book was about change, the theme would happen naturally. Second, he might not like the idea that he was changing. She was seeing it, but he might not be. She didn't want to inadvertently tamper with that.

"You have goals and smarts. But you also have a nice thread of logic that runs through your life—evidenced by how you're handling Max."

He laughed. "It always amazes me when someone assumes logic is unusual. You do realize there was a time when the world ran on logic."

"Not so much anymore." She took a pull on her beer. "Everybody's out for the next big thing, instead of the next logical step."

"Exactly."

The ocean breeze wafted over to them. She inhaled deeply. "It's so peaceful here."

"It is." He glanced around. "This might sound weird, but the place feels totally different with Max here."

"I'll bet your pool never got so much use."

He laughed. "My dog has also never had so much fun."

"You'll miss him if he leaves to live in France."

"Maybe. But I also don't want to do the wrong thing. God only knows what will happen when I go back to work. I barely have time for sleep, let alone time for a little boy. Plus, he could *choose* to live with his French cousins. I don't want him to feel pressured."

He also didn't want to be disappointed. He didn't say it. But up to this point he'd been leaning toward *wanting* Max to be raised by people he knew. Now that Grant himself was someone Max knew, he'd included himself in the equation.

All these changes gave her reason to hope that he wouldn't just shuffle Max off to a new home while he was still grieving, still trying to find his way. Grant was going to do the right thing for his little boy.

She laughed, suddenly feeling a million pounds lighter. Max would be cared for. Her book had found its legs. She could stop worrying.

The silent night air relaxed her a little more.

"So how many ghostwriting projects have you done?"

She looked over at Grant, not surprised he'd changed the subject. "Only four. One a year since I bought the ranch."

He gaped at her. "You bought that ranch immediately after your parents died?"

"I went through some horrific emotions. Made worse by the fact that they caught the guys who killed my parents almost immediately. They were two addicts looking for money for drugs. My dad apparently heard them and came out to the kitchen. The one kid panicked and shot him. My mom raced out and they shot her."

"Oh, my God. I'm sorry."

"The kids were caught just down the street. The evidence against them was overwhelming. They still had the gun on them. Had my dad's wallet. They confessed, told the story of my parents coming into the kitchen, then took a plea deal to avoid the death penalty. And it was done."

He studied her for a second. "That quick?"

"Yes. It was set in stone in less than a week."

"That must have been jarring."

"That's exactly the word for it. My parents were gone—never coming back. I felt like there should have been more to it than that. You know…some time at least to process things."

She took a breath. "Instead, I was left feeling out of sorts and unable to get myself back to normal. I tried returning to work, even flew to New York but couldn't leave the airport to go to the office. I'd broken an engagement to take the assignment of traveling for the network. I'd given up the love of my life for a job—"

"You'd given up the love of your life?"

"I was engaged when I got the network job offer. Jeff was a happy small-town guy, homespun." She smiled. "He reminded me of my dad. When I got the offer, the whole world opened up to me and I knew I couldn't refuse it. It was everything I'd studied for. Everything I secretly dreamed about. But I also knew Jeff couldn't handle having the mother of his kids in a war zone. That would not have been fair to him. So, I broke off our engagement."

"Sounds like a no-win situation."

"It was."

"Did you miss him?"

"I didn't at first. The job was everything I wanted and more." She shook her head. "I can't even explain how happy I was. And he found somebody else. I totally believed I'd made the right choice. Then my parents were killed, and the reality of life set in. The job might have been wonderful, but I didn't have a close friend who wasn't connected to the network. I also didn't have a partner. Or a home anymore. Without my parents, there was no home. When I most needed someone in my life, I was alone."

"Like Max is now."

Two days ago, his perception would have surprised her. Today, she realized he saw everything, processed everything, around him. Maybe even with more understanding than a true narcissist would have. Meaning, he might not actually be a narcissist, but simply an exacting businessman, so focused on his work he always did what he believed needed to be done—damn the consequences.

"My parents were gone. The job I'd ditched the man I loved for was suddenly irrelevant. Pointless. My life was a big, black hole and it seemed that every major choice I'd made had been wrong."

"I felt that when I woke up in the hospital."

His perception might not surprise her, but his admission had. "Oh, yeah?"

He chuckled. "Oh, yeah. I built a company that a board of directors could yank out from under me when they decided my management style was inappropriate. I'd married a woman I no longer even liked most days. And some fool on his phone almost killed me. I was like...what's the point?"

"My realization was more like there's got to be more to life than this. Or maybe there has to be a way to blend what I needed personally with what I needed professionally."

"So how did you end up with a ranch?"

"I rented a car at the airport and started to drive. After a week of hotels and fast food I found myself in Montana. Where I was reminded of nothing. I knew no one. Nothing reminded me of the love I'd pointlessly thrown away. I hadn't done a story anywhere west of the Mississippi. None of that was even vaguely familiar. And, honestly, it was a relief to feel nothing. The house was quaint. Most of the time my world was silent. I found peace and after the first year of grief, I felt better. Then the reality of the finances kicked in."

He nodded, which she took as permission to keep talking.

"I should have rented a house in peaceful, quiet Montana...or even *bought* a house. Instead, I'd bought a *ranch*."

"And now you're broke?"

"And now I'm broke. The place doesn't make money. It *costs* money. The cattle I sell only pays for the hands who work there, and part of the feed. Every cent I've earned ghostwriting goes into that money pit. Most of my retirement is gone because I need it now. If I don't do something soon, I will have to file for bankruptcy."

"Why don't you sell it?"

"It's beginning to look like that's my only option. I gave running the place my best shot. I can't make it profitable. Once we finish your book, I'll meet with a real estate agent. I'll probably take a loss...which essentially will mean ponying up the rest of my savings. But I'll be free."

"And then what?"

She shrugged. "This ghostwriting gig is pretty fun."

He laughed. "That can't be a living."

"It pays better than you think. Plus, I still have my parents' house in Pennsylvania."

His eyebrows rose. "After four years?"

"I rented it out."

"Ah."

"I should probably make a decision about that. You know... get some closure for myself."

"From what I read, closure is the thing. You can't go forward until you make peace with the loss by tying up loose ends."

"Those must have been some articles you read."

He laughed. "They were. That's the brilliance of the internet. You really can find just about anything you need to know."

He leaned back on his chair, linking his hands behind his neck. The material of his T-shirt stretched across his muscular chest, drawing her eyes to it. Attraction twinkled through her. Urges she hadn't felt in forever blossomed. She hadn't even been held by a man in four long years. The time had flown, and she had barely been aware of it. But being with Grant seemed to be waking up the part of her she'd forgotten existed.

"The danger is not checking and rechecking the information, verifying sources."

She took a quiet breath. *His* waking up her hormones was one thing. *Her* acting on her reactions was quite another. Even as attractive as he was, he wasn't her type. She liked stable, quiet, happy people. Her ex had been the epitome of the strong, silent type. A guy who wanted a family and a home in a small town like her parents'. She wasn't sure that was what she wanted now. But she'd never forgotten how happy she had been with Jeff. All because his strength came from stability. After losing everything, she now knew the importance of that.

Grant's emotions were all over the board and usually confusing. Worse, his beliefs about relationships were opposite hers.

She did not need to worry about or even pay attention to her awakening hormones. He was not the right guy for her.

"Look who you're talking to. I was on network news. Verifying was my middle name."

The night got quiet again. The peace she'd felt before returned, surrounding her like a blanket. The decision to sell the ranch was the first step to finding her way back to herself. Her real self. Then maybe she'd be ready to look for love again.

She could give Grant a little credit for the decisions that were coming so easily tonight, but only because he owned the island where her stalled-out brain seemed to be clearing. He was the first person who'd gotten her to talk about her parents, about the ranch, because in a way she knew that part of her story reflected poorly on her. Even though she'd needed the peace and quiet of Montana, the answer hadn't been to buy a business she couldn't run. Most people would see that as at least bad judgment. Others might think she'd taken a tumble off the deep end.

It had been easy to tell him, though. Not only did he understand mistakes because he'd made some whoppers, but also he was smart enough not to judge but to listen—

She saw it then. The danger. She was a serious person who wanted to mend her life. And here she was on a private island with a handsome man, somebody she found incredibly attractive, somebody she was easily opening up to. If she didn't watch herself, something could happen between them. While his good looks and charm drew her, telling her story, connecting with someone after years of being alone, was a hundred times more tempting.

Especially since she was coming out of her grief, ready to be herself again and most likely vulnerable.

She had to put some distance between them.

She rose from the patio table. "I should turn in."

He smiled at her. "Me too. I'll see you in the morning."

Her chest tightened. Sharing with him had seemed objective, but his smile was warm with intimacy. He kept saying she'd witnessed the oddest moment of his life. Now, he knew she'd screwed up royally after her parents' deaths.

They had a connection.

He rose out of politeness but that put them toe-to-toe again, as they'd been on the first night she'd stayed here—the night she knew he'd considered kissing her. The warm air filled with that kind of promise again, a kiss, a potential romance to satisfy their attraction—

She stopped those thoughts, reminding herself she and Grant were not a good match. Still, as she walked into his house, a house with which she was now familiar, the connection she felt with him strengthened, confusing her.

The sense that she belonged here rippled through her.

But she didn't belong here. She couldn't. Even Grant intended to leave this island to return to work. There was not a place here for her.

She shook her head, telling herself to stop imagining things that weren't there. Particularly those connections she was so sure she felt. They could be nothing. Grant's attraction to her might not be as strong as she thought—

No. A woman always knew when a man wanted to kiss her.

Still, it didn't have to be a problem if she kept her distance with Grant. If she couldn't, she would keep her wits about her and notice when things began turning into something they shouldn't. That was how a person survived in a war zone.

She laughed to herself. She'd been to real war zones. An unwanted attraction did not qualify as one, but the instinct for self-preservation was real and right—

Or maybe it was a sign that *all* her instincts were returning?

That she really was coming back to herself after four long years of grief and confusion.

She stopped on the stairway. She was coming back. That's why she could remember her parents without falling into a deep depression. That's why she was seeing so much into what was happening with Grant. The reporter she had been was finally waking up.

CHAPTER SIX

THE NEXT MORNING at breakfast, Grant waited until Lola arrived before he turned to Max. He didn't necessarily need Lola's support, but he did want her to be apprised of what was going on.

"We have something important to talk about."

Max said, "We do?"

Lola's attention fixed on Grant.

"Your mom gave me a letter that says you are my son. But there are reasons I believe we need to be sure of that." When Max looked confused, Grant said, "Reasons we need to confirm that."

Still confused, Max glanced at Lola.

Which was exactly why he had wanted her in the room. He was good with Max. But every once in a while, he needed backup.

"There's a test," she said. "A DNA test that will tell us for sure that Grant is your dad."

Max's gaze whipped back to Grant.

"It's a precaution."

Lola tapped Max's hand so he would look at her. "We're doing the test to make sure. So that there aren't complications down the road. But we're fairly certain you're Grant's son."

Max nodded.

Grant said, "Your mom's letter told me that you had some cousins in France."

"Mademoiselle Janine and Monsieur Pierre."

Grant didn't know why he was surprised Max knew their names. Samantha had said they spent time with them. But the little boy's familiarity with them shot the oddest negative feeling through him. Something strong enough to tighten his gut.

"Mademoiselle is a lawyer like Mom was."

The easy way he spoke again struck Grant negatively, but he ignored that in favor of practicality. Max knowing their names could make Charlie's job a lot easier. "Do you know their last name?"

"Rochefort."

Denise arrived with bacon and eggs for Grant and a toasted cheese sandwich for Max. She asked Lola what she would like, and Lola requested a bagel and coffee.

Pins and needles raced through Grant. He had no time or patience for mundane things like breakfast with Max speaking so casually about people Grant didn't know, but Max appeared to know very well.

"What does Pierre do?"

"He's a painter," Max said then took a big bite of his sandwich. "He lets me paint too." He peered at Grant. "With *oils*."

Lola said, "That sounds fun."

Max turned serious. "Oils are expensive."

Grant frowned. "Oh, do the Rocheforts have money troubles?"

Lola sent Grant a warning look at the insensitive question.

But Max shook his head. "I don't know. They live in a huge house. With a yard as big as the park by our condo where Mom took me to play."

"Oh."

Max ate another three bites of the sandwich in quick succession.

"Anyway," Grant said, "I have a friend who will be coming here this morning to start the test."

Max nodded. He quickly finished his sandwich. "Can I watch cartoons?"

"Sure."

"I'll go with you," Lola said, rising from her seat.

"You haven't gotten your bagel yet."

"I can eat it cold."

Grant heard the subtle recrimination in Lola's voice, but he had absolutely no idea what he'd done wrong. He couldn't have his doctor take the DNA swab without an explanation to Max. He also hadn't thought he was insensitive asking about Pierre and Janine.

Anger skittered through him. He hated their pretentious names—

He stopped himself. Confusing emotions buffeted him. One was fear. He hadn't even known Max three full days, but the thought of handing him over to strangers set his nerve endings on fire. Now, he understood what Lola had been telling him the day Max arrived when she'd said he couldn't hand the little boy over to strangers. But they weren't strangers to Max. They were strangers to Grant—

Who—as his father—was the one charged with protecting him. Even if that meant protecting him from the odd, probably lonely life he'd have with Grant.

The sound of Jason returning on the sea cruiser eased into the dining room. With a sigh, Grant tossed his napkin to the table and walked out of the house toward the dock.

As he reached the boat, his friend, Art Montgomery, the doctor who had cared for him when he arrived on the island to heal, jumped out. Wearing shorts and a tropical print shirt, he shook Grant's hand.

"So how are you feeling?"

"A little overwhelmed." He slapped Art's back. "Getting the DNA results will help a lot."

"I understand. You can't make decisions until you know for sure the little guy is yours."

"Right." He agreed in principle, but he thought of the French cousins and Max running into their arms and his nerves caught fire again. Deciding it had to be because he didn't know the Rocheforts, he made the plan to call Charlie as soon as Art left and have him dig up every piece of information known to mankind on the lawyer and painter, who lived on a property with a yard as big as a park.

Not that he was angry, bitter or jealous. He was just concerned for Max.

Really.

Art caught his arm. "All that's great. But I was talking about your health—your legs. Is everything okay?"

"Yeah. Great. Fine. Wonderful."

"You'd tell me if they weren't."

Grant laughed. "I count on you. So, yes. I would tell you."

They walked to the house and Grant guided Art to follow him in through the family room doors. A set of steps took them to the main floor where Max, Benjamin Franklin and Lola sat on the big leather sofa, watching television, waiting for Jeremy to arrive with Caroline.

"Hey, Max. This is my friend, Art. He's a doctor."

Art smiled at Max.

Max said, "Hi."

"Hi to you too," Art said ambling over to the sofa beside Max.

"That's Lola Evans," Grant said. "She's helping me with a project. Lola, this is Art Montgomery."

"Pleasure to meet you."

"Pleasure to meet you too," Art said, shaking her hand.

The way Art smiled at Lola sent the same weird feelings shooting through him as thinking of Max running into the arms of the French couple.

He reminded himself he couldn't have anything with Lola beyond their work relationship, but he seriously hated the idea of her with another man.

He took a cleansing breath and smiled at Max. "Art's going to take the swab we need to do the DNA test we talked about."

Max nodded.

"There's nothing to be afraid of," Art said. He pulled a swab from his bag and unwrapped it. "In fact, I'll demonstrate on your dad."

Grant nodded and sat on one of the chairs.

Still talking to Max, Art said, "I'm just going to put this in your mouth and swipe it a few times—"

Grant opened his mouth. Art put the swab in and rubbed along his cheek, demonstrating for Max.

"When I'm done, you and old Ben can go out to the pool."

Max nodded again. Lola watched him carefully. Probably looking for signs of distress. Grant appreciated that she was so protective with Max, but right now, in this minute, Grant was filled with more distress than he'd imagined a person could feel.

What would he do if Max *wasn't* his? Send him to some pretentious people in France? Forget about him?

Why the hell had he even asked for confirmation, when he could have taken Samantha's letter at face value and raised Max himself?

The questions confused him so much his breath stuttered.

Art swabbed the inside of Max's mouth and Max smiled and faced Grant. "Can I get my bathing suit on?"

"Sure," Lola answered before Grant could. "I'll even take you out to the pool, so you'll be there when Jeremy and Caroline get here."

He nodded eagerly and raced off. Art packed up the swab and headed to the door. "If I put a rush on this, we'll have an answer tomorrow."

Grant walked him outside and then to the dock. "Thanks for coming out."

"It's good for me to see you doing so well," Art said, stepping into the boat again. "You made a remarkable recovery."

"And now it's time to go back to work."

Art shook his head. "If I had an island like this, I'd never leave."

"So, what you're saying is I should look for employees willing to work here."

Art laughed and jumped inside the cruiser.

The boat eased away from the dock. Grant returned to the house, but he heard the sound of Benjamin Franklin and Max in the pool and went to the back patio.

He ambled to the chaise beside the one Lola sat on. "I thought that went okay."

Her gaze never left Max. "Nine-year-olds are tricky. I wasn't sure how much he understood. He's smart enough to know what you were doing, but I don't think he comprehended why. I also recognized you had to be honest with him. But I hope he doesn't start connecting dots and thinking you're trying to get rid of him."

All the horrible feelings Grant had when Max talked about Janine and Pierre rose again like ugly black ghosts in a graveyard. "You heard how he talked about Janine and Pierre. Pierre who lets him paint with *oils*."

Lola studied his face for a few seconds, then she laughed. "You're jealous!"

"Of people I don't know? I don't think so. But I am worried about Max, and I do see what you were saying about not rushing him into going to live with them."

"Are you inviting them to the memorial service?"

"I have a private eye who's worked for me since my divorce. If he finds them, I'll have Fletcher call them to see if they can come to the memorial."

"Makes sense."

"And if they can't, then we have to take a trip to visit them before *any* decisions are made."

She nodded.

He glanced at Max and Benjamin Franklin. "If you want to get set up, I'll wait for Caroline and Jeremy."

She rose from the chaise. "Okay. See you in a few minutes."

Caroline and Jeremy arrived almost immediately after she left. His house manager shooed Grant inside, and he headed to the office where Lola awaited him. He talked about starting his company for what felt like minutes but was actually hours.

Then he took the boys out on the boat that afternoon. But the strangest feeling followed him around all day.

The sense that this child had changed his life without even trying.

New concerns arose. He knew who he was and what he wanted. Could he suddenly change his mind about goals he'd had forever? Not only was that impractical, but also, he had to take Max's needs into consideration. Wouldn't it be better to be raised by a loving couple than a single workaholic dad?

He thought of his sister. The way she could fool babysitters and sneak out of the house. The trouble she got into that his parents never saw. Anything would be better than being raised by a parent who ignored him, left him to his own devices, forced him to figure out life for himself.

He couldn't pay attention to the crazy feelings swelling his heart in his very tight chest. He had to do the right thing. Not for himself, but for Max.

The next day Art called with the news that Max was his son. The relief he felt was overshadowed by truth. He wanted to raise Max. But for once in his life, he could not be selfish. He could not inflict the same kind of mixed-up childhood he'd had on Max.

Still, he also couldn't hand his child over to people he didn't know—

They had to spend time with the Rochefort couple.

Because the most important thing to factor into this decision was Max. It seemed that he loved Janine and Pierre but what if he didn't?

What if he wanted to live with Grant?

Would he change his plans for his future? Could he?

When they boarded Grant's luxurious jet on Friday morning, Lola glanced around in awe. The buttery brown leather seats weren't arranged in rows, but rather seating areas. Four seats in the back could have been a conversation grouping. The four seats in the front were arranged around a small table.

"Why don't you stow that laptop," Grant said, pointing to an overhead compartment in the back. "And play Yahtzee with me and Max."

She looked at Max, adorable in his black suit, white shirt and little black tie. She longed to give him anything he wanted, be anything he wanted, to help make this day go easier. But that was actually part of her problem. It had been too natural to like Grant, to simply be herself with him, so she'd decided she had to pull back. But the trip this morning pointed out that she was also getting too involved with Max and it might be difficult for him when she left.

Though she'd be as present for the sweet little boy as she could, she also realized the importance of maintaining some distance to make her leaving easier on him—the way it should be. She was not part of the little family they were making. She was a temporary employee. She was finally seeing how confusing the situation had gotten, but she could fix it.

She patted her laptop case. "I brought work."

"Yeah, we figured that," Grant said with a laugh. "But you could take a break."

The urging in his voice tempted her. She'd loved playing games with her parents as a kid. Her mom and dad had made her part of everything in their lives. But she was not really part of Max's life—or Grant's. She was hired help. She didn't want Max feeling that he had lost someone else when she left.

She stowed the laptop for takeoff but sat in one of the chairs away from the game table. "Don't forget that we have a deadline."

Grant said, "Okay. Do your thing," but Max's head tilted in question.

She wished Grant would explain to his son that they were working on a book that needed to be completed within a certain time frame. That would go a long way to helping Max understand her position in his life. But Grant said nothing more about her, just retrieved the game from a bin beside his chair.

"We can't play until the plane is in the air," he said to Max. "So, let's buckle up and get this trip started."

Max said, "Okay," but his gaze slid back to her again.

She ignored him, knowing that ten minutes from now when he was engrossed in the game, his confusion would be gone.

The plane took off and reached cruising altitude. Grant set up the Yahtzee game and he and Max began playing.

Lola retrieved her laptop. With no table in the little conversation area, she set it on her lap, which bunched the skirt of her black sheath. She straightened it then slipped off her black pumps to get comfortable for the flight.

Just as her mom had always told her to travel with an umbrella and a raincoat, she'd had Lola pack a little black dress and black pumps no matter where she was going.

"Just in case," she would say.

In the middle of reading her notes from Grant's last two sessions, Lola smiled to herself. Her mother had been a pistol. More than anything, Lola missed her unsolicited advice and folksy wisdom. She also missed her dad's bear hugs. Barbecuing on the back deck in the dead of winter—

Max cried, "Yahtzee!" and Grant groaned.

"You're the luckiest kid I know."

Max giggled but Lola winced at his poor choice of words given that they were flying to his mom's memorial service. Still, she said nothing. There were plenty of times every day when Max and Grant played together or swam together or took walks on the beach without her while she worked. Staying out of their conversation solidified the idea that she was here to do a job.

She took a breath and began arranging notes, turning phrases into sentences and sentences into paragraphs, until the pilot announced that they were landing in twenty minutes and gear should be stowed before they fastened themselves into their seats.

They taxied along the private airstrip to a hangar where a limo awaited them. Max piled in then Grant motioned for Lola to get inside before he slid onto the seat beside Max. She'd deliberately put herself on the bench seat across from them, keeping that little bit of distance, to ease Max away from seeing her as part of their family.

Grant said, "Remember what we talked about last night?"

Max nodded. "I remember."

Lola tried not to notice his serious eyes and somber expression, but the little boy's sorrow couldn't be missed.

"This might be really hard," Grant said.

Max nodded.

"If you want to cry that's okay. If you want to punch something save that for when we get home."

Max nodded again.

Lola stopped a smile. She couldn't imagine Max wanting to punch something, but apparently that was a possibility that Grant and Max had discussed the night before.

That was another thing. Max and Grant had lots of conversations when he put his little boy to bed. She wasn't there for that. And that was what really demonstrated that she wasn't part of their family.

They spent lots of time without her. As long as she maintained this distance, she wouldn't need to worry about Max missing her.

The drive to the mausoleum where Samantha's ashes had already been interred took longer than Lola had anticipated but Max and Grant appeared to be unfazed. Though they didn't speak much, neither seemed nervous. Both were quiet.

They finally arrived. The limo drove by a small line of cars then stopped in front of the building entrance. The driver came around and opened the door. Lola stepped out. Max got out. Grant slid out.

He sucked in a breath, then took Max's hand.

Max smiled up at him.

Lola's chest expanded. Grant had absolutely no idea how attuned he was with his son, but they had nonverbal communication down to a science. More than that, Max trusted Grant. She could see it in his solemn eyes.

They walked into the building and Gio greeted them. Tall with dark hair and green eyes, he said, "Hello," to Lola, squeezed Grant's shoulder in one of those male gestures of solidarity, then he stooped down in front of Max.

"Are you okay?"

Max nodded.

"That's Gio," Grant told Max. "He helped arrange most of this."

Gio smiled. Max nodded again.

Max's silence might have concerned Lola, except he was still communicating, nodding. And looking to Grant.

Gio directed them to the seats in the front row. They passed Fletcher, who waved slightly. The rest of the seats were populated by well-dressed men and women who could have been friends, coworkers or neighbors of Samantha's. There were enough people that they couldn't easily be categorized.

And no one had told her if Janine and Pierre had been found, and if they had been, if they were coming to the memorial service.

A clergyman walked behind the podium and began talking about Samantha. How smart she was. How well liked she was. What a great mom she was.

Max raised his head proudly.

Lola's chest pinched. Her parents had been buried on the same day, the same service, in side-by-side burial plots. The whole town had been there. A lot of her friends from the network had flown down for the funerals.

She'd been numb. She could barely remember what the minister had said about them. She hadn't even had anger to comfort her since the perpetrators had been caught and made a plea deal.

It had been a surreal nightmare.

The service ended. Max slid a rose in the small vase on the door of his mom's interment space. Lola didn't wonder why Samantha had chosen to have her remains put in a mausoleum. Max was too young to be given her ashes and with a place like a mausoleum, if he ever wanted to visit, he would know where to find her.

Samantha, it seemed, had thought of everything.

She must have been a great person.

Lola hoped Max would remember her.

They filed out of the small room. At the door, Grant and Max accepted condolences. From Max's polite thank-yous, it was clear Grant had coached him. He cried twice and Grant comforted him. To look at them, it was hard to believe they'd only *met* when Fletcher brought him to the island a few days ago.

A gentleman walked up to Max and his eyes widened. "Pierre!"

He stooped down and scooped Max into his arms. *"Mon fils."* He hugged Max tightly. "How are you?"

Max looked at the floor. "I'm okay."

Pierre hugged him again. "I am so sorry." He broke the hug and rose. He extended his hand to Grant. "I'm Pierre Rochefort."

Grant shook his hand. "I'm Grant Laningham."

"Oui. I have read about you. Your ideas are genius."

Lola stood off to the side. She'd seen Grant's eyes narrow when Pierre said he'd read about him. But they returned to normal when he'd called Grant's ideas genius.

"Thank you." He smiled at the man. Slightly older than Grant, Pierre had a few strands of gray in his dark hair. "Would you care to have lunch with us?"

"Actually, I arranged to fly out soon. Janine had a trial, and it was too late to ask for a continuance or for someone else to stand in for her and I need to get home."

"I'm sorry. The memorial was a spur of the moment thing," Grant said. "Max and I were talking, and we decided we needed to do it."

"I understand," Pierre said, perfectly reasonably, like someone who didn't get ruffled easily.

Lola liked him on the spot. She didn't miss the way Max eased over and caught his hand, as if he were accustomed to holding it.

"I miss you," Max said, his voice shaking.

"I miss you too." Pierre stooped to Max's level again. "And we will see you very soon." He hugged Max again. Tears filled his eyes, as he held on tightly, the bond between them evident.

He let Max go and swallowed hard. "My plane leaves in a

little over an hour, just enough time to get to the airport." He caught Grant's gaze. "But we have much to discuss."

Grant pulled in a breath. An odd tension passed between them. Grant took Max's hand and eased him beside him. Pierre looked down at Max, obviously seeing the proprietary gesture for what it was.

Grant didn't like Pierre.

Or maybe he'd just gotten his first taste of what losing Max would feel like?

Gio came over. "The superintendent of Samantha's building is waiting for us with the combination to her condo door." As if just noticing Pierre, he said, "I'm sorry. I didn't mean to interrupt. I'm Giovanni, Grant's publicist."

"It's fine. I'm on my way to the airport. It was a pleasure to meet you," he said to Grant.

In all the tension of the situation, everyone had taken their focus off Max. When Lola looked down at him, the little boy was staring at the rose he'd slid into the holder beside his mom's interment spot.

It was as if he'd suddenly realized this was the last moment he'd have of his mom. His little blue eyes filled with tears.

Pierre said, "Goodbye," and headed to the right. Gio directed Grant and Max to the waiting limo. "I have my car. I'll meet you at the building."

Grant said, "Okay."

Lola's eyes ached with the weight of unshed tears. She'd been an adult when she'd lost her parents. Max was nine. He would live most of his life without his mother. She swore she could see that realization in his face. The absolute unfairness of life filled her tired, lonely soul. It had been a long, lost four years for her. Now, Max was facing the same thing.

Holding Max's hand Grant led him back to the limo. Lola silently followed them, her heart heavy. Her emotions about the loneliness she knew Max was about to face mixed with her own loneliness and filled her with sorrow.

Max stopped suddenly. Still holding Grant's hand, he turned to face her. She kept walking until she reached them.

Looking at her through his tears, he caught her hand and started to the limo again. "You should walk with us."

The sweetness of him including her nearly did her in. All this time she'd worried that he would miss her when she was gone when the truth was she would probably miss him more.

When they were seated in the limo, Max slid off the seat with Grant and sat beside her. "It's okay."

Her tears fell. "I know."

Grant wiped away tears too. "We're going to stop at the condo, gather some of Max's things, then make arrangements for the rest to be boxed and shipped to us."

Lola nodded.

"Then we're having a nice lunch before we head home."

Max caught her gaze. "I'm going to be okay."

She smiled through her tears. "Of course, you are. Pretty soon all your memories will be of good things you did with your mom. They'll all be happy."

He nodded. "That's what my dad said."

The proud way he said "my dad" hurt her heart. Grant was taking to parenting like a fish to water, but she'd seen Max catch Pierre's hand. The decision about where Max should live might not be Grant's. Max might actually want to live with Janine and Pierre. What had been Grant's hope when Max first arrived now might be his greatest sorrow.

She was thinking exactly that that night, sitting on Grant's dock, looking out over the dark water that sporadically sparkled in the light of the moon.

"You okay?"

She turned to see Grant standing behind her. She hadn't even heard him approaching.

"Yeah. I'm fine."

Dressed in jeans and a T-shirt, as she was, he lowered himself beside her. "Long day."

"Is Max asleep?"

"Out like a light."

"He adores you."

He looked out over the water. "I love him too. I see myself in him. Tall, skinny, looking around at everything, trying to figure out what's going on. Except he has good reason to be confused. I just had bad parents."

She laughed. "You did okay raising yourself."

Grant snorted. "Right. Luckily, Max seems to have a lot of people willing to help him." He paused for a second, then said, "He didn't like that you set yourself apart from us."

She shrugged. "I don't want him to miss me when I'm gone."

Grant inclined his head. "You only miss friends if they never come around again."

She shifted on the wooden boards to face him. "Are you offering me the chance to vacation here? Because I've got to warn you, I will take you up on it. Once I dump the ranch, I'm going to need a break."

He laughed, then surprised her by putting his arm around her shoulders, shifting her so they sat side by side. "You know, one of the best things about having money is being able to find goofy little holes in people's lives and fill them."

Having his arm around her felt so right, so normal, and she was so tired that she had to fight the longing to lean against him and absorb some of his strength.

"By providing vacations?"

"Yeah. Weekends. Plane tickets. Fruit baskets."

She laughed. "Fruit baskets?"

"Not everything's about getting away."

A little too comfortable being this close to him she shifted the conversation to get them back to the real purpose of her being on his island. His autobiography. "Tell me you did that before your accident, and we will have a totally different book on our hands."

"Before my accident I didn't see anything but work."

"Getting hurt changed you?"

The look that came to his dark eyes told her that he realized she was interviewing him again, looking at angles, hoping for secrets.

"Do you ever take a break?"

She wanted to. Right now, with the remnants of the grief of her own loss mixing with Max's loss, her entire body ached. Life seemed like a long, endless, lonely road.

But she couldn't tell him that. She couldn't confide. She was an employee.

"I've got five weeks left to turn in a manuscript that's as close to publishable as I can make it. I don't have time to—"

He stopped her with a kiss. The kiss he'd almost given her twice.

Her heart stumbled. Her breathing stuttered. Everything inside her woke up and glittered with happiness. She told herself this wasn't right, that she shouldn't get involved with him, then she let herself fall into the kiss. She hadn't kissed anyone in four long years, and it was delicious—he was delicious. Soft, yet demanding.

She reached up to catch his shoulders to steady herself and the feeling of touching him sent delight shimmying through her. She liked this guy that everybody else thought was a holy terror. He'd barely shown her his holy terror side. She'd seen more of his nice guy side. She'd seen someone trying to tell his story. Someone good to a child he hadn't even known he'd had.

And he liked her.

He liked her enough to finally kiss her.

He pulled back. She blinked at him, his strong-featured face, his dark, sensual eyes. She should feel odd, uncomfortable or at least have the sense that kissing had been wrong. But nothing had ever felt as right.

"I've been wanting to do that all day. You seemed so alone."

Disappointment stopped her heart. "You kissed me because you felt sorry for me?"

He snorted. "No. I kissed you because I want you and I usually get what I want. But I need you for the book. Plus, we have a little boy to consider. No skinny-dipping. No inadvertent remarks."

She laughed. Joy tumbled around in her chest, confusing her. She might like and understand him, but she wasn't supposed to even *want* to get romantically involved with him. If that wasn't rule number one between bosses and employees, it should be. She sobered her expression. He was right. He needed her for his book and they did have a little boy to consider.

"Plus, I think anything between us has to be *your* choice." He sniffed a laugh. "Actually, I think you're going to have to seduce me. I'll take that as your proof that us sleeping together won't hurt the book or our relationships with Max."

His presumptuousness made her sputter. "Who says I want you?"

"After the way you kissed me back?" He laughed again. "Nice try. Something's been bubbling between us since you stepped onto my dock. It's starting to annoy me that you're so good at ignoring it when I'm not."

She laughed, but even as her heart told her to open up, to enjoy this, part of her wanted to run. She'd lost her parents. She'd lost a fiancé through a bad choice. She might not be strong enough to handle another loss. Plus, he was nothing like the one guy she'd loved enough to want to marry.

Still, temptation rose and swelled. There really was something between them. He'd made himself vulnerable with his admissions. If nothing else, she had to be honest.

She scooted a few inches away from him. "I'm not as good at ignoring it as you think."

He grinned. "Oh, yeah?"

"Yeah." The rapport between them amazed her, comforted her and scared her silly. How did someone become so close to a person in so little time, with almost no effort? Especially when they really had nothing in common. And with the exception of the things he'd been telling her for his autobiography, they really didn't know each other—

She scooted a little farther away.

He motioned to the distance she'd managed to put between them. "You're saying one thing but doing another. I'm also as concerned as Max was that you won't interact with us."

"I'm an employee."

"So? We like you."

"All right. The truth? I worry about Max getting attached to another person he might lose, and I don't want to get too attached either."

"To me or Max?"

"Either." She shook her head. "Both." She nudged him with her shoulder. "I feel like I'm finally coming out of four years of grief, and I can't go through that again when I lose you when I leave." She nudged him again. "You're very likable."

He laughed. "I have a hundred former employees who will dispute that."

"You have former employees who would probably gape in awe watching you with Max." She caught his gaze. "You're different. Not the same guy who got hit by that car."

"No. I *am* the same guy. We're just in different circumstances. Max needs understanding. I need time to get to know him. And you act like a person who is lost and tired. Is it so

wrong that the three of us spend the next five weeks trying
to adjust to our new realities?"

"When you put it like that, it seems like the right thing
to do."

He shook his head and laughed. "How have you survived
the past four years?"

"I have no idea. I woke up one day the owner of a failing
ranch. Trying to make that turkey work took every waking
minute of every day. I didn't have time to analyze it or myself."

"You found time for ghostwriting."

"That was about ten or twelve weeks out of every year.
The rest of the time I was a woman drowning."

"Well, that ends now. Tomorrow, you come out on the boat
with us. You might not eat all three meals, but the two you
do eat will be with us." His expression became serious. "You
need this. You're so sad even Max noticed. Let's all enjoy
these next few weeks."

Lola nodded, as her head and her heart battled. She really
did need some relaxation, some fun, some interaction with
good people while her thoughts sorted themselves.

But, oh, how dangerous that was. She could still feel his
kiss on her lips, causing the longing for more to hum through
her. But what was more? Laughter and kissing…or a real connection that would find its way into her heart and fill it—

Then break it when it was time for her to leave.

Why couldn't she be the kind of woman who could enjoy
herself, have a fling, spend time with a little boy who needed
her, then go home with good memories.

Why couldn't she put her vulnerability on hold and simply enjoy herself with no regrets?

CHAPTER SEVEN

GRANT WOKE THE next morning feeling better than he had in years. For the second time in his life, he wasn't a hundred percent sure what he was doing, but buying this island for his recovery had worked out just fine. It had been the best decision of his life.

Which would make propositioning Lola the second-best, if only because he'd learned a thing or two in the past four years about taking timeouts.

His first time-out had been necessary—maybe even forced upon him—because he'd needed to recuperate after his accident. As he'd regained his strength, living on an island had become fun, invigorating. Not fighting with his board or working every waking minute had become a chance to enjoy his wealth and his friends. It had shown him the good side of life, shown him that work had to be rewarded with rest.

He was fairly certain that was what Lola needed right now and if romance came into the picture, so much the better. Not just for him. For her. She needed a space of time when she had no worries, where she didn't ponder her future, when reality was thousands of miles away.

Because reality for him and her and even Max was that they would all be starting over. When they left this island, they'd have to establish new lives and learn how to live them.

All three of them needed this space of time before the real world bombarded them again.

Which was what made his relationship with Lola different than his relationship with his ex. There was an end date. There'd be no marriage, no living together, no arguments. Just fun.

He jogged up the stairs to the third-floor bedrooms and he smiled when he walked past Lola's suite. It might take her awhile to get the courage to seduce him, but they had plenty of time. Despite some rumors about him, he was a patient man when he needed to be.

Plus, he hadn't said he wouldn't entice her in the weeks she took to make up her mind. He had all kinds of fun things in store for her.

He reached Max's room and quietly opened the door just in case Max was sleeping. He wasn't. His son stood on the wraparound deck, looking at the water. He held the sailboat Grant had found online and had delivered to the island, along with a beach ball, a corn hole game, a few Frisbees, a bucket ball game and some extra floaties for the pool.

Closing the door, he stepped inside the bedroom. "Hey, Max!"

Max turned. "Hey, Dad."

Grant didn't think he'd ever get over the emotion that washed through him every time Max called him dad. Part thrill, part warmth, it tightened his chest and softened places in him he didn't realize he had.

"Ready for breakfast?"

"Is Lola awake?"

"Not sure. But it's not appropriate for two gentlemen to knock on her bedroom door."

Max's head tilted.

"We want to give her privacy. She could still be sleeping, or she could be going over her work notes."

Max nodded and they went inside to change him out of his pajamas and into shorts and a T-shirt, then they went downstairs to the dining room.

Denise entered with a smile. "I was thinking you guys might like French toast this morning."

Max's eyes lit. "With cinnamon?"

"Always."

Grant laughed and his thoughts when he woke whispered through him again. This really was a special space of time for him, Max and Lola. Now, he simply had to convince Lola it was okay to take advantage of it.

"French toast it is."

As if she'd timed it, Lola arrived just as Denise entered with two plates of French toast.

"If you want French toast," Denise said, "I can bring you a plate."

Grant said, "She can have mine. I'll wait."

"No waiting," Denise said. "There's more already made."

She left the dining room and Grant caught Lola's gaze. "Good morning."

Her cheeks pinkened as she averted her eyes. "Good morning."

Busy with the syrup, Max said, "Yeah. Good morning."

"Caroline's going to be taking the boys to the mainland this morning. First, they'll see a few tourist attractions, then they're going to the public beach. Caroline says it's good to be with other people sometimes. They'll also have lunch before they return."

Lola smiled at Max. "That sounds amazing."

In his simple, honest way, Max said, "I know."

"Which leaves us almost six hours to work," Grant said, as Denise set his plate of French toast in front of him.

Lola caught his gaze. Uncertainty filled her pretty blue eyes. "I'm not sure how you want to divide up the time."

She was clearly confused about how their lives would change now that he'd suggested they have some fun in the weeks they had together on the island. He would say he was about to teach her that their work and play could be accommodated in special times like the one they were in now, but he didn't want to insult her. Instead, without spelling it out, he set their schedule.

"We have a lot of work to do. You more than me. So, let's factor in time for you to process everything I've said and type up your notes."

"I can type up notes at night," she said, slathering syrup onto her breakfast. "If you want to talk the whole time Max is gone, I'm all for it."

He smiled at her, and she immediately averted her gaze.

Averting her gaze when she'd arrived in the dining room had been natural. But a second time of her not wanting to look in his eyes? That wasn't her. She was smarter, bolder, than this.

Maybe he'd misjudged her? Maybe she wasn't ready for something to happen between them?

Caroline arrived and herded laughing Max and Jeremy into the cruiser to go to the mainland. As Grant stepped away from the boat, Lola stood on the dock behind him, waving to the happy trio.

The boat edged away from the wooden platform then took off toward the tourist town.

Grant inhaled a quick breath. "We are so lucky to have Caroline."

"I know." She hadn't been pleased that Grant seemed to have arranged for them to be alone the morning after he'd all but told her he wanted to sleep with her. Not just because it was heavy handed, but because they had work to do. Seeing this as her big chance to make sure Grant didn't have any ideas, Lola added, "We need all the work time we can scrape together to get your biography written."

He faced her. Their gazes caught. She wasn't even sure they should have a romance and his tactic of getting everybody out of the house to give them privacy wouldn't push her into doing something she wasn't ready for.

Instead of making a pass or even a suggestion, he turned toward the house and motioned for her to walk with him.

"Absolutely. I've been thinking about my life...you know, things I want to get into the book and I think today might be the day I talk in detail about my work."

She peeked over at him. In a T-shirt and shorts, he looked more like a beach bum than a genius, but he was a genius. He liked his work and wanted to talk about it. In fact, he seemed eager to talk about it.

Maybe arranging for them to be alone wasn't a setup?

Relief tiptoed through her but was quickly replaced by unexpected disappointment. He was good-looking, smart, strong. Why wouldn't she want to make the most of their time together? Why did everything always have to be so serious with her?

Her life was a mess. She would be returning to Montana to face reality. He was offering her almost five weeks of not dwelling on that. Why couldn't she just let go?

Because she was afraid of a broken heart.

Which was ridiculous. If she went into this knowing it was temporary, that she was only looking for a respite, not forever, she should be able to control her emotions. Plus, she also couldn't be angry with him or herself when his autobiography was done, and she got on his cruiser and headed home. She'd been strong before her parents' deaths. And if she really was coming back to herself, she could be strong again.

She took a breath. With the sun already hot, golden rays shimmered around him. Almost as if Fate were saying, "Who cares about reality? Here he is. Yours for a moment. You know better than anyone that there is no such thing as permanent or forever. You should enjoy."

She should!

Still, she couldn't pull the trigger. Even with them alone for hours she couldn't turn to him and kiss him senseless. She needed another day or two to either assure herself she could handle this or get herself to the point where she could absolutely say no to his suggestion. Say no to kisses that felt so right. Say no to having someone she could talk to, open up with. Say no to moonlight walks on the beach, swimming, waking up with him in paradise—

Obviously oblivious to her thoughts, Grant kept talking. "I don't think people have any idea of how hard I worked. Everybody assumes that being a genius smooths your path... and in a way, it does. I see things others don't. But that doesn't mean I don't spend long hours sorting through ideas, combining ideas, figuring out how to turn ideas into products that have value. And don't even get me started on marketing."

Excitement skittered along her nerve endings. She might not be able to decide about a romance between them, but this morning she would hear what it was like to be a genius. This was the part of reporting she loved. Getting the inside story.

"Actually, that reminds me of something I've been wanting to ask. I'm telling you my life in segments. You're not just typing out what I told you. You're piecing it all together."

"Sort of." Glad he was ready to work, and give her time to think about the romance end of things, she led the way to the house. "There are two ways to tell your story. I can do it in segments like work, education, creating and leading. Or I can put it together chronologically, taking those segments you've been dictating and weaving them into a timeline. My instincts are telling me the timeline is the way to go. But I haven't made up my mind yet."

He nodded.

They spent the next two hours in the office with him talking about work. Lola was very glad for her recorder because she would be researching the technical terms he tossed around as if everyone knew them. Like most people, she had a grasp of the basics about computers, software and the way the world had changed with a few simple inventions. But Grant was a computer guy. She wouldn't sell him short by simplifying concepts that should be complex to demonstrate that he deserved the success he'd found.

They stopped for lunch, which she refused. Her brain popped with too many ideas to sit and eat a sandwich and talk about nothing. She returned to her room to search the technical things he'd spoken of so casually.

Working on the deck, she heard the cruiser return and glanced at her watch. It was after two o'clock. Grant had left her alone to work.

Watching as happy Caroline led her two boys into the house like a short string of baby chicks, she wondered about all those employees who'd complained about Grant.

Oh, she knew he probably was a taskmaster of a sort, but he seemed particularly attuned to her need for time to work on her own. Surely, he'd also realized employees needed time to implement the ideas he had in his head. What could have happened to make him lose his temper and fire so many people?

She carefully approached the subject after dinner. They'd eaten in the dining room. Max and Benjamin Franklin had had a little beach time. Then Grant had taken his little boy upstairs to get into pajamas. Now, they were alone, on the pool patio, surrounded by the sounds of the ocean and a million stars.

"Of course, I gave people time to work on projects."

"Were you the kind of boss who interrupted work sessions? Did you watch over their shoulders?"

He laughed. "Next you'll be asking if I used a whip to prod them or put a ball and chain on their ankles to make sure they couldn't leave their desks."

"So your Laningham the Destroyer name is all about that month you kept firing people?"

"That and the fact that I'm a perfectionist." He caught her gaze. "Most people aren't, you know? To them, good enough is good enough. But it can't be when you're coming up with new products." He shoved his chair away from the umbrella table. "Beer?"

As always, the patio was saved from darkness by the lights of the pool. The heat of the night air was alleviated by a soft breeze. A full, bright moon hung over the ocean.

His explanation satisfied part of her curiosity about the month before he was ousted, but not all of it. There was something missing. Maybe even something he didn't fully understand himself?

Still, she had the sense this wasn't the time to push. And even if it wasn't the night to seduce him, either, the quiet, the moon and the breeze lured her to relax.

"How about a cocktail? What do you have behind that bar?"

"What do you want?"

"I love margaritas and Cosmos...can you make either of those?"

"The margaritas are premixed. I never found a recipe for one that guests liked better than what I could buy already made. The Cosmo I'm pretty good at making."

"I'll take a margarita." She ambled up to the bar and slid onto a stool. "I have to ask. Did you learn to bartend for a reason?"

"You mean like did I bartend while I was at university?"

"Yeah."

"No. My parents paid for my education and before you say anything I knew I was lucky. I've thanked them for that."

"But?"

"No buts. I was lucky. I thanked them because it was the right thing to do."

She thought about that as he poured ice and the premixed margarita into a blender. He hit the button. The noise disturbed the perfect peace of the island for a solid minute, while he retrieved a glass and rubbed the rim in salt. When the blender stopped, he poured the frozen margarita into the glass and handed it to her.

"You are so good at that."

"I think I'm a natural." He sucked in air as he looked around the patio. "When I was recovering, there wasn't much I could do. But I noticed a hole of a sort when my friends would come down to check on me. Everybody could grab a beer but not everybody could make a cocktail. So, while they were back at work doing their day jobs, I learned to mix drinks. Got Caroline drunk twice. Denise was a better taste tester."

Lola laughed. "Who would have thought."

"Those two were as important to me and my recovery as my physical therapists and doctors. We've become close over the years. I'll never sell this place. It'll be a weekend getaway for me."

"And your two best friends."

"And my two best friends."

He grabbed a beer for himself and took a seat on the stool beside hers. "Okay, enough about me. My head's about to explode from this morning's session and you spent most of the afternoon transcribing. You've got to be tired too."

"I am."

He nudged his head in the direction of the chaise lounges.

"So maybe we just sit and watch the ocean for a few minutes. No talking. Just sipping our drinks."

"Sounds good to me."

She noticed again that he wasn't pushing her toward the relationship he was so sure they both wanted. She stretched out on the chaise, letting the sound of the surf hypnotize her.

"I was so bored during therapy."

She laughed and poked him playfully. "I thought you said no talking."

He faced her. "This isn't me talking for the biography. This is me talking to a friend."

"Okay."

"You see people in wheelchairs, and you recognize they're injured but subconsciously you're thinking they can still get around so it's not that big of a deal." He glanced out over the ocean. "But people have no idea what someone in a wheelchair gives up. What they are missing. Especially freedom."

"Sounds like your injury gave you a lot of life lessons."

"And perspective and a sense of appreciation."

"You talked about your friends coming to your aid and visiting. Did your parents help out?"

"Because they were already retired, living in Key West, they made one visit to the hospital in Manhattan and one trip here once I was stable."

Her face scrunched. "But you were injured, and they're doctors."

"Yes, and they got access to my charts and talked to my specialists and told me I was fine."

"If you were in a wheelchair, you weren't fine."

"After looking at my charts, they knew I would heal." He snorted. "Actually, that's how I took it. When my parents told me I was fine, I realized they were essentially telling me that there was nothing so broken it couldn't heal. I reasoned that meant I had to do my physical therapy and then I'd be fine."

"They didn't visit you?"

"They made the initial trip to the hospital to get the scoop on my injuries. They visited me here once. But I preferred that they stay away. Healing is hard. Therapy is hard work. I didn't want them around watching—criticizing."

Her brain went blank. *He didn't want them here.* Maybe he didn't want anybody here? Except a house manager and a cook.

And his friends, whom she would love to meet.

But that explained why he and Caroline were so close. Denise, too.

The breeze billowed around them in the darkness. She thought about who Grant had been and who he'd become, and amazement filled her. Maybe while she listened to and eventually wrote his story, she should be taking a page from his book. Learning from him. He knew how to accept things, to take things in stride. He also knew how to live in the moment, do the next logical thing, and enjoy what he had.

That's what was missing in her life. The lesson she should have learned in the last four years. Hiding hadn't helped. Losing herself in work hadn't helped.

Accepting her losses, accepting that she'd made a mistake and would have to sell her ranch, accepting that she had to rebuild her life, those had helped.

Grant had helped. Hearing his story had helped.

She finished her margarita and took the glass to the bar. "I guess I should be getting inside."

He rose from the chaise. "Me too. Tomorrow is another fishing day for Max and Jeremy."

She remembered that he'd said he wanted her to go with them the next time they went out on the boat. Temptation rose and she couldn't quite quash it. She was tired of being alone. Tired of hoping for things that wouldn't happen. Ready to accept reality and move on.

And maybe that's the realization Grant had found after his accident when he learned how to accept his life—enjoy reality instead of wishing for what couldn't be.

Enjoy reality instead of wishing for what couldn't be.

That was what she needed to do.

She felt as if someone had opened the windows of her life and let fresh air inside. Felt as if she could breathe. Felt for the first time in years that everything was going to be okay.

They walked into the downstairs family room. She turned to the left to go to the stairway, but he turned right and picked up a remote.

"Twenty minutes of a ball game wouldn't hurt."

She laughed and walked over to him again. She smiled up at him, then pressed her hands to his cheeks. "You're checking up on your team."

He winced. "Maybe a little."

"You're so interesting."

He chuckled. "If another person had said that I'd probably be insulted. Coming from you though, I know that's a compliment."

"It is a compliment."

Unable to resist, she rose to her tiptoes and pressed her mouth to his quickly, completely. But he didn't let her pull away. He caught her elbows and kept her where she was, deepening the kiss, opening a part of her that had been closed for four long years. She felt the strength of him, the surety. If there would ever be a person she could trust with her life, herself, even for only a few weeks, it would be him.

The certainty of that scared her as much as it comforted her. How could a person not fall in love with him?

That was really the problem. There was no question that she'd enjoy being with him, but could she give him up?

She'd given up her fiancé and hadn't cared as long as she was busy traveling. But when her life stopped when her parents died, she'd realized what she'd thrown away. Selling her ranch would keep her busy for a while…but as soon as it was sold and she was on her own again, would she miss Grant? Or would she regret not taking advantage of their time together?

She pulled away and he smiled at her. The urge to let go and let nature take its course with them tiptoed through her.

Then she remembered she had always been the smart one, the reasonable one. The only time she'd let go and done something without thinking it through—buy a ranch—she'd made a huge mistake.

Even if it meant she'd miss out on something wonderful, she could not afford another huge mistake in her life.

She would take the time to think this through. But the odds had gone up significantly in his favor.

CHAPTER EIGHT

LOLA STEPPED AWAY, studying his face for a few more seconds, thinking thoughts he was absolutely positive he'd never be privy to. For a woman who made her living poking into other people's lives she held her own story close to the vest. She'd told him bits and pieces, snippets of her past that showed she understood the things he'd told her, but she never gave away enough that he felt he knew the real her—the complete her.

He probably never would.

She turned to go to the stairway. "Good night."

"Good night."

Shaking his head, he picked up the remote and found the Lions game. Everything inside him pulsed with life but she'd been able to walk away.

Still, she was the one who'd initiated that kiss.

The hot, prickly feeling of success surged through him. He told himself he'd made progress that night, and to a degree he had, but in the grand scheme of things he really hadn't. Losing her parents, then making such a big life change—one that had blown up in her face—hadn't scared her as much as it had scarred her.

Oddly, that was probably why he related to her. He understood her enough that he would never push. He might try enticing her, but he'd never push her. He'd lose all the possible fun they could have together, the friendship they could probably forge, before he'd push her.

He plopped to the sofa. Two strikes and a runner on third should have held his attention, instead it kept straying to Lola. He closed his eyes remembering her softness and her strength. He had the weirdest feeling she didn't know how strong she was but if she ever picked up on that she would be unstoppable.

And tremendously fun to fool around with.

The thought made him groan and though he tried to focus on the baseball game, he couldn't. He went to the primary suite equal parts turned on and exhausted. The thought of the busy morning he'd have with the boys forced him to his bed. The time spent in the pool with them had left him depleted enough that he fell asleep immediately. Unfortunately, morning came in what felt like twenty minutes.

He crawled out of bed, just a little bit sore. Wounds from his accident sometimes rebelled, but a hot shower and some topical ointment for pain were usually enough to get him moving. Once he started moving, he simply kept moving until his body was awake and responding normally.

He and Max ate breakfast alone. He waited for Lola with the nervousness of a guy debating asking the pretty girl in high school for a date. But she never came to the dining room.

Assuming she was already working in her suite, he fought back the disappointment, then did his fatherly duties of rounding up his crew and preparing to take them fishing. When everything was on the boat, he, Max and Jeremy marched across the dock. They jumped in the boat, ready to head out.

Two seconds before he would have shoved off, Lola came running down the weather-beaten boards.

A hand on her big sunhat, she called, "Wait for me!"

Grant helped her into the boat. A little clumsy in her flip-flops and unaccustomed to getting into a cruiser, she all but fell into his arms.

The moment caught and held. It felt so normal, so natural

for her to be in his arms that he simply enjoyed her. Her crazy need for independence. The way she could get him to talk without even trying. The yearning he saw in her eyes every time he caught her off guard.

She studied his face. He couldn't tell what she was looking for and didn't know if she found it when she inched away from him, but it was one of the happiest moments of his life. He almost couldn't believe that she'd joined them—and that she hadn't pulled away when she'd fallen into his arms. He didn't feel ice chips melting away, he felt life returning to her spirit.

He grinned at her. "Nice hat."

"My mother always told me to be prepared." She took a breath, smiled at Max. "You said this would be awesome."

He gaped at her as if he couldn't believe she'd doubted him. "It is!"

Time stopped for Grant again. All his money couldn't buy the emotions that swam through him at seeing Max happy, and Lola in the boat, willing to have some fun.

The air filled with promise, and he faced his crew. "Well, let's get going then."

As he eased the boat away from the dock, Jeremy and Max—both in swimming trunks and life vests—knelt on the bench seat to watch the wake and feel the spray on their little boy faces.

Lola slipped out of the sweater she had over her tank top and shorts. Grant snickered and shook his head. Her mother must have been something for her to hold onto her advice to always be prepared as if it was the only thing she had left of her—

He frowned. Maybe it was? Memories, advice—that was it. That was all she had of her parents. He supposed if his parents had given him loving advice instead of lectures, he might want to remember it too.

But they hadn't. They hadn't been around for most of his life, and when the result of that was a tragedy, they felt they should be able to waltz in and pretend nothing had happened.

Well, he wouldn't let them.

He stopped the boat at one of his favorite fishing spots. The boys raced for the rod and bait, eager today because they knew what they were doing. The sun was hot. The kids were happy. Lola also had her face raised to enjoy the warmth that surrounded them.

He wouldn't let negative thoughts ruin this good day.

That was how *he* survived.

Lola savored the warm rays on her face, but she knew she couldn't stay that way long or she'd sunburn. She found the sunscreen Caroline always packed for the boys as Grant talked them through the process of baiting the hook and casting off. It surprised her that the boys themselves weren't fishing, but they seemed perfectly happy to kneel on the bench seat and watch Grant do all the work.

She studied the rod and noted its size, remembering from a fishing trip or two with her dad that grouper could be large— probably difficult to reel in. Which was undoubtedly why Grant was doing all the heavy lifting.

"Why not try for something smaller so the boys can fish too?"

Max and Jeremy gaped at her as if she'd said something sacrilegious.

Grant laughed. "We like to eat grouper."

"Yeah. We like grouper," Max and Jeremy echoed.

Grant had once said that Max reminded him of himself when he was younger and this morning, she saw it. Not just the physical similarities of bone structure that showed Max would someday be tall like Grant. But the idiosyncrasies.

The way they held their heads or looked out over the water. Even the way they walked.

The boys returned their attention to the water. With the rod anchored on some kind of holder, Grant watched the sway of the line. Lola got more comfortable on the seat, suddenly wishing she had a book. Not because she was bored but because it seemed to be a good place to read. While her three companions had fun, watching the line, hoping for a fish, she could be reading in the warmth of the sun with the ocean sparkling around them.

Eventually, they caught a fish. Max and Jeremy danced as Grant displayed some serious fishing skills, reeling in the big fish: the grouper they wanted.

"This is dinner," Grant said proudly. "Jeremy, do you want to stay and eat with us?"

He nodded eagerly.

Lola shook her head, wishing she could write about this. No matter what Grant said about the perfectionist he was when he worked, *this* was the real Grant Laningham. And this was the real story. Recovery and change. So much so that even a surprise like a child arriving unexpectedly hadn't fazed him.

They drove back to the dock. Max and Jeremy raced ahead to tell Caroline about the big fish.

Lola waited for Grant. She followed him to an unexpected room on the first level of his house where he prepped the fish for cooking.

She glanced around at the gray, cement block room with an unremarkable table, a ladder, some tools. "This does not match the rest of the house."

"Actually, this is the most practical room of the house."

"I suppose." She faced him. "The boys really enjoyed the trip."

"I did too." He laughed. "I'm fishing alone when there aren't any guests. I love having built-in companions."

"You also seem to like teaching them. Have you ever thought of teaching as your second act?"

He gaped at her. "You're kidding, right?"

"Imagine what you could impart to students at the university level."

He shook his head. "No. And don't suggest I do a TED Talk either."

She laughed heartily. "Are we going to work today?"

"This afternoon." He glanced at her. "Caroline will keep the kids. I thought we'd invite her to dinner too, since Jeremy wants to eat dinner here."

"Sounds fun."

"Okay. I'll meet you in the office at about two." He paused. "Unless you want to join us for lunch? I'm grilling hot dogs. There might even be potato chips."

"With all this sumptuous-looking fish for dinner? I'm saving my appetite."

She left him tending to his fish and headed to her suite where she opened her laptop. She knew Grant didn't want Max in his story, but something inside her had to write up what she'd watched that morning. Not the events, but the emotions. Max loving his dad. Grant teaching, nurturing those two little boys. Giving them not just his time but an experience they might carry with them forever.

With all that out of her system, she consulted her outline, fleshed it out a bit, took transcribed notes and began arranging them into chunks of the book.

The oddest thing happened. As she arranged, wrote and rewrote passages of his conversations, she heard Grant's voice in her head as if he were reciting the words as she typed.

She heard his voice.

She smiled. When she heard the voice of her subject, she knew the story had found its footing. She really was telling *his* story.

She felt so good about the biography that after their session that afternoon, she again showered and dressed for dinner. She tightened her long tresses into a bun at the top of her head with tendrils of curls falling haphazardly around her face and neck.

When she stepped onto the patio, the boys were in the pool with Benjamin Franklin and Caroline lounged on a chaise, enjoying a cocktail.

"You're not going to get her drunk," she chastised Grant.

Caroline snorted. "I survived the learning-to-bartend years. I now know my limit. I also know when to stay away from him because he's in the mood to entertain."

Lola laughed.

"But he's especially happy with me tonight because my family's going to Busch Gardens for the weekend, and I asked to take Max."

"Oh?" She glanced at Grant who was peering at the fish.

"Honestly, my sisters all have granddaughters. There's never been a little boy for Jeremy to run with. So, Max would be a welcome addition."

"Sounds fun."

"It will be," Grant agreed. "The kid needs all the breaks and fun he can get right now. An amusement park with a bunch of kids fits the bill." He pointed at the closed grill. "Grouper's just about ready." His head tilted. For the first time since she arrived, he really looked at her. "You dressed up again. You must be pleased with what you wrote today."

It had stopped unnerving her that he didn't merely see everything, he had a way of analyzing what he saw and keeping it in that steel trap mind of his. Instead, she accepted it. That was part of who he was, and that part was interesting and sometimes even amazing.

She strolled to the chaise beside Caroline. "Yes. I am extremely pleased. Not just with the work we did today but with the project. It finally seems like it's coming together."

"When do I get to read it?"

She frowned, pretending she wasn't sure that was a good idea, though she liked having her subjects read the story as it was evolving. But it was always better if Grant believed something was his idea. He wasn't the only one who noticed things. Noticing things was her job. She never argued with her subconscious that saw as much as his did.

"If you promise to keep in mind that this is little more than an outline that's being fleshed out, I could let you read it any time you want."

He perked up. "Really?"

"It's your story. Plus, reading at this stage might remind you of things you want to add. Points you want to make."

"I feel like I'm already hitting all the highlights."

"You'll be surprised by how much reading a draft will jog your memories."

He smiled and nodded. "Okay. Shoot me an attachment in an email."

"Okay."

"Want a drink?"

She shook her head. "It's such a hot day, I think I need water."

He rounded the bar. "Water it is." He tossed a bottle to her.

She caught it like an expert.

"You played ball."

She shrugged. "Everybody plays softball at some point in their life."

"Were you good?" Caroline asked.

"Good enough that I got a scholarship to a small university. Once I got my first two years in and knew what I wanted my major to be, I shifted to a bigger school. One with a respected journalism program."

"I saw you on TV," Caroline said. "I didn't recognize you when you first arrived because I hadn't put two and two together yet, but once Grant told me you'd been a foreign correspondent, bingo, I remembered you."

"That was a really fun time in my life."

Grant snorted. "Getting shot at was fun?"

"Meeting people from all over the world was fun. Seeing cultures. I would come home from an assignment and my parents would put on a pot of coffee and quiz me." The memory of it surprised her, not with its clarity but with the jolt of happiness that accompanied it.

Caroline laughed. "I'd probably have a million questions too."

Grant peeked at the fish, then yelled to the boys. "Dinner's almost ready. Grab some dry towels."

The boys jumped out of the pool without question. Grant brought the fish to the table, along with containers of steamed vegetables that he'd cooked on the grill too. Jeremy sat by Caroline at the table. Max sat beside Grant. Because the table was round, when Lola sat beside Max she was also beside Jeremy.

The patio filled with the sounds of everyone passing dishes of food, filling plates and taking that first bite.

The air stilled. Everyone savored. Then a communal groan rose around them.

"This is fabulous!" Lola said. "My compliments to the chef."

"I researched cooking grouper a few years ago."

Of course, he had.

"This technique is the one everyone seems to like. Now it's my go-to way to prepare it."

"Well, whatever you did, this fish is amazing."

Caroline brought up the subject of Lola's travels again and did ask a good bit of the questions she'd said she would have.

The boys gobbled their food, hardly interested in Lola's life and went inside to play a video game.

The adults stayed at the table, talking the way she and her parents had when she would arrive home from an assignment.

As Caroline nodded in response to something Grant said, and Grant rose to clean the grill, a weird sense fell over Lola. She was talking about her parents without missing them... No. She was talking with other people the way she always had with her parents and not missing them.

She was making a friend of Caroline. A handsome, sexy, extremely successful man was interested in her. She'd been swimming with Max. She'd gone on a boat. And had fun.

The feeling intensified until Lola recognized it.

She wasn't moving on with her life—a term people said when they spoke of her parents, a term she hated. The jumble of feelings she'd had since her parents' deaths had settled enough that the person she'd been was finally able to see and talk and come out again.

Grant's voice intruded on her revelation. "I'm going to save this for lunch tomorrow," he said, reaching for the platter with the leftover fish.

"The boys could eat hot dogs every day," Caroline said. "But it wouldn't hurt to toss something different in their menus."

Grant laughed. "I agree."

Lola's head tilted as she watched him. He was so different, so much more likable than he'd been portrayed before his accident. And he liked her. She also liked him. No, she was enthralled by him. The person she'd been before her parents' passing would have seduced him the night he'd told her he wanted to sleep with her.

That realization intensified, bringing some conclusions. If the fog of grief and the burden of the trouble she'd made for herself when she bought the ranch really were lifting, she would be enjoying the hell out of the rest of the time she had here. Time with Grant. Time with Max. Time on an island where no one would criticize or question her. Where she could experiment with the idea that she was coming back to life and see if it was as real as it felt.

And maybe that's exactly what she should do.

CHAPTER NINE

As GOOD AS her word, Lola had sent Grant the draft of his autobiography. Because it was mostly an outline and notes with a few fleshed-out passages, he'd read through it before he'd fallen asleep that night.

When they met in his office the next morning, he was ready with comments.

"At this point, it seems like you're highlighting my logic. It reads funny to me."

"It reads funny to you because you're the guy we're writing about." Dressed in her usual shorts and T-shirt, with her hair down, she leaned across the desk, as if trying to see what page or excerpt had made him feel odd. "That's one of the reasons I like my clients to see every stage of the book. The next time you read what we have you will be accustomed to reading about yourself."

"It's first person. My voice. I know I'm reading about myself."

"See…that right there. Knowing it's your voice is what we are aiming for."

He frowned at her. She grinned at him. Her pretty blue eyes were lit with excitement. Even her pert little nose looked cute this morning.

"So, we're on the right track?"

"We are," she assured him in her confident, happy tone. "But if you want to discuss the logic thread, I'm using that to demonstrate that you weren't a bad person or even a task-master—" His eyebrows rose.

"You're driven by common sense and logic."

He understood what she was saying. He simply wasn't sure he liked it. "You make me sound like an android."

"In the first draft maybe. But as we flesh out the story, we'll flesh out your character."

"Now it sounds like we're making things up."

She laughed gaily. "No. We'll be adding layers to your personality so that the logic thread will recede into the background of the story. It will still be there, guiding readers, but it will be more subtle. And they will be accustomed to the way you worked when we get to the point where we have to talk about the month you got rid of an employee every day… the month that led to you being fired."

He said nothing. She might have avoided mentioning this before now because she'd latched on to a reasonable explanation for his behavior and was setting that up. But a shimmer of a memory rose in him. His sister. Her suicide. Gio working his magic to keep the story out of the press.

He tried to fight the memory because, like Max, he didn't want his sister in his autobiography. Her death might serve to explain things, but it felt wrong. Like an excuse for bad behavior. He didn't make excuses. He took responsibility.

Plus, Lola was better at making his actions sound reasonable than she knew. She was portraying him as human, as a person who made mistakes but moved on. When the time came to talk about the reason his board fired him, she would describe him being out of control that month because they were behind schedule. After the buildup to that point, people would see his temper as the natural result of a perfectionist not being able to get his work done.

He knew that's how she would handle it. Because he knew that's how she saw it. She was extremely good at what she did, not just a pretty face on the news. Though her face was extremely pretty, especially when she was happy.

When he realized pondering his life and the book had stopped, and he was just sitting in his chair, staring at her, liking the way her hair flowed around her and the happy expression on her face, he snapped himself back to real life again.

"What you're saying is that we're on schedule."

"I think so. In another two weeks this draft won't be a draft. It will be a manuscript and then we'll nitpick."

He laughed at her choice of words. "I am known for that."

"Which is why there's time built in for you to nitpick to your heart's delight."

"Or we could spend that time on the boat."

She laughed. "You got me out once—"

"Max got you out once. I haven't made any headway in getting you to relax."

She leaned back in her chair. "Sure, you have. I've had drinks with you. We've also sat on your patio enjoying the breeze."

"And you always questioned me. Interviewed me. I'd like a night when we could just be ourselves."

"Really?"

"You know, with Caroline taking Max for the weekend, we could fly to the Virgin Islands." As the suggestion formed in his mind, he liked it more and more. "We could have fancy private dinners. We could dance in the moonlight… and stay over."

"Stay over?"

"I'd book us separate rooms."

He watched as she considered that. When she didn't reply, he said, "Think it through. This time next month you will be on a ranch in Montana. Probably slogging through wet fields with a real estate agent, hoping he or she has a client on the line who wants it. And you'll be cursing yourself, thinking you should have taken the tropical getaway with me."

She laughed. "Yeah. I haven't forgotten that whole mess is waiting for me."

"So come away with me."

He rose from his seat behind the desk and leaned against it, in front of her. "This time next month, I'll be facing work the likes of which I haven't done in four years. I didn't leave in good standing. The world's moved on without me. It's going to be the challenge of a lifetime...so maybe do it for me?"

Her eyes softened. She really was a nice person. Someone who genuinely connected with others. Someone who felt deeply. He couldn't imagine what she'd gone through when she lost her parents. But he knew enough from what happened after he lost his sister to understand why Lola had broken.

"All right. We can use a rest. We'll return with our minds fresh and ready to go back to work."

The shock of her agreeing hit him like a punch in the gut. Still, he pretended to be casual. "Okay. I'll make the arrangements."

He walked behind the desk again. They talked about the book a bit more, first themes, then whether it was best to set out the story in topics or write it on a timeline, a chronological order of events. In the end he decided he liked the timeline. Technically, what he'd already read followed a timeline so why mess with something that was working?

Then she asked about his first company, which led to him admitting his humble beginnings, sleeping on Brad's couch so he could put all his money into his start-up. That segued into talking about the lawsuit that had nearly crushed him until he saw at trial that the testimony about his product was an advertisement that it was a step forward in software development and suddenly sales went through the roof.

"Interesting."

He sighed. "What's interesting now?"

She laughed. "I don't mean interesting as a way to nudge you to explain. It really is interesting that you saw that the trial itself was an advertisement for your software."

"I see everything."

"Yeah. You do."

She stretched, appearing to ease a kink out of her back before she rose, but all he saw was softness, feminine curves.

"I think that's enough for today. Especially if we're going away. I'll need to have all this transcribed and integrated into the document so I can rest while we're gone."

He nodded, still unable to believe she'd agreed to go away with him, but not about to question his luck. He knew he'd probably never get this chance again. As she walked to the door, he called, "Pack for two days."

She stopped. "Two?"

"Caroline said they were going away for the weekend. That's two days."

She sniffed a laugh, shook her head and walked out of the room.

He got on the phone. If he only had two days, he would make the best of them.

Friday morning, Max grinned foolishly as he headed to the door with Caroline and Jeremy.

"We'll be back on Sunday night. Probably late," Caroline said, guiding the two boys who walked ahead of her. "Did you talk to Denise about spending time with Benjamin Franklin?"

Grant said, "She said she'll bring her kids to feed him so he'll get some playtime."

Caroline laughed. "I doubt he needs that. That old, tired dog might be happy to see us go."

Grant snorted.

Lola watched him and Max, looking for signs that time

away wasn't a good idea. But Max was excited, and Grant was like a kid before Christmas. Either he needed this break from suddenly becoming a dad and trying to organize the story of his life—

Or he was excited about the *other* things this trip could mean.

Fear tried to steal her breath. In her room, finishing her packing, she reminded herself she wasn't a person prone to fear. She'd traveled the world. And she really had been shot at.

Plus, Grant had said that if anything happened between them, she would have to initiate it.

She had no reason to believe he'd changed his mind. Especially since he'd said he was booking two rooms.

Ten minutes later, she met him in the foyer.

"Ready?"

She smiled at him. "Do you really think a little scruff on your jaw and sunglasses will keep people from recognizing you?"

He hoisted his duffel bag to his shoulder. "You'd be surprised what throws people off. Plus, where we're going is exclusive. There will be people there who don't want to be recognized either. If they recognize me, there'll be like a silent pact that passes between us. Everybody's there for privacy and to relax. Nobody fangirls another guest."

"Well, this should be fun."

He motioned for her to leave the house and head for the dock. Instead of Jason, Grant drove the cruiser, surprising her. He docked in a spot with his name on it then a limo took them to a private airstrip on the mainland. Even on a private jet, the flight to the Virgin Islands was a little longer than Lola expected. Another limo met them and took them to a dock where they boarded another boat that took them to the quiet island filled with trees.

She was just about to mention that she hoped the resort

was worth the effort to get there, when they arrived at a white beach with a main building that looked like a big tiki bar and a cluster of smaller tiki huts surrounding it.

Grant pointed at it, as an employee of the resort unloaded their bags. "That's the common area, used mostly for registration. Over there—" he said, pointing to the right "—is a piano bar. Just beyond that is a five-star restaurant."

"Wow." She glanced around. "This certainly beats the accommodations in a war zone."

He laughed. "Yes. It's a different kind of travel than what you're accustomed to."

With a resort employee scurrying to take their bags to their villa, they checked in then walked along a cobblestone path through gardens and wild foliage, toward their private oasis. When they turned left and walked twenty or thirty feet along a path thick with trees and plants, she realized they'd probably been passing well-hidden villas all along.

Grant opened the elaborate leaded glass door and they stepped into a great room. Dark beams in the ceiling contrasted the white walls. Folding doors had been opened to expose their private section of beach where two well-padded chaise lounges awaited them on the white sand that led to the bluest water Lola had ever seen.

"Wow."

"I've been here before. You can mingle or your stay can be totally private, a two-day retreat where we don't have to talk to anyone."

"I thought you said you were getting us two rooms."

"This villa has two bedrooms."

His answer was so casual that she wondered if he even remembered that he'd said he wanted her to seduce him.

She didn't have time to ponder that as he pointed right, outside the folding doors, to a patio with a linen-covered table. "We can eat all three meals there. We can have a chef come here to cook for us. Or we can order off a menu." He smiled. "Like room service."

He gestured beyond the table to a pergola with white linen strips that wove through the beams, which could be drawn for privacy or left as they were to allow sunbathing.

"We can get massages there and even have drinks by the pool." A silver cart covered in white linen didn't quite conceal the refrigerator below the main tray that sat beside a sparkling pool. "I asked for the place to be stocked with beer, wine, water and the makings of margaritas."

She couldn't stop another, "Wow," as she gazed at the absolutely perfect space filled with cool sea air that blew in through the open doors. "So, this is how the other half lives."

"I wouldn't say half." He laughed. "The lucky one percent is who you'll meet here."

She faced him. "If we decide to mingle."

He shrugged. "If we decide to mingle."

"You're seriously not afraid of being recognized?"

He laughed. "I told you. Even people who recognize me won't approach us. Everybody's here for privacy. Everybody respects that."

He plopped on the sofa. "What do you want to do?"

"I think a walk on the beach would be nice."

"Me too. Then we can have lunch and swim. But after that I have something special planned for dinner."

"Really." She'd brought out her flirty voice. Not just because she could see how much trouble he'd gone to to make their two days whatever they wanted them to be; but because they were delaying real life. Living in the moment. She refused to spoil the fantasy for herself or him.

He laughed, rose from the sofa, and slid his arms around her waist. "You're not going to charm the surprise out of me so don't even try."

"I've gotten you to tell me more about yourself and your

life than you probably planned. I'll bet I can get you to spill your secret evening."

"You're on. Of course, I should warn you that I intend to sleep by the pool most of the afternoon, so your badgering time is limited."

She sniffed. "I don't badger."

"You could though," he said, before dropping a quick kiss on her mouth. "You have that in you. Like a determination to get the story could inspire you to push until you made politicians weep."

He headed for the open doors to the beach.

She scrambled after him. "Oh, yeah? So why do you like me then?"

He stopped, faced her. Rather than tease, he got deadly serious. "You keep me on my toes. I like that."

She laughed, then slipped off her shoes before following him out into the sunshine, eager to get *her* toes in the soft white sand.

They walked fifteen minutes out and fifteen minutes back. Enough to feel the tension leave their bodies. Warm from the sun, they spent an hour playing in the pool, then true to his word, he fell asleep on a chaise lounge. A few minutes later she drifted off too. Two hours after that, she awoke, totally awed by the fact that she'd let herself rest.

When she saw the time, she left the pool area and went to the room in which the hotel staff had put her luggage. It all felt weird. She knew he wanted her. Yet he had her things put into a separate room. He held her hand walking along the water. Yet he hadn't made a pass at her.

She thought about it all in the shower, washing her bounty of hair and rinsing off sunblock. He showed her he liked her without being overbearing. And without seducing her. He'd said that was her choice, so she'd have to do the seducing.

She simply wasn't sure how. He was different than anyone

she'd ever dated or slept with. For as interested as she was in him, she also recognized he was special. Something inside her didn't want to risk the relationship they had by saying or doing something wrong. And sex changed things. Even between friends. *Especially* between friends.

And then there was their working relationship. How would that change?

Wrapped in the soft white robe provided by the resort, she left the bathroom and headed to her duffel bag. She'd packed her little black dress and actually considered wearing it but decided to save it for the following day when they might eat at the restaurant or visit the piano bar.

She carried it to the closet to hang it, and when she opened the door, three gowns sparkled at her. One was red. One was pale blue. The third was basic black, with subtle sequins that made it sparkle in such a way that it looked like it was moving.

She hung her simple sheath in the closet, then examined the gowns. All three were her size. She considered that this was another service of the resort, then she remembered that Grant Laningham was the most organized problem solver she'd ever met.

And he had a big plan for this evening.

Maybe a plan that required her to wear a gown?

A thrill of happiness danced through her. It was like playing dress-up. And if he hadn't had them sent to her room, and the resort provided them, then maybe she would surprise him by showing up at dinnertime dressed like a princess.

This night was all about fantasy. They'd left reality behind for a few days. She would more than play along. She would do her part.

She carefully did her hair and nails, listening for signs that Grant had come in from his extremely long nap by the pool, but she heard nothing. Considering that her room was at the end of a long corridor she realized she might not hear him enter the great room.

When her hair, nails and makeup were done, she slipped into the red dress. Though it was gorgeous, she wanted to try on the pale blue. That one she loved. Strapless, in a simple style that caressed every curve of her body, the dress was subtly sexy. It was tasteful enough that she could have been going to the opera or even dinner in Manhattan. But the way it flowed over her curves left nothing to the imagination about the shape of her body.

It was naughty but not obvious. Just what she wanted.

Unfortunately, she didn't have shoes to match. Then she laughed. Who cared? If they were staying in their private oasis for the evening, why not be barefoot in a gown?

If they were going out, she could make do with her black pumps. After all, they'd be hidden beneath the flowing skirt.

She left her room and stopped. Hundreds of candles had been placed around the main room.

Careful, she walked down the corridor. When she reached the great room, she saw Grant standing in the center. Dressed in a tux, he held a single red rose.

Her heart stuttered. "This is lovely."

He gave her the rose and held out his hand. "This is just the start." He nodded once and music flowed around them. She noticed a string quartet standing in a corner of the patio.

She put her hand in his and he drew her to him for a quick kiss. The feeling of being Cinderella flitted through her.

"Dinner is on the patio."

She followed him out to the linen-covered table with tall candles and a bottle of champagne chilling in a bucket beside it. As he pulled out her chair, an older gentleman, also in a tux appeared by the side of the table. He set salads at each place.

Grant said, "Thank you."

The waiter said, "The main course is chicken marsala risotto."

She smiled at Grant. "Sounds wonderful."

He leaned across the table. "Wait until you see dessert."

"I'm drooling already."

He laughed and dug into his salad. "In all the excitement, we forgot lunch."

She thought about that. "Huh. I guess we did."

"You wouldn't notice because you're a two-meals-a-day person. But I was starving."

"Yet you waited for me."

"I am a gentleman."

She laughed and tasted her lemon arugula salad. "So good."

"That's another thing I like about you. You're not afraid to eat."

"Not when I'm hungry."

They finished their salads, ate the chicken marsala and groaned with pleasure over chocolate cake with raspberry syrup. Then he took her hand and invited her to dance in the moonlight by the pool. The quartet played softly in the background while they nestled together, enjoying the evening breeze and each other.

The time for talking had ended with their meal. The fantasy of being the only two people in the world took its place as they slow danced to the soft music. She wouldn't let herself think about tomorrow or her troubles. She wouldn't let her thoughts drift to where he might be this time next month. Tonight, he was hers and that was all that mattered.

It was also enough to get her to tilt her head a bit so she could kiss him, softly at first, to not disturb the mood. But as the kiss continued, it took on a life of its own, deepening, and filling her with pleasure-induced boldness.

She smoothed her hands down his back as his hands found

the closure of her dress. Surprised, she pulled back. "We're not alone."

"Yeah, we are. Listen."

She realized the music had stopped. She'd been so engrossed in the kiss she hadn't noticed.

She smiled at him. "But I'm supposed to be seducing you."

"I'd say we've always been seducing each other."

That made her laugh. He kissed away the sound in the darkness, as he undid the catch of her dress and let it puddle to the patio floor.

"You're barefoot."

"I know." Basking in her boldness, she undid his tie, then all the buttons of his silky white shirt.

Standing in the moonlight in only panties had to be the most decadent thing she'd ever done, yet a sort of rightness filled the tropical air, along with the sound of waves caressing the shore.

He looked around. "This place isn't made for first times when everything has to be perfect." He caught her hand and led her inside to the room across the hall from hers. He didn't close the door, just pulled her to him and began kissing her again.

It had been so long since she'd been held, touched, that a reverent feeling stole through her. It tried to sabotage her courage, so she took a breath, stepped away and gave him a nudge that knocked him to the bed.

But he caught her hand and tugged her with him. He kissed her, lowering her to the soft comforter. Everything was special, perfect, but she wanted the fun. She wanted the freedom. With another bump to his shoulder, she rolled him to his back and took control of the kiss. She liked this guy, and he liked her. The pleasure of that alone intoxicated her.

Her hands roamed his chest, while his found her breasts, then slid to her bottom. They'd been building to this from the minute she'd met him, but the fruition of her dreams was nothing compared to the reality of touching him and tasting him.

Her tongue drifted down her torso, but stopped when she found a long, thin scar. Reality stumbled through her. He'd been hurt. Nearly killed. But without that accident and an unexpected four years of being off the grid, she never would have met him, never had this wonderful space of time when he was just hers.

Emotion spiked. The memory of how fleeting life was mixed and mingled with the knowledge that in this moment he was hers.

They came together in a roar of desire. Tingling with arousal, she groaned with need as their passion set the world on fire. None of her past relationships had ever felt like this. But she was glad. Grant was special. Now, in her memories, he would always be.

Afterward they lay nestled together. His arm beneath her shoulders, he stroked his fingers down her bicep.

"You know what?" he said, pulling his arm from beneath her. "I'm getting the champagne."

She sat up. "Good idea."

He returned with a new bottle, popped the cork and poured a glass for each of them. As he sat on the bed again, he shook his head. "Has anyone ever told you how perfect you are?"

"You mean, physically? That's just the good luck of mother nature. And it's nothing more than symmetry. Everything is proportional and balanced."

He leaned forward and kissed her. "Yeah, well, I love your symmetry."

She giggled at his silliness. "And there are parts of you I also love. Actually, you're just about physically perfect too."

"You saw the scars. I'm not perfect."

Laying her hand on his cheek, she held his gaze to make sure he knew she meant what she said. "You're more perfect than you think."

He leaned in and kissed her again, softly, as if thanking her for her confidence in him, but this time he didn't stop. As if he couldn't get enough of her, he kissed her until arousal rose, and the champagne glass in her hand felt clumsy and unwanted. They might have just made love, but she hadn't lied when she said he was more perfect than he thought. Everything about him appealed to her—even his scars. His accident hadn't just changed him; in some ways it had made him whole.

She warned herself not to make a big deal of how wonderful and perfect he was to her. She had to bring herself back from expecting too much or even wanting too much. This was a fling. That was the one thing she knew for sure. Each of them had lives to work out. This time next month, she'd be in Montana.

In a way, she really was Cinderella. When their time was up, their affair would be over. They would go their separate ways. She had to enjoy him now.

She pulled back, took a sip of her champagne then set her glass on the bedside table. She took his glass and set it beside hers.

"I'm sensing you have a plan."

She nudged him enough that he fell back to his pillow, then she straddled him. "Just appreciating the moment."

"Which is exactly what I wanted. A little time away to enjoy ourselves."

She kissed him to shut him up.

He laughed against her mouth, and she saw it: the thing that made their being together perfect. They weren't taking themselves too seriously. And both loved to laugh. To savor. To enjoy.

She spent the next five minutes showing him just how much there was to enjoy, then he rolled her over and joined them again. Pleasure intensified until she wished, if only fleetingly, that this could never end.

But she didn't let the notion stick. They had things to do. Lives to gather up and restart. When his autobiography was done, they would go in different directions and probably never see each other again.

CHAPTER TEN

THEY WOKE LAZILY the next morning. He kissed her soundly, then got out of bed to use the bathroom. When he returned, teeth brushed and face splashed with warm water, she was gone. But she slipped into the room a few seconds later.

"I thought it would simplify things if I used my room."

He caught her to him and kissed her. Even the few inches shorter she was than him somehow made everything about her sexier. They made love again then showered together before dressing in shorts and lightweight tops.

In the great room, he pointed to the open doors. "Walk on the beach?"

"I think I'd like to tour the common area of the resort. We woke so late we didn't have breakfast. I'd love lunch."

He put his arm around her and directed her out the folding doors. "Whatever you want."

They walked along the shore until they reached the public beach for the resort. Men and women in colorful beach attire sat on blankets or chairs, reading, chatting and enjoying the day. He directed Lola to cut to the path leading to the resort and entered the space with doors folded open to give the place an outdoor feeling.

They ate lunch, swam, had another private dinner and another amazing night together. But time slipped away too quicky and suddenly it was Sunday morning. Lola slept so soundly he hated to wake her, but he couldn't seem to leave the room. He almost couldn't believe she would go back to Montana, and he'd probably never see her after that. Even if she came to his island to decompress after the sale of her ranch, he wouldn't be there. He'd be in a city, starting his new company.

He also couldn't ask her to move with him. Wherever he was going, his life would be chaotic. No matter how good his intentions, he wouldn't have time for her. She'd be alone most of the time. That would inevitably result in a breakup that would hurt them. He'd already played out this scenario with one wife. He didn't need to repeat it with a woman he adored.

It was better to simply let her go—restart *her* life.

Still, his chest hurt when he thought about her departing his island, saying goodbye to her—and mere days later handing Max off to two strangers in France. Trying to assuage the awful ache, he got out of bed, grabbed his phone and headed to the kitchen. He made a single cup of coffee and walked out to the patio. With a few clicks on his phone, he called Caroline.

When her face appeared on the phone screen, he said, "Is Max there?"

"Yeah, they're eating cereal in front of the hotel TV. Then we're going to head south, back home again." Her eyes lit. "How is *your* trip?"

"It's great. The break we both need from the book. The place is perfect. Beautiful. Sinfully luxurious. I'm going to have to give you a few days at this beach to thank you for being so good to Max."

"Max is a pleasure to have around." She laughed. "But book me a whole week and I'll call us even."

He snorted. She was a better negotiator than he was some days.

Max walked into the camera view. "Hey, Max!"

"Hey, Dad!"

Caroline gave him the phone.

"Are you having fun?"

"Busch Gardens is awesome."

He laughed at Max's incessant use of *awesome*. "No kidding. Lola and I will be back late this afternoon. Caroline says you guys are starting home now. You'll probably get there before us."

"Okay."

He smiled. "See you soon," but he suddenly envisioned himself only having phone conversations with his son, who would be across an ocean. With the time differences, they'd have to schedule their calls—

His mind rebelled at the idea that their contact would be so limited and frustrating. He silenced it. Though he'd met Pierre at the memorial service, he hadn't contacted the Rochefort couple yet to talk about Max. Plus, he had to be honest about what his life would be like after he set the wheels in motion to produce the ideas he'd been working on the last year. His days would be filled with meetings. He'd need office space, employees—

Hell, he'd have to pick a city before he could produce the products he envisioned. It amazed him that no one had thought of these things, or even accidentally stumbled across the software tools that so obviously filled needs. But if there was one thing he'd learned about his brain, it was that he saw things differently. It was a blessing and a curse. But it was also a gift. Something he had to use. He could see the future. He had the talent and imagination to bring that future to life. That was his purpose.

And he'd seen Max catch Pierre's hand at Samantha's memorial service. Max loved him.

He said goodbye to Max, then took a solid breath, telling himself to stop thinking about the future. He'd never before whined about the responsibility of having talent. Yet, this morning, in the soft sunlight, watching a glistening pool, he wanted nothing more than to be lazy, to take long weekends at resorts, travel—show Max the world—and work, but not at such a frenetic pace.

But he knew himself. He knew that once he started working again, his life would be absorbed. He wouldn't stop when eight hours had passed. He pushed harder at nights. He did the work. He got things done—

Because that's how he worked. Full-on. Every cell in his brain engaged.

He wished it was otherwise. He wished he could punch a time clock and work like a normal person.

But he couldn't. He'd already been through this with his first company. If there was one thing he'd learned from that experience, it was to accept who he was and use who he was to make the world a better place.

He had three weeks to soak in everything he could and establish a relationship with his son that would survive living apart.

Then responsibility demanded he break away and do his duty.

Lola opened her eyes to find Grant giving her a slight shake.

"We have a limo coming in forty minutes."

She groaned and closed her eyes again. "Already?"

"Sorry. I've been up for two hours. I video chatted with Max who had fun but clearly is ready to come home. That means we need to be there too."

"Damn it. That's probably the only thing you could have said that would keep me from begging for another day."

He leaned down over the bed to kiss her. "We can come back, you know."

She still hadn't opened her eyes. "Promise?"

"Absolutely." But unless they stole away for another few

days before the book was finished, he knew that was wishful thinking. He didn't say it. He refused to destroy the spell they'd been weaving. It would break soon enough on its own.

Returning to her room, she showered and dressed, then packed her duffel and overnight bag. Hotel employees came around to gather them and Grant instructed them to bring the three dresses from the closet.

"I bought them," he said, scrolling through his phone. "You never know when we'll want to play dress-up at the house."

She laughed and headed out to the limo as the resort employees packed it with their things. They took the boat to the island with the airstrip and got into Grant's jet. After a flight that felt far faster than the one to the resort, they were back in South Carolina, where they took another limo and another boat and arrived at Grant's dock to find Max waiting for them.

As soon as Grant stepped on the gray boards, Max launched himself at his dad, hugging him around the waist. Grant stooped down and caught him to his chest, giving him a proper hug.

Lola imagined that Grant and Max probably hugged when Grant put him to bed, but she'd never seen them so filled with emotion over being together again. The sight stole her breath. There was no denying their connection. But there was also no denying that all their problems—especially the knowledge of a future spent apart with Max on another continent—surrounded them.

She would be leaving before Grant took Max to visit his French cousins. But the father/son separation was coming too. Because Grant was re-entering his real world. And she had to re-enter hers. Get a job. Support herself. Sell her family home—

"Lola?"

She brought herself back to the present. Then Max hurled

himself at her, hugging her waist. Her heart slid to her throat. Love emanated from him, along with heartfelt joy.

"I missed you guys."

Grant slipped his arm over Max's shoulders. "We missed you too."

"Me too," she said, her voice a hoarse whisper. No matter how wonderful those two days had been and how wonderful the next few weeks could be, this was not her life. She had no permanent place with Max and Grant.

A little voice whispered through her brain. *Are you sure?*

Of course, she was sure.

Once you sell your ranch, you're free to do what you choose. Stay here. Find a job in the city where Grant settles.

And what if Grant didn't want her for anything more than a passing fling? They'd both gone into their relationship knowing it would end.

She also knew Max loved his cousins. His voice rang with it every time he talked about them. He'd hugged Pierre. Taken his hand at the memorial service. There was more to his life than either she or Grant knew.

The three of them together was temporary.

But what if it wasn't?

The persistent argument in her brain annoyed her. How dare her thoughts nudge her to reach for something that couldn't be? Still, she looked around, really saw the easy love Grant had for Max and Max had for Grant, as she remembered the intensity of the feelings she and Grant had shared in the Caribbean.

What if you're the glue that makes it possible? What if yours is the voice Grant needs to hear?

The thought stopped her. She wouldn't let herself even consider that they could stay together. Or that she was the person who made it all work. Or that hers was the voice of experience Grant needed to advise him.

She'd lived through the loss of both of her parents. She knew the upcoming separation would be more heartbreaking than Grant could imagine. Grant had a child he clearly loved. And Max might have lost his mom, but he and Grant had bonded. Still, Grant's experience with his parents wouldn't let him see that family, blood ties, were not something to be taken lightly.

He and Max needed each other. Yet he was letting Max be raised by someone else so he could go back to work.

It suddenly seemed all wrong.

What if Grant sending Max to Paris was wrong and what if hers was the voice he needed to hear about *that?*

What if that was her place here? Telling him to take the first step of keeping Max, so they could take all the other steps that came after?

Heading to the patio door with Max, Grant faced her. "Coming?"

She looked at the little boy, the tall man. A new future popped into her overly busy, overly optimistic brain. She could see herself living here with Grant and Max. Making friends. Making a real life like the one she'd had in her small town growing up. Christmas. Siblings for Max. Bedtime stories. Manic breakfasts as everyone tried to get out the door for school and work.

Oh, God.

It made perfect sense.

Except Grant needed to go back to work. And even if he found room for Max in his life, *she* was the one for whom there was no place. His marriage and divorce had taught him that.

Plus, he'd said what they'd had was temporary. Wouldn't she be foolish to believe there might be more for them and have him tell her he didn't want her?

CHAPTER ELEVEN

THE NEXT MORNING, Lola awoke to noise and confusion. She'd slept in Grant's bed, but he was nowhere in sight. She slid out from under the silky sheets and into the clothes she'd worn the day before so she could sneak up the flight of stairs to her room, quickly shower and dress for the day.

When she walked out of her suite wearing shorts and a T-shirt, with her hair in a ponytail, the noise greeted her again. It sounded like ten people all trying to talk over each other. She followed it to the dining room where Grant and Max were having breakfast with an older couple—

Grant's parents.

She'd seen their pictures several times when she'd gathered data for his autobiography. His father was tall like Grant, but he had fair hair and blue eyes. While Grant got his height from his father, he had his mom's coloring. Dark hair. Dark eyes.

His father rose as she entered the dining room.

"No need to stand for me. I'm hired help."

His father chuckled as he sat again.

Grant said, "Mom, Dad, this is Lola Evans, the ghostwriter Gio hired. Lola, these are my parents Ron and Teresa."

His mother gasped. "Oh, it's so nice to meet you! Everybody gets everything about our Grant wrong. He's the nicest guy in the world."

Grant frowned at his plate. Not as much as glancing at either parent, he said, "Mom. I'm not nice. I'm a dictator when I work. I'm gonna own that."

Teresa snapped open her napkin and set it on her lap. "You're supposed to be a dictator. You're the boss. You know what needs to be done and how to do it. Your job is to get others to do what you say. Sometimes that means being strict or difficult."

Lola blinked. Wow. The about-face from how nice Grant was to the assertion that he was supposed to be a dictator left Lola's head spinning. But hadn't Grant warned her his parents were workaholic physicians who had affairs and left their children to their own devices?

Deciding to tread lightly, she took her seat and politely said, "It's nice to meet you both too."

Grant's dad said, "So what's the scoop? When's this thing going to be done?"

"We have a very narrow timetable," Lola said, peering at Grant to see if he was signaling for her to not say anything more. He wasn't. His attention was on Max, even though his father had asked a question.

She smiled at his parents. "I hope to be done this week in order to get two weeks of editing in."

His father waggled his eyebrows. "Anything juicy in there?"

Grant rolled his eyes and looked away.

Again, Lola replied. "It's a very straightforward story," she said, answering the question without really saying anything. "Your son's a hard worker. It comes through in the book."

His mom beamed with approval. "That's great." But her comment went unanswered. The table grew silent.

Grant's dad shifted a bit as Denise served his breakfast. When she pulled away, he said, "We're going to swim with the boys this morning."

Lola said, "You are?" then peered at Grant again.

He thanked Denise when she served his bacon and eggs. Then he said, "Caroline will be with them too."

Lola nodded and attempted to smile as everything tried to knit together in her brain. Grant not talking, insisting Caroline be with the boys when his parents could be watching them—

Grant wasn't merely holding himself back from talking. He did not trust his parents with Max.

It seemed extreme, except being a parent was new to Grant, and he clearly hadn't liked the way his parents raised him.

Denise brought Lola a plate of bacon and eggs and fried potatoes as she'd made for everyone else. As if nothing was wrong, the elder Laninghams told story after story about their yacht club and card club and the events they attended.

"Last year we went to the Kentucky Derby," Ron said. "Best time we've had in forever."

When Grant said nothing, Lola said, "It must have been wonderful."

Grant tossed his napkin to his plate and rose from the table. Facing Lola, he said, "I'll be in the office."

Then he walked out.

After another ten minutes of listening to the Laninghams, Lola finished her breakfast. Caroline arrived with Jeremy and shooed the boys upstairs for Max to get into his bathing suit.

Then she faced Grant's parents. "Grant texted and said you'll be swimming with us."

"Yes. We were hoping to stay a few days but with the autobiography and all, Grant said he needs the privacy."

Lola said nothing, still trying to work all this out in her head.

Clearly softening the blow, Caroline smiled and said, "Yes. He's very busy."

Lola rose from her seat to go to her room to gather the things she'd need to work with Grant. Facing his parents, she said, "It was nice to meet you."

Looking clueless, they both smiled, nodded and said it was nice to meet her too.

She left the dining room shaking her head. Either his parents were so clueless they were delusional—

Or they hadn't been expecting a warm reception?

It bothered her enough that she almost asked Grant about it when they went to his office to work. Instead, she noted the fine aura of tension that surrounded him. He'd had enough stress for one morning, so she led him back to the discussions of creativity, a topic he seemed to love.

That afternoon, she watched him listlessly wave goodbye to his parents as Jason drove them back to the mainland to catch a flight to Key West.

Her story took another turn. Except it might be another one of those things she wouldn't be allowed to use. He hadn't forgiven his parents for ignoring him and his sister. He'd thanked them for paying for his education. He'd accepted that their version of love wasn't effusive and warm. But he hadn't forgiven them for his childhood.

It seemed petty for a guy who always thought in terms of logic.

But thinking about her own childhood, she knew it was the bonds she and her parents had formed over daily things— doing dishes, making popcorn and watching TV together that filled her with love for them and brought her home after every assignment to share the joy of her career.

If they'd been cold, or distant, or made her feel like she wasn't as important as their jobs and their charity work, she'd be a very different person right now.

And that was the part of the story she knew couldn't make it into the autobiography, even though it explained a lot.

A few days later, Grant and Lola were discussing the fact that they were very close to a final draft. They'd closed in on everything but his decision to go back to work. This morning he'd tell her that segment of his story, then she would not only put it into the book chronologically; she would also smooth out the sections where it affected the overall story.

Otherwise, the manuscript was strong. The book was just about done. Even as a nonwriter Grant could see that.

But while he was grateful that his autobiography was close to being done, he also knew that sending the manuscript to Gio meant Lola could leave. He didn't want to think about it, much less actually talk about it, so when his phone rang and Charlie's name came up on caller ID, he stopped to take the call.

Setting his phone on his desk, he said, "It's the PI I hired to check out Janine and Pierre." Then he hit the button to put the call on speaker. "Hey, Charlie!"

"Hey, Grant! I finished the deep dive that you asked me to do on Janine and Pierre Rochefort."

"Spill it."

Grant listened as Charlie rattled off details of Janine and Pierre's lives. Though Lola appeared to be looking at her notes, he knew she was listening too.

Janine was a well-respected lawyer.
Artist Pierre seemed like a kept man.
No gambling.
No alcoholics anonymous.
Bills paid on time.
Neighbors loved them.

Even with that information, Grant still had itchy feelings about Pierre but that was because he didn't really know anybody who didn't have a job except his ex-wife after she married him. And the impressions she'd given him were not positive. But he forced himself to see that it was good that Pierre didn't have to be somewhere every morning at nine o'clock. He painted in a studio in a small building in their backyard. He would always be around for Max.

Max would always have someone. He wouldn't be alone. He wouldn't feel like an annoyance or a problem.

This was for the best.

"I guess the next move is mine."

Charlie chortled. "I guess it is. If you need anything else, you know where to find me."

Grant disconnected the call.

Lola caught his gaze. "What was that all about?"

"After we met Pierre at the memorial, I called Charlie. Pierre seemed like a nice enough guy and Max clearly knew and liked him." He winced. "But I've been rich too long. Before I retreated to this island, I had a battery of lawyers who fought all the frivolous lawsuits brought against me just because I have money."

"Really?"

"Do you know how many hit-and-runs I was supposedly in? People believe I'd rather settle than go to court...so I hired a bunch of lawyers willing to take people to court for the things I hadn't done. I refused to be an easy mark for con men."

"I guess that makes sense."

"Because I'm used to people seeing me as a cash machine, I wanted the lowdown on Pierre and Janine. I didn't want Max living with them if they only saw him as a meal ticket—since I'll be paying child support and for anything Max wants. I also needed assurances that they weren't drug addicts or gamblers or even workaholics like me."

She took a second to think that through and for once didn't question his choice. Or ask for more information about his choice. Or demand his reasoning. She'd met his parents. If she couldn't understand his decisions about Max after that, she never would.

A few seconds went by, then she simply said, "Okay. Now what?"

"Now, we finish the book." And enjoy Max for the rest of the time he had before he began his quest to return to work in earnest. He felt the same way about Lola. Their time together was running out. He wanted every second of that too. The best way to get it was to keep working on the book, not turn it in early and have her leave. Not fly to France with Max and lose the child he'd only met a few weeks ago. But greedily hang onto this time.

He fought the sadness that threatened. Not because it surprised him—personal problems had never before interfered with his work—but because they still had almost two weeks. No one was taking the time away from him. Even if he had to think of creative ways to stall, he would.

"You're not going to call them?"

"My lawyers will make first contact. Then Max and I will fly to France together. I'd rather talk to them face-to-face, really see the relationship dynamics, make sure this is what *Max* wants before we discuss anything."

She hesitated but eventually said, "I guess that makes sense, too."

He sighed. "Look, I know you don't want me to give up Max. You don't even have to say it. But I've thought about this every way I could, and I know Max would be the one to suffer if I made the wrong choice."

She took a breath as if she were about to argue, but he saw something change in her eyes before she said, "Okay."

"Okay," he said, ready to get them back on track. "What were we talking about?"

She consulted her notes. "The day you decided to go back to work."

He laughed. "I didn't actually *decide* to go back to work. It was more like my brain woke up and started spewing ideas at me." He shook his head. "It was odd. I'd spent years like a hamster on a wheel, waking up, doing the stretches I had to do to be able to get to the dining room for breakfast, then swimming—which always loosened me up—then spending time on real therapy with two physical therapists, and then swimming again. Tired in the afternoons, I'd actually nap. Evenings I'd watch the Lions. Read. Keep up with friends. Then go to bed and do it all over again the next day.

"Work never entered my thoughts. I don't think I had the mental energy for it. Therapy is exhausting. Then one day I started thinking about artificial intelligence."

Her somber expression shifted to excitement. "Oh...that's interesting."

"I'm not going to tell you what I came up with. That's not going into the book. What I can say is that things just started connecting in my brain. What if this did this? What if that was expanded? What are practical applications?"

"And you came up with things?"

"Yes."

She stopped writing and studied him. "It must be amazing to see what's next before anyone else does."

"It's a blessing and a curse. But don't put that into the book. This is just us talking."

She nodded.

"Change is like a wave. Think back to your first cell phone. I'll bet you didn't have it long before you got a better one. Then smartphones came on the scene and suddenly we had enough power in our hands to see the people we called, listen to music, research anything, make videos of our lives, read books, craft a novel, take courses online, do our banking, bill clients—all with something that fits in the palm of your hand. It didn't happen overnight, even though it felt like it to consumers. But behind all that technology were the people who saw the possibilities and couldn't rest until they figured out how to make it happen. They didn't eat. They rarely slept. They couldn't. Work wasn't an obsession. It was more that discovery and implementation are intoxicating. There's an odd bit of fear in there too. With your brain popping with answers, you can't risk losing something—forgetting an option. You must act while the ideas are real and alive—before you forget them."

"Is that what's happening with you? That you have a million ideas that you're worried you'll forget?"

"No. I'm still in the possibilities stage. Once I start working, the practical application ideas will be like a tsunami."

She studied his face again. "It's going to take over your life, isn't it?"

"Yes."

"And you won't have time for Max at all, will you?"

They were back to the conversation that had begun after Charlie called. He didn't understand why she needed proof that his life was about to change, but now was the time to silence her doubts. "No."

Her expression shifted again. Her question became acceptance. "Then we really should make the best of these last weeks."

He caught her gaze and held it, assuring himself that she understood the truth of what he was saying. It wasn't just Max who was leaving. She would be too. He didn't want her to go. She didn't want to go. But they both knew she had to.

"We will."

Because he knew this time, these feelings, were what he would hold onto when he was running on adrenaline, working without sleep, connecting things and concocting things.

He returned to talking about how his thoughts built slowly, how he'd studied the current technology, read all the scientific papers written, delved into the dark web, listened to chatter and reconnected with the few people on the planet who could be called his peers.

He watched her expression as she realized he wasn't exaggerating when he said he wouldn't have time for Max—

Or her.

It hurt his heart to think about losing them, especially with their time running out, but if he held onto them, they'd be lonely and bored and eventually grow to hate him the way his first wife had. And he'd hate himself. Hate that he left them alone. Question his decisions. His commitment. Lose sleep over being disconnected and single-minded.

He'd hate himself for becoming his parents. He'd seen firsthand the damage they'd done by trying to be parents when their time had to be spent elsewhere. He would not ruin anyone's life because of his work.

It was better this way.

CHAPTER TWELVE

AFTER LUNCH, Max and Jeremy headed to the beach to throw a ball with Benjamin Franklin. Grant went to his office. Lola raced to her room to grab another notebook. She wouldn't let herself think about their discussion about Max that morning. Twice she'd almost argued with Grant, but both times she'd shut herself down. Not because this wasn't any of her business, but because Grant was a serious man who didn't take things lightly. He'd clearly thought this through.

Even if he was wrong.

Coming down the stairs, she groaned at the thought that insisted on haunting her. As much as her brain had told her she could be the voice Grant needed to hear, she did not trust it. She thought with her heart. Grant thought with his brain. She'd learned her lessons the hard way about listening to her heart. Hearts could long for things that couldn't be. Brains were a lot more practical.

When she entered Grant's office, he stood behind the desk, staring out at the ocean. Just from his posture she could tell something was wrong.

"Grant?"

He turned.

"What's up?"

"My lawyers called Janine and Pierre. They're ready for us to come to France whenever we're ready."

Lola tried to sound excited when she said, "That's great."

He said, "Yes. It is," but his voice was tired. And that little whisper about being the voice he needed to hear rose up again, so strong this time that she couldn't fight it.

She took a breath and said, "What are you doing? Why are you sending Max to France when you want to raise him?"

"I can't."

Desperation for Max filled her, and she understood why these thoughts wouldn't leave her alone. That little boy loved his dad and Grant loved his son. Surely, everything else could be worked out. "I say you can."

Grant shook his head. "You know what I think? I think your incredibly nice parents gave you a different perspective of life than what happens in the real world. If I raise Max, he will become the little boy who doesn't have anyone show up for his class plays or recitals or science fairs because I will have lost track of time and missed it. The question here isn't whether I should raise Max. It's whether I'm unselfish enough to see that he deserves better than me.

"Do you think I don't want him? That I don't want to watch him grow up?" He sucked in a breath and looked at the ceiling. "I do not want to hurt him the way my parents hurt me."

"They might have hurt you in the past. But I saw them jumping through hoops to get your attention or get you to talk the day they were here. And you literally froze them out."

"It was the best I could do."

"I get that. But your parents' openness and getting Max are like an opportunity for you to start over. Change your life. Have the things you never had."

He gaped at her. "No."

"Because you can't forgive them?"

He shook his head as if he couldn't believe they were having this conversation. "You're ghostwriting my autobiography. Yet, you haven't asked me why I never talk about my sister."

She frowned. "I assumed you didn't think she had a place in a biography that was more about your business life than your personal life."

"I never talk about her because she's dead."

Lola blinked. "What?"

"When your parents aren't ever around, you learn how to manipulate babysitters. It was so easy for her to sneak out at night by pretending to go to her room to study and then slipping out the back door. But more than that, we had absolutely no guidance. It was like our parents believed we'd magically mature as our bodies got bigger.

"Sneaking out to be with her friends led to other things. Eventually, she was a full-blown addict. She ran away because she couldn't hide it anymore. She also hated herself. Hated who she was. Had absolutely no self-esteem. When I found her years later, no matter how much I tried to help her she couldn't get herself together. Eventually, she was found dead in an abandoned building in Los Angeles. She had committed suicide."

Torn between sympathizing with him and confusion, she said, "How did I not find that when I researched you?"

"I had Gio bury the story. Not for me. Not for my parents. To give her a little dignity."

"I'm so sorry—"

"Thank you. But I've adapted. And she's finally at peace." He rose from his seat. "But let's just say I know the damage a bad parent can do. When I say I won't expose Max to that, I know what I'm talking about. I might have turned out okay—found my way without any guidance—but she didn't have a snowball's chance in hell."

With that he left the room.

Lola's breath shuddered in her chest. She didn't know when his sister had died, and she also had no way of finding out given that Gio had buried the story. But if it was around the time of Grant's meltdown when he fired half his staff, which resulted in his being kicked off his board, losing his marriage, getting hit by a car, that made sense. Her loss could explain Grant making mistakes, angering his board, and pushing his unsuitable wife to the point that she filed for divorce. It might also explain why his parents barely visited him around the time of his accident. He didn't *want* them around.

Dear God. That explained so much.

And that was probably something else she couldn't put in the book. Not if he'd had his sister's suicide covered up—for his sister. To give her some dignity.

Her heart ached. Tears filled her eyes. Grant had suffered a lot more than anybody would ever know.

Because he'd never let her put any of this in his autobiography.

That night, she slipped into Grant's room. After leaving his office without working that afternoon, he'd been sullen at dinner, but she'd thought he would return to the family room after putting Max to bed. She'd expected him to pretend nothing was wrong, make a pass, sweep her off to his room.

When he didn't, she showered and put on a pretty pair of pajamas and went there on her own. He was in bed, sitting up against the headboard, wearing navy blue pajamas and black frame glasses, watching a baseball game on the big screen TV on the wall that was usually hidden by a walnut cabinet.

She laughed. "What's this?"

"Maybe another slice of the real me. The only time I wear glasses is when my contacts are out, and I want to watch TV before I fall asleep."

She inched over to the bed. Without asking permission, she slid under the covers and eased her way over to him. Putting her head on his chest, she said, "I'm sorry."

He snorted but buried his fingers in her hair. "You're sorry? For what?"

"For making you talk. For pushing you when I shouldn't have."

"I just thought it was your aggressive reporter skills."

She took a breath. "No. Truth be told, I love seeing you with Max. I think you need him as much as he needs you... but I also see that you know yourself. Sometimes you're even brutally honest."

She pulled herself up and brushed a quick kiss across his mouth. He caught her elbows and kept her where she was, kissing her deeply, completely. The easy intimacy between them calmed her the way it always did. She'd never had a relationship like this, a person she could talk with so casually about the most important things. It might be because she'd been interviewing him for weeks and knew every corner of his life. Especially with his admission that day.

He was such a good guy, and he didn't see it. And it hurt her heart that he didn't.

She ran her palm against the soft top of his pajamas. "Oh... I like these. Let's take them off."

He laughed. "You, too."

"Race?"

He shook his head, kicking off his pajama bottoms with very little effort before he reached for the top. Without opening buttons, he caught the hem and pulled it over his head, tossing it across the room.

She wrinkled her nose. "I prefer a more mannerly approach."

He threw himself across the bed and yanked her to him. "You weren't very mannerly the other night."

"You bring out the best in me."

His deep-throated laugh filled the room and gratitude relaxed her a little more. She'd taken him to what had probably been the lowest point in his life that day, but she'd also brought him back just by coming to his room, being herself, accepting that their relationship was strong enough to handle the mistake she'd made by pushing him.

Love for him filled her soul, but she stopped it. What he'd told her about Max applied to all of his life. In a little over a week, she'd go home. She'd never see him again because their paths wouldn't cross. If she took him up on his invitation to vacation on the island after she sold her ranch, he wouldn't be here. He'd have already started his new life. She desperately wanted to enjoy him while she could, but she had to hold back her heart. Or at least keep her feelings in check.

Their kisses and caresses grew more heated, hungrier, and she felt the first crack in her armor. She'd never been as connected to anyone as she was to him. Even as she needed him, she wanted to be everything to him too.

She wouldn't let herself acknowledge that his work meant more to him than she did. That was an endless loop. She forced herself to be present, to enjoy making love, to sleep snuggled against him.

Try as she might to be happy, Lola had spent the next day miserable, knowing this wonderful life she'd begun creating was coming to an end. But there were two positives. First, these would be the best memories of her life. Second, her ability to connect with people had returned. Once she handled the sale of the ranch and found a new job, she would settle in a city where she would make friends. She could also reconnect with her old friends and bring them into her life again.

This wasn't the end. It was *an* end. But technically once she left this island, she would be starting a new chapter in her life. Actually, she'd be starting a whole new life, and in some ways, she believed she had Grant to thank for that. In others, she knew meeting Grant might have been a coincidence. She'd reached the point where it was time she moved on. He'd been in the right place at the right time to be part of it.

After only a few minutes, she stopped thinking of it from her own perspective, if only to force away the blues, and she focused on what was about to happen with Max.

Watching him playing with Jeremy and Benjamin Franklin, a few good ideas came to her for easing the transition. She didn't mention any of them to Grant until Max was tucked away in bed and Grant had come to the pool patio to find her.

"I was thinking maybe it might be a good idea for you to have Max call Janine and Pierre...you know. To sort of make a path for when you visit."

He shook his head. "I know this is going to sound selfish, but I don't want that interfering with the time we have left." He took a breath and expelled it quickly. "Besides, it's clear he knows them, clear they're close enough that they'll pick up their relationship as if there hadn't been a pause."

She nodded and dropped the subject. He hadn't shut her down because it wasn't her place to mention it. He'd stopped the conversation because he was feeling the end as much as she was. She heard it in his voice. He couldn't hide that from her now. They had a little over a week and he wanted it, every minute of it. Even though another person might consider that selfish, she had come to realize Grant hadn't had a lot of love in his life. Was it so wrong for him to want to savor this?

No.

In the same way, she didn't want to think about the ranch she had to deal with when she returned to Montana. She didn't want to consider job possibilities. She didn't want to think about never seeing Max again. That would all happen soon enough. She wanted to breathe the salty air, bask in the sun, enjoy being with Max and make memories with Grant.

Period.

Because she could also see how much he wanted this life. How much it hurt him to give it up.

She caught his hand, pulling him to her so she could kiss

him. For the first time since she'd begun interviewing him, she saw what other people called his selfishness as dedication. A burden he couldn't shake. She also saw how his parents' haphazard way of raising him, and losing his sister because of it, had bruised his soul. Out of necessity, he would be a long-distance parent, so he could allow his son to be raised by a couple Max knew and loved. His child would have love twenty-four-seven.

They kissed in the moonlight, making another memory she could tuck away, then went back to the house.

He opened the bifold door, walked into the game room and twirled her around as if they were dancing. "Sleep with me tonight."

She laughed. "I sleep with you every night."

"I know. I just like asking and having you say yes."

He liked the assurance that she would be there for him. It was equal parts romantic and heartbreaking.

So they danced in the game room, then kissed their way to his second-floor suite and made love as if they didn't have a care in the world. As if they didn't know all this would end in the blink of an eye.

A week later, in the office, she handed him her three-hundred-page draft. "I'm emailing this to Gio this morning."

He glanced at it then up at her. "This is it?"

She nodded. "This is it. Your life. Every segment blended together. Every chapter a masterpiece."

He snorted. "Right."

"Hey, that's my work you're snorting at. All you did was talk." She took a seat on the chair in front of his desk. "I have about a week before I get the copy-edited version."

"Are you being overconfident?"

"They said there wasn't time for a draft. There'd be no content editing. This is my best work. Their editors will take a crack at finding holes or problems in the copy edit, but I don't think there will be many."

His eyes met hers slowly. Their usual sparkle was gone. He knew this was it. They hadn't even had a work session in days while she polished sentences.

"So you're leaving?"

"Honestly, I'd prefer to wait here for the edits and then to do them here."

He perked up. "My island is at your disposal."

"That's good."

He winced. "I'm not going to be around much. While you were polishing that thing, I've being doing video interviews with prospective employees. I have four more this morning."

"Are you sleeping with any of them?"

He frowned. "Virtually?"

She laughed. "I'm staying the extra few days because I like being with you, but I can swim with the boys and walk on the beach myself. The only thing I really need you for is at night."

He grinned. "You're the devil."

"Not even a minion. I like you. I'll take what I can get while we're waiting for edits."

His grin grew. The sadness disappeared from his eyes. "Sounds good to me."

"Okay. I'll email this, then I'll probably put on my swimsuit."

"I'll be talking to—" He reached for a paper on his desk. "Jim Billings, Josh Neville, Angel McDermott and Pete Farnsworth."

She walked around the desk and kissed him. "Sounds like I'm getting some real pool time."

He kissed her back. "Enjoy."

But when she walked out of his office, his grin receded. He was interviewing, beginning to choose staff. Gio had three prospective office spaces ready for him to see and choose from. Purely out of selfishness, he'd decided to locate his new company in Charleston, South Carolina. It was close enough that he could get back to his island in under an hour. He could still live in his beach house. Especially if he created a small apartment for himself in whatever space he rented for his offices—somewhere he could grab a nap if they pulled an all-nighter. It would be one less horrible shift he'd have to make in the big changes about to happen in his life.

When these interviews were done and he'd chosen office space, he and Max would be going to France to make the biggest change of all.

All this would be gone. Not just his son but the easy kisses and the real conversations with someone who liked him enough to challenge him—

He shook his head to clear it of the sadness and sense of loss and set up the first video call. Gio had sent him two piles of résumés. He'd weeded through them, choosing the best of the best. Then Gio had made first contact, because most people couldn't believe they were being contacted by Grant Laningham. They would dismiss email correspondence from him as a hoax or spam.

Once they agreed to an interview based on the company being created, its goals and mission statement, then Gio told them the company was being started by Grant Laningham. Half had declined based on Grant's reputation. Of the other half, he suspected a high percentage of them had only agreed to a video interview out of curiosity.

Which gave him about ten real candidates. But he only needed a handful of employees in the beginning. Once he got things off the ground, he'd find people as the workload grew.

Of the ten, he'd spoken with three already. He'd speak with the next four today and the final three tomorrow.

The first guy was a curiosity seeker, but Grant gave him

enough information that by the end of their call he was excited for the project. The second candidate, a flashy woman
with a PhD and tons of work experience with NASA, wasn't
interested. The third guy ate an apple through the first five
minutes of their hour-long call, but he was a decent candidate, so Grant kept him on the list.

The fourth guy was standoffish and questioned Grant brutally.

Eventually, the guy cut Grant off with a sigh. "This is a
waste of time. I have a good job."

"I'm offering you a better one."

He had the nerve to grimace. "So, you say."

"You think I'm not smart enough to know my vision is
revolutionary. That everybody involved will make money.
That we'll potentially change the world?"

"You've been out of the game awhile, Grandpa."

Grandpa? What the hell kind of crack was that? "I was
injured."

"Almost killed." He nodded thoughtfully. "I remember."
He snorted. "Because I remember just about everything about
everything."

For the first time in his life, Grant felt like he was getting
a peek at what he must sound like to normal people.

"I've got a nice résumé and a cushy job. The only reason
I took this interview was out of curiosity."

"Cushy jobs aren't cutting edge."

"I worked cutting-edge research and development once.
It's not all that it's cracked up to be."

"Where were you working?"

He named a high-profile company. "I was developing a
multi-universe game."

"Game?"

"System. The game could be whatever the players wanted,
depending on their imaginations and skill set. You could play

in one universe or seven. You could hone it down to your own city and your own enemies or you could try to rule a galaxy. The game could be a hundred different games. Meaning we had to plan for any contingency. Be smarter than any potential player."

"Interesting. I'm guessing you hated the long hours?"

"I loved the challenge."

Grant would have too. "So, what didn't you like?"

"The letdown when it fails."

That was interesting. And also explained why Grant had never heard of it. "Didn't you go through beta tests and get opportunities to fix things? How could it fail?"

"No real market. It was a thing of beauty, and consumers didn't want it. The people who did want it couldn't afford it."

Grant laughed. He found it hard to believe real gamers wouldn't have found the money for it. "Are you sure you weren't just in love with it because it was yours?"

"It was a diamond among coal in the video game world."

"That's too bad."

"No. It was poor planning."

"Probably." And poor marketing, if this guy was telling him the truth. "But I would think you'd want to clear your name. Show the world it wasn't you…it was management who failed."

"What?" His round face reddened. "You're challenging me?"

"I probably could. I could also probably teach you a thing or two."

He snorted. "Right, Gramps."

Grant's nerve ending shivered. He wasn't a babysitter or a mentor. He was a genius trying to find people to help him bring a vision to life. He didn't need an arrogant, angry pain in the butt.

"Okay then. I'll be reviewing my notes… You'll hear from Gio if you make the cut."

The guy said, "Whatever," and clicked off the call.

The guy had hung up on him, as if trying to insult him. Grant raised his eyes to heaven. Pete Farnsworth would have to work a little harder than that to insult him.

Still, when he left his office and went upstairs to get into swimming trunks, Pete Farnsworth's arrogance followed him upstairs and eventually outside to the pool.

He knew he'd been that arrogant as a newbie. He'd also created things that changed the world. That guy had nothing to be so self-important about.

Or maybe Pete Farnsworth wasn't self-important as much as he was bitter about having failed?

Grant didn't know. He also didn't care. The guy wasn't making the cut.

They swam that day and took Max to the beach that night to play with glow sticks. The next day Grant interviewed another three people. Two very boring candidates caught his eye, if only because neither of them called him grandpa. They'd be great people to do the day-to-day grunt work required. And that's what he was looking for. People who could *execute* his ideas.

The next day Gio texted Grant to have Lola in his office in ten minutes for a video call. When they were all together, Gio gushed.

"I loved it. I wouldn't change a word. Copy editors are still going over it with a fine-tooth comb. The publisher is also insisting on fact verification."

Grant bristled. "It's my life. I know what happened."

Lola brushed it aside. "Fact checking is normal, Grant."

Gio said, "They want three more days."

Grant peeked at Lola then glanced at the computer monitor again. "Three more days?"

Gio winced. "Sorry about that. I know that cuts your revision time down to two days, Lola, but it was the best I could do."

She smiled. "That's fine."

Gio gushed a bit more then they signed off.

Grant laughed. "You called that one."

"I did. I saw the deadline and worked it all out in my head."

Grant's computer buzzed with another incoming call. A glance at the screen told him it was Janine and Pierre.

He and Lola exchanged a look before he answered it. "Hey... What's up?"

"We hadn't heard from you after we spoke to your lawyers," Pierre said. "We thought we'd check in."

"Everything's great."

Pretty blonde, Janine said, "You don't have any more information about when you'll be visiting with Max?"

He knew they were really asking if he was stalling. They didn't know about the biography, but technically it was done. They didn't know he'd begun interviewing employees to start a new company. They didn't know that the six he wanted to hire were enough to set up an office and get organized.

All they saw was a guy who'd almost accidentally gotten custody of his child—the child they loved. They'd told Grant's lawyers that because Samantha was alone, they'd always believed they'd be raising Max. Grant's lawyers had told them all that would be discussed when Grant and Max came to Paris.

And maybe the time for stalling was over.

"Actually, we could get on a plane tonight and be at your house around noon tomorrow."

Janine's face blossomed and glowed. "Really?"

He understood why. Max was a wonderful kid.

Pierre stuttered. "We can be ready for you any time."

"Good."

Janine said, "We'll see you tomorrow then."

Grant said, "Tomorrow."

When he disconnected the call, Lola gave him a confused look.

He sighed. "There's no point in putting it off."

She said, "Okay," and he suddenly realized she thought he was leaving her when they'd just gotten a lucky three-day extension.

"I want you to come with us."

"Oh."

"Have you ever been to Paris?" he asked enticingly.

She frowned. "Actually, no. I'd always said I'd attach a visit to Paris onto one of my assignments but never made it happen."

Their work done, he rose from his seat. "That's because you were always eager to get home to talk with those really great parents of yours."

She laughed and stood, too. "I was."

"So, come with us."

As he walked around his desk to stand in front of her, she took a breath. "This isn't going to be easy."

His voice softened. "I know. I'm not going to tell Max that he's staying until he's happily settled. Then I'll explain that I'll visit as often as I can and call at least once a week."

"Do you think you'll get time for monthly visits?"

"I think I'm going to hire an assistant who will force me to make time."

She laughed. "A bulldog?"

"I do like a good bulldog." He smiled and caught her around the waist to haul her to him. "You wouldn't be interested in the job, would you?"

CHAPTER THIRTEEN

IT WOULD BE the perfect compromise. She could take the job as his assistant, make sure he ate and slept and put visits with Max on his calendar—refusing to accept any excuse for why he needed to cancel.

There would be no canceling visits with his son.

But she'd be a different kind of employee than the subcontractor ghostwriting his autobiography. She'd be in the daily grind of his work. She'd become part of a world that pushed him and punished him.

They wouldn't have any personal time. And even if they did, she could see their relationship deflating, turning into something that didn't have the life or romance it had here because of the confusion of working together. Their roles would change.

What they had would die.

That would hurt more than walking away now. At least now, they had good memories and a soft spot in their hearts for each other.

She pretended he was teasing. Maybe he was? "Oh, you wouldn't want me for an assistant. I'm accustomed to having assistants. And I'd bark at you."

He laughed, taking the tension out of the room, making her believe he really had made that suggestion as a joke.

"I'm the only one who gets to bark in the office." He kissed her quickly. "Thank you for coming to France with me. This *is* going to be hard."

She knew it was. She also saw that he finally understood just how difficult it would be. While that was good, understanding wasn't going to make things easier.

She followed him out to the pool where Max, Jeremy and Benjamin Franklin were swimming.

"Max, you want to come out here for a second?"

Max nodded and swam to the ladder. Unconcerned, Jeremy picked up the Frisbee and tossed it for Benjamin Franklin who eagerly raced after it.

Lola sucked in a soft breath. The boys had made friends. Benjamin Franklin's life had found a new purpose—

And this time tomorrow all of that would be gone. The pool would be silent. The dog would spend most of his days sleeping in the sun.

Grant sat on the edge of a chaise lounge. Lola sat on the one beside it. Max ambled over.

"What's up?"

"Lola and I have been talking to Janine and Pierre."

The little boy's eyes lit. Some of Lola's worry softened. She remembered how Pierre had hugged Max and Max had clung to Pierre's hand.

"We're going to fly to Paris tonight to see them."

Max's mouth fell open in disbelief, then he jumped for joy. "All right!"

More heaviness fell from Lola's heart. She watched Grant force a smile. "I'll have Caroline pack for you. Then I thought we'd all spend the afternoon on the boat."

Max nodded eagerly again.

Lola didn't wonder whether she should join them. Max was enthusiastic and that was great. It really did take away part of the worry about the choice to have Janine and Pierre raise Max. But Grant needed this.

An hour later, the warm sun lulled Lola into contentment

as Grant and the boys put on life vests and jumped into the ocean.

"Hey, sleepyhead!" Grant called.

Max seconded that. "Yeah. Put on a vest and swim with us."

She waved her book. "The last time I was out on the boat I realized this would be the perfect place to read. I came prepared."

Grant shook his head. "Nope. Read on your own time. We're swimming."

Realizing this was a losing battle, she said, "Okay, but I don't need a life vest."

She dove off the boat into the water and surfaced beside Grant. He shook his head. "You really always have to do things your own way, don't you?"

She laughed. "Sometimes." She caught his gaze. "Does it bother you?"

"I think it makes you interesting."

Their attention caught by something shiny, the boys swam off. Grant watched them. "He's going to miss this."

Shielding her eyes from the sun, Lola said, "You could arrange for him to spend two months here with you in the summer."

"I can never really predict I'll have that much time off. But I see what you're saying. With the new office only about forty minutes away from the island, lots of things about my life could be more easily managed. But I'm just not sure I can be available for two months."

"You can't make a schedule?"

He glanced at her. "That's actually the point. Ideas and answers to problems come at their own speed. I could clear my calendar, and on the day he arrives for the summer, I could finally figure out something in my work and get so involved I don't come home."

Not wanting to go over this yet again, Lola said, "Well, think about it."

"I will."

"Good. Because if you could work that out, it would be the perfect way to be in his life. To help him to realize that you are his dad and you do love him."

Grant's eyes grew solemn and sad. "I do love him."

Which was why she'd agreed to go to Paris with him. No matter how difficult Grant believed leaving Max was going to be, she knew it would be a hundred times harder and he would need her to be there for him.

They boarded the plane for the overnight flight. Lola's suggestion of Max spending two months on the island had followed Grant the rest of the afternoon and through the drive to the airport. He loved the idea of having Max spend summers with him and would try to make it happen, but he wouldn't tell Max about it to prevent disappointment if he couldn't work it out.

Dressed in pajamas and tucked under a cashmere blanket, Max fell asleep first and woke first. When Grant yawned and stretched to wake himself, it was to find his son dressed in jeans and a T-shirt, sitting on one of the chairs by the table, amusing himself rolling the Yahtzee dice.

"Hey. What's up?" He glanced at his watch. Six o'clock in South Carolina. They'd been sleeping like rocks for hours. At least, he hoped they had. "Did you sleep?"

Max nodded eagerly.

"Everything okay?"

He grinned. "Yeah."

Grant suddenly understood. Max was eager to see Janine and Pierre. Staying at the island had been like a vacation. But his reality was that he'd lost his mother and the two people who were most like family to him were Janine and Pierre.

Max wanted to be with them.

Easing his chair in the upright position, quietly so he didn't wake Lola, Grant said, "Okay. I'm going to shower and get dressed too."

In the shower, he worked to shake off the feelings that tumbled through him as he acknowledged that Max loved Janine and Pierre and they were more family to him than Grant was.

Sliding into khakis and a polo shirt, he experienced the kind of emotions he'd never felt before. Any guilt or odd thoughts he might have had about allowing Janine and Pierre to raise his son disappeared, but they were replaced by his own sense of loss. He'd never in his life loved anyone the way he loved his son. And he couldn't raise him.

Still, the more important consideration was that Max loved his cousins and wanted to be with them. Grant's emotions didn't count, Max's were the ones that counted.

Grant didn't talk much on the drive to their home. He'd rented a car so he'd have transportation for the few days they would be in France. He knew he had to get Lola back to the States once the copyedit of his autobiography was returned. But he wanted to spend time with Max and Janine and Pierre to make himself a part of their family before he went home and lost himself in work.

They arrived at the French provincial style house in the country on what appeared to be acres of ground. Pretty gray and brown stone created a timeless look and feel of a country estate. The perfect place for a child to grow up.

Janine and Pierre ran out to meet them. Max threw himself into Janine's arms and she hugged him fiercely. "I'm so sorry about your *maman*."

Tears filled Max's eyes and Pierre took him from Janine to hold him. "We will love her forever and never forget her."

Max nodded. Pierre squeezed him tightly.

Janine glanced at Grant. "Can we help with bags?"

He shook his head. "We don't have a lot. I'll be shipping other things later."

She nodded her understanding that Grant didn't want to say too much in front of Max. He hadn't yet talked with Janine and Pierre about Max living with them. So he couldn't tell Max yet.

Pierre slid the little boy to the ground and took his hand. "We have new chickens."

Max said, "All right!"

Pierre and Max walked into the house and through the corridor to the kitchen of the open-floor-plan downstairs and out the back door.

Janine said, "He's taking him out to the coop."

Grant nodded stiffly. The house was perfect, a cozy family home. A wonderful place for a little boy to run with a big yard to play in and a chicken coop that Grant could see through the sliding glass doors leading to a perfect patio.

He shouldn't have been angry or negative and Lola reminded him of that as they whispered to each other in the darkness before falling asleep after an afternoon of getting to know Janine and Pierre and watching Max happily interacting with them.

The next day, Max played with Pierre in the backyard, painted with him and in general was like his sidekick. Midafternoon, Grant, Janine and Lola sat by a big window, having coffee, watching them.

"He's always loved Pierre," Janine said with a laugh. "You know, if you wanted to spend the rest of the day in the city, we wouldn't mind."

Grant's gaze stayed on Max. He was happy. There was no doubt about that. But he'd also been very happy on Grant's island. He didn't know how a kid could look so at home in two places, but Max did. For as much as Grant tried to adjust to leaving Max behind, he simply couldn't do it.

His eyes on Max, he said, "I think we'll just stay here."

Janine nodded.

They hadn't yet out-and-out discussed custody. No one had even hinted that Max would be staying with the Rocheforts when Lola and Grant returned home, but Janine's behavior almost indicated she thought it a foregone conclusion.

Knowing what he did about his work and parenting, and how happy Janine and Pierre were to have Max, this should be a no-brainer. He should want his son to have a secure, happy life with two wonderful people...but something held him back.

His phone buzzed with a video call, and he frowned. "I'm sorry. I have no idea who this is, but I have three potential office spaces to look at when we get home and six newly hired employees who might be getting cold feet."

"Go. Answer it," Lola said, batting her hand. "We're fine."

He walked through the foyer of the big house and into Janine's office. Closing the door, he clicked on the call only to have the face of Pete Farnsworth rise on his screen.

"Dude."

Grant frowned. Not just at the weird greeting, but he was fairly certain Farnsworth had hung up on their last call. "What do you want, Pete?"

"I was thinking about the job."

A crazy kind of hope rose in Grant. Pete Farnsworth had been the smartest, most experienced person he'd interviewed. He'd love to have him on staff. He could actually see himself freeing up some of his time by handing off some of the more difficult work to Pete. Which would translate to time for visits with Max.

But he didn't want to give that away. He said simply, "Yeah?"

"I've been thinking about the bits you told me about your new products, and I got some ideas. You don't need to pay me or thank me. I just like where you're going with the artificial intelligence stuff, and I want to share a few thoughts."

Grant blinked. "I can't take your ideas. My legal people would shoot me."

"I told you. You don't have to pay me. I just see all the potential—"

"I think you want to be part of this project."

Pete sighed. "I have the easiest job in the world. And I don't want to be your grunt. I'm a supervisor here. I'm staying. If you want my ideas, you know how to reach me."

With that he clicked off the call and Grant rolled his eyes. Technically, that was the second time Pete had hung up on him.

As he returned to the table in front of the window, Lola said, "Who was that?"

"Remember the kind of grouchy guy I talked to last week? Well, he had some ideas for my projects that he wanted to share."

Lola laughed but lawyer Janine's eyes grew huge. "Without any sort of agreement in place he was going to just *give* you ideas?"

Grant shook his head. "I told him my legal people wouldn't let me take his ideas."

"If you asked me," Lola said, "he wants in on the project."

"I know he does," Grant agreed. "But he has a solid job and the last big project he worked on failed so he was fired."

"No confidence," Janine suggested.

"He's got lots of confidence. And from what I dug up on him before I called him last week, he deserves to have it, but he's holding back because he likes his salary and easy hours. I'm not going to beg him or make promises. Life is sometimes about risk. He needs to either man up or get comfortable with the fact that his cushy job will never allow him to make a real contribution. That's why he wants to give me ideas. He wants a place at the table. But he doesn't want the risk."

"Well, that's his loss," Janine said.

Grant laughed. "You investigated me, didn't you?"

"No more than you investigated us."

"At least we both know we don't make decisions lightly."

Janine's eyes softened. "No. We do not."

Dinner was chicken legs coq au vin with salads and side dishes. Max ate as if he'd never eaten before. He teased with Janine and gazed at Pierre with adoring eyes. By the time the evening of playing the French edition of Pictionary was over, whether Grant liked it or not, he felt the push he needed to give Max the right life.

Still, it broke his heart when he took Max upstairs to watch him get ready for bed. As he was tucking him in, Janine, Pierre and Lola came in to say good night. Max happily said good night as if he was ready for a solid night's sleep, but when everyone headed for his bedroom door, he said, "Can you stay a minute, Dad?"

Grant smiled and returned to the bed. He sat on the edge as everyone trooped out and closed the bedroom door.

"Am I staying here?"

Grant's mouth opened, but nothing came out. Max's blue eyes were solemn and intense. The kid was just a little too observant. But this was also a conversation they needed to have.

"It's not a done deal. I haven't even really spoken to Janine and Pierre about it but we're all thinking about it."

Max nodded. "Oh... Because I don't want to."

That surprised Grant so much he blinked. "You don't want to live with Janine and Pierre?"

"I like them, but I never had a dad. Now I do. I want to stay with you. I want to have a dad."

Swallowing back a groundswell of emotion, Grant tucked the blankets around Max. "You know what? I never thought of that. I just looked at the big picture. With Janine and Pierre you'd have a mom *and* a dad."

"Pierre's not my dad. *You're* my dad."

Grant's eyes filled with tears. He hadn't had one inkling of how much those words would mean to him. "Yeah, and I like being your dad."

"And I like being your kid."

He pressed his lips together, giving himself a minute to compose himself but also to gather up every nuance of this moment so he would remember it forever.

"I like having you as my kid... My son."

Max grinned, happily, easily, as if they hadn't just had the most profound conversation of Grant's existence and that life was a simple thing. Maybe for Max it was. Or maybe Grant made life hard when it didn't have to be. He had no idea how this would work, but he did know he'd make it work. Because right now, nothing else in this world mattered except the opportunity to raise his son.

Still, just to be sure, he said, "You're saying you want to come home with me?"

Max nodded eagerly. "And Benjamin Franklin and Lola and Caroline and Jeremy and Denise."

Grant saw it then. The family he'd created. All this time, he'd known what he wanted, and he'd been building toward it. He just hadn't realized it.

He leaned down to hug his son and Max partially sat up to accept the hug.

"Okay, we leave tomorrow morning. Before we go, we'll talk with Janine and Pierre about you coming here for visits."

Max nodded again.

"And maybe we'll have them come to the island for Christmas or New Year's—"

"Let's make them come for Halloween."

Grant laughed and rose. He had no idea why Max had suggested Halloween, but there was no way he'd break the happiness of the moment. "That would probably be fun." He took a breath. "I'll see you in the morning."

"I'll see you in the morning, Dad."

He walked downstairs, returning to the living room where they'd been playing Pictionary and sat down with a sigh.

Astute and observant, Janine said, "What did he want?"

"To come home with me. He'd figured out that this trip was me dropping him off to live with you and he told me that he wanted to live with me." Because he liked having a dad. *A real dad.* And Grant liked being a dad. But he wouldn't tell anyone else that. That would stay between him and his son.

Pierre looked sad. "He doesn't want to live with us?"

"I'm sorry."

Janine surprised Grant by grabbing his hand and squeezing it. "Don't be sorry. He loves you. I could see it. And we love him, but he can visit us. *You're* his dad."

Grant rubbed the back of his neck. "That's approximately what he told me. And I told him that he could visit you as much as he wants, but also we'd love to have you come to the island for visits."

Janine said, "That sounds lovely."

"And I've always wanted to paint something from the States," Pierre said.

Confident in a way he'd never been before about anything other than software, Grant said, "We'll make this work."

They talked a bit more then Grant and Lola excused themselves to go to bed. When they were under the covers, she nestled against him. "You seem happy."

"I'm beyond happy. Remember how we talked about happiness once and I said I didn't believe it was a permanent state?"

She laughed. "Yes."

"And how I told you I thought your parents were the exception to the rule or some such thing?"

She laughed again. "Yes."

"I get it now."

She sighed with contentment as she cuddled against him. "I hoped you would."

"I do." He closed his eyes, savoring her softness. He wanted to tell her that with Max's life sorted out, it was time for them to talk about her staying, too. But he couldn't do that. Not only did he have no idea how he would make his life work now that he had a son living with him. But also, her life needed to be straightened out. For all he knew, their fling might have been just the moment of happiness she needed right now. Maybe after she sold her ranch and looked at her life, other plans could have more appeal.

Especially going back to work. At one time, she'd been an important voice in American journalism—

And she'd broken an engagement, left a man she loved, to have that career. Proof that she loved working, loved being her own person.

And proof that he shouldn't try to hold her back from restarting her life, from having what she really wanted.

No matter how empty it made him feel.

CHAPTER FOURTEEN

MAX AND GRANT were so happy, so content on the return to the island that Lola couldn't stop watching them. Caroline and Jeremy danced for joy when the cruiser pulled up to the dock. Grant had made a call to tell them the news about Max staying, and they had been thrilled. Even Jason whistled a tune as he grabbed their things and took them into the house.

Grant hugged Caroline. When she pulled away, her eyes were misty. "You know I will do everything in my power to facilitate things."

"Thank you. Gio found three potential office areas for my new company within forty minutes of the island. So all my time won't be eaten up in travel. But I still have to pick one. Also, about half the new staff is from out of state. I'm probably going to have to assist them with finding places to live."

Caroline laughed. "I have connections. I can help you with that."

Walking with Caroline, he headed off the dock toward the house. "After that we have to find a school for Max. And I was thinking about hiring a nanny—"

Standing on the dock, Lola continued to watch them. Jeremy and Max making plans to swim. The dog dancing around the boys. Grant talking to Caroline like the employee that she was, giving her assignments that would ease the transition from single Grant to single dad Grant who was also putting his new office in a city close enough that this island could remain his home.

A breeze ruffled her hair and she realized she was still standing on the dock, beside the boat. No one had missed that she wasn't following. Father and son were both still basking in the decision that Max would stay with his dad. Caroline had work to do.

Technically, Lola had work to do. She had to go over the copyedits. Then she had to go back to her ranch. It wasn't home but it was the next logical thing on her to-do list, as Grant would say. She needed to sell it and then find another job so she could also make a home the way Grant was.

Grant, Caroline and the boys entered the house through the entry by the pool patio. The door closed. She still stood on the dock.

Then her phone beeped. Seeing it was Gio, she answered it. "Hey, Gio."

"Have you looked at the copyedits?"

"We just got back from Paris. I'm still on the dock."

"Get to your computer, take a look, call me if there's anything troublesome."

"Okay."

"And by the way, when you look at your deposit for payment, it's going to be a little more than you expect."

"What? Why?"

"Grant told me to double your fee."

Her eyes widened and her heart stuttered. That was a lot of money. "What?"

Gio laughed. "If there's one thing you should know about Grant Laningham, it's that he appreciates a job well done. You were a star, Lola. We needed you and you came through. Thank you."

Confused and a little dazed, she took a breath. "You're welcome, but the original amount was fair."

Gio chuckled. "Never argue with a bonus."

Remembering her bills, she laughed. "I guess I won't."

She walked into the house a little shell-shocked. It struck her that Grant was paying her for more than the book. He was thanking her for the advice she'd given him and the way she'd helped him turn his life around. She could have thought that insulting, except she saw logical Grant's purpose. She'd helped him. So, he was helping her in the way she most needed his help.

No one was around as she climbed the stairs to her room. Taking her laptop out to the table on the deck outside her room, she looked at the copyedits. With everyone busy, she started checking the changes made by the editors and the comments in the margins. She worked through dinner and was still working when the sun set.

A little after ten, she pulled away from the work. She rolled her back and shoulders to relieve some of the tightness then walked to the kitchen to make herself a sandwich. The room was totally different with no one there. Not noisy and happy. Shiny and silent.

Not in the mood for an empty room, she took her sandwich with her as she looked for Grant. Seeing lights on the pool patio, she headed out but when she got to the pool, she saw Grant and Max sitting on a chaise. Grant pointed out constellations. Max nodded, enjoying his dad.

Something wonderful fluttered through her. Max hadn't simply needed his dad. Grant needed his child. They also needed this time together to bond for real. Now that they had chosen each other, chosen to live together as a family, things would be different. The next few weeks would be about sorting that out.

She took a few steps back, then turned and walked inside the house again.

The horrible feeling of being unnecessary filled her. With

the autobiography done, there was no place for her. An odd hollow sensation flitted through her. Not just that she wasn't needed but that she wasn't a part of things.

Because she wasn't. Max and Grant were settling in. Caroline was taking over some of Grant's planning—

Denise cooked. A nanny would be hired.

And her troubles still loomed large in her mind. A failing ranch. An unsold house in Pennsylvania. Employment to procure.

It was time to go back to Montana.

That's why Grant had added the money. He knew she would be leaving. He knew she would need cash for a fresh start. Even if she sold her ranch at a break-even price, thanks to him, she'd have money for her fresh start.

Tears filled her eyes. He really did see everything.

Most of her clothes were still packed from Paris. She could easily leave tonight.

Sandwich in hand, she returned to the kitchen where a sheet with the phone numbers of all the household employees was tacked on a bulletin board. After calling the airline and getting a flight to Montana in the morning, she found Jason's number and dialed it.

"Hey. It's Lola. I'm sorry to be calling so late but I need to go to the mainland. I'm flying out early tomorrow morning—" Not exactly a lie. She did have a flight to Boseman in the morning, but it wasn't so early that she couldn't have spent the night. But she didn't want to stay. She didn't want to feel like extra baggage anymore, or worse, interrupt Grant and Max as they basked in the happiness of being together. "Is it possible for you to come and get me?"

"Sure. Not a problem. I'll be right there."

They hung up the phone. Lola went upstairs to put her computer in its carrier. She packed the rest of her things, then took her luggage to the front foyer. Jason arrived in fifteen minutes. She saw Grant intercept him, so she gathered her things and raced out to the beach in front of the dark dock.

"Here's my duffel, computer and overnight bag," she said to Jason. "I'll be there in a minute."

He nodded. "Okay. I'll be waiting."

As he walked away, Grant said, "You're leaving?"

"That's always been the plan."

His eyes softened with confusion. "Weren't you going to tell me?"

"Of course, I was going to tell you. Jason just got here a little sooner than I'd thought he would. I have a world of trouble to get back to—"

He put his hands on her waist, pulled her to him and kissed her. "Stay another day. The trouble will still be there."

Temptation nearly overwhelmed her. She loved his handsome face, loved his ideals, loved his intelligence—

But she'd seen what his work ethic had done to one marriage. Now, he had Max—who needed his attention more than she did.

"I can't. You know...don't put off until tomorrow what you can do today."

"More wisdom from your mom?"

"I think Ben Franklin said it first."

He laughed, given that his dog was also Ben Franklin. "All right I get it. But staying one or two days won't hurt."

Today it was one or two days but at the end of those days, would he coax her to stay some more...and would she be depriving Max as much as she would be shortchanging herself? She had to move on. Anything she had here was temporary.

"Really. I have to go. I've lived with my grief and the ranch and the mess I made of my life for too long. It's time for me to fix things too." She bounced up and kissed him quickly, but as he always did when she kissed him, he caught her arms and kept her to him, so he could kiss her the right way.

She let herself sink into the kiss, let herself enjoy it and memorize every sweep of his tongue because she never wanted to forget this. Then she pulled away and smiled at him. Her heart ached. Her soul shimmied with sorrow. But she wanted him to remember her happy. She wanted his thoughts of her to be filled with good times, not a struggle.

"Thank you for everything."

His eyes searched hers as if he couldn't believe this was the end. Finally, he said, "You're welcome. Offer still stands for you to come back to decompress after your ranch sells."

She smiled, and said, "I know," but she'd never return. What they'd had was a once-in-a-lifetime thing. If she came back, while he was working and too busy for her, she'd only sully the memories.

The temptation to kiss him again was so strong that she pivoted away before she could and raced to the boat. Raincoat over her forearm, umbrella in her hand, she jumped in on her own and settled in quickly so Jason could head out before she or Grant changed their mind.

She caught her flight in the morning. That flight connected with a flight that connected to a third flight that would take her to Boseman. On the third flight, a dark, quiet flight with very few passengers, she let herself cry. Not because she was sorry that she'd connected with Grant but because she would never find anybody else like him.

And she'd lost him.

Grant spent most of the night staring at a whiskey bottle. He wanted to drink. He would have appreciated the numbness the alcohol would have brought after only a few shots. But he had a son. *A son.* A little boy who had changed his whole world.

A relationship with Lola in addition to that was out of the question. Yes, he understood that Lola could have helped him with Max, but the worry was that he'd take advantage of her as a built-in babysitter and then she and Max would both miss him.

And he'd have another huge emotional failure.

Two if he counted Max.

His priority had to be his son.

But he would miss Lola. Ridiculously. Unlike his ex, Lola spoke his language. Smart, funny at all the right times, serious in the others, she had a personality that meshed with his. It wasn't just about sex with them. They'd had *that* connection.

Eventually, he left the pool patio and went to his room where ghosts of Lola haunted him. After an hour or so he fell asleep, but his alarm went off at six. Normally, he could have hit the snooze button, but he knew Max woke early.

He went to his little boy's room and discovered he was correct. Max was already gone. Probably in the kitchen, telling Denise how to make French toast.

Correct again, he found Max kneeling on a stool by the center island and Denise laughing over his breakfast order.

"A peanut butter sandwich and pickles?"

He nodded. "Sweet and sour. My mom always said that was a good thing."

Denise laughed again.

Grant walked into the room. "I'm not having peanut butter sandwiches and pickles."

Denise said, "Thank goodness."

"I want eggs," he said, knowing that might pique Max's interest. "And home fries and bacon."

Max said, "I like bacon."

"Hmmm. Maybe you want to change your breakfast order."

Max considered it, then said, "No. We'll just add bacon to the peanut butter sandwich."

He laughed. "Come on. Let's go to the dining room and give Denise space to work."

Max jumped off the stool and led Grant into the dining

room. When Max settled, thoughts of Lola returned. He'd never told her he loved her, but he felt more for her than he'd ever felt for another woman. He had to have loved her and he'd never said it.

Regret swelled in his chest. She should have known that he loved her.

Denise brought their food and Max chattered about what he and Jeremy intended to do that day. At the end of his list of activities, he glanced around. "Where's Lola?"

Oh, Lord. In all the confusion of coming home the day before and her leaving, and him wishing he could have a shot of whiskey, he'd forgotten to tell Max that Lola had left.

He took a breath. "Well, she finished the book—" At least he assumed that's what she'd done after they'd returned the day before. "It was time for her to get back to her ranch."

Max perked up. "She has a ranch?"

"Yes, but she wants to sell it."

Max looked at him as if he were crazy. "But she could have chickens."

Grant laughed. The simplicity of his thinking was equal parts interesting and fun. "No. She has to get on with her life."

From the expression on his face, Max clearly had no idea what Grant was talking about. "She has to find another job."

"Find another book to write?"

"Maybe. But she used to be a reporter. One of those people on TV or the internet who goes to places where things are happening like wars or earthquakes and she gets the story."

Max's face fell. "She's going to war?"

Grant almost groaned realizing he was going about this all wrong, giving Max all the worst ideas. "No. I don't know what she's going to do but I assume she will go back to reporting."

Unfortunately, thinking about her going to war wasn't any more comforting to Grant than thinking of her alone on a ranch in the middle of nowhere, trying to figure out how to make ends meet or hoping a real estate agent could find her a buyer—

He took a breath to stop his worries. She was a capable woman and he'd doubled her salary. She would more than pull through this. She would sell the ranch and find a great job and have a wonderful, happy life—

With a normal guy. Because that was the real problem. Grant wasn't a normal guy. He was a genius who believed he had to use his talent for the betterment of humanity.

Jeremy and Caroline arrived as Max was finishing his pickle. The boys raced out of the room and up the stairs so Max could get his swimming trunks on.

"Lola left last night."

Caroline said, "What?"

"Book is done. She has a ranch she needs to sell. And she wants to jumpstart her career."

Caroline deflated. "I liked her. I'd *hoped* you'd realize how special she was and convince her to stay."

"I tried," he admitted. "But we both know that I'm going back to a job that will consume me and now I also have Max."

"She didn't want to be second fiddle? That doesn't sound like her."

"It isn't her. That wasn't how she felt. She just… I just… I would hurt her, Caroline. Her parents were murdered. She's lived off the grid for four years. She's finally ready to re-enter her world—wouldn't it be selfish of me to beg her to stay?"

Caroline looked at the ceiling. "I don't know. I just saw you two had something special and I believe when two people have something special they find a way to work things out."

"I hadn't been able to in my first marriage. I have no reason to believe I would now."

He left the room and headed for his office. A flurry of emails showed that most of the staff had accepted his offers of employment and were dealing with Caroline about housing, but he still had to look at the office space.

A rush of adrenaline poured through him as he rounded his desk. He did want to go back to work. But even as he thought of the enormity of his new projects he deflated. He might want to work but he didn't want to go back to that *life*. The price of it was high. All of his time. All of his brain. All of his energy.

And companionship. He would always be alone because he would never drag another woman into the life he would be re-entering.

He sucked in a breath. Like it or not, this was who he was. He had to accept it.

He called the real estate agent Gio had used and spent the day with him going through the three potential office spaces. He finally decided on a building after the manager agreed that he could turn the far corner into a small apartment with a bedroom and bath and kitchenette.

Paperwork in hand, he returned to his island and walked to his office to store the copy of the leases that his attorneys were currently reviewing. He slid them into a file folder and then a drawer. As he turned to leave, his computer announced he had an incoming call.

Thinking it was Janine and Pierre, he was surprised to see the face of Pete Farnsworth pop up on his screen when he answered.

"Pete?"

"Yeah. I talked with a lawyer who said it was a simple thing for you to get some sort of agreement drawn up. Like you and I will chat about your new projects, and I'll give you input for which I do not expect to be paid."

Grant laughed. Fate must believe he needed comic relief because Pete's persistence and insistence on giving him his ideas was funny.

"It's still a no."

"Look, man, the world wasn't built by one person and you're not the only genius around. I could do your job."

Grant knew he was arrogant, but that was a little beyond arrogant.

"And I'm not asking you for money. Just to be a part of things."

"Oh, I get that," Grant said. "But you don't want to come to work for me."

"I don't want to lose the sure thing I have."

"But you do want to be a part of how the world's changing."

"Yes. But you know my story. I failed my first time out. Helping you but not really working for you would be like a cushion from failure."

"While you kept your easy job."

"It's a living."

Unexpected empathy for the guy rumbled through him. He remembered how it had felt working for the first software developer who had hired him. He remembered feeling hemmed in. He remembered the frustration of working for someone else. Especially when they wouldn't implement his ideas. He knew what it was like to be smarter than his boss. He knew what it was like to have big dreams and no avenue to pursue them. He more than empathized with Pete. He'd lived a big chunk of his life.

"Are you sure there's no way to resurrect that game of yours? Do you own any piece of it?"

Pete paused. "I didn't own any of it. But what does it matter now?"

"Maybe contact your old employer. See if you can buy the licenses."

Pete snorted. "I'm guessing they want more for it than I have."

"I could back you."

"Really?"

"I might make it a provision of employment. If I front you the money to get the license for your game so you could do some upgrades and release it yourself, then you have to come work for me."

That resulted in a laugh from Pete.

Grant rolled his eyes. "Look, I'm a master at figuring out what people want, and I can tell you two things. First, *you* want that game to succeed. Second, you want to be boss."

Grant glanced at his résumé and confirmed a few things in his education and experience before he said, "How would you like to be *me*?"

"What?"

"I don't want to run the show anymore. I have a son now. But I still have all these great ideas. I want to explain my ideas to someone who will understand them and let that person run with them."

Pete's face fell. "What?"

"I'm hiring you to run my R&D. I'll buy back your game for you. I'll hire a CEO and a financial manager for the new company. All you have to do is create the products."

He sat forward. "Are you serious?"

"Completely. Like I said. I have a son. I just realized I want to raise him. That means I can't be at the office twelve hours a day or work seven days a week. I need somebody like you to translate my ideas into software and software into products."

Pete stared at him.

"I will come into the office, get progress reports, chair meetings where we'll brainstorm. I'll also manage the CEO and financial guy." He laughed. "This could be fun. Me running the show without all the work. You getting to infuse my vision with your ideas." He paused and held Pete's gaze. "Take the job. I'm giving you a chance to change the world and myself a chance to have a life. All you have to do is say yes."

CHAPTER FIFTEEN

LOLA SAT ON the front porch of her ranch house the next morning, sipping a cup of coffee, after a long meeting with her foreman. She'd explained that she intended to sell the ranch and told him to continue doing what they had been doing. The hope was that the new owners would keep him and the hands, the way she had when she took over the place, and she'd try to negotiate for that, but there were no guarantees.

There might not be guarantees, but seeing the expression on his face, Lola had decided right then and there that she *would* work that into the deal with the new owner—if a new owner could be found.

She sat back in her chair, uncomfortable in her jeans and T-shirt when she was accustomed to wearing shorts or a sundress. But she wouldn't let her mind drift back to Grant's island. Instead, she nestled her hands around her coffee and reminded herself to take it one day at a time.

The sound of an approaching helicopter interrupted her peace and quiet and she took a breath. Her real estate agent had said he'd be at her ranch first thing in the morning. And this was first thing in the morning.

She rose, finished her coffee as she walked into the house and back to her kitchen. She put the mug in the dishwasher before she went outside again and headed across the field to meet the real estate guy.

Her heavy boots easily navigated the wild grass that grew

in the field by the bunkhouse. Head down, she pushed her way to the clearing where the helicopter had landed.

Twenty feet before she would have gone as far as she could and still be clear of the blades, she stopped. A guy jumped out and headed her way.

The closer he got the more she squinted. He looked like Grant. He *was* Grant.

She stood frozen. He looked so different in jeans and a plaid shirt—and boots. Her beach bum was wearing cowboy boots.

She laughed, then her breath stalled. Their first goodbye had been difficult enough. She wasn't sure she would survive a second.

When he reached her, he grabbed her and twirled her around. He set her down, kissed her soundly and said, "You look like a cowgirl!" He tweaked her nose. "So cute."

She stared at him. The kiss had robbed her of the power to think and reminded her of everything they had. But they'd been down this road. There was no scenario in which a life together for them worked.

"Don't think I didn't notice your boots."

He laughed. "When in Rome—"

"Why are you here?"

He tweaked her nose again. "I came here to bring you home."

Her heart stuttered. Didn't he know how much she wanted that and how hard it would be to turn him down again?

"You know I can't come."

"Because of selling the ranch? Max thinks we should keep the ranch. You know. Get some chickens."

She stared at him again. "What are you talking about?"

"Max loves chickens. You saw him with Pierre's chickens."

When she only gaped at him, he slid his arm around her shoulders and turned her toward the house. "Okay. Since you seem a little slow on the uptake, I'll catch you up."

The feeling of his arm across her shoulders was so right that she could have nestled against him. But he was acting as if their lives were simple, happy, easily fixed lives and they weren't. She couldn't pretend everything was fine.

"I was tossing the paper copies of my new leases on my desk, when I got another unexpected video call from that guy Pete...the one who wanted to give me ideas for no money."

Confused about where this was going, she said, "Yeah, I remember him."

"This time he'd called me to tell me my lawyers could easily write up an agreement that would allow me to talk with him about my ideas and use them for no compensation."

"That guy was weird."

"No. That guy really wanted to work on the projects I'd told him about when I interviewed him. So, while he was talking, I figured out what he really wanted, something he couldn't refuse, the license for the game he'd created that had failed—and my job."

"Your job?"

"I hired him to be me."

Her face scrunched. "What?"

"It all fell into place in my head while he was talking. I'll be hiring a CEO to run things and an accountant to keep track of the money... So why not hire someone to manage the research and development team? Pete was a little shocked at first too. But when I explained that I'd work as much as I wanted and be hands on, but he would be in charge he was totally in agreement."

"Can you do that?"

"I just did."

"No. I mean can you stand back and let somebody else shepherd your products?"

He took a breath. "Yeah. Easily. I'm not a kid anymore. I don't have to prove myself. I know things take time. I know there is no prize at the end for the person who makes the most money or has the most accomplishments. I know that living is about being happy."

She stared at him.

But she still wasn't sure what his job had to do with her. She'd figured out before she left that she had to be careful with the position he relegated her to. Not that she didn't want to be a mom to Max or be the happy, lucky woman who slept with Grant…but she needed more.

She wanted *everything*.

"So what do you say?"

"So what do I say about what?" she mimicked because she wasn't going to be the one to make any suggestions. If he hadn't figured this part out on his own, then she couldn't go back with him.

"Are you coming home with me?"

She glanced at the ranch to avoid him seeing the hope in her eyes. She had such strong feelings for him that she couldn't believe he didn't have those same feelings for her. But she couldn't pull them out of him. They had to be real. Natural. Spontaneous. From the heart.

"Seriously. If you're dragging your feet because you'll miss this place, Max really thinks we should keep the ranch."

She turned so she could catch his gaze. "Really? This is about Max?"

"Well, yes and no. Even if I didn't have Max, I think meeting you might have steered me into realizing that I'd already been through my workaholic phase, and I wanted a life." He smiled and took her hand. "You are that life."

The hope that swelled in her stole her breath. "Really?"

"Yes. I've slept in with you. I've worked in the morning but not in the afternoon because of you. You make me romantic and spontaneous when the only thing I used to think about was work, finding the next big idea. And you've told me enough about your parents that you've made me believe there can be another kind of life. A better life."

She smiled at him.

He stopped a few feet shy of the porch and slid his hands around her waist. "I don't want to do this without you. None of it. Create a company. Raise a son. Figure out how to be normal. I want you with me because you make me better and I love you for it."

"You love me because I make you better?"

"I think I love you because you're you. Cute. Funny. Sexy. Wonderful."

It was the last part that made her believe him. She didn't want to be a sidekick. She wanted to be his woman.

She rose to her tiptoes to kiss him. This time he didn't have to catch her arms to extend the kiss. She could have kissed him forever.

Breaking away, he smiled at her. "You're so much fun."

"No. I might be fun, but you're happy." She paused, thought it through then laughed. "I make you happy."

"And that's funny because…"

"You didn't believe in happiness."

He laughed. "I didn't but I was coming around."

"All you thought you'd ever be was content…and here you are… Happy."

He took a breath, looked at the sky, then looked at her. "I wasn't that bad."

"You were. You definitely were." She took his hand and led him to the porch. "And I'm going to see to it that you never feel that lost and lonely again."

"I'm going to make sure you stay happy too."

She stopped to kiss him. "I will as long as you stay with me."

He grinned. "Who'd have thought."

"Who'd have thought what?"

"That telling the world the truth about my life would change it."

"You didn't tell the world the truth about your life. You only told me. And I don't think the truth changed your life as much as it changed you."

"Well, whatever." He glanced around. "So are we keeping this place or what?"

"If Max wants it—"

He laughed. "It might take a couple of million to clean it up and make it work...but we've got a few million hanging around with nothing else to do."

She kissed him again, then led him into the house, up the stairs to the bedroom. If the real estate agent arrived, they never heard him.

But it didn't matter. They weren't selling the ranch. They were keeping it.

And getting chickens.

EPILOGUE

THEY MARRIED THE following year in a spring wedding on
the beach. She wore a simple white gown with a veil that was
twenty feet long. It brushed the sand, but not often because
the light netting caught the breeze and billowed around her
more than it fell to the ground. Her old friends from the network had been invited, along with Grant's two best friends.
His parents had also come, staying at the beach house with
the family. They adored Max. But more than that they wanted
a second chance. Grant was now in a place where he knew he
had to forgive them. He wasn't there yet. But he was close.

Toward the end of the evening, with guests milling around
the pool, drinking wine and dancing to the band tucked in
the corner of the pool patio, Caroline came up to them.

"If you don't ditch these people soon, you're not going to
get to Paris."

Lola smiled. "I can't wait for Paris."

"With all the times you've taken Max to Janine and
Pierre's, one would think you'd already seen the city."

Grant put his arm around Lola. "We were saving it for
our honeymoon."

Caroline rolled her eyes. "Kids. Seriously. What am I
going to do with you two?"

"Besides, we might wait a day so we can go to Pierre's
first showing in the US."

Caroline rolled her eyes. "He told me over Christmas that no one ever wanted to see his paintings."

Lola laughed. "Times change."

But Grant had also bought a gallery. It didn't hurt to give Max's cousins some motivation to visit more often. Besides, that's what Grant believed money was for. To fill little holes in people's lives.

Lola glanced around. "Times really do change. Look at us. We're very different than we were last year."

Grant caught her hand and twirled her around. "Yes, we are."

Caroline shook her head. "Thanks to Pete Farnsworth."

Grant looked around. "Where is he by the way?"

"In the living room, debating Max about something in his new game. Last time I was in there, he was getting frustrated."

Grant laughed. "Meaning, Max is probably right."

"Apple doesn't fall far from the tree," Lola said.

Caroline laughed. "No, it sure doesn't."

With that she walked away, and Grant laughed. "When are we going to tell her about the new baby?"

Lola leaned in and kissed him. "When we get back...and after we tell Max."

Grant smiled, then slid his arm around her and walked her to the crowd milling around the pool. Never in a million years would he have thought he'd have so many friends, so much love, in his life.

But here he was...the luckiest guy in the world.

* * * * *

WEDDING DEAL
WITH HER RIVAL

KATE HARDY

MILLS & BOON

To Archie and Dexter,
best Edit-paw-ial Assistants ever.

CHAPTER ONE

WILL YOU MARRY ME? Catriona tried the words out in her head.

They sounded utterly wrong.

But she didn't have any other option. She'd analysed every line of her grandfather's will, and his lawyer had made it watertight. Whatever Catriona chose to do, she'd become Viscountess of Linton; under Scots law, the oldest child inherited the title, regardless of gender. But, if she didn't get married in the next six months, then under the terms of James Findlay's will the castle and the estate would be split between her three half-brothers—and she'd get nothing.

She sighed.

This wasn't about greed. She couldn't care less about the money. But she did care about the castle; it was the one place where she'd been happy when she'd been growing up. She knew that Tom, Lachlan and Finn wouldn't look after Lark Hill Castle. They didn't know the place or feel about it the way she did. Under the guidance of their mothers, they'd simply sell the property and land to the highest bidder, not bothering about what happened to the tenants or the people who worked on the estate—or to the castle itself. She hoped that her misgivings were ill-founded but, if her fears were right and they followed in their father's footsteps, every last penny would be gone within a year.

James Findlay—the Fourteenth Viscount of Linton, to give him his correct title—had known that Catriona would be a safe pair of hands and would see herself as the custodian of Lark Hill. If she inherited the castle, the tenants would all keep their homes and get their roofs fixed; everyone would keep their jobs; and she'd also find a way of making the estate look after itself to the point where she'd be able to give the boys something to help them set up their future. At least, that was her plan.

So why, why, *why* had Gramps put that ridiculous clause in the will to say that she had to get married, first?

He knew how she felt about marriage.

Her parents had married eight times between them, for pity's sake. If her father hadn't died ten years ago, there would've been at least two more. Thomas Findlay seemed to have suffered from a bad case of five-year itch after his divorce from Catriona's mother, divorcing, remarrying and producing another child roughly every five years. Catriona's mother was on her fifth divorce.

And then there had been Catriona's own mistake, seven years ago, when she'd got engaged to Mr Very Wrong. Thankfully she hadn't actually married Luke, but the way her engagement had imploded had destroyed her last vestiges of belief in romantic love. As far as she was concerned, 'love' was simply a marketing device designed to sell cards, flowers and little cutesy knick-knacks that nobody really wanted. It certainly didn't last. Thanks to her parents and Luke, she'd learned her lesson—and she'd learned it well.

With her elbows propped on her desk and her chin resting on her interlinked fingers, Catriona stared at the will, her eyes narrowed. She had to be married within six months of the reading of her grandfather's will. Though the will itself didn't specify how long the marriage had to last. Or that she had to be in love with her husband... So it didn't technically have to be a *real* marriage.

In which case, all she had to do was find the perfect husband. Someone who would agree to marry her for, say, a year—and then walk away with everything he'd brought into the marriage and nothing from Lark Hill.

All the men she knew outside work were either married or in a serious relationship with one of her own friends, so they weren't suitable. That left her colleagues. The ones she'd consider trusting to do the job were already married.

Except one: Dominic Ferrars. And he was the last person she could ask.

Not because she didn't trust him; he definitely had integrity. Though most people became corporate lawyers because of the high salary. Was that what drove him? She knew Dominic was an ambitious workaholic, and he was in the running for the next partnership in the legal firm where they both worked. As was she, on both counts: which was probably why they tended to rub each other up the wrong way, she thought wryly. Asking him for help would feel beyond awkward. How would she react if their positions were reversed and he asked her to marry him for a year? If she were honest with herself, she'd probably scoff in amused disbelief.

But, try as she might, she couldn't think of any other man she could ask to be her temporary husband.

Hating having to ask for such a personal favour, but knowing that the future of Lark Hill and the tenants depended on her, she typed out an email. Then she deleted it, rewrote it, deleted it again, and finally settled on:

Are you free for a business discussion at some point in the next week? Half an hour should be enough. Suggest over lunch. Thanks, CF.

She stared at the message glumly for a few more seconds, then sighed and pressed 'send'.

A business discussion? Over lunch?

Dominic Ferrars stared at the email, puzzled. What business could Catriona Findlay possibly want to discuss with him outside the office? And actually taking time for lunch? She usually ate a sandwich at her desk while she dealt with paperwork. He was pretty sure it couldn't be anything to do with the partnership race; she was as ambitious and competitive as he was, and she'd want to win the position on merit.

Which left...what? The more he thought about it, the less of a reason he could pinpoint.

There was only one way to find out. And he was intrigued enough to do it. He replied.

12.30 today, Luigi's? DF

The Italian sandwich bar just round the corner from their office sold excellent coffee and even more excellent paninis. More to the point, they'd be able to find a quiet table there and discuss whatever this 'business' was.

His email pinged again.

Thank you. See you there. CF

He concentrated on paperwork and put the meeting out of his mind until twelve-twenty. And then he made sure he was at Luigi's for half-past twelve on the dot.

So was Catriona. Wearing her usual navy business suit, crisp white shirt, and the kind of shoes that looked elegant but he'd just bet she could run in them if she needed to. She wore minimal make-up, no jewellery apart from a practical watch and a very discreet pair of pearl studs in her ears, and her dark hair was cut in a sleek, shiny bob. The whole image screamed expensive lawyer with a razor-sharp mind: which was exactly what she was. And he pushed aside the fact that she was also really pretty. That wasn't relevant and he wasn't even going to think of her in those sort of terms.

'Thank you for coming to meet me, Dominic,' she said. 'Lunch is on me. No strings,' she added swiftly.

Dominic inclined his head in acknowledgement. 'Thank you.' She was carrying a slim satchel-style briefcase, so clearly she'd brought either documents or a laptop with her. He wondered again why she hadn't simply spoken to him before or after work in the office. 'I'm intrigued by this "business" discussion.'

For a second, she looked intensely uncomfortable. *Interesting*. Catriona Findlay wasn't easily flummoxed. This must be something big.

'Let's order, and then we can discuss it,' she said.

'Sure.'

Once they'd ordered—and why wasn't he surprised that she drank plain black coffee rather than a frothy cappuccino?—they found a quiet table.

Close up, he could see that her eyes weren't quite the piercing ice-blue he'd always thought they were; the edge of her irises were almost navy. In other circumstances, and if she were any other woman, he'd admit to the attraction and maybe ask her out to dinner. But this was Catriona Findlay, who intimidated most of the lawyers he knew. She didn't suffer fools at all, let alone gladly.

So instead he waited for her to start the conversation.

'Thank you again for agreeing to meet me,' she said.

As openings went, it was polite enough. But he'd noticed the fleeting expression in her eyes that said she really didn't want to be having this conversation.

Curiouser and curiouser, he thought. This definitely felt like an *Alice in Wonderland* moment. 'You said half an hour,' he mused, doing his best to look casual but watching her very closely indeed.

'Yes. So I'll cut to the chase,' she said, and took a deep breath. 'Will you marry me?'

What?

Was he going mad? Had he just dropped into some weird parallel universe? Or had his fiercest rival for the next partnership in their firm just asked him to marry her?

Dominic stared at Catriona, too stunned to answer.

Marry her?

According to the office grapevine, she dated even less frequently than he did. All her energies went into her job—a job that she did extremely well, to be fair, and any legal firm would be lucky to have her as a partner.

Why would a woman so totally focused on her career want to get married?

And, more specifically, why did she want to get married to *him*?

Marriage wasn't on his agenda. Not when his goal was to become partner of a top London law firm. By concentrating on his career, he'd ensure he earned enough so his family never had to struggle again.

'I take it that your silence means no,' she said. 'OK. Thanks for your time, and I'm sorry for wasting it.'

Just as she was getting up to leave, he found his voice. 'Hold on. Firstly, our lunch hasn't arrived yet. And, secondly, you haven't heard my answer.' Where had that come from? It sounded almost as if he were about to say yes. 'Which is "why?",' he added swiftly.

For a long, long moment, she paused. And then she sat down again. 'This is a confidential discussion,' she said.

'Then why didn't you book one of the meeting rooms at work?'

'I...' She looked blank.

Whatever this was about, it had really disconcerted her. Even though he didn't really like her very much, he could sympathise with the fact that she was clearly in a tricky situation and was finding it hard to ask for help. 'As you said, it's confidential. I'll respect that,' he said.

'Thank you.' She took a deep breath. 'It's complicated.'

He'd expected better from her. She was good at cutting to the chase. 'Give me the short version,' he said, knowing she'd see it as a challenge.

'I need to get married,' she said, 'to fulfil the conditions of a will.'

He scoffed. 'Which is the plot of just about every soppy romantic movie going.'

She raised an eyebrow. 'And you know this because you watch a lot of soppy romantic movies?'

There was the quick and slightly acerbic wit she was known for. 'No. My sisters do.'

'It's also very Jane Austen,' she said, her eyes narrowing to ice-blue slits. 'Marriage and inheritance is pure *Pride and Prejudice* territory. So you can drop the intellectual snobbery. Not that there's anything wrong with soppy romantic movies.'

Was she saying that *she* liked soppy romantic movies? No way. Dominic would've pegged her as someone who watched French art-house films and didn't need the subtitles. Maybe Catriona had a soft side—one she kept very well hidden. He suppressed his smile at the idea of her being even remotely fluffy. 'All right. Explain.'

'The quick version: if I don't get married within the next six months, my grandfather's estate goes to my three half-brothers. Which he would emphatically not want to happen.'

'Then why make it a condition of his will?'

'I've asked myself that since the moment his solicitor gave me a copy of the will,' she said dryly. 'And I'm still coming up blank.'

He looked at her. 'I didn't have you down as the kind of person who was motivated by money.'

'I'm not. And I don't plan to cut the boys off with nothing.'

He waited, but she didn't elaborate about her brothers. He'd had no idea she even had any brothers. There were no family photographs on her desk: nothing personal at all, now he thought about it. 'Why did you ask *me* to marry you?' he asked.

'Because you have integrity,' she said.

Yes, he did. It was something he prided himself on. But Dominic was shocked to realise that her acknowledging that pleased him. It shouldn't bother him what she thought about him, good or bad. 'There are other people in the office who'd fit the bill,' he said. 'You said this was a business discussion.'

'It is.' She blew out a breath. 'The marriage needs to last for about a year, to give me time to sort out the estate properly and fairly.'

Which sounded to him as if she definitely wanted her brothers to get their share of the estate. His first instinct had been right: she wasn't the greedy sort.

'I'd also expect my husband to walk away at the end of

that year,' she added, 'with a no-fault divorce, and no claim on the estate. Just as I'd have no claim on any of his assets.'

She was suggesting a marriage of convenience. Though the convenience was purely hers, he noted. 'What reason would your intended spouse have to marry you? Apart from being bowled over by your warmth and charm, of course,' he added.

Her eyes narrowed, and he knew he'd scored his point. He felt the tiniest bit guilty for sniping at her, but he knew she could give as good as she got. If anything, she could probably give better. Most of the lawyers he knew tried hard not to be on the end of one of Catriona's sharp looks or crisp words. She was the only person he'd ever met who could be scrupulously polite to someone while, at the same time, making it very clear she thought they were completely in the wrong. He'd been on the receiving end of some of those looks, himself.

'You want the partnership,' she said. 'Marry me for a year, and I'll step out of the running.'

Which was the equivalent of dropping the partnership in his lap.

And it was also incredibly insulting, because the implication was that she thought the partnership already had her name on it. He thought it might be a bit less clear-cut than that.

'So I'd marry you for your warmth, charm *and* your humility,' he said, making sure she could hear the slight edge to his voice.

She sat back in her seat and winced. 'I apologise. That didn't come across quite the way I intended it to.'

'You have a point.' Even if it annoyed him. 'You're my only competition, at this stage. If one of us steps down, the other will automatically get the partnership,' he said.

'Instead of it being you, me and briefcases at dawn,' she said lightly.

He'd get the partnership. The recognition of his hard work. The bonus would pay off his mother's mortgage and let him help his sisters out, too. Everything he wanted—everything he'd worked for—finally his. All he had to do in return was to be her husband for a year.

He was seriously tempted to say yes.

But this was Catriona Findlay. They'd rubbed each other up the wrong way since the very first case they'd worked on together, when they'd had opposite views on how the case should be run; in the end, she'd been right, and although she hadn't crowed about it he'd felt that she'd judged him.

He hated to admit it but she was one of the brightest people he'd ever met, so why hadn't she found a way round the terms of the will? There had to be more to this than simply needing a marriage on paper. He needed to know all the details, and think about what it meant for both of them, before he agreed.

He indicated her briefcase. 'I assume you've brought the will with you?'

She retrieved a large manila envelope from her briefcase and handed it to him. 'If you can find a loophole that means I don't have to marry, then I'd be grateful—because I can't find one.'

Catriona's attention to detail was legendary. If she hadn't found a loophole, it was highly unlikely that he'd be able to see one. But Dominic looked anyway. And looked again. What he read was enough to make him ignore his favourite panini in the world—prosciutto, mozzarella, spinach and roasted red pepper with a smear of pesto—when their waitress brought it over.

'You're inheriting a castle in Scotland,' he said.

'Yes.'

Her expression said, *I've already told you that, so less of the dimwittery.*

He looked her squarely in the eye. 'And, since your grand-father's death—my condolences, by the way—you're a vis-countess.'

At least this time she squirmed. 'Yes.'

'Do they know about this in the office?' Though he couldn't remember anyone mentioning her recent bereavement, let alone the fact that she now had a title. Catriona Findlay kept her cards so close to her chest that you couldn't even see the backs of them.

'It's not relevant to my job.'

That was a no, then. 'Technically,' he pointed out, 'I should be calling you "my lady".'

She rolled her eyes. 'We work for the same firm. You know perfectly well my name's Catriona. Or Ms Findlay, if you want to be formal.'

In other words, she wanted to be judged on her work, not her title. He liked that.

'And your youngest brother is called...' He stared at the will again. '*Finn* Findlay?'

'Half-brother,' she corrected. 'None of us has the same mother. And I'm pretty sure the rest of us are all very grateful that Finn's mother didn't get the chance to name any of us.'

'You'd make a wonderful Fifi,' he said blandly. 'Fifi Find-lay.'

She said nothing.

'Fifi Froufrou Findlay,' he suggested—because that un-ruffled surface made him want to push her just that little bit further.

He saw the grin, the nanosecond before she masked it, and it took his breath away. He hadn't known that Catriona could smile like that, and he was glad he was sitting down because his knees had actually gone weak. Talk about hoist by his own petard. He'd meant to rattle her, but instead he'd succeeded in thoroughly rattling himself.

'Mitzi would've called you Ferrari. Or maybe Fergus,' Catriona said, equally blandly.

His own grin was barely suppressed—along with surprise that they shared the same sense of humour. He'd had no idea. It was a moment of pure joy—like an unexpected shaft of early morning winter sunlight turning a frost-covered lawn into a carpet of diamonds.

Then he switched to analysis mode as he ate his sandwich and read the document again. 'So you've got three half-brothers—all with different mothers, born five years apart.'

She rolled her eyes. 'It's pretty obvious that my father had a five-year itch. Fall in love, get bored, fall for someone else. There was another one after Finn's mother, but he died before he could marry her. He clearly made a bit more effort with my mother, because she lasted almost twice as long as the others.' She shrugged. 'Or maybe that was simply because she was the first.'

Dominic wasn't sure whether Catriona seemed more embarrassed or sad; and it sounded as if she wasn't close to any of her half-brothers. His own father had been just as selfish as hers seemed to be, putting his own needs before those of his family, but at least Dominic had been able to depend on the rest of his family and he was close to his sisters. It looked as if Catriona didn't have anyone.

'Why didn't your grandfather want the boys to inherit anything?' he asked.

There was a little pleat in the middle of her forehead, a tell-tale sign that she was concentrating. 'He thought they were growing up like my father, under the influence of their mothers. Feckless. He wanted the estate looked after properly and he was worried that they wouldn't do that.'

Whereas it was a given that Catriona would look after the estate properly without needing to be told. She was a perfectionist.

'Though I also don't think it's fair that I should get everything, and I intend to do something about that.' She frowned. 'But I can only do once the castle's on a sound financial footing.'

'That's reasonable—and realistic.' Which was a good combination, in Dominic's view. But it left her with a problem. One that would've made him as antsy as she looked, right now, were he in her shoes. 'You're right. There aren't any loopholes,' he said. 'You have to get married to inherit the castle. Does that affect the viscountcy?'

'No. Under Scots law, it goes to the first-born, full stop. Which is me. For the record,' she added, 'if you married me, you wouldn't become Dominic Ferrars, Viscount of Linton. I'm afraid nobody would be calling you "Your Lordship".'

That comment was enough to make him want to don a kilt and kiss her stupid, until she begged him to—

No.

He dragged his mind back from that little scenario. Where the hell had that come from? Catriona was pretty, yes, but she was nothing like the women he dated. He didn't date that often, but he always made it very clear that any relationship was strictly for fun because he was concentrating on his career; he'd remained friends with most of his exes as well. Catriona Findlay wasn't the fun type.

The fact he could imagine kissing her, wasn't helpful.

At all.

'And the land isn't entailed?' he asked, trying to keep his mind completely on business and well away from the idea of how her mouth would feel against his.

'No. The land and title used to go together, but over time

they've become separated. As I'm sure you're aware,' she said, 'entailments were made to help families ensure that the estate wasn't split up into smaller and smaller chunks with each generation, so the estate could support the holder of the title. But, if you had a dissolute child who was likely to gamble the entire estate on a game of cards, then the entail wasn't quite so helpful.'

Yeah. His father would definitely have gambled the whole lot on a game of cards, then made a hasty exit and left someone else to pick up the pieces. Just like he'd done to Dominic's mum.

'To break an entail, all you have to do is persuade the heir to agree to break it,' Dominic said, thinking out loud because Catriona obviously knew that, too. 'Did your father agree to do that?'

She shook her head. 'He didn't need to. Lark Hill's entail was broken more than a century ago. And I've been Gramps' heir since I was about five years old.'

'If you'd always known you'd inherit the castle—' and eventually become the Viscountess of Linton, after her grandfather's and her father's death, he reminded himself '—then why didn't you study estate management instead of law, or at the very least qualify in Scots law rather than English? Why are you working in London, not Glasgow or Edinburgh?'

'Because my father was still alive when I went to university, and Gramps could've altered his will at any time. I wanted to keep my options open rather than taking things for granted,' she said.

That sounded plausible. He wasn't going to quibble. 'Did your grandfather cut your father off completely?' he asked.

'No,' she said. 'Gramps left him money—just not the castle. Except, as my father died before Gramps did, that bequest went back into the estate.' She sighed. 'The castle needs a custodian who'll nurture it, update it and pass it on safely to the next generation. My father would've mortgaged Lark Hill to the hilt to buy an exclusive car.' Her eyes narrowed, betraying just how even the thought of it made her angry. 'Money that would be better spent on fixing the roof, battling the damp, installing a biomass boiler and developing the kind of amenities that attract paying visitors without causing ecological damage. Not to mention paying the inheritance tax.'

If spending the money carelessly was what her father would've done—and his own father would've seen it as a way of funding his gambling habit—then Dominic backed her grandfather's decision completely.

Catriona had been very specific about where the money needed to be spent, so she was clearly a realist and knew exactly what problems the estate faced. 'I think I understand the situation,' he said. 'What are your plans for the castle?'

'It needs a bit—no, a *lot*,' she corrected herself, 'of repair work. I need to sort that out, sell enough paintings to cover the inheritance tax, and then plan how I can make the estate support itself and generate an income for the boys.' She wrinkled her nose. 'Well, Tom's twenty-five and Lachy's twenty, so I suppose they should be classed as men. Finn's fifteen.'

At twenty and twenty-five, the two oldest half-brothers were surely capable of helping her. The fact she hadn't even suggested working with them to sort out the castle made him wonder what kind of men they were. Entitled and spoiled? Or they just hadn't reached her impossibly high standards yet? They were still young, so he wouldn't expect them to tackle the estate in the same way as she would; but surely they could've given her some kind of support? Had she turned them down, or had they not even offered in the first place? 'But?'

She spread her hands. 'They still need to find out who they are and what they want from life. And they make me feel as if I'm middle-aged, not thirty-five,' she admitted. 'Especially as, technically, I'm old enough to be Finn's mother.'

'Younger siblings have a habit of making you feel middle-aged,' he said wryly, thinking of his sisters.

'Yours, too?'

That rueful smile—it felt almost as if they were on the same side, instead of rivals, and that ruffled him. 'My sisters know who they are and what they want to do,' he said. 'But, yes, they've had their moments.' He looked at her. 'Are you going to leave the firm to manage the castle?'

'No. At least, not completely,' she said. 'I'll need to take a sabbatical until I've sorted things out.' She sighed. 'Which I think might take me a year.'

'Strictly speaking, then, you've already ruled yourself out of the partnership race,' he said. 'In which case, I could simply sit back and wait for it to drop into my lap.'

She spread her hands. 'If I don't marry, I won't inherit the castle and I won't need the sabbatical. Which will mean I'm very much still in the running for partner.'

'That might be a risk I'm prepared to take,' he drawled.

'It's always disappointing when you find out that your instincts about someone are wrong.' She reached over to take the manila envelope.

He held on to it. 'I didn't say I wouldn't help you.'

'You didn't say you would,' she countered.

'This needs a considered answer. I need time to think about it before I decide whether to agree or refuse,' he said.

She'd schooled her face into careful neutrality; he didn't have a clue what was going on in her head. Complicated didn't begin to describe her, and he wasn't sure whether that intrigued him or annoyed him more.

'How long do you need?' she asked.

He wanted to check out the differences between English and Scots law and really think about what this meant—for both of them. 'A day or so? And I might have some questions for you before then. Let's meet on Sunday morning to discuss it.'

'All right.' She paused. 'I'd better give you my mobile number, in case you want to send me any questions beforehand.' She took a business card from her briefcase and scribbled a number on the back.

He punched the number into his phone and texted her, keeping his face expressionless.

Yo, Fifi.

She glanced at the screen and this time there was a definite twitch at the corner of her mouth. A mouth, he suddenly realised, that was a perfect cupid's bow. How had he not noticed before that her lower lip was so full and lush? So kissable?

'Why, thank you, Fergus,' she said, batting her eyelashes at him, and it was all he could do not to laugh.

She checked her watch. 'I'd better head back. You know the drill: clients and paperwork. See you later. And thank you again.'

Then she was gone before he had a chance to say anything else.

Married.

For a year.

In name only.

And he'd be made partner.

The decision was his. Yes...or no?

CHAPTER TWO

NOT A WORD. Not a single word.

By Saturday afternoon, Catriona was decidedly twitchy and glaring at her phone, willing it to make a sound.

If Dominic had any difficult questions, surely he would've contacted her with them by now? The fact he hadn't convinced her that tomorrow he was going to say no. In the meantime, he was clearly enjoying the power game by making her wait to hear from him.

Well, she wasn't playing.

She'd just picked up her phone, ready to call off their proposed meeting and tell him not to worry about it because she'd sort the situation out herself, when her phone pinged.

Meet you tomorrow morning outside Tower Hill Tube Station—Roman Wall side?

Technically, she could wait a while before texting back, to play him at his own game; but she knew that the waiting would annoy her just as much as it would annoy him. She'd rather make this as straightforward as possible.

Fine. 11?

Perfect. Wear something you can walk in. Weather fore-
cast sunny, for once. Thought we could walk down the
Thames path. See you by the Roman Wall.

Butterflies suddenly fluttered through her stomach, as if
he'd just arranged a date with her, though she knew it was
nothing of the kind. They would be discussing business: a
marriage of convenience that would give them both what
they wanted. So Catriona told herself not to be so ridiculous. But, even so, on Sunday morning she felt another of
those odd little flutters in her stomach as she laced up her
trainers and shrugged into her coat. Quivers that increased
when she walked out of the Tube station and saw Dominic
standing there; in walking boots, faded jeans and a fleece-
lined rust-coloured jacket to keep out the late autumnal chill,
he looked a lot more approachable than the shark-in-a-suit
he was at work. His short dark hair was brushed back from
his eyes, which were hidden from the bright November sun
behind a pair of sunglasses; he looked like just another tourist taking a selfie next to the Roman Wall.

'It's only Roman up to the third layer of tiles, you know,'
she said, walking up to him. 'Anything above that's medi-
eval.'

'Says the woman who's heiress to a castle,' he said. 'A
castle in Scotland, which repelled the Romans.'

'Look up the Antonine Wall,' she said dryly. 'And, just
for your information, there's a Roman fort in Edinburgh.'

'I stand corrected,' he said, pushing up his sunglasses
and looking her straight in the eye.

She wasn't sure if the glint in his brown eyes was teasing
or a challenge, and it made her feel wrongfooted. 'I wasn't
trying to score points. Gramps was a bit of a history nerd,'
she said, wanting to explain. 'I inherited that gene.'

'Uh-huh.'

The question that had haunted her for days was mirrored in his expression: it made no sense that James Findlay, a man who cherished history, had put a clause in his will that would threaten the future of Lark Hill Castle. Why had he done it?

'As it's not raining, for once, let's go for that walk,' she said.

He gave her a little half-smile that made the fluttering in her stomach turn briefly into a tornado. 'Supplies, first.' He shepherded her over to the nearest coffee shop, bought them both coffee—and clearly he'd noticed how she drank her coffee, because he ordered exactly what she liked without needing to ask her, or suggesting that she might like one of the Christmassy options—and handed her a reusable cup.

'Thank you,' she said. 'The next coffees are on me.'

Dominic answered her with another of those unsettling smiles.

This time, her whole skin felt as if it was tingling.

How ridiculous. She didn't react to anyone like that, let alone her greatest rival. They'd never socialised outside work before, unless it was during some kind of team event: the sort of thing where she always found an excuse to leave early. And, although this wasn't a date, in a weird way it felt like it. Even more weirdly, she actually felt *shy* in his company. Shyness was something she hadn't experienced in years, and it made her antsy. She was used to knowing exactly what she was doing.

'Have you worked out yet why your grandfather made marriage a condition of you inheriting the castle?' he asked.

'No. Your guess would be as good as mine.'

'How? I didn't know him,' Dominic said.

'Precisely my point,' she said. 'The people who did know him have no idea. The family solicitor doesn't know. Mrs

MacFarlane—who's been our housekeeper ever since I can remember—doesn't know.'

'What about your half-brothers?'

'They weren't close to him or to my late grandmother. And that wasn't my grandparents' choice, before you ask,' she added. 'My father's next three wives weren't keen on traipsing up to Scotland from Cornwall, Sussex and Kent, respectively.'

'Does that mean you don't know them or their mothers very well, either?'

'The boys and I haven't spent much time together,' Catriona said. Once she'd been old enough to realise what both her parents were like, she'd made the effort to try and stay in touch with her half-brothers; but the boys' mothers had discouraged anything more than a birthday or Christmas card or gift. She'd just had to wait until they were old enough to rebel and contact her for themselves. But even then it wasn't like having a proper family. Not like the way her best friend's siblings teased her but absolutely had her back.

If they'd been a proper family, she would've talked to her half-brothers about the will in the certainty that they'd help her come up with a plan.

As things stood, she was on her own—and she knew it. Which was why she was trying to recruit Dominic for her team.

'I'm not judging you,' Dominic said.

'Good.' Because she'd skewer him if he did. 'Did you have questions about the…' She could hardly call it a marriage. 'Business deal?' she amended.

'I've thought about it,' he said. 'And it doesn't sit well with me. Yes, I want the partnership—but I want it on the grounds that I'm the best one for the position.'

'If you're that concerned about it,' she said, 'you could

always ask the partners the hypothetical question.' If Catriona hadn't backed out, would he still have been the one they'd chosen?

His eyes were hidden by the sunglasses he'd pushed back down again, but his irritation was clear in his voice. 'You're not helping your case.'

'I take it back,' she said, wincing. 'I didn't actually intend to insult you.' And, given what she was asking of him, he deserved some honesty from her. 'This whole inheritance thing has rattled me enough to make me unprofessional in the way I'm handling the situation. If I was the one choosing the new partner—your personality and smug mansplainer tendencies apart,' she added, just because honesty cut both ways, 'I'd pick you, because you have the edge over me when it comes to seeing the big picture.'

Dominic wasn't sure what had surprised him most: that Catriona had confessed to being all at sixes and sevens, that she thought he was the better candidate for the partnership, or that she'd zeroed in on his strengths and only made one searing comment—similar to the one he would've made about her, because he thought she was an ambitious, abrasive ball-breaker and he was glad his desk was the other side of their open-plan office from hers.

Her candour disarmed him enough to admit, 'Actually, I think I'd pick you because you have a better eye for the small details. Especially the ones that can flip a case on its head.'

Before she masked her expression, she looked as surprised as he'd felt.

They'd never actually complimented each other before.

Now he thought about it for the first time and realised that perhaps they complemented each other, too. With his strength being overall strategy and hers being a quick grasp of details, they could make a formidable team.

'Thank you for the compliment,' she said.

'You're welcome. And thank you for yours.' He took a swig of coffee, but it didn't do much to clear his head.

Could he and Catriona work together in some kind of partnership?

'If I agreed to do it,' he said, 'how would you see it working?'

'We'd have a quiet wedding, stay married for a year—at least until I've got things at Lark Hill running the way they need to be—and then apply for a quiet no-fault divorce,' she said. 'And we'd have a prenup.'

'You and I both know prenups aren't legally enforceable in the UK,' he said.

'But the courts will uphold one, provided we meet the conditions,' she reminded him. 'We both have independent legal representation; we both disclose full assets, liabilities and debts; there's no pressure, duress or misunderstanding to sign; it's fair; and the paperwork's drawn up properly and filed twenty-one days before the marriage.'

She'd listed every single condition without having to look them up—and she worked in corporate law, not family. This was a woman with a prodigious memory, never to be underestimated. 'I'm pretty sure that we can give a decent brief to our respective lawyers,' he said. 'All right. I'd be happy to sign a prenup. But what about your grandfather's lawyers? Will they consider that a marriage of convenience fulfils the conditions? Or do we have to convince them that it's real?'

'His lawyers,' she said, 'would probably advise a marriage of convenience as the best way forward. Gramps didn't actually specify that the marriage had to be real, so this is my only workable loophole.' She blew out a breath. 'On the other hand, I need to convince the boys the marriage is real, or they could challenge me—particularly if their mothers have something to say about it—which would mean an expensive legal case that neither the estate nor I can afford. I want Lark Hill to stay in the family and I want the castle to be a going concern.'

'So we're going to have to pretend the marriage is real?'

She gave a single, definite nod of her head. 'At least until they believe it.'

'What would convince them?'

'If we can prove that we know each other well,' she said. 'Which means we have to do some homework. Learn about each other. Ask questions. Make notes. Test each other until we're word-perfect on any answers.'

'Like that film my mum loves, where Andie MacDowell wants an apartment with a greenhouse, and Gerard Depardieu needs a green card—so, even though it's illegal, they help each other out,' he mused.

'My mother loves that film, too,' she said. 'It must be a nineties' idea of grand romance, though I don't think my mother actually married any of her husbands for a green card.' She shrugged. 'She's on her fifth divorce.'

It sounded as if Catriona had grown up without the kind of stability in her life that his mum had given him. If she'd had a new stepfather every few years, how did she get used to constant change? His own family had been in deep financial trouble, following his father's departure, but he and his sisters had always felt loved and wanted; whereas he thought that Catriona might be the archetypal 'poor little rich girl' who had plenty of money but whose family had no time for her.

A sudden tightness in her expression told him she'd realised that she'd told him more than she'd intended.

'If we're echoing the film: I inherit my castle, the way Andie MacDowell gets her dream apartment; and you get your partnership rather than Depardieu's green card,' she said. 'Though what I'm asking you for isn't illegal, and you don't need to be married to get the partnership.'

'Marrying you takes out the competition for the partnership. Plus, it has the bonus of making you indebted to me,' he said.

She wrinkled her nose. 'That's not who you are.'

'It also feeds my knight on a white charger complex.'

This time, she laughed. 'You don't have one of those, either.'

Interesting. She didn't think he wanted to feel superior or desperately needed. 'So who do you think I am?' he asked, genuinely wanting to know the answer.

'A workaholic who wants to prove himself,' she said. 'Ambitious. I think what you want is public recognition of your talent and the fact you've got there by sheer hard work, not by family connections or the old boys' network.'

Which was right on the money. Scarily so. He'd never met anyone before who'd really understood who he was, deep down. He wasn't sure whether the fact that Catriona seemed to have worked it out—and so fast—was more worrying or intriguing.

'Though,' she said, 'I've always wondered why you do so much *pro bono* work.'

'It balances out the corporate shark stuff,' he said. He wasn't going to tell her the real reason. 'Aren't you going to ask me what I think of you?'

She shrugged. 'An ambitious workaholic: much like you.'

One who didn't use family connections either, he thought.

'Ambition is probably why we've always rubbed each other up the wrong way at work,' she added.

'Maybe. But I think you hide behind the image of being a scary ball-breaker,' he said. 'I'd like to know what's behind that image.'

'My image,' she said, 'is like the hoardings you see round the scaffolding of ancient tourist attractions in Italy. Painted with exactly what's underneath it, or what will be underneath it once the cracks are fixed. The tourist attractions, I mean; I don't have any cracks and I don't need fixing.'

He didn't believe her.

He wanted to know what was really underneath her painted hoardings.

Though he knew that a bulldozer approach wasn't going to work. He'd be better off trying something more oblique. 'You said you wanted to give your half-brothers a share of the estate but without selling any land. Tell me about the castle,' he said instead.

'Currently, it's supported by tenant rents and some investment income. Until I've scrutinised the figures properly, I can't tell if the investments are good enough, though I suspect they're probably not or Gramps would've sorted out the roof and the boiler before now,' she said. 'I'm absolutely not going to put up the tenants' rents, so I'll need to look at the castle itself and work out how it can make money.'

'Guest accommodation? Hosting weddings?' he suggested.

'You could be describing practically every castle in Scotland,' she said dryly. 'Not to mention all the stately homes in England. Lark Hill needs to offer something different. Something to make the castle stand out—and make enough money to support the estate.' She paused. 'What do you think of when you think of Scotland?'

'Tartan,' he said. 'Do you have your own tartan?'

'I'm ignoring that,' she said, narrowing her eyes at him.

'All right. Scotland to me is kilts, Loch Ness, mountains and Highland dancing—the stuff over swords. Oh, and bagpipes.'

'Keep going,' she said, and he wondered how much of this her steel-trap mind was remembering.

'Whisky. Heather. Honey. Porridge. Salmon.' He thought a bit more. 'Grouse. Haggis. Cattle with big horns. Will that do?'

She nodded. 'For starters, I'm ignoring kilts. We're on the coast, so it's no to a loch and absolutely no to fictitious monsters. The castle's on a hill rather than a mountain, as you might have guessed from the name. We're not in the Highlands, and dancing won't bring in enough money; and it's a no to bagpipes as well.'

She was demolishing everything he suggested, he noticed. Not even questioning or considering any of it. And that annoyed him. If she wanted to work as a team, then why wasn't she treating him as her equal?

'Whisky—we don't have a still. There's no heather on the hill; very probably no to honey—to the best of my knowledge, we don't have bees on the estate; and, although some of the tenants have arable land and probably grow oats, I don't know whether the quantities would work for commercial production of Lark Hill brand porridge, granola or oatcakes. No river, so it's a no to salmon. Grouse—even if we do have them, that's an absolute no to shooting. I'll ignore haggis. Some of the tenants have cattle, but I'm not sure whether or not they're Highland cows.'

'Is this a game where you shoot down every single thing I say?' he asked, damping down the fact he was impressed by how she'd retained everything he'd said—*and* in order.

'No,' she said, though he noticed she didn't remark on how harshly she'd come across or how it might have made him feel. Today, it was as if she didn't have any emotions; there was no trace of the sense of humour and wicked grin that had captivated him in their lunch meeting.

'Your non-Scots point of view is useful, actually,' she added. 'It helps me think and sort out what's viable.'

Did she consider herself to be Scots, even though she had a very English accent? Interesting. He thought a bit more. 'My sisters love *Outlander*.'

'We're not *quite* going to be able to offer our guests time travel, even if we could offer historical dress and traditional dinners,' she said wryly. 'And, again, the books were meant to be set in the Highlands.'

'Much further north than you. Got it. Given that you're on the coast, how about islands?'

'There are islands around Edinburgh,' she said, 'but they're mostly uninhabited, and none of them belong to Lark Hill.'

'Shortbread?' He gave her a sidelong look. 'In a tartan tin.'

She narrowed her eyes at him. 'Basically, what you're telling me is that when you think of Scotland, it's tartan, food and scenery.'

'Yup.' He loved the way she'd chopped up his list and categorised it so swiftly. 'So what's the castle like?'

'A lot of the rooms are shut off, with the furniture covered in dust sheets, so they don't have to be heated,' she said. 'At the moment, "shabby chic" is probably the best way to describe it.'

But something in her expression told him that it meant something more to her than that. And her very stubbornness in wanting to save the castle, despite it being a huge challenge, tempted him to join her. Be a team with her.

A team.

Despite his earlier reservations, he was pretty sure it could work. They were very different people—but combining their strengths would make them a formidable pair. Besides, if he agreed to help her he'd get the partnership: and then he'd need to find himself a new challenge.

Saving the castle with her might be just what he needed.

And he wasn't going to listen to the little voice in his head that was pointing out it wasn't just the business side of things that attracted him: it was Catriona herself.

Not relevant.

Not true.

He'd push her a bit further, first. Find out if she would work with him. And then he'd accept her offer. 'Let's try brainstorming this the other way round,' he said. 'Tell me what Lark Hill means to you.'

Home.

It was the only place Catriona had felt settled, as a child. The only place she'd felt wanted.

Not that she was going to admit that to Dominic.

Even if she sold her flat in Primrose Hill and paid off the mortgage, she knew that any capital raised plus her savings wouldn't last long in propping up the castle. The estate needed to change so it could support itself.

And Dominic was waiting for an answer.

'History,' she said. 'It's been in my family for centuries.'

'From what you've told me, the building will need a major overhaul to make it suitable for visitors,' he said. 'On the physical asset side, you have the castle, its lands and its tenants.'

'I'm not fleecing my tenants by putting up their rent,' she said again. 'Gramps always said that with rights came responsibility. I agree with him.'

'That brings us back to the castle and its lands,' he said. 'Which means you need to look at using either the buildings or the land to make money. The history angle could be useful. On balance, we're looking at tourism or production.'

We.

Did that mean Dominic saw them as a team?

Catriona had never considered being a team with him, before. But that was what she was asking him to do, wasn't it? If he married her, they'd be Team Domiona, or maybe Team Catrinic. Neither sounded right, to her ears.

Team Fifi-Fergus.

She shook herself. Now that was *really* ridiculous.

Of course they weren't a team.

But they could be.

The idea made her feel warm all over; it shocked her that she was even considering it, but maybe she and Dominic could be a partnership. His grasp of the big picture and her grasp of details would work well together. They'd dovetail. They'd probably—no, *definitely*—argue, but they'd dovetail.

'There are a lot of things we could do with the building. A hotel or holiday apartments and a restaurant—which, as you say, lots of other Scottish castles and stately homes can offer. But we could offer organic food grown locally, either by the castle itself or by the tenants,' he said. 'A shop showcasing local craftspeople and local produce. An education centre, even, if there's something specific to the site—flora, fauna or something big historically.'

'That's the tourism side,' she said. 'And you mentioned production. There are outbuildings.'

'Which gives us options. They could be fitted out as accommodation; or, if we went the production route, either as workplaces or sales outlets.'

'Production.' She thought about it. 'You see Scotland in

terms of food. If the tenants grow enough oats, maybe Lark Hill oatcakes?'

'And is there something special about the oats?' he asked. 'You need a niche to differentiate yourself. Gluten-free, maybe? Or something else—my youngest sister has eczema and she swears by oat-based toiletries.'

'I like that idea,' she said. 'We could make shampoo, cleanser and moisturiser in bars and wrap them in compostable packaging rather than put them in plastic pots. Provided we have the raw materials and the figures stack up.'

'Sustainable's a good way to differentiate Lark Hill,' he said. 'If we produced food-based items, we could use compostable packaging, too. Or drink. If there's space for a still in the cellars, we could consider small-batch production. Lark Hill special malt.'

'Can you actually make whisky from oats?' she asked.

'I have no idea. In America they use rye. So I guess you could use another grain.'

'Though, even if we had the right grains to make whisky, we'd need an expert to make it for us. Not to mention the cost of a still and whatever else you need to make the whisky, getting a licence, and how long the whisky would need to be aged,' she said. 'It'd be years before we could start selling it, let alone pay off the cost of production.'

'So that's another no?'

'It'll stay on the list of potential options,' she corrected, 'but it'll be a long-term project rather than a short-term one.'

He looked at her. 'All right, Your Ladyship.' At her narrowed eyes, he smiled. 'I think you've answered all my questions. I accept your proposal.'

CHAPTER THREE

DOMINIC HAD AGREED to marry her.

Catriona wasn't sure whether that was relief or fear flooding through her veins. Maybe a weird mixture of both. 'Thank you,' she said.

'When do we need to do the deed?' He did a quick internet search on his phone. 'If we want to get married in less than a week, we'd have to go to America.'

'But we also need to have the prenups done twenty-one days before the wedding,' she reminded him. 'That'll take three or four days to sort out anyway, so we might as well give the twenty-nine days' notice to marry in England.'

He nodded agreement. 'When we give notice, we need to name the venue.' He paused. 'Do you want to get married at Lark Hill?'

Catriona had to remind herself to breathe.

She'd once thought to get married at Lark Hill. When she'd been younger and foolish, and fallen in love with her personal trainer at the gym. She'd thought that Luke loved her back and had secretly dreamed about a winter wedding at the chapel in the castle grounds. She'd be wearing a lacy cream dress topped with dark green velvet cloak, to go with the Findlay tartan, and a crown of cream rosebuds in her hair; she'd carry a bouquet of cream roses and heather. Luke would be wearing a kilt with a Prince Charlie jacket and a rose prettied up with heather in his buttonhole. Her grandfather would walk her down the aisle, something romantic would be played on a harp, and it would be snowing outside…

Except she'd discovered that Luke had the same flaw as her parents: the same inability to be faithful. When she looked back, the signs had been there right from the start; but she'd so wanted to believe that she was wrong and love really did exist that she'd ignored them.

Then she'd been forced to face the truth. Luke had claimed that she was cold and he'd needed to find warmth elsewhere; but if he'd really loved her surely he would've taught her to be warmer? Anyway, being reserved wasn't the same thing as being cold. But the experience had made her vow never to get involved with anyone again. And she'd stopped believing in love.

'The castle isn't licensed for weddings,' she said. The chapel was a different matter; but it felt wrong to have the kind of wedding where you walked down the aisle when it wasn't for real. 'I think it'd be best if we had a register office ceremony. The nearest one to the office, so we can get married at lunchtime and be back at work in the afternoon,' she said.

'A wedding like that wouldn't convince my sisters—or my mum,' Dominic said. 'I don't think it's likely that'd convince your mum or your half-brothers, either.'

'It doesn't matter what my mother thinks,' Catriona said. 'She'll be too busy to attend the wedding, in any case.'

'But it matters what the mothers of your half-brothers think—and your half-brothers themselves,' he pointed out. 'Otherwise, as you said, they could contest the will.'

Dominic was absolutely right, and it irritated her. 'I don't want a massive wedding. I'm definitely not going to do the fussy dress and veil and flowers bit. That isn't me.' She squashed down the memories of the wedding she'd once wanted. At least this one—ironically, as it was a fake—would be honest. 'The whole point is to have a quiet, understated wedding.'

'Like the quiet, understated shark-in-a-suit lawyer you are?'

'That,' she said coolly, 'is exactly how I'd describe you.'

'Just as well our children will never ask me how you proposed to me,' he drawled.

That stung. Which was crazy, because she didn't want children. She didn't want to fail a child, the way her parents had failed her. And she absolutely wasn't planning to have a baby with Dominic Ferrars. 'I used the right language. Four little words,' she reminded him stiffly.

'But you didn't go down on one knee.'

Did he really think she wasn't going to rise to a challenge like that? Well, then. Let him learn not to underestimate her in future. She dropped to one knee, batted her eyelashes at him and held up her hands in supplication, ignoring the tourists who'd stopped in a little crowd to watch them. 'Dominic Ferrars, I know you've already said yes—but, as you want it the traditional way, will you marry me?'

'Go on, my son! Say yes!' someone catcalled.

They both ignored the crowd, and Dominic hauled her back to her feet. 'Point taken, Your Ladyship,' he said coolly.

'Catriona,' she reminded him.

'Catriona.' He folded his arms and stared at her.

The crowd, denied of the smooch and the declaration of love they'd expected, grumbled and moved on.

And Catriona felt as if she'd lost the point rather than scored it.

'Let's walk,' he said.

'Sure.' Though walking didn't settle her thoughts, the

way it usually did. And, despite the sunshine, it was chilly enough for her to wish she'd brought gloves. Had she made a mistake in asking Dominic to marry her? Or had this been her grandfather's way of saying that he knew Lark Hill would be a total millstone round her neck, and the only way he could stop her being dragged down by it was by putting that ridiculous clause in the will, so she could refuse to inherit the castle and at the same time keep her conscience clear?

The more she thought about it, the more muddled it became.

'What if you fall in love with someone, the day after you marry me?' Dominic asked, breaking into her thoughts.

She scoffed. 'That'd be highly unlikely.' How could she fall in love, when she knew first-hand that love didn't exist? Though she didn't want to argue that particular point. 'But, if I do and if he's worth waiting for, then he'll think I'm worth waiting for, too,' she said. She looked at him. 'What if *you* fall in love with someone, the day after you marry me?'

'That'd be highly unlikely for me, too; but your answer works for me,' he said.

Why was it so unlikely that he'd fall in love—or that someone would fall for him? When she looked at it objectively, Dominic Ferrars was easy on the eye. More than easy, with those soft brown eyes, those gorgeous cheekbones and that beautiful mouth. And he might not irritate other women in the same way that he irritated her.

And that was another point. One that needed addressing, if they were going to make this work. 'We need to convince people that the reason we've never got on before is because we're so similar. But then, when we realised those similarities are things we have in common, we spent more time together and eventually fell for each other, so we got married.'

'That might convince your side,' he said, 'but it won't convince mine.'

'Do we need to convince yours?'

'If we want yours to stay convinced, then probably,' he said.

'Your family will want to come to the wedding?' She shook her head. 'I'm not good enough at acting to carry that off. I want a small, quick legal ceremony, not a huge fuss.'

'Why are you so against weddings?' Dominic paused, as if thinking about it, then answered his own question. 'You said your dad was married four times,' he said. 'And your mum's on her fifth divorce. I guess that'd make anyone twitchy about weddings.'

Not to mention her failed engagement, but Dominic didn't need to know about that. She nodded, but said nothing, glad that he wasn't going to push her further.

'Then our cover story should be that you want to marry me, but you don't want a fuss since your parents have already cornered the wedding market.'

'We could take a half day, change into something that looks vaguely wedding-like for the register office, and it'll be just you and me—and two witnesses we borrow from the street,' she said. 'If that works for you. Though, before this goes too far, don't you want to get married properly—I mean, to someone you love and who loves you back?'

For someone who clearly didn't believe in love, Dominic thought, it was surprising that she'd asked. 'No,' he said. 'Marriage isn't in my game plan.' He'd done his share of responsibility and bringing up a family when his sisters were small. With his mother working several jobs to keep their family afloat, he'd learned to do housework and to cook, and he'd got a paper round as soon as he could. His mum had refused to let him contribute to the housekeeping, but she couldn't stop him buying her a bunch of cheap flowers and chocolates for the girls after he'd been paid on a Sunday morning.

In sixth form, he'd had a part-time job in the local coffee shop at weekends, and had done two evenings a week washing up in the local pub kitchen; during his university years, he'd lived at home to save costs and swapped his kitchen job for working behind the bar three evenings a week as well as being an intern in a local solicitor's during university holidays. He'd landed his training contract through hard work and grit rather than family connections, and after he'd qualified as a solicitor he'd spent one last year at home to make sure both his sisters were on the way to being settled.

Only then had he gone to London and allowed himself to climb the ladder. His aim was to be able to support his family and make sure he was their safety net—that they'd never have to live under the shadow of debt, ever again. When he'd met Catriona, he'd had her measure from the start: ambitious and privileged. Although now he was beginning to realise that might be what she wanted people to think, and underneath that layer of privilege was a very different person.

'A marriage of convenience works for me,' he said.

'OK. So we get married, and then maybe…maybe you come to Scotland with me? And, after a week's "honeymoon" at the castle—' she actually did the finger quotes, as if to make it clear to Dominic that she meant nothing of the kind '—you come back to London and I stay at Lark Hill.'

'And then what?'

She shrugged. 'You get the partnership, I sort out the castle, and we divorce in a year's time.'

'For a details woman, you've missed out something fairly crucial,' he said.

'What?'

'Your family,' he said. 'When are you going to announce the marriage?'

'When we're at Lark Hill,' she said.

'How? Are you going to call them?'

She shook her head. 'I'll send them a text,' she said. 'Or maybe an email.'

'My sisters,' he said, 'would be up in arms if I did that. As would my mother.'

'And your father?' she asked.

Of course she'd notice what he'd quietly left out. 'I don't have any contact with my father,' he admitted.

'Why?'

He decided to answer a question with a question. 'Would you have much contact with yours, if he'd still been alive?'

'Only insofar as I'm the heir to Lark Hill. The one who might have a bit of influence over the purse strings,' she said dryly.

'There's your answer,' he said.

She blinked. 'Was your dad like mine, then?'

'Absent, for most of my life,' Dominic said. 'I haven't seen him since my mum was pregnant with my youngest sister. That was when he walked out on us, for someone else.' Leaving his debts behind him, though Catriona didn't need to know that. Or how bad those debts had been.

'I'm sorry,' she said.

'Not your fault,' he said.

'Did your mum ever remarry?'

'No,' he said. 'Though she's been seeing someone for the last three years. The girls and I think he's perfect for her, but...' He spread his hands. 'Let's say my father left her with a few trust issues.'

'It sounds as if you and I have similar issues,' she said.

'A dad who did whatever he wanted, whenever he wanted—and who left us when we were small.'

Except Dominic had a mother, two sisters and an extended family who loved him. It sounded as if the only people Catriona had been close to had been her grandparents—neither of whom was still alive.

How hard her grandfather's funeral must've been: saying goodbye to the last person she'd been close to.

And it couldn't be easy for her now. She was taking over as the viscountess, shouldering the management of the castle and its estate, and having to step back from a job she loved. Although he suspected Catriona might have originally been offered her job at the firm through family connections, he couldn't fault her work ethic. She put in the same kind of hours that he did and she was good at her job.

He curbed the impulse to take her hand, because he was pretty sure she'd hate that. She wasn't the demonstrative kind at work. If you needed a hug, Catriona Findlay wasn't the go-to person. She was completely self-sufficient and made it clear that she expected everyone else around her to respect that.

Though now Dominic had a much better idea of what had made her so self-sufficient in the first place; and he rather thought that her painted hoardings had a few layers beneath them, despite her protests.

The silence between them was easy rather than awkward as they walked along the Thames path. When they reached Embankment and he judged that she had her equilibrium back, he said, 'Want to break for lunch and make a list?'

'Sure. My bill.'

'You paid for lunch on Friday,' he pointed out.

'And you paid for coffee this morning.'

'We're not keeping score, Catriona,' he said gently.

'You're doing me a huge favour,' she reminded him.

Not just for her; their deal would help him achieve everything he'd spent years working for. 'If I'd been the one who needed to get married for inheritance reasons, would you have accepted my proposal?' he asked.

She wrinkled her nose. 'I would've needed time to think about it. And I would've had questions.'

'You've given me time and answers. I've thought about it and my answer's yes. So lighten up a little,' he said.

'Sorry. I'm not good at...' She flapped a hand.

'Doing the fluffy stuff?' he suggested.

She gave him a wry nod.

'I think,' he said, 'we both might need some carbs. And there's a pub not far from here that does the most amazing macaroni cheese.'

'Sounds great.' She gave him a dazzling smile.

At the pub, she waved away the menu. 'I'll take your recommendation,' she said.

'Glass of wine?' Dominic asked.

'Whatever you're having,' she said.

Glad that she wasn't a wine bore, he ordered them both the macaroni and a glass of chianti.

'While we're waiting for the food, we might as well make a start on the getting-to-know-each-other dossiers,' he said. 'Let's start with family. Your grandfather was James Findlay, and your grandmother was...?'

'Morag.'

He made a note. 'Your father was Thomas, an only child who died ten years ago; your mother is...?'

'Victoria.'

He didn't ask if Catriona's mum had been named after the queen or if Catriona was related to the English royal family;

he knew her response would be arctic and that wouldn't be helpful. 'Aunts and uncles?' he asked instead.

'No,' she said. 'My father was an only child. My mother fell out with her family when she married him, and never really made it up with them after the divorce.'

'Why? Because they didn't think the son of a viscount was good enough for her?' They certainly wouldn't approve of *him*, then, Dominic thought. His background was much more modest.

'I doubt it. More that my mother does things her way.' Catriona shrugged. 'Yes, I could've got in touch with them when I was older. But I had better things to do with my time than chasing after people who clearly weren't interested in me.'

That sounded as if Catriona had been hurt by their abandonment, at least when she was younger, but her expression said very clearly that she wasn't going to discuss it. Instead, he asked, 'What does your mother do?'

'Marries people,' she said.

Clearly his surprise showed in his face, because she sighed. 'My mother doesn't actually have a job. She lives off a combination of divorce settlements and a trust fund. She likes yachts, parties, Ascot, that sort of thing.'

The way she said it made it sound as if Catriona didn't like any of that. And he had the distinct feeling that she didn't like talking about her mother, either. 'OK. Your half-brothers. Tell me about them.'

'Tom surfs, Lachy's into his computers, but hasn't bothered with university and doesn't have a job at the moment either, and Finn...' She shook her head. 'Finn's your average stroppy, testosterone-fuelled teen. And their mums all come from society backgrounds, so they don't have to worry about money.'

He could see why the idea of the estate being in their control worried her. Being so young, they wouldn't have enough life experience or maturity to shoulder the burden of running the castle. 'Anything else?'

She spread her hands. 'We're simply not a close family. Clearly yours is different. Perhaps I could trouble you for the same information.'

She made it sound as if this was a business brief, instead of telling her about the people he loved. And this had the potential to be a deal-breaker. 'My grandparents died a few years ago. My father isn't part of my life and didn't have any brothers or sisters. My mum's called Ginny, and she's a manager at a supermarket.' He lifted his chin. This was the point where he might decide not to help Catriona, after all, depending on her reaction. 'When I was growing up, Mum worked several part-time jobs. Cleaning the school first thing, being a domestic cleaner in the morning and afternoon, doing a shift as a school dinner lady at lunchtime, and doing a shift stacking shelves in the supermarket in the evening.'

'That's a tough schedule. I can see where you get your work ethic,' she said, and Dominic realised he'd half-expected Catriona, as a viscountess, to be scathing of his background.

But there was no judgement in her face, no scorn or censure; whereas he'd judged her, and got it badly wrong. Catriona's family might be snobs, but she wasn't.

'My middle sister Tilly's thirty-one,' he said, 'and she's currently on maternity leave with her son. She's an office manager. Suzy, the baby of the family, is twenty-eight; she's a personal trainer.'

Was it his imagination, or did Catriona just flinch? Why

would the idea of a personal trainer make her lose her equilibrium? He filed that one away for later.

'And you're close to them?' she asked.

'We have a family Zoom call at eight o'clock every Wednesday night, without fail. Except for the night that Tilly was in labour, when we thought it was only fair to let her off.' Catriona let out a soft chuckle at that, and he continued, 'And we were all waiting for Joe to ring us and tell us the second she had the baby. Plus, Birmingham's an easy drive or train journey at the weekend. I go home for my mum's Sunday lunch once a month. And they all know they can come and stay with me, any time they like.'

'You don't have much of an accent,' she observed.

'I've lived in London for a long time now, so it's softened. But it comes out a bit stronger when I visit home.' He smiled at her, then asked, 'When was the last time you saw your mum or your b— half-brothers?' he corrected himself swiftly.

'My mother...' She thought about it. 'I guess sometime in the spring. The boys were at Gramps's funeral, a couple of weeks ago.'

Obviously her mum hadn't been there. He winced. 'Sorry. Tactless.'

She shrugged. 'I already told you we weren't close. By the way, you've missed out aunts and uncles. As you know, I don't have any.'

'My mum has three older sisters. They get together once a month—funnily enough, it's usually the same weekend I go home. Sunday lunch tends to be a barbecue in the summer,' he said. 'At Christmas, they take turns hosting. It's a bit of squash, with all the kids sitting on folding garden chairs at a pasting table, and everyone brings something as a contribution towards dinner.' Just thinking of his family made him smile, remembering all the warmth and the shared laughter. Catriona didn't have that, which he imagined must make her feel pretty lonely.

'Sounds fun,' Catriona said lightly, and gave him her best smile, hoping he wouldn't see the wistfulness underneath. What would it to be like, to be part of a big extended family?

Her own Christmases had always been spent at Lark Hill. And they'd always been small-scale, just the three of them, her and her grandparents, and occasionally Mrs MacFarlane—the housekeeper—rattling around in the castle. The turkey that lasted for days, until they were all utterly sick of turkey sandwiches, turkey salad, turkey fricassee and turkey soup. Her dad was never there for Christmas because he always had a new family to attend to, her half-brothers were busy with their own families and she was never invited there anyway, and her mum always preferred to spend Christmas with friends in Monaco, Hawaii, or somewhere else where children were surplus to requirements.

Even though Catriona was no longer a child, she still didn't fit in with her mother's lifestyle.

'We play charades and board games,' Dominic continued, 'take assorted dogs for a quick walk and get back in time to have pudding watching the King's Speech. The usual family stuff. Uncle Glenn's homemade wine is a rite of passage, and Uncle Bill brings his guitar. His band plays the local pub circuit, so he's the one who gets us all singing, whether it's carols or Christmas pop songs—and he always makes my mum and her sisters sing "All I Want for Christmas is You", wearing fluffy Santa hats. Nobody cares that everyone is slightly out of tune because they're too busy enjoying themselves.' He looked at her. 'You?'

'Me?'

'Christmas traditions,' he said. 'You must have some.'

None—and she didn't want him to pity her. Time for a diversion. 'It's Hogmanay all the way in Scotland rather than Christmas. First footing, "Auld Lang Syne" and fireworks.' They'd always done the first footing and sung the song, though she'd watched other people's fireworks from her bedroom in the turret rather than enjoying them close up. Mrs MacFarlane had bought sparklers, a couple of times, but that was about it. Hopefully Dominic wouldn't press her for details until she was ready to admit just how quiet the holiday season always was for her.

'Right.' He made a note. 'What did you want to be, when you were small?'

Loved.

She pushed the thought away. 'The usual,' she drawled. 'A doctor or a lawyer. You?'

'A trapeze artist,' he said.

She shook her head, surprised. It was the last thing she'd expected, and it intrigued her. 'Why a trapeze artist?'

'One of the people Mum used to clean for gave us tickets to the circus when I was about eight. I was spellbound,' he explained. 'It wasn't one of the circuses with animals— I would've wanted to set them all free—but a people one, with clowns and acrobats and fire-jugglers.'

'I've never been to a circus,' she said.

'I haven't, for years,' he said. 'But that high-wire act made me think about the world and what was out there.'

'Have you ever done one of those circus skills courses?' she asked.

He smiled. 'I've thought about it, but things get in the way. You know how it is.'

Work. Yeah. Though in other ways she was grateful that work took up all her time. It meant she didn't have time to get close to other people and be let down again. 'What made you decide to become a lawyer?' she asked.

'I wanted to do something that would make a difference,' he said. 'Plus, I knew it'd pay enough to help me support my mum and my sisters.' He paused. 'You?'

'One of my teachers suggested it. And it was a good fit,' she said.

'Did you go to school at Lark Hill?'

'No. I was a day pupil in London until I was about seven,' she said. 'Then I went to boarding school.'

'You went to boarding school at the age of *seven*?' He sounded shocked.

'My parents both went to boarding school.' She shrugged. 'It was a given that I'd do the same.' Just her time there had started when she'd been a few years earlier than they had.

'But didn't you—well, miss your family?'

If hers had been close, the way his sounded, she would've hated being torn away from them to go to school. But her family wasn't close. Boarding had taught her to be self-sufficient, and the bullying had given her a thick skin. 'It was OK,' she said. 'And I went to Lark Hill in the holidays.'

'So you lived with your grandparents rather than with your mum?'

'During the holidays. And I was lucky. Some of the international students didn't get to go home until the summer holidays.'

'OK.' He blew out a breath. 'Sorry. It's not my place to judge.'

'It is what it is,' she said. 'You get used to it.'

'I didn't mean to drag up difficult memories.'

'You didn't. It's fine.' But her smile felt over-bright, and she could see in his eyes that he could tell.

The macaroni cheese saved her from having to talk for

a bit, but in a way that was a bad move because it gave her room to think. To realise how different their upbringings had been. Dominic's family had clearly struggled financially, but it sounded as if he was really close to his mum and his sisters. Catriona had never wanted for anything money could buy; but, with parents who regarded her as something that curtailed their fun and grandparents who were firmly part of the stiff-upper-lip brigade, she'd never really felt loved.

Which was probably why she'd fallen so hard for Luke. He'd given her everything she'd thought she wanted.

Except it had all been for show. And she'd found out the hard way that Luke had been in love with the idea of dating the granddaughter of a viscount rather than in love with her. With the idea of marrying into money. And he'd had the nerve to call *her* cold?

'Pudding?' Dominic asked, when they'd finished the pasta.

'Just coffee, please,' she said.

He ordered two coffees when the waitress cleared their places, then looked at her. 'Right. We've done family, and sort of education. What were your A levels?'

'English, history and economics,' she said.

'Same as mine, so that's easy to remember.' He gave her a wry smile. 'And I'd guess yours were all top grades.'

She nodded. 'Same for you?'

'Yes.' He paused. 'Then obviously you took a law degree. Where did you go?'

'Brasenose. Oxford,' she clarified. 'You?'

'Birmingham.'

He'd said his family lived in Birmingham, she remembered. 'Did you live at home rather than going away to uni?'

'It worked out for the best,' he said.

It sounded as if he'd stayed at home to lessen the financial burden on his family. She respected that. 'And you did your Legal Practice course and training there, too?'

'Yes. And I assume you did all yours in London?'

'Yes.' He didn't need to know that she'd done her training at a different firm. Ashamed of how badly she'd been taken in by Luke and what a fool she'd made of herself, she'd moved on as soon as she could after she'd split up with Luke and had lost contact with everyone at her old firm. 'What do you do when you're not at work?'

He raised an eyebrow. 'According to my family, I just work. Which I'm guessing is the same for you.'

'I read historical novels. Historical non-fiction, too.'

'Crime for me,' he said. 'Not the gory stuff—I like the clever ones with puzzles to solve.' He smiled. 'I go to the gym after work to clear my head. Suzy's designed me a tailor-made HIIT programme so I don't get bored.'

Luke had designed her a tailor-made programme, too. If only she'd kept their relationship purely business instead of being stupid enough to fall for a charmer who'd turned out to be as much of a cheat as her father. 'I'd rather walk in the park,' she muttered.

'Even on wet days?'

She looked away. 'Yes.'

'So you like fresh air and green spaces. Got it,' he said. 'I won't ask you to join me in the gym. Though it might be fun to spar with you.'

'Spar?'

'Boxing,' he said. 'It's great for clearing your head after a rubbish day. Ten punches, ten burpees, ten star jumps, rinse and repeat. By the time you're sweating, you're ready to conquer the world again.'

'I'll take your word for it,' she said.

'Anything else apart from reading? Music? Cinema?'

'I sometimes listen to the radio.'

'What sort of music?'

'Classical. And I might go to the theatre if there's something special on.' She paused. 'You?'

'I'll go and see any band with a decent guitarist,' he said. 'Probably Uncle Bill's influence. He did try teaching me, but I was never good enough to be in a band. Though he also taught me how to appreciate good guitar playing. Blues, rock, a bit of folk.'

That surprised her enough to look at him. 'You like going to see music?' It was a side to him she'd never expected.

'There's nothing like being in a crowd, all singing along with the band to your favourite songs,' he said.

'It's not something I've ever really done,' she said.

He batted his eyelashes at her. 'And there was I waiting for you to tell me that you're a bagpipes virtuoso. How disappointing of you, Fifi.'

She couldn't help smiling. His sense of the absurd was infectious. Why had she never really noticed before that he had this dry, whimsical streak? 'Apart from the fact I can't play them, I'm pretty sure you wouldn't enjoy virtuoso bagpipes, my dear Fergus.'

'I'm prepared to give it a go,' he said. 'Actually, I love Celtic folk-rock. How far is Lark Hill from Edinburgh?'

'Half an hour or so—obviously depending on the traffic,' she said.

'Then I'll find us a band to see on our honeymoon,' he said.

Honeymoon.

Was he expecting a real honeymoon? One with handholding and smooching and...? Catriona wasn't sure what terrified her more: the fact that she could actually imagine holding Dominic's hand and smooching with him, or the fact that a deeply buried part of her actually liked the idea of doing it.

This wasn't supposed to happen. This was a business deal, not an emotional one.

'It's a marriage of convenience,' she said, trying to stop the sudden panic running through her.

'But it's meant to look real. If we don't do anything fun on our honeymoon, surely it'll look suspicious?'

She didn't dare ask him what his idea of fun was. If it chimed with hers, she'd really be in trouble.

He smiled. 'Besides, just because it's fake, it doesn't mean we can't enjoy it.'

The pictures that put inside her head stopped any words at all coming out. And that scared her even more. Since Luke, she hadn't let herself think about dating, kissing or making love. She'd buried herself in work, because in her view work was a lot more reliable than relationships.

'You can show me all the things you love about Lark Hill,' he continued. 'Your favourite bits of Edinburgh.'

Sharing with him.

Being like a proper couple.

Part of Catriona yearned for it. The Dominic she was getting to know was the kind of man she'd like to be with. Quick mind, absurd humour, seriously attractive.

The way he was looking at her made her wonder if it was the same for him. If he was seeing past her professional face to who she really was, deep inside. And that was even more terrifying.

She stared at him mutely, not knowing what to say.

'Catriona. No strings,' he said gently.

This whole thing had been her idea in the first place.

So why did it suddenly feel as if she'd completely lost her judgement?

CHAPTER FOUR

WHAT HAD HE said to make her look so tense? Dominic wondered. Had it been suggesting taking her to a gig? Or was it
the idea of having fun on their honeymoon that rattled her?

But he'd agreed to help her, and he wouldn't go back on
his word.

'Ready for a bit more walking?' he asked. Moving helped
him think better, and right now he felt as if he needed all
the help he could get.

'Great idea. I'll sort the bill,' she said, and disappeared
before he could suggest going halves.

If she was like this with him now, they'd never convince
her half-brothers that their marriage was real.

How was he going to get her to relax with him?

When she reappeared, they headed back out to the river.
She didn't initiate conversation, and the silence between
them felt more and more awkward. In the end, he stopped
dead. They might as well face the problem head-on. 'Catriona. This isn't going to work.'

She lifted her chin. 'You're right. And I'm sorry. I shouldn't
have asked you to help me.'

'No, I mean if we're going to convince people that we're
married for real, we need to...connect.' He grimaced. 'That
isn't how I meant it to sound. I'm not being sleazy. I mean
we need to be a bit more relaxed with each other.'

'To be honest, this isn't really in my skillset,' she said. 'And, learning what I have so far, it's unfair to you—and to your family. You're close to them. They'll be hurt if you don't invite them to your wedding.'

He liked the fact that, even though she wasn't close to her own family, she could appreciate how his family might feel about him getting married. 'They'll be fine about it if I tell them the truth,' he said. 'And your family's unlikely to be in touch with mine, so we won't have any issues with my family accidentally outing us. I'm assuming you don't have a big social media presence.'

She shook her head. 'Nothing that's outside the office. Social media's not really my sort of thing.'

He wasn't surprised. It wasn't really his, either. 'Then it's not going to be a problem.'

'This whole thing is a mess,' she said. 'But getting married is the only way to keep Lark Hill going.'

'If your dad had been still alive and he'd been the heir,' Dominic said, 'would anyone have been surprised if he'd sold up?'

'No,' she admitted. 'But I'm not my father. And I won't judge myself by his standards. It's not so much what other people think of me and what I do—it's what *I* think of me. I couldn't forgive myself if I let everyone down.'

She set high standards, he thought—and she reserved the highest ones for herself. Part of him wanted to give her a hug, and tell her to relax a bit, but he was pretty sure that would be the quickest way to make her barriers shoot straight back up again. He tried a different tack. 'Would you forgive anyone else, in your shoes?' he asked.

She spread her hands. 'That's academic, because it isn't anyone else. It's *my* responsibility.'

Time to back off. 'OK.' He gestured to the path ahead. 'Shall we?'

They walked on. The silence between them still wasn't companionable, but it wasn't completely awkward, either. It was more as if they were giving each other space to think and work out how they felt.

When they eventually stopped at another café just past Battersea Power Station on the other side of the river, Catriona asked, 'Are you completely sure you want to go ahead with this, Dominic? Because the divorce will mean you can't get married in a church when you meet the love of your life.'

Something he'd never found and wasn't looking for. Or hadn't been, until now. The fact she'd asked unsettled him slightly. Did he want a grand, passionate love? Or was he content to be focused on his job, the way he'd been until now? 'I'm thirty-five,' he said. 'How likely is it that I'm going to meet someone?'

She frowned. 'At the risk of fuelling your ego, you're reasonably good-looking—don't women queue up to date you?'

So she found him physically attractive, too? That sent a very pleasurable flutter down his spine. 'Thanks for the compliment, but I'm happy as I am,' he said. 'I'm focusing on my career. In a way, you're doing me a favour because marrying you takes me off the market and saves me a few dull explanations.'

'We're on the same page, then,' she said. 'We need to make some plans. Prenups and booking the register office.'

Between them, they agreed which firms they were going to use for the prenups, and settled on the register office closest to their office: Camden Town Hall, just behind the station at King's Cross. Luckily, Catriona lived in the area for that particular office, so they didn't have to give notice in a different place. And trust her to have a handle on the smallest details, he thought.

'Which room do you want?' He angled his phone so she could see the page. The iconic marble staircase was listed as an option for just the bride, groom and two witnesses; or there was a small room with plush sofas and a neutral décor for a slightly larger group.

'I'd prefer the more private option,' she said. 'That staircase is beautiful, but it feels very...*public*.'

His thoughts exactly. 'We'll book the small room, then.' He paused. 'Are you absolutely sure you want to do it this way?

She nodded. 'There's no point in making a fuss when it's not a real wedding.'

He wondered if that bothered her—if she'd dreamed of a wedding when she was young, the way his sisters had. But he knew that asking her would just make her close up on him, and he wanted to break down the barriers between them, not add to them.

He scrolled down the list. 'There's a slot at three o'clock tomorrow. Does that work for you?'

She checked her diary. 'I have a phone call booked in with a client, but I can move it.'

'My afternoon of paperwork can fit round anything,' he said, and booked the appointment.

Now what?

She was looking twitchy, as if she didn't know what to do now, either.

Weird how they seemed to unsettle each other. Though he was pretty sure she'd deny it if he raised the subject, and he didn't want her to know that she could fluster him. At the end of the day, she was still his rival at work. Showing weakness would be a bad tactical move. He'd think about it and find a better way to get her to open up. 'I guess we ought to do more of the dossier stuff,' he said instead.

'Maybe we can do it in chunks?' she asked. 'I don't think I can face doing any more of that today.'

'Maybe we can make a list of questions,' he said.

'Good idea. We'll swap lists tomorrow.'

'Sure.'

'I…um…guess I'll see you at work in the morning,' she said.

Right then, she looked really vulnerable, he thought. And, yes, maybe she was from a privileged class: but that didn't mean she was facing something easy now. Dealing with her grief at losing the last member of her family she'd been close to, having to give up the partnership she'd worked hard for, shouldering the responsibilities of her grandfather's estate, and having to handle what sounded like a difficult family.

Going to boarding school at the age of seven was probably what had made her so self-sufficient, but he still had the distinct impression that Catriona was lonely. Whereas he could pick up the phone and call a dozen people who'd be straight by his side if he asked, he had the feeling she didn't have anyone.

Poor little rich girl.

Though what he felt about her wasn't pity. She intrigued him; now he was starting to get to know her, he realised that she wasn't who he'd thought she was. The real Catriona, the one she kept hidden, was someone he thought he could actually like. More than like, if he was honest about it: the glitter in her eyes and the suspicion of a dimple when she smiled made a wave of heat wash through him.

'I'll walk you to the Tube,' he said.

'You really don't have to.'

'I know you're perfectly capable of looking after yourself.' He suspected she'd had to do that for a very, very long time. 'But it's the way I was brought up. Humour me,' he said. 'I'm guessing you've had enough socialising for today, so we don't have to make small talk. But I'll walk with you.'

Those ice-blue eyes softened slightly with what he thought might be gratitude. 'Thank you.'

He did exactly as he'd said, walking with her to Pimlico tube station without making her talk about something deep or irritating her with small talk. Their trains home were on different lines, so he said goodbye to her on the station concourse and headed for his flat.

Later that evening, he rang his mum to let her know what was going on.

'Are you sure this is a good idea, love?' Ginny asked.

'Yes. It means I get the promotion.'

'But is that the way you really want to do it? I mean, getting *married*—that's a huge thing,' she said.

'I know. I didn't want you to get the wrong idea and think I've fallen in love,' he said.

'That's the only reason why you should get married—because you love each other,' Ginny said. 'Don't let what happened with your dad put you off marriage. Our Tilly's happy. And Suzy's hinted that she and Lou might be moving in together. I wouldn't be surprised if there was a wedding on the cards there, too.'

Dominic coughed. 'What about you and Ray?'

'We're fine as we are,' she said immediately.

'I rest my case, Mum,' he said.

'Love, I know we were lucky and people helped us when we needed it most,' Ginny said, 'but you've more than paid that back with all the *pro bono* work you do. You don't have to get married.'

'It's a business deal, Mum, I make partner if I do this. It

means financial security for all of us.' Though, at the same time, he knew there was a little more to it than that. Now Catriona had started to let him see a glimpse of who she was beneath the painted hoardings, he discovered that he was intrigued by her.

'When's the date of the wedding?' Ginny asked.

'About a month. I'll let you know the exact date once we've been to the register office tomorrow,' he said.

'Who are going to be your witnesses?' she asked.

'We'll ask two strangers off the street,' he said.

'Absolutely not,' Ginny said. 'If you're going through with this, then I want to be there—and so will Ray. And Tilly and Suzy. And Joe and Lou. And baby Aiden.'

'But—'

'No buts,' she said firmly. 'Catriona needs to be there for the family video call on Wednesday. We want to meet her.'

'Mum, the whole point of me telling you about it now is because it's not a real wedding. It's so she can sort out her family business and I get the partnership,' Dominic said. 'You don't need to meet her and you don't need to drag all the way over to London to be our witness.'

'It's not negotiable,' Ginny said. 'I'll speak to you on Wednesday. And your sisters,' she warned, 'might want to talk to you before that.'

They did. Tilly and Suzy tag-teamed him in a video call, and both of them raised the same arguments as their mum had.

In the end, he said, 'I've always supported you both in what you want to do. Can't you do the same for me?'

'But you're not doing this for *you*, Dommy, are you?' Suzy protested.

'We're helping each other. The deal is she gets the castle,

and she steps out of the partnership race to leave the way clear for me.'

'You would probably have won that anyway,' Tilly pointed out.

'Thanks for the vote of confidence, Tillykins, but there are no guarantees I would've got it,' Dominic said. 'If I had to choose between us, I'd find it a tough call. And do you know what this means? A uni fund for Aiden, at the very least. And I can pay off Mum's mortgage. Build that extension for you. Give our Suze a hand with the deposit on a flat.' Tilly, who'd clearly been trying to interrupt him, closed her mouth. He'd finally found the way to show her that the partnership would do a lot for all of them.

'I still think it's a bad idea,' Suzy said, 'but we'll be fair and hear what she has to say on Wednesday.'

Dominic knew he was going to have to explain a few things to Catriona before she spoke to his sisters. 'All right. I'll talk to you then,' he said.

On Monday, Catriona and Dominic left the office at different times, headed in different directions, and met at the register office five minutes before their appointment.

'We need to talk before we do this,' Dominic said.

Catriona felt her stomach twist. 'You've changed your mind?'

'No, but I told my mum last night.'

She schooled her expression to what she hoped was careful neutrality. 'And?'

'She doesn't think it's a great idea, but she'll support us.' He wrinkled his nose. 'You know we said we'd pick witnesses off the street?'

'Yes.'

'It seems that's superfluous to requirements.'

She narrowed her eyes at him. 'How?'

'We have six and a half witnesses,' he said.

'Six and a *half*?' She didn't quite understand.

'My mother and her partner, my sisters and their partners—and my nephew. Aiden isn't old enough to understand or even speak yet, but he'll be with Tilly and Joe. He's the half.'

Her quiet, businesslike wedding was rapidly turning into something else, and her chest felt tight.

'I'm afraid I haven't quite finished. You know I have a weekly video call with my mum and my sisters? They want you to be there for it, this week.'

Catriona frowned. 'Why? Don't they know it's a business arrangement?'

'That doesn't change anything.' He flicked into the message app on his phone and handed it to her. 'See for yourself.'

The messages from his sisters made it very clear they expected to meet her.

She winced. 'I'm sorry for causing a row with your family.'

'There's no row,' he said. 'But I was thinking: my sisters are both on social media. They know I want to be partner, so they'll help us if it means I get what I want. They'll post the sort of things that will convince your family that this is real.' The horror she felt must've shown on her expression, because he said, 'You don't have to go on social media yourself. Though it'd probably be useful for Lark Hill to have social media accounts, once we've decided on the way forward.'

We again.

But they weren't really a 'we', were they? She was on her own, the way she'd always been. 'Maybe,' she said.

'They've already pointed out that we need an engagement ring.'

She shrugged. 'We can use my grandmother's engagement ring.'

'You don't want something just for you?'

She thought of Luke. How he'd swept her off her feet and bought her an expensive flashy diamond, even though secretly she would've preferred a smaller and prettier ring, like her grandmother's. She'd given the flashy diamond back to him, along with all the things he'd left at her flat. 'No,' she said. 'I like my grandmother's ring, actually.'

'At least let me buy the wedding rings.'

'Provided they're plain, and not expensive.'

He looked at her. 'You don't wear much jewellery, do you?'

'Just a watch and earrings.' She gestured to the pearl studs in her ears. 'My grandparents gave me these on my twenty-first.'

He raised an eyebrow. 'Is that something to do with your mother?'

He was sharp to have picked that up, Catriona thought. 'Let's just say "dripping with diamonds" would describe her perfectly,' she said dryly. 'That's not me.'

'OK. We'll do it your way,' he said.

Thankfully, there was a space in the schedule for one of the small rooms on the date they wanted, so they were able to book the room for Tuesday the fifth of December as well as sort out the paperwork.

'What's the situation with your prenups?' she asked as they left the register office.

'I briefed them first thing this morning. They should be back at the end of tomorrow afternoon,' he said.

'Good. Same with mine,' she said.

'Business meeting after work tomorrow?'

She nodded. 'Plus. I need to see Lewis—' the managing partner of their firm '—this afternoon to sort out my sabbatical.' She held his gaze. 'And to withdraw from the partnership opportunity.'

Fulfilling the terms of their deal. She was giving up so much for the castle. Dominic hoped it was worth it, for her sake. 'Thank you. I assume we're going back to the office separately.'

'Yes. It's pointless fuelling the office grapevine. I'll message you later.' Her face looked slightly pinched, 'And thank you, Dominic. You've helped this all be less—well, painful.'

And all of a sudden his heart ached for her. 'Did you want to invite your family to the wedding?'

'There's no point,' she said. 'My mother will be busy.'

Too busy to attend her daughter's wedding? How selfish could the woman get? Well, he already knew that Catriona's mother had left her daughter's upbringing to boarding school and her in-laws. Dominic couldn't understand it; his own mother would drop everything if one of her children needed her. Catriona's mother needed a reality check, he thought grimly. Or maybe Catriona really was better off without her.

She messaged him later that afternoon to suggest meeting at seven the following evening—to give them both a chance to read through each other's prenups. He'd just bet she'd stay late in the office.

He messaged back.

Fine by me. How did it go with the partners?

They're giving me the year's sabbatical I asked for. And I kept my side of the bargain; I'm surprised they haven't already asked you in to discuss the partnership.

Almost the second after he'd read Catriona's message, the managing partner's PA rang him to ask him to see Lewis in his office.

This was it.

The moment he'd worked so hard for.

He'd finally reached the pinnacle.

And he was shocked to find his stomach full of butterflies.

The managing partner smiled when Dominic walked in. 'Congratulations are in order, Dominic. I'll cut to the chase. We've been very pleased with your work and we're delighted to offer you a partnership.'

It was everything Dominic wanted. A partnership in a prestigious firm of London solicitors. He'd be able to support his family, just the way he'd always planned.

Of course he was going to accept the partnership.

Though he'd expected to feel differently when he'd achieved his goal. As if he were walking on air, triumphant, instead of this weird flatness seeping through him.

He had a pretty good idea what was at the root of his feelings. *Second-best.* The words echoed in his head. And he needed to know. 'If Catriona hadn't ruled herself out of the running, would you still be talking to me?' he asked.

'That's very direct,' Lewis said.

Dominic simply waited.

'You obviously know Catriona's stepped down,' Lewis said.

'I also know why,' Dominic said. 'And that she's taking a year's sabbatical.'

'Interesting,' Lewis said. 'We were all rather under the impression that you and Catriona were deadly rivals.'

They had been. But everything had changed over the last few days. 'You haven't answered my question.'

'It's a moot point.' Lewis smiled at the legal pun.

'Not to me.'

'We hadn't quite decided,' Lewis said. 'It was very, very close.'

'In other words, no.'

Lewis sighed. 'It was very, very close,' he said again. 'We really hadn't decided. It could've gone either way.'

'Then maybe,' Dominic said, 'we need to have a slightly different conversation.'

Lewis blinked. 'You're turning down the partnership?'

The hint of dismay in the managing partner's eyes, quickly masked, made Dominic feel a bit better. Maybe he wasn't second-best, after all. 'No.' That was the point of his deal with Catriona: that he'd get the partnership. 'But it's unfair that Catriona's personal circumstances should disadvantage her, when the situation's not of her making.'

'What exactly are you suggesting?' Lewis asked.

'In a year's time, you'd potentially have space for two partners: ones who bring very different but equal abilities to the table. I'm better at overview and strategy, but she's better at details.'

Lewis raised an eyebrow. 'Your point?'

If Lewis valued him enough to make him partner, then so would quite a lot of other people in London. Which put Dominic in precisely the negotiation position he needed. 'If the decision was so close, why choose between us at all? Particularly when our skills complement each other. Make me a partner now, and promote Catriona when she's back from her sabbatical.'

'I see,' Lewis said. 'That's very gallant of you.'

'It's a business decision,' Dominic said. 'She'd be an excellent partner.'

'Do you think she would've suggested the same, if your positions had been reversed?' Lewis asked.

Dominic thought of the way Catriona had told him how she wanted to get the estate to work—without ripping off her tenants or cutting out her half-brothers. 'Yes, actually. I do.'

Lewis was silent for a moment, and then sighed. 'I agree. She would. And you have a point. It's what's made it so difficult to choose between you.'

'I'm glad you see things the way I do,' Dominic said.

Lewis rested his elbows on his desk and steepled his fingers. 'All right. I'll need to talk to the rest of the partners.'

'But they'll be guided by your view. Which is that two partners with a broad skillset between them will make an unbeatable team.' Dominic smiled.

'And that,' Lewis said, 'is exactly why you'll make an excellent partner. You see the bigger picture. Welcome to the team.' Lewis smiled. 'And I'll talk to the partners and then Catriona, in due course.'

'Thank you,' Dominic said. 'And perhaps we can hold off announcing my news until she's on sabbatical. Otherwise it feels like gloating.'

'Quite the moral compass you have there,' Lewis said dryly.

'Added strength,' Dominic said, smiling. 'You don't build a strong team by trampling on them. You do it by empowering them.'

CHAPTER FIVE

THE FOLLOWING EVENING, Dominic met Catriona at a wine bar far enough from the office that they were unlikely to bump into a colleague. He bought them both a glass of white wine, and they found a quiet spot.

'Have you had a chance to look through everything?' he asked.

'Yes. Have you?'

He nodded. 'I'm happy.'

'Ditto. Though I notice you've asked for a clause to make it clear that you're not responsible for Lark Hill or the mortgage on my flat, and I'm not responsible for the mortgage on your flat,' she said.

'So our assets will be separated.'

'It's the wording you've used,' she said. 'What haven't you told me?'

He should've known she'd pick that up. Her eye for detail. 'I guess I should disclose this—and you need to know the whole story before tomorrow,' he said, 'but this is about my family and I want to keep it confidential.'

'I'd never gossip about you.'

He knew that, but he remembered what it was like to be talked about. The way the other mums at school had avoided his mum at the school gate. The whispers. The shame. It still made him feel slightly sick.

'My father left us when Mum was pregnant with Suzy.' He looked away. 'He had a gambling problem. I know addiction is an illness, and I should feel sorry for him, but I just can't. Not after what he did to Mum.' He looked her straight in the eye. 'He hadn't paid the mortgage for months, and he'd hidden all the mortgage company's letters so she didn't have a clue that they were in so much debt or were near to the house being repossessed. He'd also wiped out their joint savings and maxed out their joint overdraft.'

Catriona winced. 'All their finances were in joint names?'

'Yes. When he walked out on Mum and left the country with another woman—someone he'd met in the casino— he also left her with all the debt.' He closed his eyes for a moment. 'Our house was repossessed the week after Mum gave birth to Suzy.'

'That,' she said, 'was incredibly unfair. And surely there's something in the rules that says you can't make a new mother homeless?'

'You'd think,' he said. 'Though, even without all the extra debt from the missed payments, Mum couldn't afford the mortgage on her own. Despite the fact that she wasn't the one who'd run up the debts, she was liable for them because they were in joint names. My father had skipped the country, so she was the easiest one for the bank to go after.' He frowned. 'The local solicitor gave her some advice, *pro bono*. She had the joint account frozen. But, even when the house was sold, the money wasn't enough to pay off the debts. She ended up having to declare bankruptcy. My grandparents and my aunts and uncles did what they could to help with babysitting, and my grandparents made sure we always had food on the table, but Mum hated the fact she had to rely on them for help.'

'None of it was her fault.' She looked at him. 'Your mum sounds an amazing woman.'

'She is.' He was fiercely proud of her.

'That's why you really do the *pro bono* work in family law, isn't it?' she asked. 'Not just to balance out the corporate stuff, like you told me, but because someone helped your family when you needed it most, and you're paying it forward.'

Again, Catriona had zeroed in on the salient point. 'Yes. Though if you tell anyone that I'll deny it.'

'I wouldn't drag your family into it,' she said. 'I'm sorry they had a tough time—and I'm not surprised you're fed up with me whining about inheriting a castle.'

'You're not whining. You're trying to do the right thing.' He raised an eyebrow. 'Before you asked me to marry you, I thought you were rich, spoiled and entitled.'

She nodded her head slowly. 'That's fair,' she said. 'It's probably what I am.'

He shook his head. 'You come from a rich family—but nobody spoiled you. And you're not entitled.'

'Before I asked you to marry me,' she said, 'I thought you were ambitious and probably in the job just for the money. But the money isn't for you, is it? It's about being able to support your family.'

'And never being in a position again where I have to rely on the kindness of other people,' he said. 'And you want to help your half-brothers. Except it sounds to me as if they're the ones who are spoiled and entitled.'

'They seem to be, at the moment, but I'm hoping it's partly because they haven't worked out who they really are yet. My father seemed to go for a particular type of woman, so they're going to have to work pretty hard to battle the selfish genes.' She gave him a wry smile. 'They weren't sent to stay at Lark Hill, the way I was, so they never really got to know our grandparents and they don't see the castle the way I do.'

'If I were in your shoes, I'd get married to inherit the castle,' he said.

'If I were in your shoes...' She paused. 'I hope I'd be decent enough to help you.'

'You would be,' he said, meaning it. He'd learned that she had a strong moral compass, and he liked that. Liked *her*. 'Funny. Last week we probably wouldn't have chosen to work together. This week, we're planning our wedding.'

She chuckled and it was a sound he was quickly becoming to appreciate. He'd love to hear it more and see her loosening up when she was with him.

'Acting as a team. Weird, indeed,' she said. 'Thank you for being honest with me, Dominic. I can see why you don't have any time for your father.' She paused. 'Did he ever apologise, or try to pay any of the money back to your mum?'

'No.'

'That's atrocious. If he ever comes back into this country, I want to know and I'll make sure he sees justice in court,' she said. 'And I'll personally see to it that he apologises. Sincerely.'

Dominic was pleased that she was immediately on his mother's side. 'Being married to me means there would be a conflict of interest and you couldn't be on the prosecution's team,' he reminded her.

'Then we'll brief someone we trust to do it for us,' she said.

We.

Was she, too, starting to see them as a team?

'Sounds good to me,' he said. 'I was thinking, tomorrow

night you might as well come and have dinner at my flat before the call. Is there anything you don't eat?'

'No allergies and I'm not fussy,' she said. 'Can I bring wine or pudding?'

'I'm not much of a pudding person,' he said. 'You don't need to bring anything. Just yourself.'

'All right,' she said. 'What time?'

'Seven? It'll give us time to eat and plan our strategy before the call,' he said. Though it wasn't just that, was it? If he was honest with himself, it meant he'd be able to spend a bit more time just with her.

'Works for me,' she said.

There was a pinker tinge than normal to her cheeks. Was she, too, starting to want to spend time with him? Or was he just fooling himself, confused by an attraction he'd never expected to feel?

She glanced at her watch. 'I'll see you tomorrow, then. Let me know your address. And we'll get everything signed by Friday.'

On Wednesday evening, Catriona felt oddly nervous. She really should've checked the dress code with Dominic. Her office suit clearly wouldn't pass muster with his family, but jeans felt too casual. In the end, she went for a simple black woollen dress.

Dominic's flat was part of a converted yellow-brick warehouse overlooking the river. When she pressed the door intercom, he buzzed her through. 'I'm on the third floor,' he said. 'There's a lift or stairs—your choice.'

She took the lift; he greeted her at his front door—wearing jeans and a round-necked cream sweater, which made her feel overdressed. But what did you wear when you 'met' your convenient husband-to-be's family for the first time on a video call?

'Welcome,' he said.

'Thank you.' She took a box of good crackers, a bunch of black grapes and a paper-wrapped package from her bag. 'My contribution to dinner,' she said.

He raised an eyebrow. 'I did say you needn't bring anything.'

'Remember when you insisted on walking me to the tube station on Sunday when I said you didn't need to, and you asked me to humour you because it was the way you were brought up?' she asked. 'This is the same thing. My grandparents always taught me to take a gift for my host or hostess. You're not into sweet things, so I couldn't bring chocolates, and flowers didn't feel right. Humour me.'

'All right. Thank you.' He sniffed the package. 'Ooh. Would I be right in thinking this contains a very nice ripe Camembert?'

'At perfect ooziness,' she said.

'Wonderful. Thank you very much indeed. I can always be won round by cheese.' He grinned. 'There's another product idea for you: Lark Hill cheese.'

She didn't think that grin was for show: this was the real Dominic, the man behind the professional at work, full of enthusiasm.

And he was still thinking of things to help the castle, even without her asking. It made her feel as if he was becoming as invested in the project as she was—and not just because it meant he'd make partner. He was doing it because they were a team.

Which was scary and thrilling, all at the same time.

'Let me put this in the kitchen. Feel free to hang your coat up. Then I'll give you the tour.'

She hung her coat on the rack by his front door and followed him into the galley-style kitchen. The flooring was stripped oak planks, the cupboards were shiny white, the walls were painted a soft duck-egg-blue and the worktops were mid-grey granite. Everywhere was incredibly tidy; only the kettle was on display on the worktops.

'The bathroom's opposite,' he said, gesturing to the doorway. 'The living room's through here.' The room was an enormous square; one wall was almost entirely glass, with French doors and blinds she guessed were for sunny days. There were two comfortable-looking sofas; against one wall was a desk, next to a bookcase, which she could see was stuffed with a mixture of legal textbooks and the crime novels he'd told her were his favourites. There was a cabinet next to the bookcase, stuffed full of vinyl albums, with a turntable on top; an electro-acoustic guitar and amp sat on the other side. Six chairs were tucked neatly around a dining table, which was set for two.

On the neutral-painted walls, there were a couple of seascapes, which looked to her like original watercolours rather than prints; on the mantelpiece, there was a scattering of framed photographs, all showing Dominic with his family—everything from his formal graduation picture to candid snaps in the garden. They were the kind of pictures she didn't have, apart from her graduation photograph with her grandparents, and she pushed down the wave of longing. His family wasn't going to become her family, she reminded herself. Not when their wedding was just for convenience. She was perfectly fine on her own. Always had been.

'It's a very nice flat,' she said.

'I like it,' he said. 'There's a communal garden—not that I really get time to use it—and the balcony is lovely in summer.' He gestured to the French doors. 'The view's pretty good.'

The river was ink-dark at this time of night, with lights reflected in the water. Catriona recognised the lit-up shapes of the Shard and the Fenchurch Building. 'I bet this is stunning at sunrise and sunset.'

'It is,' he said. 'I tend to keep the blinds open, except when it's blazingly hot.'

'Mine's a duplex on the top two floors, so I don't have a garden either,' she said. 'Just a terrace with a few pots of geraniums and the like. Though it's only a few steps to Regent's Park, so I can wander through the rose gardens and up Primrose Hill whenever I want.'

'That sounds good, too,' he said.

'I noticed your record collection, by the way. Would that be your Uncle Bill's influence?'

'And the guitar, yes.' He smiled. 'He taught me years ago that vinyl sounds so much better than digital.'

'With all the scratches and hisses?'

'You don't lose bits of information, the way you do with an MP3 that has to translate analogue to digital and back again,' he said. 'And the sound's warmer. Can I get you a glass of wine?'

'If you have camomile tea,' she said, 'that would be perfect.'

He grimaced. 'Afraid not. I can do builder's tea.'

She shook her head. 'Then a glass of water would be lovely, thanks.'

'Have a seat,' he said, gesturing to the table.

Dinner turned out to be a seriously good chicken tagine scattered with pomegranate seeds and pieces of preserved lemon, served with greens and some fluffy couscous. 'This is really lovely,' she said, impressed by his cooking skills.

'Thanks. I like messing about in the kitchen. It relaxes me,' he said.

She raised an eyebrow. 'Your kitchen's spotless. There's not even the tiniest hint of mess.'

'If you'd seen it half an hour ago, you wouldn't be saying that,' he said with a grin.

Oh, that grin. It was boyish, slightly goofy, and it made her heart feel as if it had done a somersault.

Which was ridiculous. And she wasn't supposed to be thinking about him in those terms. Their marriage had nothing to do with any foolish feelings of attraction, and everything to do with sorting out her grandfather's estate.

'Are you OK?' he asked.

'I'm a bit nervous about meeting your family,' she admitted.

'They'll be fine. Well, they might grill you a bit,' he said. 'But that's because they're worried about me.' He rolled his eyes. 'Despite the fact I've explained the situation to them.'

Which didn't reassure her in the slightest. What if one of them decided to object formally at the wedding?

'Maybe we should've eloped to Las Vegas,' she said.

'They would've given you a harder time if we'd got married without telling them,' he countered.

All the same, her stomach was tied in knots by the time the video call took place. And it seemed that his sisters had congregated at their mother's house because only one screen came up on his laptop.

'Catriona, this is my mum Ginny, my baby sister Suzy, and my middle sister Tilly with my nephew Aiden,' Dominic said, introducing them swiftly. 'Everyone, this is Catriona.'

'Hello,' Catriona said.

'Nice to meet you,' Ginny said, though her tone was slightly reserved.

Suzy was the one to raise the tough issue. 'Dommy says you have to get married or you can't inherit the castle and it'll go to your half-brothers instead.'

Which sounded horrible.

'It's not about greed,' Catriona said. 'It means the tenants won't have to worry about a change in ownership that might lead to a rent increase or even giving them notice, and the castle stays in my family instead of being sold off to the highest bidder.'

'But you're both supposed to be hotshot lawyers,' Tilly said. 'You were Dominic's main competition for the partnership.'

Catriona flushed. 'Yes.'

'Then why can't you find a loophole to get round the will?' Tilly asked.

'Because there *isn't* a loophole,' Dominic said.

'And he said you don't get on very well, because you're rich and ent—'

'Tills, drop it,' Dominic cut in, looking pained.

'She's right. We need to be open about this. Yes, in the past Dominic and I rubbed each other up the wrong way professionally,' Catriona said. 'We're both focused on work and we both think we're always right. Obviously we've clashed.'

'And you chose him as the one to marry?' Suzy asked.

'He has integrity,' Catriona said; glancing at the man who very soon would become her husband. 'I trust him.' She wasn't lying; she did trust him and that was something she hadn't done for a long time. Not since she'd discovered Luke's betrayal...

'And you're giving up the partnership race for him?' Tilly asked.

'This way we both get what we want,' Catriona said.

Ginny looked thoughtful. 'Will this be the first time your family's ever heard of Dommy?'

'Yes,' Catriona admitted.

'In their shoes,' Ginny said, 'I'd suspect this was a fake marriage so you can meet the terms of the will, and I'd contest it.'

'The castle needs extensive repairs. We can't afford a court case,' Catriona added, 'which is why I need to convince them it's a real marriage.'

'Are they coming to the wedding?' Tilly asked.

Catriona winced. 'No. Just the three of you, your partners and the baby.'

'What about your mum?' Tilly asked.

At Catriona's headshake, Suzy frowned. 'There's nobody on your side?'

'My best friend moved to New York six months ago. And she's pregnant, so I don't want to drag her over here on a plane. This is going to be a quiet wedding,' Catriona said. 'Which I think most people would understand, given that I buried my grandfather a couple of weeks ago.'

'My condolences,' Ginny said, and it seemed genuine.

'I trust her, too. I told her about our situation with my father,' Dominic said.

'And I'll respect that confidence. I'm sorry you had a rough time,' Catriona said.

'It is what it is. Gambling's an addiction, and addiction's an illness,' Ginny said. 'The man I married would never have neglected his children or cheated on me. The gambling changed him.'

'I would still have wanted to punch him on the nose for what he did,' Catriona said.

Ginny gave her a wry smile. 'I wanted to, believe me.

But my focus was on the kids. And I was lucky that my family helped us.'

What would it be like to have a family that pulled together like that? Catriona wondered. Not that she'd ever know.

'You're going to need help convincing your brothers,' Tilly said. 'What are you wearing?'

'My work clothes will be fine,' Catriona said.

'That wouldn't convince me,' Suzy said. 'You need to wear something that looks a *bit* bridal. Skip the veil, but you need flowers.'

'Agreed,' Tilly said. 'What are you doing on Sunday?'

'I...' Catriona couldn't think of an excuse quickly enough.

'Good. You're coming to Birmingham,' Tilly said. 'We'll go shopping.'

'But—'

'You don't have time?' Suzy asked. 'Then we'll order some things in your size. Lou can do a trial run of your hair and make-up, and her best friend's a florist so she can sort out the flowers. And then, on the day, you throw your bouquet at Lou.' She gave Catriona a broad wink. 'Which is a discussion for another time.'

'Bring a couple of pairs of shoes with different heel heights with you,' Tilly added with a smile, 'so then you'll know what shoes to get to go with the dress.'

'I know it's not our planned weekend for Sunday lunch, but I'll cook,' Ginny said.

'Talking of food, what about the wedding breakfast?' Suzy asked.

'We hadn't planned one. It was meant to be a quiet wedding with just the two of us and two witnesses off the street,' Dominic said. 'Stop steamrollering my fiancée.'

His fiancée.

And he was standing up for her.

Catriona was perfectly capable of standing up for herself—and she knew that Dominic knew it, too—but she kind of liked the way he'd taken her part. And she liked his family. Yes, they were a bit over the top, and their reaction to the whole situation was ridiculous enough to make her smile; but they were enthusiastic, and they clearly loved Dominic to bits. This was the kind of family she could enjoy being part of—except this wasn't a real relationship.

'It's not about steamrollering,' Tilly said. 'You're getting married in four weeks. In December. Most places will be booked up with Christmas lunches. But you absolutely can't get married without at least having lunch. What time's the wedding?'

'One o'clock,' Dominic said.

'Maybe just book somewhere nice for lunch at two, so we can toast you with bubbles—and then you'll have the photos to show your brothers, Trina,' Suzy said.

Trina?

Nobody had ever shortened her name.

But Catriona didn't have time even to think about how that made her feel, because then Tilly asked, 'Are you officially engaged yet?'

'That's going to be on Friday,' Dominic said.

'You've chosen the ring?' Suzy asked.

'We're using my grandmother's,' Catriona said.

'That's nice. Tradition. And you'll be sure to post it on social media,' Tilly said. 'Maybe with a picture of your grandparents at their engagement, if you've got one.'

'I don't do social media,' Catriona said. The idea of it made her skin itch. Why did you need to have your life on display for other people? Why put yourself up to be judged?

'You need to convince your brothers,' Suzy said. 'Play it safe and take pictures on your phone.'

How daunting it all felt.

Dominic clearly realised that Catriona had had enough, because he said, 'OK, guys. Grilling over. We'll see you on Sunday.'

Catriona had just about enough presence of mind to say goodbye, but her mind was reeling when Dominic ended the call.

'Sorry. I'm used to the way they are, but it looks as if you found them a bit much,' he said.

A bit much? His family was *terrifying*. But they were also caring and kind. Enchanting. Not that she wanted to tell him. She wasn't ready to expose all her weaknesses. 'I can see where you get your energy from,' she said instead. She raised an eyebrow. 'And the bossiness.'

He grinned. 'Why, thank you, Fifi.' But then his smile faded and he took her hand and squeezed it briefly.

Her skin felt as if it shimmered where he'd touched it, and little flickers of something she didn't want to name started low in her belly.

'I'll drive us on Sunday,' he said. 'I normally get the train home so I can do some work on the way, but if I drive it means we can escape whenever you need to, instead of being tied to the train timetable.'

She hadn't expected him to be so thoughtful—or to realise that, coming from a family that was as distant as you could get, it was likely that she'd find a family like his overwhelming. 'Thank you. I'll—um—see you tomorrow.'

'Have you got a taxi booked?'

'Tube,' she said. Before he could offer to walk her to the tube station, she added, 'And the walk on my own will help me get my head round things. Thank you for dinner.' And then she left before she could land herself in an even deeper muddle.

By the time she got back to her flat, Catriona found Suzy and Tilly had already set her up in a WhatsApp group with them, and there was a screenful of messages. They were clearly taken with the idea of wedding planning—but beneath it was a kindness she found humbling. She was a stranger, and they were helping her. For their brother's sake, admittedly; but it was good to feel that she had a team.

She answered their questions, sent them a snap of the ring, and then sent a private message to Dominic.

Your sisters are lovely.

They have their moments. Tell me if they get too much.

All of this was too much. She'd sworn she'd never have a wedding again. But they were right: all of this was necessary to save Lark Hill. Her home. She'd just never expected to bring a whole new family into it. And then she smiled in spite of herself. Because clearly Dominic was a package deal, and that package was loud and brash...and unexpectedly wonderful.

CHAPTER SIX

On Thursday, Suzy and Tilly sent Catriona an array of dress pictures.

Suzy warned:

Don't show Dommy. It's bad luck for the groom to see the dress.

Even though it wasn't a proper wedding?

Catriona chose the plainest dresses, and sent her thanks.

On Friday lunchtime, she signed the prenups with Dominic, with their lawyers as witnesses; and on Friday evening they met up after work, ready to take an engagement photograph for her brothers—and, more importantly, their mothers. She'd assumed that they'd go to a bar somewhere—maybe one with a pretty flower wall, or fairy lights—or to dinner, but instead Dominic shepherded her to the Regent's Canal at Little Venice, where a boat was waiting for them.

'A private cruise?' she asked, surprised.

'It's been quite a week,' he said. 'I thought you might like the chance to chill out. Privately.'

'Thank you.' It was exactly what she needed. 'Has Lewis talked to you about the partnership yet?'

'Yes. When you're on leave, we'll announce the deal.' He looked her. 'Otherwise it feels like rubbing your nose in it.'

'That's decent of you,' she said.

He shrugged it off. 'You would have done the same.'

'Even though I'm an ambitious ball-breaker?'

'Now I know you better, I realise that isn't who you are,' he said. 'But you don't suffer fools gladly.'

'Not anymore.'

He raised an eyebrow. 'That sounds like an interesting story.

'Dull,' she corrected. 'Maybe some other time.' She could see in his expression that he'd ask her about it at some time in the future. She'd make sure she was ready, with all the emotions taken out. Cold, hard facts. And proof that she learned from her mistakes.

He helped her onto the boat and introduced her to the captain. The covered viewing deck at the front of the boat was twined with twinkly fairy lights, and there was a huge fluffy blanket on the seat behind the table—clearly aimed at couples who wanted to snuggle up together. Which *wasn't* her and Dominic.

'It's so we don't freeze,' he said, seeing where she was looking. 'Given it's a November evening.'

'Uh-huh,' she said, sitting down and draping the blanket over her lap.

He sat down next to her, did the same, and then leaned to the side and brought out a willow hamper.

'I wasn't planning to starve you,' he said, and swiftly decanted the hamper's contents onto the table: a charcuterie and cheeseboard with crackers, mini plum tomatoes, olives and baby figs.

If this had been a real date, Catriona would definitely have been swept off her feet. As it was, she was just very close to it. This was one of the most romantic things anyone had ever done for her, and it was just the kind of food she enjoyed most.

'It's the perfect setting for an engagement,' she said. 'You've done a great job.'

'Thanks, though I haven't *quite* finished.' He flicked into a streaming app on his phone, and a few moments later gentle piano music floated into the air—the sort of music she really loved. He'd clearly remembered what she'd said.

Then he reached under the table and brought out two champagne flutes and a chilled bottle of champagne, deftly dealt with the cork and poured two glasses. He handed one to her, then raised his own glass in a toast. 'To you,' he said. 'Because you've changed the way I think about things, this last week.'

'You've changed the way I think, too,' she said. Particularly about him. How had she got him so wrong?

'I vote we eat before we do the taking-pictures-with-ring business,' he said.

'And I need to give you the ring anyway,' she said. She took the old-fashioned blue velvet box out of her bag and gave it to him.

'May I?' he asked.

'Sure.'

He opened the box. 'That's really pretty. Do you know how old it is?'

'It was my gran's, but she and Gramps married in the early sixties and I think this is Edwardian. It might have been her grandmother's,' Catriona said.

'What would she think of this wedding?'

'My grandmother was practical above all else,' she said. 'I think her marriage to Gramps was—well, dynastic, rather than a love match. But I'm pretty sure they grew to love each other. He missed her badly after she died.' And she missed both of them.

'To your grandparents,' he said, lifting his glass again.

'Grannie and Gramps,' she said, blinking back the threatening tears.

Once they'd finished the picnic—and most of the champagne—Dominic turned to her. 'Ready for this?'

'Ready,' she said.

He took the ring from the box and slid it onto her finger.

And this felt very, very different from the last time a man had slid an engagement ring onto her finger. This time, she wasn't in a spin and head over heels in love; but, this time, even though the engagement was fake, it felt real. As if Dominic was quietly making a promise that he intended to keep.

He took a photograph of the ring on her finger, and one of her holding her hand up in the traditional 'I said yes' pose.

'I've had instructions from the girls,' he said, pulling up a message on his phone. 'We need a shot of me holding your hand, ring uppermost.'

'OK,' she said.

He slid his palm underneath hers, and her skin tingled where he touched her. Which was crazy, because she and Dominic weren't in the least bit attracted to each other. She was just letting the situation sway her, she told herself. All the same, she found her fingers curling round his. And when she looked at him—were those little flecks of gold in his irises, or was it just a reflection of the fairy lights?

'And there's another one we have to do,' he said, carefully following the instructions in the text. 'Your left hand on my cheek to show off the ring. Me leaning in for a kiss. Both of us having our eyes closed.'

The tingling in her skin spread.

'Close your eyes,' he said. 'This is our first kiss as an engaged couple.'

Except they weren't a couple. They weren't really engaged. And was he *really* going to kiss her?

'Relax,' he said. 'Pretend I'm your dream man. The actor you fell in love with when you were fifteen.'

'I...' Her breath hitched.

'Relax,' he repeated. 'Just think about kissing someone you'd really, really want to kiss.'

The world felt as if it was tilting sideways when she realised that the person she was thinking of, right at that moment, was Dominic Ferrars.

'Imagine he's close,' Dominic whispered. 'Close enough for you to feel the heat of his skin next to yours. And any second now his mouth's going to touch yours. It's just the two of you. Under the stars on a deserted beach, with the water swishing softly across the sand.'

Catriona could hear water swishing and, even though she knew it was the Regent's Canal rather than the sea, she could imagine that she was standing on a beach with her fiancé.

With Dominic.

'Think of that first touch of his mouth against yours. Soft, sweet, a declaration of love to seal your engagement,' he continued, his voice hypnotic.

With her eyes still closed, Catriona felt her lips parting and her head tipping back, inviting a kiss.

Dominic had no idea who Catriona was thinking of. But the softness in her face, the way she arched towards him with her eyes closed, was his undoing. He couldn't stop himself leaning towards her.

This was supposed to be for social media. For them to make an official declaration of their engagement to the world.

And instead it felt like an intensely private moment. As if the scenario he'd just suggested was true: the two of them, on a deserted beach, about to kiss. His mouth was millimetres from hers.

Dominic had just about enough presence of mind left to glance at the screen of his phone and check that they were somewhere in the right place for the photograph.

And then he closed his eyes and touched his mouth against hers.

It felt like an electric shock.

Particularly when she kissed him back, all sweet and enticing. Her mouth was so soft against his, and he wanted more. He wanted her to feel the same kind of sparks that were igniting in his head. He dropped his phone on the seat and drew her closer. The hand she'd rested on his cheek slid round to the back of his neck, and she opened her mouth, letting him deepen the kiss.

He'd kissed women before. Kissed women he liked. Kissed women he might've been able to love.

But kissing Catriona was like nothing else he'd ever experienced.

It felt so right.

And it shook him to the core.

When he finally broke the kiss, he stared at her. 'Um… Sorry. That wasn't supposed to happen.'

'Nothing happened,' she said swiftly. 'It was just for the photographs.'

But something *had* happened. There had been a connection between them he hadn't expected, and he was pretty sure it was the same for her, too. Her eyes were wide and her mouth was parted, her lips plump and tempting.

It flustered him; now he knew what it felt to kiss her, he wanted to do it again. And again. Until they were both dizzy.

Though was that longing or worry he saw in her eyes?

He couldn't be sure, so he backed off. 'Just for the photographs,' he echoed, knowing that he was lying and it had been a lot more than that.

Somehow he managed to make polite conversation through the rest of their boat trip. Once they were on land again, he called a taxi. 'You're on my way home,' he said, 'so I'll drop you off.'

'Thank you.'

When the taxi stopped, she looked wary. 'Would you, um…?' she began.

Yes, but he also knew it wouldn't be sensible and he needed time to get his head back in the right place. 'I've got some work to catch up on,' he fibbed. 'See you Sunday. It takes two and a half hours to get there; shall I pick you up at half-past eight?'

'I'll be ready,' she said.

He just hoped he managed to get his common sense back in place by Sunday. But he smiled and, once the light went on in her flat, he asked the cabbie to take him back to Islington.

On Sunday morning, Catriona was waiting outside her front door as Dominic pulled up to the kerb. He glanced at the clock on the dashboard: twenty-eight minutes past eight. He was early, but she'd been earlier.

'I hope you haven't been waiting long,' he said.

'Only about a minute,' she said.

'What's all that?' he asked, gesturing to the bags she was holding.

'Flowers for your mum, and a little thank-you for your sisters and Lou,' she said. 'And coffee for us.'

'You really didn't have to,' he said, 'but thank you. Mum and the girls will be pleased.' He stowed her bags safely in the car, then opened the passenger door for her. At her raised eyebrows, he said, 'This doesn't mean I think you're an incapable little woman, because you're nothing of the kind. It's how I was brought up. You open the door for your passenger.'

'Good manners rather than patronising works for me,' she said. 'Thank you.'

He climbed into the driver's side. 'Feel free to adjust the heating and put whatever you like on the radio.'

He wasn't surprised that she picked a classical music station; and he also wasn't surprised that she took refuge in her coffee to avoid talking.

But eventually she spoke. 'Dominic, I need to tell you something before we see your family.'

'Oh?'

She took a deep breath. 'This isn't the first time I've been engaged.'

Now that *did* surprise him. 'What happened?'

'I thought I'd learned from my parents' mistakes,' she said. 'Except I didn't. He thought a big flashy diamond ring gave him licence to cheat. I found out when I came home early from work, one afternoon. He was in bed—*my* bed—with someone I didn't know. I know everyone makes mistakes and you should give people a second chance, but it turned out that his affair had been going on for a while. And she wasn't the first. So I packed his things, made him give me my key back—and changed the locks. And then I moved.'

'I'm sorry he let you down so badly,' Dominic said.

'I let myself down,' she said. 'I should have seen through him. He was in love with the idea of marrying a viscount's granddaughter, of marrying into money. But he tried to make me feel it was my fault, for being cold.'

Her tone was even, but Dominic was starting to be able

to read what she kept hidden. That accusation of coldness had really hurt her. Catriona wasn't cold, when you got to know her. She definitely used her intellect as a shield, but she *cared*.

'Now I get why you really didn't want a diamond engagement ring.' He frowned. 'Though, if your grandfather knew about this, that makes the clause inexcusable as well as even more unexplainable.'

'He didn't know the full story of why I broke up with Luke,' Catriona said. 'Grannie was ill at the time. I didn't want to burden either of them.'

'That's hard,' Dominic said. 'But, even though this isn't the same kind of engagement, I can assure you I won't cheat on you. That's not who I am.'

'That's why I picked you as my convenient husband,' Catriona said with a glance at him.

'You know what you said about wanting to punch my father? That's how I feel about your ex, right now,' Dominic said.

'You might come off worse,' she warned. 'Luke was my personal trainer.'

So *that* was why she'd flinched about his sister's job. And why she preferred to walk in the park rather than train at the gym. Dominic's heart ached for her, though it wasn't from pity. It was something he couldn't define.

'I keep in shape. I'd rate my chances,' he said. 'Not all men are cheating scumbags, you know.'

'I know. I'm just disappointed that my judgement was so poor, given what my parents were like.' She wrinkled her nose. 'I'm sorry. I should've told you before.'

'No, but I'm glad you told me.' He paused. 'And it won't go any further than me.'

'Thank you,' she said.

* * *

Dominic's family were all there to greet them at his mother's house. To Catriona's surprise, Ginny greeted her with a huge hug. She couldn't remember the last time anyone had done that, and it felt strange: as if the barriers she usually kept around herself were starting to melt.

'Oh, sweetheart, they're lovely,' Ginny said when Catriona gave her the flowers. 'Thank you.'

Dominic's sisters followed up with hugs, as did Tilly's husband Joe, Ginny's partner Ray and Suzy's partner Lou. Clearly Dominic's family were openly affectionate.

The girls allowed her enough time to have a coffee, then whisked her up to Suzy's room to try on the dresses.

All the ones she'd picked out were serviceable enough, but Suzy had added another. 'One of my friends designed this, and I think it's perfect for you.'

The dress was knee-length with a Bardot collar, in ivory silk; it was cinched in at the waist and had a flared skirt that fell to just below the knee. It wasn't the kind of style Catriona would have chosen, but Suzy had gone to a lot of effort, so she tried it on.

'That's definitely the one,' Tilly said.

Catriona stared at her reflection and felt as if her tongue was glued to her mouth.

'It's perfect,' Lou agreed.

And it was a million times better than the dress Catriona had once dreamed of wearing on her wedding day.

Lou did a mock-up of her hair and make-up, and Ginny came in to give the final verdict. She stood in the doorway, looking stunned. 'Catriona, you look absolutely amazing! I want to hug you—but I don't want to spoil the dress.'

'Give us ten minutes, and she'll be back to normal and you can hug her,' Lou said.

After that they ran through the flowers and the wedding breakfast.

'Have you ordered a wedding cake?' Suzy asked.

'I wasn't going to bother,' Catriona said. 'Dominic's not a fan of cakes or puddings, and it's a small wedding.' She smiled at Ginny. 'Can I help you with lunch, Ginny?'

'All done. Sit down and have a glass of bubbles,' Ginny said. 'Dommy, there's a bottle in the fridge, if you could go and open it for us.'

'Sure,' he said with a smile.

'I...um...wanted to say thanks for your help,' Catriona said, and quietly dished out the gift bags she'd brought with her.

'You didn't need to do that! But thank you,' Tilly said, looking pleased.

'Can we open them now?' Suzy asked. At Catriona's nod, she did so. 'Oh, wow. This is seriously posh stuff. Thank you so much.' She pulled her in for another hug.

Catriona realised she was going to have to get used to the hugs. Dominic's family were all seriously tactile. 'You're welcome,' she said. 'You've all put a lot of work into helping us, and I appreciate it.' She felt the colour rise in her cheeks. 'Though I realise it's because of Dominic.'

'Now we're getting to know you,' Tilly said, 'it's for you as well.'

Catriona couldn't remember the last time she'd taken part in family Sunday lunch with any more people than her grandparents and Mrs MacFarlane; but she found herself really enjoying it. Even when Dominic's uncles and aunts arrived unexpectedly.

'I know you wanted to get to know Dominic's young lady properly and we were supposed to butt out,' one of his uncles said, 'but how could we pass up the chance to meet her? I'm Bill.'

'Of the guitar fame,' Catriona said.

Bill looked pleased. 'Dommy talks about my music?'

'I told you we'd fill you in later. *Don't* scare her away,' Ginny admonished. 'Catriona, this is my sister Shirl and her husband Bill, my sister Di and her husband Andy, and my sister Angie and her husband Glenn.'

'Who'd've thought it? Our little Dommy, getting married at last,' Shirl cooed.

'We've waited for *years* for him to bring a girl home,' Di added.

'Stop it, you two. You'll make the poor boy blush,' Angie said. 'But come here, Catriona, and let's give you a welcome hug.'

It sounded as if Dominic's aunts and uncles all thought the wedding was a real one.

'Go with it,' Dominic murmured in her ear. 'Think of it as a trial run for convincing your half-brothers.'

'How did you meet?' Angie asked, giving her a hug.

'We work together,' Catriona said.

'Love among all the legal fine print,' Shirl said with a grin.

'And the wedding's next month?' Di gave a very pointed look at Catriona's stomach.

'It's not a shotgun wedding, Auntie Di,' Dominic said, rolling his eyes. 'We just…didn't want to wait.'

'So what are you having as the first dance?' Bill asked.

'No dancing. We're driving to Scotland almost straight after wedding,' Dominic said.

'Which bit of Scotland?' Glenn asked.

'Roughly east-south-east of Edinburgh,' Catriona said.

'If you leave London at three, you'll be lucky to get there by eleven, even without any hold-ups,' Bill said. 'You might be better off going the next day and doing more of the journey in daylight.'

'And that means you'll be able to have a couple of glasses of champagne with us to toast your wedding, instead of just a sip to keep you under the limit for driving,' Shirley said.

'It's going to be a very small wedding, Auntie Shirl,' Dominic said gently, 'given that Catriona recently lost her grandfather. Just Mum, the girls and their partners.'

Shirley bit her lip. 'Oh, love, I'm so sorry.' She gave Catriona a hug. 'You were close to him?'

'Yes,' Catriona said. Although it wasn't anything like the closeness Dominic had with his family, it wasn't a complete fib; she'd been closer to her grandfather and her grandmother than to anyone else in her family.

'Raise a glass to him on the day, love,' Bill said kindly. 'He'll know.'

'Yes.' She barely managed to get the word past the lump in her throat.

'I didn't mean to make you sad, love. Come on, we'll do a family sing,' Bill said.

'Bill,' Ginny said warningly.

'No, Gin, music's just the thing when you're feeling low,' he said. 'Back in a tick. I'll just nip out to the car.'

He returned without the guitar Catriona was expecting.

Catriona blinked as he checked the tuning of the instrument. 'Is that a *ukulele*?'

'It's easier to carry around than a guitar,' Bill said. 'You're a music fan?'

'Classical, mainly,' Catriona said.

'Ah.' Bill smiled, and played a piece that Catriona recognised instantly.

'The Prelude from Bach's cello suite,' she said. 'That's lovely. Thank you.'

The next thing she knew, he'd switched into a Beatles medley and everyone was singing along. She was shocked to find herself joining in when he segued into the Abba songs that everyone knew.

Dominic put an arm round her shoulders, squeezed her briefly and dropped a kiss on her hair. She knew he was doing it for show, to convince his aunts and uncles that this was a real courtship, but the sudden longing for contact was too much for her and she slid her arm round his waist. She felt him tense in surprise, and then he shifted just that little bit closer. And she could almost believe that he was singing some of the words of the songs to her. That this was going to be a real marriage, not a fake.

All too soon it was time to go back to London.

'Your family's lovely,' Catriona said when they were back on the motorway. 'You're so lucky to have grown up with all that...' The word 'love' caught in her throat.

'We have each other's backs,' he agreed. 'We're all out in force in the front row when Bill's band is playing, getting everyone dancing and singing. Aunty Shirl's a teacher, so when they do the summer fundraising fair we all donate raffle prizes and help man the stalls. Anyone needs a hand, we're there.'

What would it be like if her half-brothers did that? If they came and helped her with Lark Hill? But it was pointless wishing because she knew it wasn't going to happen.

'Your aunts and uncles are so disappointed about being left out of your wedding,' she said. 'I feel really guilty.'

'They understand it's a quiet wedding.'

And it wasn't a real one, she thought, so it shouldn't matter. Besides, what was the point of wishing for a real family wedding when they weren't actually going to be her family? It would only make it harder when she and Dominic had their quiet, amicable divorce and he walked away. She couldn't afford to get close to them.

'I've been thinking,' she said. 'Maybe your uncle's right about the drive. It isn't fair to Mrs MacFarlane, making her wait up and worry about us. We'd be better off going to Lark Hill the day after the wedding.'

He shot her a sidelong glance. 'Is this your way of telling me you're planning to go back to work, after the wedding? Except you can't, because you'll be on sabbatical. You're clearing your desk out, the evening before. Not that you have a lot to clear out.'

'It's inefficient to have clutter everywhere,' she said. Though she knew what he meant. She was about the only person in the office who had nothing personal on her desk, not even a pot plant. It had never bothered her before, but now she started to wonder if she was seriously out of step with the rest of the office—and the rest of the human race.

'I notice my sisters have given you a nickname,' he said.

She nodded. 'Trina.' At first, she'd found it strange; then she'd seen the affection behind it, and she secretly liked it.

'It sounds softer if you drop the first syllable of your name,' he mused. '"Trina" sounds like a girl who has fun. "Catriona" is the serious, scary lawyer.'

Precisely why she'd never admit to it in the office. But it still made her smile—as well as reminding her of his own nickname in the family. 'Like the difference between Dominic the London lawyer and "Dommy" who kicks a ball around in the park with all the family kids?'

'Something like that. So who are you in Scotland?' he asked.

'Just me,' she said.

'The Viscountess of Linton.'

'I'm still not used to the title,' she said. 'I intend to be on first-name terms with the tenants. Most of them have known me since I was tiny anyway.'

'If you're still just you,' he said thoughtfully, 'then you're fair, honest and hard-working.'

'Like Gramps,' she said.

He reached over to squeeze her hand briefly. 'You'll do a great job. And you'll bring something of you to the role, too.'

Except she didn't do personal. She kept everything brisk and businesslike. She'd prided herself on being professional; now, she was starting to wonder if that was enough.

When Dominic parked by her house, Catriona asked, 'Would you like to come in for a coffee?'

He was pretty sure she'd only invited him out of politeness, but he was intrigued to see what her flat was like. If it gave him any more clues as to who she really was. 'Thanks. That'd be lovely.'

Her flat was in a four-storey Georgian terrace; the houses had pale yellow bricks, tall, white-painted sash windows, and glossy black front doors with a rectangular fanlight above.

'Most of the houses are divided into flats,' she said as she unlocked her front door. 'I'm on the top two floors.'

He followed her up the stairs to her flat, where she let him into the black-and-white-tiled hallway.

'It's a bit of an upside-down house,' she said. 'The bedrooms are on this floor.' She indicated one of the doors. 'That's the bathroom. Come up.'

There was another landing at the top of the stairs, and a black-and-white-tiled corridor. 'Living room,' she said, gesturing to one door, 'my office, and the kitchen. Would you prefer tea or coffee?'

'Coffee, please,' he said.

He followed her into the kitchen; the kitchen units were glossy cream, teamed with pale wood countertops and terracotta tiled flooring. A single door led to what he assumed was the terrace. There was a pale square wooden table with four chairs tucked neatly round it. Everything was incredibly tidy, and the only things on any of the work surfaces were the kettle and an expensive-looking coffee machine.

'That's a bean-to-cup machine, isn't it?' he asked.

'Because I don't want to put pods into landfill,' she said. 'Besides, this way I get to choose my blend.' She gestured towards the living room. 'Take a seat,' she said, 'and I'll bring your coffee through.'

As he'd half-expected, her living room was organised and uncluttered, just like her clear desk policy at work, and it told him almost nothing about her. The room contained two small plain olive-green sofas with a small square coffee table next to each, and a sideboard which had a single brass lamp with a glass shade on top of it. It felt more like a show flat rather than a home.

The built-in bookshelves on either side of the chimney breast contained legal textbooks, historical novels and a few volumes about Tudor history; they were all shelved in strict alphabetical order by author surname, he noticed, and although he didn't recognise many of the names it was a fair bet that each author's novels were shelved in chronological order. It was clear that Catriona liked things orderly.

There was an antique carriage clock on the mantelpiece; it sat next to a silver photograph frame, which held a photo of Catriona at graduation with what he presumed were her grandparents. They were all smiling, but there was definitely an air of reserve about her grandparents: so very different to his own family. He remembered his own graduation, celebrating with his entire family. He had a feeling that Catriona's graduation celebrations had been an awful lot quieter.

There were no cushions or throws or any of the soft touches his mother, sisters and aunts had in their homes. There was a gilt mirror above the mantelpiece, a standard lamp by one of the sofas that was clearly used as a reading lamp, and the single piece of art on the walls was a small gilt-framed oil painting of a castle overlooking the sea. He wondered whether it was Lark Hill.

He couldn't resist peeking through the heavy brocade curtains; outside, there was a row of Georgian houses, and behind that he could see the greenery of Regent's Park— or what would look green on a spring morning rather than a winter night.

Catriona came in and handed him a mug of coffee, then took two coasters from a drawer in the sideboard and set one on each table. He had to hide a smile, because he knew she kept a coaster in her desk drawer at work, too. Was this how posh people lived, with everything kept hidden away?

The coffee was excellent, but he wasn't surprised—or that she was drinking what looked like chamomile tea. Her painted hoardings were very much back up, and he was beginning to think there was a layer of steel and barbed wire underneath. What would it take to persuade Catriona to let anyone close—to let *him* close? he wondered.

'It's a lovely flat,' he said.

'Thank you. I like it. It's a quiet road and it's near the park.' She looked at him. 'I moved here seven years ago.'

He remembered she'd said that she'd moved after she'd discovered her fiancé's infidelity. Not wanting to dwell on tough memories for her, he changed the subject. 'Is that Lark Hill?' he asked, gesturing to the painting.

'Yes. Gramps commissioned it from a local artist when I

was born, and my grandparents gave it to me for my twenty-fifth,' she said.

'And they're the ones with you in your graduation photo?'

She nodded. 'I probably should've asked my mother, but you could only have two guests and my grandparents were the ones who sent me weekly letters and chocolate when I was a student. I thought they'd enjoy it more than she would. And it was a lovely day. Sunny, bright, Oxford at its prettiest.'

If he'd studied away from home, his mother would've sent him a care package every week. It sounded as though Catriona's mother had clearly decided that giving birth was the limit of her familial duties, and had practically abandoned her daughter afterwards. No wonder Catriona was so aloof. 'My graduation was on a sunny day, too. Mum and Ray came to the ceremony—there was a limit of two tickets per graduand, but everyone else was waiting outside for me and they took a gazillion photos.' He laughed. 'Everyone took turns wearing my mortar board and having their photo taken with me. We spent the rest of the day celebrating, and it was good to share the day with them all.' He winced. 'Sorry. I know family stuff isn't the same for you.'

'It is what it is,' she said with a shrug. 'I've come to terms with it.'

Dominic wasn't quite so sure. There was something wistful in her eyes. He finished his coffee. 'Can I wash this up?' he asked, indicating his mug.

'No, it's fine,' she said, and took the mug from him.

'Guess I'll see you tomorrow, then,' he said, following her into the hallway.

She put the mugs on the kitchen worktop, then headed down the stairs to the front door.

He leaned forward and kissed her on the cheek. Her eyes

went wide, and there was a distinct slash of colour across her cheekbones. Maybe she wasn't quite as immune to this thing between them as she acted.

'If we're going to convince your brothers that the wedding isn't a fake,' he said, 'we need to be comfortable with each other.'

'True.' But she didn't make a move towards him.

What he really wanted was for it to be like it had been on the boat, when she'd loosened her guard and kissed him. Though that in itself was scary, telling him that he was already getting too close to her. All the same, he kissed her other cheek, just to make the point. And then it was oh, so easy just to angle his face slightly and kiss the corner of her mouth. To move closer and tease her lips with his, tiny nibbling kisses intended to provoke her. And he thoroughly enjoyed the moment when she snapped, slid her arms round his neck, and pulled him closer. He let her set the place, and his pulse rocketed when she deepened the kiss.

This wasn't his imagination.

There was a definite spark between them. A spark he would never have known existed if she hadn't suggested the wedding deal. But now he knew—and he wanted more.

She pulled back. 'Comfortable enough for you?' she drawled.

Was she saying that kiss had all been an act? That she'd played him, the way he'd kind of tried to play her? 'Maybe,' he said, affecting a coolness he definitely didn't feel. 'It's a start.'

'Goodnight, Dominic. See you in the office.' Though, despite the calmness of her tone, he could see the glitter in her eyes. That kiss had affected her as much as it had affected him.

The question was: what were they going to do about it?

CHAPTER SEVEN

DOMINIC BROODED ABOUT it all the way home. It was a dilemma he couldn't really discuss with anyone.

Where did you take your fiancée-who-wasn't-really on a date-that-wasn't-really, on the grounds of getting to know each other better so they could look relaxed when they stood next to each other at *their* wedding, instead of as if they were scared the other might accidentally scald them? Especially when you discovered that actually, you were really attracted to your fake bride-to-be and you thought she might feel the same about you?

This was bizarre. He'd never been in a position before where he didn't have a clue where to take his date. But Catriona was so guarded and self-contained that he couldn't work out what sort of thing she might like.

Checking the internet didn't help. The 'first date' ideas in winter were all just too samey. Going to glitzy, Instagrammable bars; wrapping up warm for a walk in the park and then having hot chocolate together; a winter brunch.

What he needed was something that would make them have to get close and physical.

Dancing? Except Catriona preferred classical music, which pretty much ruled out a nightclub.

He couldn't imagine her ice-skating at any of the seasonal pop-up rinks, either.

She'd grown up in a castle and she read historical novels. Maybe he could take her to a museum? Except their visit would need to be outside office hours, which in most cases would mean a weekend. He was pretty sure she'd like something like the Queen's House at Greenwich, with its amazing staircase, or maybe something more unusual, like the Petrie Museum of Egyptian Archaeology.

Maybe he should just ask her what she'd like to do.

Considering their office was open plan and she was only a few feet away...everyone would hear their conversation. So he'd do it a more subtle way.

Assuming that, like him, she turned her phone to silent when she was at work, he texted her.

Yo, Fifi. You busy at the weekend?

Why? was the answer.
Typical Catriona, giving nothing away.

Wondered if you wanted to go to the Queen's House in Greenwich. Or a museum. Would suggest this evening but can't find any open late. Maybe British Museum on Friday's late opening?

Either would be nice.

Cinema tonight? Maybe we could go to one of the live theatre screenings, if there's one on.

Sounds good. Let me know what time.

He checked the listings, found one at a cinema the other side of Regent's Park from her flat, and booked their tickets, then texted her the details.

Film starts at seven.

Thank you, Fergus.

That cheekiness in her reply made him smile. Then:

This is the cinema chain that delivers food and drink to your seat, yes? If so, I'll buy drinks and food.

Perfect. Meet you outside Baker Street tube station after work?

It was only a couple of stops on the Circle line from St Pancras to Baker Street; he left the office first, and waited for her outside the tube station entrance. She'd clearly caught the train after his, because she was only five minutes behind him.

'This was a really nice idea,' she said. 'I haven't been to the cinema for ages.'

'Me, neither.' He paused. 'I thought if we spent some time together, we'd get used to each other and we won't look awkward in the wedding photos.'

'That's a good idea,' she said. 'And this is the cinema, so I guess maybe we could hold hands through the film?'

'Or, as we have a sofa, put our arms round each other?' he suggested. 'Then perhaps we can go for a drink and discuss the film afterwards.'

'That works for me,' she said. There was a tinge of colour in her cheeks which Dominic found endearing. Strange how someone who was so confident in her job was so awkward when it came to anything close and personal.

He took her hand and they headed for the cinema. They ordered pizza and a glass of red wine each, found their seats on one of the plush sofas, then made themselves comfortable.

Once they'd eaten their pizza and the film had started, he slid his arm round her shoulders. She stayed absolutely rigid against him at first, but gradually she nestled in closer and eventually rested her head on his shoulder. Dominic was very aware of her warmth against him, and how long it had been since he'd last sat like this with one of his dates. He had a feeling it was even longer for Catriona.

Sitting here with her in semi-darkness, watching a performance by actors at the top of their game, was hugely enjoyable. And he liked the fact that Catriona seemed to be relaxing with him at last.

At the end of the film, they headed for one of the nearby wine bars. Because it was a Monday evening, it was relatively quiet and Dominic really enjoyed discussing the performance with her.

Eventually the bar staff announced last orders.

He stared at her in shock. 'How did that happen? Sorry. I didn't mean to keep you out so late.'

'I enjoyed it,' she said. 'Maybe we can do this again.'

'I'd like that, too,' he said. He glanced at the window. 'It's raining. I'll call us a cab and drop you off on the way back to mine.'

'But I'm not on your way.'

'You are, if we take the scenic route,' he said with a smile. He booked a taxi on his phone app, and kissed her goodnight when the cab pulled up outside her flat. 'We'll wait here until your living room light comes on,' he said. 'So I know you're in safely.'

Even though she lived in a very safe area, Catriona appreciated the way Dominic was looking out for her. Luke certainly hadn't cherished her like this, and he'd been her real fiancé, not her fake one.

And she found herself really aware of whenever Dominic was sitting at his desk in the office. He caught her eye across the room several times during the week, though she was relieved he didn't suggest having lunch together, because she didn't want the rest of the team to know that she was sort-of dating him. Or, worse, why she was doing it.

But they had dinner out in Covent Garden on Thursday night, and she enjoyed walking hand in hand with him around the piazza, taking in the lights and the music and the people.

'One for the dossier. Ballet—yes or no?' she asked as they walked past the Royal Opera House.

'I've never been,' he said. 'But I'm guessing the music means you like it?'

She nodded. 'The music, the movement and the costumes. And I had ballet classes when I was small.'

'I've always thought of ballet as being for posh people,' he said.

She grinned. 'Would you be stereotyping me there, Fergus?'

'I don't know any other viscountesses to compare you with, Fifi,' he said. 'But, if you like ballet, then I'd be happy to go to a performance with you.'

'All right. I'll get us tickets to *The Nutcracker*,' she said.

'And maybe you'd like to come to a blues night with me?'

'If you can step outside your comfort zone,' she said, 'I can step outside mine. Just let me know the dress code.'

'Whatever you're comfortable wearing,' he said. 'Is there a dress code for ballet?'

'Tutu?' she suggested.

'Is that a dare?' His eyes sparkled wickedly, and she knew he'd do it.

'That would almost be worth signing up for social media, to get a picture of you in a tutu,' she said with a grin.

'I could handle the office,' he said, 'but not my sisters. Will my office suit do?'

'Yes.' He looked seriously good in a suit.

He leaned close enough to whisper, 'But you could always wear a tutu for me. A private dance.'

'It's years since I did a class. I don't even have shoes, let alone a leotard and tutu.'

'You could improvise.' He nibbled her earlobe and, despite the coolness of the night air, she suddenly felt hot all over. Because now she could imagine herself in an intimate setting with Dominic. Candlelight. Dancing for him in a chiffon skirt...

'Whatever just put that expression on your face,' he said, 'I'd love to know.'

She blushed furiously, but didn't dare share it, because she was rapidly getting out of her depth. 'Ballet tickets,' she said instead, knowing that she was chickening out. 'Any particular night—except Wednesdays, obviously, because that's reserved for your family?'

'Any night except Wednesdays,' he said.

On Saturday, they visited the Queen's House, and Dominic took a photograph of Catriona sitting on the famous Tulip Staircase.

'You know they're really fleurs-de-lys, not tulips?' she asked. 'So it ought to be the Lily Staircase.'

'And they're not really painted blue—it's smalt, made from pondered cobalt glass,' he said. 'It's the first geometric self-supporting spiral staircase built in England.'

She grinned. 'You looked it up before we came here, too.'

'Of course. I can't have you being better-informed than me,' he said.

'Oh, now that sounds like a challenge,' she teased, enjoying the sparkle in his eyes.

'How to out-nerd a nerd. You're on.'

She raised an eyebrow. 'You're calling me a nerd?'

'It takes one to know one,' he said, and kissed her lightly. 'My nerdiness just happens to be in different areas.'

Yet they *fitted*. And part of Catriona was starting to wish that this was real, instead of being part of their project of getting used to each other so the wedding photographs would look authentic. That they were a real couple, wandering through an ancient house with their arms round each other.

Over the next three weeks, they spent more time together. After the ballet, Dominic admitted that he was surprised by how much he'd enjoyed the performance and wouldn't mind seeing more. And at the blues club, Catriona was surprised to discover that she really liked eating hot quesadillas and drinking cold beer with him, and then watching the show from the front row, with Dominic standing behind her with his arms wrapped round her, swaying in time to the music.

He was doing so much for her. She wanted to do something special for him, and a bit of sleuthing on the internet found her the perfect thing. She booked it for the Friday evening before the wedding and managed to keep it secret from him; the only thing she'd tell him was that he needed to meet her at her flat at quarter to seven, wearing a long-sleeved T-shirt, trainers and tracksuit bottoms—but not baggy ones.

'Are we doing a workout together, or something?' he asked when she opened the door. 'Because I thought...'

That she didn't do the gym, after Luke. She appreciated the fact that he didn't rub it in her face. 'It's an "or something",' she said, closing the front door behind her.

He narrowed his eyes at her. 'Where are we going?'

'For roughly a ten-minute walk. And we'll come back here to eat, afterwards. Stop asking questions,' she said.

When he persisted with the questions, she stopped dead. When he turned to her, she stood on tiptoe, slid her arms round his neck, and kissed him.

It silenced him for about five minutes.

'Workout clothes,' he said as she led him along the street. 'You're not taking me to a ballet class?'

She laughed. 'No tutus involved. Not even a dance belt and tights for you,' she said.

'How disappointing, Fifi.' A little later, he suggested, 'Trampolining?'

She almost told him he was getting warmer, but she didn't want to spoil the surprise. 'Not trampolining.'

'But it must be some sort of workout. Fencing?'

'No.'

'Kick-boxing?'

'No.'

He went quiet, and she could practically see the cogs turning in his head.

But finally he seemed to realise that she wasn't going to be drawn, and the questions subsided.

'I promise you'll like it,' she said.

'Boxing?'

'No. Nothing you'd do in a gym.'

'I give up,' he said.

'Good. Just through here.' She ushered him into the foyer of a community centre. And she was thrilled that she actually made his jaw drop when she introduced him to the woman who was giving them a special taster session in trapeze skills.

'You remembered what I told you about when I was eight,' he said. 'How long have you been planning this?'

'Ages,' she said.

He wrapped his arms round her. 'You're amazing,' he said softly. 'Thank you. And you're doing it with me?'

'I'm absolutely terrified,' she said, 'but, yes, I'm doing it with you.'

'The static trapeze isn't as scary as a flying trapeze,' Celeste told her. 'What I'm going to do is teach you both the basics, and then we're going to put together a small routine to music. It'll only be about a minute, but it'll be fun.'

'What if I fall off?' Catriona asked, thinking of how much a fracture would potentially hamper her.

'That's why there are crash mats underneath the trapeze,' Celeste said with a smile. 'Several of them, two deep. But people don't tend to fall off. You'll be fine.'

Celeste took them through a warm-up, then showed them how to get up on the trapeze. Dominic went first, and Catriona was amazed by how gracefully he moved. He looked slightly nervous when Celeste encouraged him to stand on the bar, but then a wide smile crossed his face.

'It's even better than I dreamed it would be,' he said when he'd dismounted and it was Catriona's turn. 'I can't believe you did this for me.'

'I wanted you to have some fun,' she said.

'And how.' He stole a kiss. 'I might run away from the office to do more of this…'

Catriona gripped the ropes very tightly, but managed to point her feet the way Celeste encouraged her to. 'It's like ballet, except in the air,' Celeste said. 'Think of the shapes.'

Dominic caught her eye. *Tutu*, he mouthed, and she couldn't help grinning back.

They changed places every few minutes, taking turns on the trapeze. By the third go, Catriona found herself relaxing, but Dominic was clearly in his element.

Finally, Celeste put on some music Catriona recognised.

'It's the waltz from Shostakovich's *Jazz Suite*,' she said.

'This one always makes me think of the trapeze,' Celeste said. 'And we're going to put everything you've learned together.'

'Is it OK if I film Dommy's routine, to show his mum and sisters?' Catriona asked.

Celeste gestured to Dominic. 'Your call, sweetie.'

'Sure,' he said, but there was something unreadable in his expression.

She filmed him getting onto the bar, moving his body into a graceful horizontal arch before going upside down, getting back up on the bar and onto his feet, then wrapping himself round the rope on one side, sliding down to a sitting position, and doing a forward roll around the bar.

'That felt amazing,' he said, when he got back onto the floor.

'It looked pretty impressive from here, too,' she said.

'Thank you.' He smiled at her. 'Your turn to get up there and strut your stuff.'

She didn't feel as fluid as he'd looked, though the ballet classes she'd taken at school meant she was comfortable with the arms and pointing her feet, but she went through the routine.

'You were both fabulous,' Celeste said. 'Did you enjoy it?'

'It was incredible. Better than I dreamed it would be, when I was a kid,' Dominic said. 'I loved it. Do you do longer courses?'

'I do one that covers all the aerial skills,' Celeste said. 'Silks, hoops and ropes, plus the trapeze. I can give you the details.'

'Yes, please. I'd definitely like to do it,' Dominic said.

'I think I'd prefer to watch,' Catriona said with a smile. 'I enjoyed doing this tonight, but it's a little bit too far out of my comfort zone.'

They walked back to Catriona's flat, with Dominic's arm round her shoulders and hers round his waist.

'I'm blown away by what you did for me,' Dominic said. 'I've always wanted to do that. And I only told you about it briefly.'

'You know my reputation. I pay attention to detail,' she said, though secretly she was thrilled that he'd liked her surprise so much.

'Details queen—no, make that empress,' he said. 'I'll be buzzing for a week after that.'

'I'm glad you enjoyed it. But I think I'm strictly sidelines for the scary stuff,' she said. 'Support crew, that's me.'

'You're amazing,' he said.

She was starting to think that about him, too. But she couldn't let herself get carried away. They'd be married on Tuesday, and then they'd be applying for divorce next Christmas. That was the deal, and she needed to remember that.

Back at her flat, she began cooking them a stir fry.

'I must be able to do something to help,' Dominic said.

'I bought everything ready-prepped,' she said. 'It's going to take five minutes of stirring.'

'Can I lay the table?'

'Already done.'

'Make you a cup of tea?'

'No.'

'Then I'll loiter,' he said, leaning against the doorframe with his arms crossed. 'You know, you called me "Dommy" tonight.'

'Did I?' She felt her eyes widen. 'Sorry. It slipped out.'

'I liked it when you called me that,' he said. 'Trina.'

'I'm not sure I like my name being shortened,' she muttered, to cover her confusion.

'It suits you, actually. Not the formal you, in the office, but the you outside. You're like a rose, with layers and layers until you get to that soft, sweet heart.'

One that didn't exist, according to Luke. 'I'm not soft and I'm not sweet. Lawyers aren't sweet!'

'Your painted hoardings,' he said, leaning forward to boop her nose, 'don't do you justice.'

Oh, help. If he carried on complimenting her like that, her knees would go weak. And she couldn't afford to let herself fall for him for real. 'Go and sit down. Dinner's nearly ready,' she said, ushering him out of the kitchen.

Something had changed between them. Something she couldn't define, but when he kissed her goodnight—under the usual excuse of it being to make them comfortable with each other for the wedding photographs—it felt like a real kiss. As if he meant it. Her blood fizzed as his mouth brushed hers, tempting and cajoling until she kissed him back.

She was going to have to be very, very careful.

It was the day before the wedding.

The day she left work. Officially on sabbatical for a year, to sort out some family business; but would she ever come back to the office?

Catriona pushed down her worries and made sure she'd handed over all her projects thoroughly. At the end of the day, she cleared out her desk and was about to slip out quietly when Lewis, the senior partner, came over. 'Can I see you for a minute in my office?' he said.

Was he going to tell her privately that he'd made Dominic the new partner, out of courtesy, because she'd been his rival? She couldn't think of any other reason for him to want a private word. 'Sure,' she said. 'So Dominic's getting his promotion?'

'In due course, my dear,' Lewis said with a smile.

But when he opened his door to usher her in, she realised that everyone in the firm was crowded into his office.

The second thing she noticed were the champagne flutes and bottles of champagne on his desk.

Maybe this wasn't going to be a private word, after all, but a public celebration of Dominic's success. And she was pleased for him—after all, she'd stepped down from the partnership race, and he was doing his side of the bargain tomorrow. Just…at the same time, part of her felt a bit wistful. This could've been her celebration, as the new partner.

But she'd made the deal with Dominic, and he deserved it, so she'd smile.

'I know you thought you were going to get away without any fuss, Catriona,' Lewis said, 'but we couldn't let you go without giving you a toast.'

What?

This wasn't about Dominic?

'We know you're coming back next year,' Sophie, one of the other partners, said. 'But you've been here a long time, and we wanted to wish you well in your sabbatical.' She handed over a large envelope which Catriona assumed held a card signed by everyone, plus a beautifully wrapped rectangular box.

'We hope you like it,' one of the others said.

She opened the box carefully to reveal a really gorgeous fountain pen.

'Thank you,' she said. 'It's lovely. And it's really kind of you all.' She hadn't expected this at all. Maybe a private, 'All the best and keep in touch' from the partners, but she knew she had a reputation for being driven and focused on her work, and she'd never really felt that her colleagues liked her. Respected her, yes; but that wasn't the same thing. She didn't have Dominic's easy charm. People would come to her for help with a knotty legal problem, but not for anything personal.

She thanked each of her colleagues individually, and somehow managed to make polite small talk until people started slipping away, and then quietly said her goodbyes. Dominic had already left, and she felt obscurely miserable on the way back to her flat.

Tomorrow was the wedding and the day after they were driving to Scotland; she'd decided which letting agency to use for her flat and which storage place for the things she wasn't taking to Scotland, and had planned to do that quietly after Christmas. There was nothing else to be done and, for the first time since she could remember, she was at a complete loss about what to do next.

She was about to resort to doing online word games— her secret vice—when her intercom buzzed.

Odd. She wasn't expecting a delivery or any visitors. 'Hello?' she said.

'Special delivery,' Dominic said. 'Can I come up?'

'Of course.' She buzzed him up, then opened her door.

'Hey. I thought you might be feeling a bit flat,' he said as she let him in. 'I know I would be, in your shoes.'

'I've worked there for nearly seven years. It's a long time, and life's going to change a lot for me tomorrow. Well, except my name. That's not changing.'

'Indeed, my dear Viscountess of Linton,' he said dryly.

How did she tell him that she always felt as if she was on the outside, looking in? But she didn't want him to pity her, so she did what she always did and stuffed her feelings back down inside.

'Did you know about the leaving do?'

'Yes,' he said. 'They were having trouble thinking about what to get you.'

'The pen's lovely. Very thoughtful.'

But they both knew it was the kind of gift you'd get for someone you didn't really know—a pen was *safe*.

'I got you something else,' he said. He took a small velvet box from his pocket. 'As you wouldn't let me get you an engagement ring.'

Her eyes widened. 'But...'

'I hope you'll like it,' he said. 'I know you don't like flashy stuff.'

Her breath caught as she opened the box. It was a delicate pendant—and it was exactly like her grandmother's engagement ring, a ruby surrounded by old-cut diamonds so it looked like a daisy, on a narrow gold chain.

'That's beautiful,' she said. 'Dominic—I don't know what to say. I wasn't expecting anything. And this is just...'

It filled her with wonder that he'd read her so well. And she didn't know how to explain it, so she hoped he could see it in her eyes as she looked up at him.

'I'm glad I got it right,' he said, and smiled.

'I didn't buy you anything.'

'That's not how presents work, Catriona,' he said. 'I wasn't giving this to you in the expectation of receiving something. I thought you might like it, that's all. I wanted to give you something for *you*. Something pretty and understated.'

So unlike the flashy diamond Luke had bought.

This was perfect. The exact sort of thing she would've chosen for herself. It was the nicest thing that anyone had ever bought her.

'Would you help me put it on?' She handed the box back to him.

'Sure.'

He took the necklace from the box; she felt his fingers against the nape of her neck, and then the pendant hung at the perfect height against her skin.

'Come and see,' he said, and drew her over to the mantelpiece.

She stared at her reflection, then caught his gaze in the mirror. 'It's beautiful. Thank you.'

'You're very welcome,' he said. And then he spun her round to face him. Brushed his mouth lightly against hers.

This wasn't for show. It felt as if it was for real. And she wasn't sure whether she was more terrified or delighted.

He stepped back, his expression completely unreadable. 'I'll see you tomorrow at the register office,' he said. 'Goodnight.'

Part of her wanted to ask him to stay; but how could she do that? This thing between them was a business arrangement. Besides, even though it wasn't a real wedding, she was mindful of the old tradition that it was bad luck to see the groom on the day until she walked down the aisle. She'd never thought herself the superstitious sort, but she didn't want to take any risks.

'Goodnight,' she whispered, and she let him see himself out.

CHAPTER EIGHT

THE NEXT MORNING, Catriona woke early, feeling decidedly antsy. Partly because it wasn't a normal Tuesday, and she wouldn't be going to the office; and partly because it was her wedding day. A wedding that would save her childhood home—but would also make her life complicated, because the way she was starting to feel about Dominic Ferrars made her feel distinctly vulnerable.

Muffling herself in a thick coat and walking up Primrose Hill to watch the sunrise didn't make her feel any better.

Was this all a huge mistake? Should she have just let Lark Hill be sold and the money divided between the boys?

But Lark Hill wasn't about money. It was about the people who lived on the estate. The history. The responsibilities her father would've shirked. The responsibilities she needed to shoulder.

She could do this.

She *had* to do this.

She'd arranged for Dominic's mum, sisters and Lou to get changed at her flat before the wedding, and Dominic was hosting the men of the party and baby Aiden. They arrived at ten, with a flurry of bags and paraphernalia.

Ginny gave her a hug. 'I know this must be hard for you, love. I wish you'd got someone on your side coming to the wedding. It feels as if we're taking over.'

'It's not a real wedding,' Catriona reminded her. Even though part of her wished it could be, and she knew she was supposed to *look* like a bride today. Happy. Looking forward to the future with the man she loved. Counting the seconds until she walked down the aisle to him, hardly able to wait to say her vows.

They'd chosen the vows together. Something they could say with total honesty: *I promise to be faithful and loyal, to respect and cherish you, to support you through the good times and the bad.*

No false declarations of love.

But the words had resonated deep inside. If she were in a real relationship, it was exactly what she wanted. To be faithful and loyal, and know that her partner would do the same. To be respected and cherished, just as she would do to him. Support.

And she couldn't help but wonder: if you added all those things together, wouldn't the sum be greater than the parts? With the added physical attraction between them—an attraction she definitely hadn't admitted to and neither had he—wouldn't that be *actual* love?

But she wasn't looking for love. She was looking to save the castle. And Dominic was helping her. They'd made a deal. A marriage of convenience, when his family deserved something real.

'And I'm sorry I'm depriving you of a real wedding. You're all so nice and you don't deserve this.' The words burst out of her, along with a tear she couldn't blink back in time.

Lou wiped away the tear that spilled over. 'Hey, it's bad luck to cry on your wedding day, even if it isn't a traditional one. Plus, it'll be harder for me to do your make-up if you're all blotchy.' She nudged Catriona. 'Give us a smile—that's better.'

'And anyway, today means we get to dress up a bit and see Dommy and have a nice lunch out with you, too—we're all fine with this,' Tilly said.

'But we all think your family seriously needs someone to shake some common sense into them,' Suzy said. 'The way they treat you is terrible.'

'Forget them. Today,' Ginny said, '*we're* your family.'

Catriona had a huge lump in her throat. 'Thank you. I, um, can I make you all some coffee? Or would you like bubbles? There's champagne in the fridge. A couple of bottles.'

Suzy gave her a hug. 'Bubbles are perfect. Dommy told us you're a cheese fiend, like him, so we brought crumpets and cheese with us because I bet you were too nervous to eat breakfast.'

'I was,' Catriona admitted.

'Do you mind me taking over your kitchen? I promise I'm not as messy as Dommy probably told you I am,' Suzy said.

'That's fine. I can't remember the last time I had crumpets,' Catriona said. 'Thank you.'

'You know, it's a shame this isn't a real wedding, because you fit right in with us,' Tilly said.

Nobody had ever said that to Catriona before, even her best friend, and she had to blink again.

'No tears!' Lou said. 'Let's get the bubbles open—and we need photos.'

'My job!' Suzy said, waving her phone. 'Say "crumpets and cheese".'

Finally, hair and make-up done, they all finished changing into their wedding outfits.

'You look amazing, Catriona,' Ginny said. 'Your grandparents would've been so proud.'

'It's all thanks to you all. If you'd left me to it, Dominic and I would've just got married at lunchtime and gone back to work,' Catriona said.

'You deserve better than that,' Ginny said.

Then Catriona's phone pinged. 'Our taxi will be here in five minutes.'

It gave them just enough time to pack everything they needed to take with them, and then it was time to head for Camden Town Hall.

Dominic paced up and down outside Camden Town Hall. Ridiculous, he knew, but he felt as nervous as if this was the real thing.

What scared him even more was that Catriona could tempt him to *want* this to be real. But she was as self-contained as the rose he'd said she reminded him of, full of layers. Or maybe she was like a daisy, hiding away in the grass and not letting anyone really see her.

Except he thought he was beginning to see who she really was—and, the more he got to know her, the more he liked her.

'Their taxi's here,' Ray said. 'It's bad luck to see the bride. Go and wait for her in the room. Joe, Aiden and I will bring them all in.'

'OK,' Dominic said. Why was it that he felt as if this was his driving test and every single exam he'd ever sat, plus every job interview he'd done, all rolled into one?

The door to the room they'd booked was open. He knocked on it, more out of courtesy than anything else, and walked in.

'Good afternoon, Mr Ferrars,' the registrar greeted him.

'Good afternoon,' he said. 'Everyone's here.'

'Don't worry. All grooms feel nervous, however small

or large the wedding,' she said with a smile. 'We'll try to make this as easy as we can for you.'

A couple of minutes later, his mother walked down the aisle on Ray's arm and took her seat, followed by Tilly, Joe and Aiden, and then Suzy and Lou.

'You look gorgeous,' Suzy said. 'And I'm glad you listened to me and wore the bow tie to match your buttonhole.'

'You look gorgeous, too,' he said. 'All of you.'

Then Catriona walked into the room and every word vanished out of his head. She looked stunning, in a knee-length ivory dress with a cinched waist and a Bardot neckline, baring her shoulders. She was carrying a bunch of white gerberas, the stems taped together and the heads in a ball, softened with gypsophila and accented with eryngium like the one he wore as a buttonhole. There was a headdress of pearls and crystals wound through her short hair, rather than a veil. She wore her usual pearl earrings, but he noticed that she was wearing his ruby-and-diamond pendant.

And she was walking down the aisle to him.

It wasn't a real wedding. Of course it wasn't. They were both clear on that.

But it felt like one, and he couldn't shift that feeling.

'You look amazing,' he whispered as she came to stand beside him.

'So do you,' she whispered back, an almost shy blush tinging her cheeks.

Again, the unexpected feelings slammed into him. *She thought he looked amazing, too. She'd gone all shy when he'd told her his own reaction.*

The registrar took them through the ceremony, and he could barely pay attention because he was so focused on the woman standing next to him.

Then they came to the legal bit.

'I declare that I know of no legal reason why I, Dominic Ferrars, may not be joined in marriage to Catriona Findlay,' he said.

Catriona echoed his declaration.

And then it was the contracting words. 'I, Dominic Ferrars, take you, Catriona Findlay, to be my wedded wife,' he said.

'I, Catriona Findlay, take you, Dominic Ferrars, to be my wedded husband,' she answered.

Rings. Where the hell had he put the rings? He rummaged in his pocket, panicking slightly that he'd messed this up and it was all going wrong; but then Joe stepped forward and handed him a small velvet bag. Dominic tipped the two plain gold rings into his hand and slid one onto the ring finger of Catriona's left hand. 'I give you this ring as a symbol of our marriage,' he said. 'I promise to be faithful and loyal, to respect and cherish you, to support you through the good times and the bad.'

Words they'd chosen together which had deliberately not included the L-word. At the same time they were vows he would stand by. Vows he believed in. Faithfulness was a definite, given her background. He'd be loyal to her, and he knew she'd be the same towards him. They respected each other. They'd support each other through the good times and the bad.

The sticky bit was cherishing.

Would she let him cherish her? Or would it make her back away?

She took the other ring, and he could feel her fingers trembling slightly as she slid the ring onto his finger and repeated his vow.

There was definite trepidation in her eyes, too. She was nervous, clearly feeling as mixed-up about this as he did.

They'd stick to their bargain; that wasn't in doubt. He had the partnership and she had the castle.

But cherishing.

The more he'd got to know Catriona, the more he liked her. And it made him antsy, because he hadn't ever felt like that towards anyone he'd dated. She'd once been engaged for real and been let down; it was one of the reasons why she didn't let anyone close. But would their marriage of convenience change things?

Because being convenient didn't necessarily mean their marriage couldn't be real...

'I'm delighted to pronounce you husband and wife,' the registrar said. 'Congratulations. Now I'd like you and your witnesses to sign the register.'

He signed his name: *Dominic Ferrars*.

Catriona's eyes crinkled very slightly at the corners, and she signed *Catriona Findlay*.

'I'd like to introduce the newlyweds, Dominic Ferrars and Catriona Findlay,' the registrar declared.

If this had been a real wedding, Dominic wouldn't have insisted that she changed her name. He'd want her for who she was: Catriona Findlay, his clever rival with her eye for detail and refusal to compromise.

'You're meant to kiss the bride, now, Dommy,' Tilly called.

Catriona gave him the very tiniest nod, and he kissed her. Her mouth felt soft and sweet and full of promise as it moved against his, and he had to stop himself pulling her closer and kissing her harder.

On the steps outside, they paused for wedding photos, and Suzy and Tilly scattered the white delphinium petals Catriona had chosen as confetti. 'And now for a very traditional bit,' Catriona said, and threw her bouquet straight at Lou, who caught it and grinned back.

Suzy kissed her girlfriend and said, 'I think that might just be a sign,' and everyone laughed.

The hotel was literally a two-minute walk away, so they cut through the streets; people smiled at the wedding party, wishing them well.

Catriona had managed to book a small private dining room; lunch was beautifully presented and tasted even better.

'What happened to the speeches?' Tilly asked when the hotel staff had cleared everything away.

Dominic and Catriona looked at each other. 'I think we can dispense with speeches,' Catriona said. 'It's not exactly a traditional wedding.'

'Well, there's one tradition we can't dispense with,' Ginny said, and gave a signal to the waiter.

'Mum?' Dominic asked.

And then the waiter brought in a platter covered with a silver dome.

'This is from Di,' Ginny said. 'She knows it's only a small wedding and our Dommy's weird about puddings, but she didn't want everyone else to be deprived of cake.'

'Auntie Di makes all the family cakes,' Tilly confided to Catriona. 'And they always taste as amazing as they look.'

Family. They were including her, Dominic thought. He glanced swiftly at her, wondering if his family's enthusiasm would all be too much; but there was a softness to her smile that made him think she was relaxed, even enjoying it.

The waiter lifted the dome to reveal a small cake, beautifully decorated with gerbera and eryngium.

'We showed her the wedding flowers, and she made them out of sugar,' Suzy said.

'I'm stunned. That's so lovely,' Catriona said. 'We'll send her flowers to say thank you.'

'That's sweet of you—but what she really wants,' Ginny said, 'is for us to video you two cutting the cake.' She gave them both a speaking look. 'Cutting the cake, and kissing.'

'We can do that,' Dominic said.

'Of course we can do that,' Catriona said.

She wanted him to kiss her?

Or was she trying to play a part, trying to make this look real to convince her family?

He and Catriona posed for a photograph, with the cake, and then the waiter gave them a silver knife to cut it.

'Videoing in three, two, one—*now*,' Ginny said, holding up her phone.

They cut the cake, and Dominic kissed her lightly. Though, weirdly, it made all the blood in his veins feel as if it were fizzing.

'Thank you for the cake, Auntie Di,' he said to the camera.

'It's the most beautiful cake I've ever seen—it matches our flowers perfectly,' Catriona added. 'Thank you.'

It tasted as good as it looked; even Dominic, who normally wasn't keen on sweet stuff, liked his aunt's cakes.

'This is where I wish Bill had managed to teach me to play the ukulele, so I could've played a first dance for you,' Ray said.

'Way ahead of you,' Tilly said. 'We also need some first dance pics. And Bill recorded something specially for you.'

That was going too far. He needed to stop this before Catriona backed away. 'We don't have time. You'll be late for your train,' Dominic said.

'No, we won't. We can spare four minutes,' Tilly said. 'Mum—you're in charge of the camera.' She gestured to

Dominic and Catriona. 'You got away without speeches, but you *don't* get away without a first dance.'

'We're under orders,' Dominic said, and held out a hand to Catriona.

'I can't remember the last time I danced,' she said, but to his relief she took his hand.

'Guess you'll just have to trust me to lead,' he said, 'though I have no idea what Bill might be thinking.' Unable to resist the idea of dancing with her any more, he spun her into his arms.

Tilly pressed 'play' on her phone, and the first chords of 'Moondance' floated into the air, played on an electro-acoustic guitar.

The perfect song. He smiled and drew her close. 'Your dress is perfect for this,' he whispered. And he couldn't help adding, '*You're* perfect for this.'

The first dance. *Their wedding dance.* And the way Dominic danced with her to the song, a slow and sensual sway, made Catriona feel giddy. He spun her out and then back into his arms, making the skirt of her dress flare out. And then, when the song ended, he bent her back over his arm theatrically, and pulled her back up again before kissing her.

She forgot about their wedding guests. As far as she was concerned, nobody else was in the room. All she could think of was the touch of his mouth against hers. The feel of his heart thudding against hers. The warmth of his skin. How much she wanted him...

When he broke the kiss, he looked as dazed as she felt.

'And that's a wrap. I think Uncle Bill's going to forgive you for not letting him play at your wedding,' Suzy said.

Just for show. This was just for show, Catriona reminded herself. But, so far, their wedding day had felt very real indeed. Something that scared and thrilled her in equal measure: because who knew where this might lead?

'But you're right—we do need to make a move for the train,' Ginny said. 'But we'll send you pictures and videos soon.'

With almost military efficiency, Dominic's family got themselves ready for travelling. Catriona and Dominic went next door to the station with them, to wave them off.

Ginny hugged Catriona hard before they went through the barriers. 'You're one of us now,' she whispered. 'I don't care if this isn't a real wedding and you're not changing your surname to Dommy's, you're *still* one of us.'

It put a huge lump in Catriona's throat when Tilly and Suzy said exactly the same.

They waited until his family had given them one last wave before boarding the train; then Catriona realised with embarrassment that she was still holding Dominic's hand. Biting her lip, she gently released it.

'So that's the wedding done,' she said.

'And you can officially claim Lark Hill tomorrow,' he said.

'Thank you.' She took a deep breath. 'Your family are just so lovely. I can't believe your aunt made us that cake, and your uncle recorded a first dance for us.'

'I had no idea they were going to do that,' he said.

'We'll send flowers to your aunt,' she said, 'and a bottle of whatever your uncle's favourite is to him.'

'Bourbon,' he said, and grinned. 'Though I'd love to see you give him a lecture about how proper Scots single malt is better.'

'I'll remember to do that some time,' she promised. She looked at him. 'So I guess this is where we each get a taxi back to our own respective flats.'

'For a little while,' he said. 'With us having such a short reception, I thought today might feel like a bit of an anti-climax, so I booked us something for this evening. But we need to change out of our wedding clothes, first, otherwise you'll freeze.'

Weirdly, that felt as if he was cherishing her, and the lump was back in her throat. 'OK. I'll be guided by you,' she said.

'Just wear something warm. Layers. I'll come over to pick you up,' he said. Then, to her surprise, he leaned forward and kissed her lightly on the mouth. 'You look stunning,' he said.

'You scrub up pretty well, too,' she said. 'And I noticed how your bow tie matches your buttonhole.'

'Couldn't let the Empress of Details down,' he said, and his eyes crinkled at the corners.

How had she ever thought this man dislikeable?

'I'll call you a cab,' he said, and flicked into the app on his phone. 'OK. It's on its way. I'll wait with you, and then I'm getting the tube to my place. I'll text you when I leave for yours.'

It didn't take long for the cab to come.

If the cabbie thought it strange that a bride would be on her own in the cab in her wedding dress, he didn't say anything. Though his rueful, 'Good luck, love,' made her wonder.

But a kiss, a first dance and a bit of cake didn't make their wedding real, she reminded herself. This was all part of a business deal. Dominic had his partnership, and she had her castle. End of story.

She changed into jeans and a long-sleeved T-shirt with another sweater over the top, took off her make-up, and carefully removed the hair vine Lou had woven through her hair, putting it back in its box. But she kept the pendant on, because it made her feel special.

Her phone beeped, and she picked it up, expecting a message from Dominic; instead, it was Ginny, sending her the photos and videos from their wedding day.

She leafed through them. They'd definitely convince her, she thought. The two of them standing in front of the registrar, looking nervous. Dominic gazing into her eyes as he slid a wedding ring onto her finger. Dominic kissing her. The two of them laughing as confetti floated down over them. Cutting the cake. Dancing together.

The kissing and the closeness they'd practised had definitely done the trick. They looked comfortable with each other. Close. Like lovers…

Except they weren't really lovers. Luke had made it clear she wasn't good at relationships. It was his excuse for cheating on her, to find the warmth that she lacked.

Maybe she should text Dominic and tell him that she had a headache and she'd see him tomorrow.

On the other hand, he'd clearly gone to some trouble to arrange something for this evening, and it would be rude and churlish of her to turn it down. Not to mention the fact that she'd discovered she actually wanted to spend time with him.

She'd just finished a mug of camomile tea when Dominic texted her. 'Five minutes.'

She was ready outside to meet him. He wouldn't tell her where they were going, but eventually they ended up at Greenwich, on a shuttle minibus to the Observatory.

'The Planetarium at night?' she asked, surprised.

He nodded. 'It's something I've always wanted to do. See the stars properly, and this is the best place in London.'

She knew somewhere better. 'The stars look amazing at

Lark Hill,' she said. 'Keep your fingers crossed for a clear night, this week.'

'Have you got a telescope?' he asked, looking intrigued.

'No. But we can get up on the roof,' she said. 'And we might see meteors. Or the Northern Lights, if we're really lucky.'

'That would be amazing.' He grinned. 'I'll hold you to that.'

He held her hand all the way through the lecture, and then they looked at the stars through the telescope together. Dominic's pleasure in the stars was infectious, and Catriona enjoyed every minute.

When the event was over, they ended up walking along the river at Greenwich, their arms wrapped round each other, enjoying the Christmas lights. Strictly speaking, they didn't need to practise being comfortable together anymore: they were married. But she was enjoying the closeness, so she didn't pull away.

Back at Primrose Hill, Dominic kissed her goodnight on the doorstep.

Catriona almost, *almost*, asked him to come in. To stay.

But what if he turned her down?

Not wanting to take the risk, she said, 'Thank you for this evening. I'll pick you up at ten tomorrow.'

Was that disappointment or relief she could see in his face? She was good at reading clients, but utterly hopeless when it came to Dominic.

'Goodnight, Catriona,' he said. 'See you tomorrow.'

She stared at herself in the mirror as she brushed her teeth. Married. She didn't look any different. Didn't *feel* any different.

Except.

She couldn't get over the way his family seemed to have taken her to their hearts.

'Be sensible,' she reminded her reflection out loud. 'You're going to have a week's honeymoon—which will be spent working—and then Dominic's going back to London. You'll apply for a quiet no-fault divorce next Christmas. And that's an end to it.'

She slept badly that night, but a cool shower and washing her hair made her feel better, and coffee had her back to normal. Almost.

She drove to Islington to pick Dominic up, and he put a small case into her car. Clearly he was the sort to travel light.

'So tell me more about the castle,' he said as they left London behind.

She gave him a quick potted version of the castle's four hundred years of history.

'And does it get its name from larks who nest there?' he asked.

'The hill itself is in the shape of a lark—though actually that's pareidolia,' she said.

'I'm going to have to look up that word,' he said. 'That's the thing about you, Catriona. You make me think.' He fiddled with his phone. 'You mean it's like the face on Mars that isn't really a face. Cydonia.'

'Something like that,' she said. 'The idea is that the slope of the hill is the back of the bird, and the castle's the head.'

'Pareidolia.' He savoured the word. 'I'm so getting that word into my next report.'

'Seriously? In a legal report?' She laughed. 'I'd like to see that.'

'Challenge accepted,' he said with a grin. 'You'd better think up a good reward.'

Oh, the pictures that put in her head. She was glad to

have the excuse of needing to concentrate on driving, because no way she was telling him what she was thinking.

They shared the driving, but outside of London it quickly grew foggy; the journey dragged on, making both of them tired.

Catriona glanced at the clock. 'I can't believe how long it's taken us to drive here. It's taken us more than twice the time it usually would.'

'How far have we got to go?' he asked.

'We've gone past Durham; that's two hours or so from Lark Hill in normal weather. Except obviously today's not normal.'

'And driving in fog is driving me insane. I vote we stop and stay somewhere overnight, get some rest and hope it's better weather tomorrow,' he said.

'There's a motorway service station coming up. We could stop there and see if there's a hotel and they have a couple of rooms?' she suggested.

But everyone else had obviously had the same idea, because of the weather. 'I'm sorry. I can only offer you one room,' the receptionist said. 'And it's a double, not a twin.'

'We'll take it,' Dominic said. 'Thank you.'

They took their cases to their room, and Catriona called Mrs MacFarlane to let her know the weather was bad so they were staying at a roadside motel and would be at Lark Hill late tomorrow morning. They ordered room service pizza on the grounds they were too tired to move.

'Do you want the first shower?' Catriona asked when they'd finished eating.

'I'll be a gentleman and let you go first,' he said.

She showered as quickly as she could, and changed into her favourite pyjamas: a navy vest top and long navy pyjama pants covered in tiny white daisies. She discovered that Dominic's preferred nightwear was a faded band T-shirt teamed with jersey shorts.

'You look all in,' he said. 'Early night?'

'Early night,' she agreed.

He switched his phone to a playlist of soothing classical music; they climbed into bed, made sure there was the biggest possible gap between them, and Catriona closed her eyes in the hope that he'd think she'd fallen asleep almost immediately.

She woke a couple of hours later to discover that she was wrapped in Dominic's arms, and her hands were under the T-shirt he wore as a pyjama top, her palms flat against his back.

If she had any common sense, she'd untangle herself and move to the edge of the bed again; but instead she found herself snuggling closer.

He shifted and moved closer so his cheek was against hers, then dropped a sleepy kiss on the corner of her mouth.

The next thing she knew, they were kissing—really kissing.

Then he stopped. 'I know we're married, but this wasn't the deal.'

Of course he didn't want to get closer to her. Hadn't she learned from Luke how bad she was at relationships? She shrank inwardly, feeling gauche and stupid and hideously embarrassed.

Her misery must've communicated itself to him in the way she held herself, because he kissed the corner of her mouth again. 'By that I mean, I don't want to take advantage of you—and I also don't have any condoms.'

'I'm on the pill,' she blurted out. 'Not because I sleep around, but because my periods are horrible.'

'I definitely don't think you sleep around,' he said, 'and, just so you know, I don't, either.'

It must've been a combination of strain and lack of sleep affecting her brain, because she said, 'So there's no reason why we couldn't...'

He went very still. 'Are you saying...?'

In answer, she lifted her hand and stroked his face.

He twisted his head and pressed a kiss into her palm.

She kissed his mouth.

He sighed her name and kissed her properly.

She couldn't remember the last time she'd been kissed like this, and white-heat desire shimmered through her. All she was aware of was Dominic: the warmth of his body, the way his hands felt against her skin, the thud of his heartbeat. She wasn't sure who removed whose clothes, or when, or how, but finally they were skin to skin—and it was oh, so good.

She gasped his name as he entered her. He went still for a moment, letting her adjust to the feel of him—and then he began to move, and every single thought went out of her head.

The next morning, when Catriona woke, she was still naked—as was Dominic. They were wrapped in each other's arms. And she didn't have a clue what to say.

'I didn't expect...' Her voice tailed off.

'I don't know how to behave with you this morning either,' he admitted. 'I think we were both tired last night—not thinking straight. We acted on...well.'

They'd acted on their instincts. On the attraction that had been growing between them ever since she'd first suggestion the marriage. Reacted with their bodies instead of their heads.

She took a deep breath. 'It's officially our honeymoon.' She paused. 'Maybe we could be honest about the fact that we...' She felt her face heat, but made herself continue through the ridiculous wave of shyness, 'That we're physically compatible. And we know this is a temporary thing. We could...enjoy each other's company.'

Echoing colour slashed across his cheeks. 'For a week.'

Was he going to turn her down? She couldn't quite meet his eyes. 'We could call it honeymoon privileges,' she mumbled.

'So I get to wake up with you in my arms for a week.'

Was that a hint of longing she could hear in his voice? So he wasn't pushing her away? Relief surged through her, followed by an urge to tease him. 'Unless I wake first.'

'Quibbled like a lawyer.'

She grinned. 'Well, Fergus. That's what we both are.'

'Honeymoon privileges. I like that idea.' He kissed her again. 'In fact, my dear Fifi, I like it a lot.'

Enough for them to be too late for breakfast, and they ended up having to get bacon rolls and coffee from the service station.

'This isn't quite the sort of breakfast I should be offering a viscountess,' he said.

'There's nothing wrong with a bacon roll,' she said. 'Though I admit I usually have porridge for breakfast.'

'Even at Lark Hill? I expected you to have a breakfast room with a sideboard and silver salvers.'

'We do.' She might as well tell him the rest of it and get it over with. 'As well as a dining room, a drawing room, a morning room, a ballroom, the library and the study. But they don't all get used. It's too expensive to heat enormous rooms that aren't in use all the time,' she said. 'The kitchen, the morning room and Gramps's study are all we heat on the ground floor, and the bedrooms that are in use on the first floor.'

'How many bedrooms are there?'

'Six on the first floor.' Honesty compelled her to add, 'More on the second. A couple more reception rooms.'

He blinked. 'The castle has three storeys?'

She squirmed. 'Yes. It's a castle, Dominic. They tend to be a bit on the big side.'

'I can't imagine living in a place with that many rooms.'

'Look, it's not as if we have an acres-long dining table and sit at opposite ends and shout to each other during meals,' she said crossly. 'Well, we do have a big dining table,' she amended, 'but we normally eat in the kitchen.'

'Right,' he said.

'A couple of centuries ago, you needed something that big because people came to stay for house parties and you needed the space to accommodate them all and their personal servants.' His raised eyebrows made her wince. 'Think about it. Back then, everything was done by hand. Imagine all the dust a coal fire produces—and how long it'd take to sweep a carpet or a floor instead of vacuuming. You'd need a lot of people to get everything done.'

'I guess,' he said. 'So Mrs MacFarlane lives in?'

'Yes. Though she's not a servant, and I don't expect her to wait on me. She's a very valued member of the household.' She narrowed her eyes at him.

'Got it,' he said. 'And she's the only one who works in the house?'

'She used to have help in the house when I was younger, because Lark Hill would be way too much for one person to manage, but the rooms we don't heat nowadays are dust-sheeted and only get a spring clean once a year. When, yes, we do hire in extra help.' She looked at him. 'Look, it's not a royal palace with sixty million rooms. It's the English equivalent of the Big House in the village.' She frowned. How had they managed to get from laughing about breakfast to arguing over her background?

'I'm sorry,' he said. 'I'm just trying to get my head round where you come from.'

'I'm just me,' she said.

'I don't mean to make you feel awkward. Actually, it's a bit daunting for me, going to your family's castle. My family live in ordinary houses. I'm the odd one out with the flashy flat in London.'

'You earn every penny of your salary,' she said. 'You've worked hard. You made partner on merit, not from social connections. That's something to be proud of.'

'Careful, Fifi. It sounds as if you're on Team Ferrars.'

'Maybe,' she said, 'I am. Just as you're on Team Findlay.'

He raised his mug in a toast. 'Team Us.'

'Team Us.' She took a sip of her coffee. 'Now the fog's cleared, it'll be a nice drive this morning, with the hills on one side and the sea on the other. You do the first half,' she said, 'because I know the road and it'll be a chance for you to enjoy the scenery of the second half.'

'Deal,' he said, and kissed her.

CHAPTER NINE

DOMINIC ENJOYED DRIVING along the coast. Catriona had been right about it being a pretty route; there was a touch of frost on the grass, and everywhere sparkled. They stopped halfway to grab a coffee, stretch their legs and for Catriona to text Mrs MacFarlane with their expected time of arrival, and then she took over the driving.

As she turned off the main road, he could see a hill and a castle in front of them. Clearly you could see for miles from the castle, too; back in the day, it would've been a good defensive position. 'I assume that's Lark Hill?' he asked.

'Yes.'

A short time later, she pulled into an entrance and stopped in front of a pair of ornate, heavy iron gates. He helped her open them, and then closed them behind the car after she'd driven through.

The driveway went up the hill, which wasn't quite as steep as it had seemed from the distance. At the top was a green oval lawn, with deep shingle surrounding it and the castle.

'It was originally a carriage drive,' she said. 'It's easier to turn a horse and carriage round in a circle. We still have the old stable blocks, though they've been used as storage for years. Grannie rode when she was younger, but I don't ever remember horses being here.'

'That's a stunning building,' he said, staring at the castle. The three-storey square building was built of honey-coloured stone, with turrets at all four corners, the windows were tall sashes painted white, there was a porch jutting out with a large archway, and four stone steps that led to a wide, glossy black door.

She parked next to the house; they took their cases out of the car and walked up the steps. She opened the door to reveal a wide stone-flagged entrance hall; in front of them was a sweeping staircase up to the next floor.

Catriona called out, 'Mrs Mac?'

A woman he judged to be in her late fifties bustled into the hall and greeted her with a smile. 'Catriona, hen, I'm so glad you're home safely. I was worried about you yesterday in all that fog.'

'Thankfully it's a better day for driving today,' Catriona said, smiling back. 'Mrs Mac, I'd like to introduce you to my husband, Dominic Ferrars. Dominic, this is Mrs MacFarlane, our housekeeper. Or Mrs Mac to me, since I was very small.'

'Welcome to Lark Hill, Mr Ferrars.' Mrs MacFarlane greeted him with a warm handshake. 'Now, the kettle's on, I'll make coffee. Or tea, if you prefer.'

'Coffee would be lovely, thank you,' Dominic said, 'but please call me Dominic and I really don't expect you to wait on me.'

'Whisht, it's my job,' Mrs MacFarlane said, but she looked pleased.

'We'll take turns in cooking,' Catriona said, 'and the washing up is our job, not yours.'

'We'll discuss that later, hen,' Mrs MacFarlane said. 'I made soup and bread this morning for lunch. I thought I'd cook salmon for dinner tonight.'

'Thank you, that's perfect,' Catriona said.

'I assumed you'd want to be in your room rather than the master suite,' Mrs MacFarlane said, 'so I made up the bed there.'

'Thank you. That's perfect. Apart from the fact that it would feel odd to be in Gramps' and Grannie's room, my room has a better view,' she said. She looked at Dominic. 'Let's take our cases up, and then I'll give you the grand tour. Mrs Mac, did the valuers send the report through?'

'It's on your gra—*your* desk, in the study, hen,' the house-keeper corrected herself.

'Valuers?' Dominic asked.

'For the inheritance tax,' Catriona said, 'and I asked them to take note of the work that needs doing, so hopefully they've assessed the roof, the heating and the bit of damp I've been worrying about in the boot room.'

Boot room? It was the first he'd heard of it. How many more rooms were there she hadn't told him about?

She hefted her suitcase. 'Right—follow me.'

Her room was at the back of the castle, on the first floor. The first thing he saw was a king-sized four-poster bed in dark wood, with a solid headboard that stretched halfway up the walls, an ornately carved post at each corner and deep red velvet curtains.

'Do they go all the way round when they're closed?' he asked, indicating the curtains.

'They do indeed,' she said, 'which is very good in winter because it keeps the warmth in.'

There was a large wardrobe, a bookcase and a chest of drawers on one wall, a dressing table in front of the window, and a table with a lamp each side of the bed. In the middle of the dark oak floor was a thick pile rug, the sort that you weren't allowed to step on in a stately home and that he guessed was worth a great deal of money. In the corner of the room was a turret, which held a comfortable-looking sofa and a desk. He went over and glanced out. 'You have a turret in your bedroom.'

She winced. 'It's not that fancy.'

'Yes, it is. But what a view of the gardens and the sea. It's stunning.'

'Which is why it's the best room in the house.' She joined him at the window. 'Sadly, the gardens aren't like they were when Grannie was alive. We still have a gardener who cuts the lawns and does the pruning and weeding, but nobody's added to her rose garden or developed anything else. I kind of feel guilty we've let her lovely flowers go to a low-maintenance thing, but something had to give and Gramps was never really bothered about plants. We have photos somewhere of how they used to look.'

'It might be worth restoring them,' he said, 'because people will pay to visit gardens. And that leads to scope for a tea shop, even if it's a pop-up thing.'

'Definitely one to add to the list of potentials,' she said, 'but first I need to look at the roof, the damp and the boiler, and work out the order in which they need to be tackled. I might end up having to extend my sabbatical.'

'I know you could do the project-managing in your sleep,' he said, 'but that's an awful lot of worry on your shoulders.'

She shrugged. 'It comes as part of the responsibilities, I guess.'

'Do you resent it?' he asked. 'Giving up everything you worked for?'

'In a way, yes,' she said. 'I'm good at my job and I would've made a good partner. But I'll do a good job here, too.'

'Is there a way you can do both?' he asked. 'Get Lark Hill up and running the way you want it, hire someone to manage it, and come back to London?'

'Maybe. Or I could switch my career path and become a judge,' she said. 'Work part-time here and part-time in court. But I've got time to think about that.'

It sounded to him as if she'd already put some thought into it.

And if she didn't come back to London...what would that mean for them? She'd said this morning about honeymoon privileges. What about when the honeymoon was over? Did she expect them to lead separate lives, or would she consider any kind of compromise? He had no idea what she wanted. He wasn't sure what he wanted, either. The day before their wedding, he would've said that they were about to embark on a marriage of convenience, and they'd have a quiet amicable divorce in a year's time.

Last night had changed everything. He hadn't expected making love with Catriona to be so amazing.

Leaving that thought to work itself out in the back of his head, he asked, 'So what's the plan for today?'

'Lunch,' she said. 'Then I'll give you a proper tour of the castle. And, if you don't mind, I'll be taking the probate survey with me to check they've covered everything.'

'Anything I can do to help?' he asked.

'Maybe cast your eye over the report and check if I miss anything,' she said.

Catriona Findlay didn't miss details, Dominic thought, but he smiled. 'Sure.'

After a lunch of excellent Scotch broth and home-made bread, Dominic went room by room with her through the house. As she'd said, most of the rooms were dust-sheeted. There were several windows that needed mending because the sashes had decayed, damp patches in some of the top rooms where guttering had broken so water dripped through the mortar and through the walls and a very suspiciously damp corner in the boot room, as well as the work on the roof that she'd mentioned.

'And this is where you come out to watch the stars?' he asked.

'When I was small, yes. Grannie would give me an oil-cloth to sit on and a blanket to wrap up in,' she said. 'She taught me the constellations. But I haven't sat up here for years. I guess, now I'm older, I'm more aware of the risks. Actually, I think we'd get just as good a view from the turret, and it'd be safer.'

'Do you know a good tradesman who works with listed buildings?' he asked.

'Gramps has a list, I think,' she said. 'If they don't have all the specialties covered between them, I'm pretty sure one of them will be able to recommend someone.' She grimaced. 'The sooner I put this into in a list, the less daunting it's going to feel. And, talking of daunting, I'd better face the music and let my mother and the boys know that we got married yesterday.' She took her phone from her pocket, typed out a brief message, added some of the pictures Ginny had sent her of the wedding, and pressed 'send'.

That evening, he and Catriona were sitting in the morning room, going through the paperwork, when her phone shrilled.

'It looks as if the boys have all read their messages,' she said. 'They're video-calling me. A joint thing.'

'Do you want me to give you some privacy?' he asked.

'No. It's fine,' she said. 'I probably ought to introduce you to them.' She took a deep breath and answered the call. 'Good evening, Tom, Lachy and Finn.'

She sounded cool, calm and collected—but Dominic noticed that her free hand was clenched, betraying her tension.

'What the hell do you mean, you got married yesterday?' one of them asked, sounding aggrieved. 'Is this to do with the will?'

'Because it's the first we've heard of you even *dating*,' another said.

'Yeah. My mum said you'd do something like this, to cut us out of our rightful inheritance,' the third said.

Dominic was shocked by the aggression in their tone. Catriona was their older sister. His own family would never dream of talking to him like that. Part of him wanted to grab the phone and ask who the hell they thought they were; but Catriona needed support, not someone taking over and interfering. He moved closer to her, making sure he wasn't visible on screen, and laid his hand over her clenched fist briefly to let her know he was there and on her side.

'The timing of the marriage is to do with the will,' Catriona said. 'But my husband isn't.'

That was a bit of a grey area, Dominic thought. Because their marriage *had* all been to do with the will…until last night.

Was she saying that she could see this being a real marriage? His heart beat a little bit faster at the idea.

Though right now wasn't the time to ask her about it.

'You sent pictures of you in a wedding dress,' the youngest said, 'but how do we know you didn't just dress up for it?'

'Yes. Where's the marriage certificate?' the oldest-looking brother asked.

'They're mailing it to me in the next ten working days,' she said. 'Which is standard procedure, so don't start thinking there's any conspiracy. And I wasn't dressing up, Finn. It was a real cake, a real first dance, and real signatures on the register in Camden. You're all perfectly welcome to check.'

There was general muttering from the three of them.

'In answer to your mother, Finn, I'm not cutting any of you out. My plan is to make sure you all get something. Before I can do that, I need to get the estate in a position where it's supporting itself and making money that I can split with you. I've spent this afternoon going over the probate inventory and checking what remedial work the castle needs, and tomorrow I'm seeing the tenants. And then I have the fun of going through the accounts. Unless any of you would like to offer help?'

The three of them were silent.

'I thought not,' she said. 'I'll send you the photographs I took this morning, and a copy of the probate inventory, so you can see it all for yourself how much work needs doing. But at least Gramps, unlike our father, left a will, which makes sorting everything out a lot easier.'

Between them, the brothers scoffed, rolled their eyes and muttered something Dominic couldn't quite catch.

'You're welcome to come and help with executor duties,' she said. 'Just let me know when you plan to arrive, and I'll get a room un-dust-sheeted for you.'

There was silence.

'In the meantime,' she said, 'let me remind you of our father. He died when you were fifteen, Tom; Lachy, you were ten; Finn, you were five. What do you remember of him?'

'The car he said I could have when I was grown up,' Lachy said. 'It was like James Bond's.'

'Hang on—he told me *I* could have the car,' Tom said.

'I don't remember the car. I don't really remember him very well, either,' Finn admitted.

'Because you were very young when he died, Finn,' Catriona said. 'I barely saw him after he left my mother for yours, Tom—which isn't a pop at you, by the way, it's just telling you how he was with me. Even before that, he and my mother used to drop me here at the castle so Gramps and Grannie could look after me while they jetted off to some Caribbean island for a party. Except the party would turn into quite a bit longer than a weekend.'

Dominic could see from their expressions that this was a revelation to them—and not a pleasant one.

'Dad used to turn up in that car,' Lachy said, 'and he'd take me out somewhere. He'd drive too fast, and we'd do all the things my mum wouldn't have approved of.' He frowned. 'And then I wouldn't see him for months.'

'Same here,' Tom said. 'Except he'd stay on the beach, drinking brandy and flirting with whoever was sitting near him, while I was surfing. He'd never come in the water with me.'

'I remember a trip to the zoo, and he bought me a stuffed tiger that was bigger than me,' Finn said.

'So what you're all saying is he didn't show his face often, and when he did he was larger than life?' Catriona asked.

Her half-brothers agreed.

'Our father,' she said, 'lived fast and died at the age of forty-nine, with four divorces behind him and no will. Sorting out his estate took me quite a lot of time.'

'I don't remember getting any money when he died,' Tom said. 'Unless you made sure any inheritance was tied up until my thirtieth birthday or something like that.'

'I couldn't have done that,' she said, 'and, besides, there wasn't any money. Because he was divorced and died intestate, we would've inherited everything equally between the four of us, but I'm afraid our father did everything on credit. A life of partying isn't cheap. Yacht hire, hotel bills—for a gaggle of hangers-on as well as himself—and the very best champagne,' she said. 'And I wouldn't be surprised if he'd been doing drugs as well. If I'd been Gramps, I would've cut off the funds and made him work. Given him a purpose in life, something to strive for.'

'And that's what you're going to do to us?' Tom asked.

'There *are* no funds for me to cut off, right now,' she said. 'And I'm afraid your mothers calling me a ball-breaker isn't going to conjure up a magic money tree.'

There were collective winces on the screen. 'You know about that?' Finn asked.

'I know everything,' she said tiredly. 'When you're twenty-five years old and four women think you're holding out on them, they don't tend to mince their words.'

'Hang on. There are three of us. Or was your mum one of the four?' Tom asked.

'No,' she said dryly. 'My mother's independently wealthy. Or she was, until she developed a taste for expensive weddings and trading in the current spouse for a new model. Much like Dad.'

'So who was the fourth woman who had a go at you?' Finn asked.

'The woman he divorced your mum for, Finn. Except she had a miscarriage, or my guess is we would've had another baby brother.' She spread her hands. 'And he died before he could marry her, so she wasn't entitled to anything, even if there had been any money. She wasn't very happy about that.'

'Gramps left you everything,' Tom said. 'Is that because you're the oldest?'

'Without looking it up,' she asked, 'when was Gramps's birthday?'

The silence told Dominic that none of them had a clue. Which shocked him: he knew all the birthdays in his own family.

'Right,' she said dryly. 'Do you know mine? And don't

start whining that women are the ones who sort that sort of thing out, and you're not girls.'

'No,' Tom admitted. 'But you always remember my birthday.'

'And mine,' Lachy agreed.

'And mine,' Finn said.

'So do you still all think I'm going to cut you off with nothing?'

There was another silence.

'Well, I'm glad I've embarrassed you into seeing the truth,' she said.

'The castle's going to be a money-pit,' Tom said. 'My best mate's parents live in a listed building that needed a new roof. It cost a fortune. And it took for ever to sort out.'

'Which is what I'm expecting to be the case here,' she said. 'But it needs doing. I think Gramps thought the three of you would sell up if he left it to you.'

'Of course we would,' Lachy said. 'You said there's damp, the roof needs fixing, and it needs a new heating system. It makes sense to let someone who actually likes doing that kind of stuff do it. Save yourself the hassle.'

'Lark Hill isn't being sold on my watch. Nor's any of the land,' she said. 'I'm selling some of the art to cover the inheritance tax, and I'll send you all a full record of what I do.'

'What about the tenants? Can't they pay more rent?' Tom asked.

'I'm not increasing the rents.' She blew out a breath. 'Gramps taught me that with rights come responsibilities. We have a duty to our tenants to look after them, not fleece them.'

They said nothing for a while, as if digesting what she'd said.

'What about the new husband?' Tom asked. 'If he's real.'

'Ask him yourself.' She glanced at Dominic, who moved closer.

'Good evening. I'm Dominic Ferrars,' he said.

'And you married Catriona yesterday. How come none of us have heard of you before?' Tom asked.

'If you don't even know your sister's birthday,' Dominic said dryly, 'you're hardly going to know if she's dating someone.'

'How do we know you're not a gold-digger?' Lachy asked.

'You might want to check out how much a qualified senior solicitor earns in London,' Dominic said. 'And, if you all think that life's all about how much money you have, then I think you've got a fair bit of growing up to do.'

'Can we lower the testosterone level a bit, please?' Catriona asked, nudging him.

He smiled at her. 'Sure.'

'So how long have you been dating my sister?' Finn asked.

'I've known her for about seven years,' Dominic said.

'How do we know she didn't just marry you to get the castle?' Tom asked.

Dominic smiled, turned Catriona to face him and kissed her very thoroughly. 'That answer your question, boys?' he asked.

Finn pulled a face. 'That's so gross. Old people kissing.'

Dominic grinned. 'I'm twenty years older than you, yes, but that isn't *old*. And kissing isn't just for teenagers.'

'It's the first time I've seen Catriona blush,' Tom said.

'If you have anything constructive to say,' Catriona said, sounding cross, 'then I'll listen. Otherwise, I think we're done with this conversation.'

Tom shrugged. 'Whatever. Bye.' His part of the screen went blank.

'Yeah,' Lachy said. 'Bye.'

* * *

Which left Finn. Catriona was expecting him to flounce off, too, but instead he asked, 'Were you serious?'

'What? About being married to Dominic?' She rolled her eyes. 'I'll send you a copy of my wedding certificate, when it gets here.'

'No. I mean about helping. There are formal gardens at Lark Hill, right?'

'Which are not top of my priority list,' she said.

'You said you want to make the castle pay for itself,' Finn reminded her. 'People pay to visit gardens.'

'And you need public liability insurance for paying visitors. I need to cost it.'

'If the figures work,' Finn said, 'then I could come and look after the gardens.'

'Is that what you want to do with your career? Horticulture?' Dominic asked.

'Maybe,' Finn said.

'You're sixteen in April. You've got two more years at school,' Catriona reminded him.

'Two more years in *education*. It doesn't have to be at school,' Finn corrected. 'I could do an apprenticeship.'

'I'd need to discuss that with your mother,' Catriona said.

He sighed. 'So that's a no.'

'Your mother has parental responsibility for you until you're sixteen, Finn,' Dominic said, 'so we have to abide by her decisions. But if you want some help in finding information about a career in horticulture, we can do that.'

'Thank you,' Finn said. 'Lachy and Tom don't know I have a greenhouse. I don't want them taking the piss out of me.'

'Ignore them if they do,' Catriona said. She'd had no idea he was into gardening—and this was the first time he'd confided anything to her. She wanted to encourage him. 'What do you grow?'

'Chilis,' Finn said. 'If there's a decent-sized greenhouse at Lark Hill, I could probably grow enough to go into production. I was thinking Lark Hill chili sauce, made from Scotch Bonnets grown in Scotland. If you open the gardens to the public, that means you can have a tea shop and a plant shop—and you can sell home-made goods in the tea shop. Like my chili sauce.'

'That,' Catriona said, 'is going on my list of possible businesses. If you're serious about this, Finn, then I want you to write me a business plan.'

'I've never written a business plan,' he said. 'How do I do that?'

'Find a template on the internet,' she said. 'But make sure the source is sound.'

'Something from the government or a charity aimed at supporting businesses for under-twenty-fives would be a good start,' Dominic added.

'What if it's not good enough?' Finn asked.

'Then you'll learn where the gaps are and what you need to know to fix them,' she said. 'Rinse and repeat, until you get it right. Just like when you revise a subject for exams and work out where your gaps are. Just so we're clear, this isn't me being mean and refusing to help you; I want you to think for yourself and work out where you need to ask for help, because you'll learn a lot more that way than if I sit down and do it for you.'

'Got it,' Finn said, and gave her a genuine smile that took her breath away. 'If school was like you, I wouldn't hate it as much as I do.'

'I'll take that as a win,' Catriona said. 'Write me a draft

plan. I'll see what we have here by way of greenhouses. And we'll look at your career options together.'

'Thank you,' Finn said. 'And…um…congratulations to you both on the wedding. And I'm sorry I wasn't very nice to you. I'll send you that plan tomorrow, Catriona.' Awkwardly, he ended the call.

'I didn't expect that,' she said, looking thoughtful. 'It sounds as if the baby of the family might be growing up.'

Dominic rubbed a hand over his face. 'Even though he thinks I'm a potential gold-digger, and we're both ancient.'

'He was very grossed-out by you kissing me,' she said. 'But, actually, that was genius. I think that convinced them more than anything I said.'

'I see what you mean now about your family not being like mine,' he said. 'I assume your grandparents were a little less…' he paused as if searching for the right word '…combative?'

'They were. But they were quite reserved and formal,' she added, wanting to be truthful.

'I think Finn might come good.'

She shrugged. 'We'll see.'

'By the way, I didn't step in when they were giving you a hard time because I'm not going to insult you by playing the knight on the white charger,' he said. 'You don't need one. Half the barristers in London are terrified of you.'

She remembered what her sort-of stepmothers thought of her. 'Do you think I'm a ball-breaker?' she asked.

'You can be,' he said. 'But only when it's necessary, and I think it's because nobody's really been on your side before.'

'Uh-huh.'

'You're not a stereotype, Catriona. You're like Cleopatra with her infinite variety,' he said.

'That's how you see me?' She stared at him. '*Antony and Cleopatra* was my A level set text.'

'Mine, too,' he said. 'And, yeah, that's how I see you. Enobarbus the low-born soldier, seeing Antony's "enchanting queen". Because you are. Enchanting.'

She blinked away the tears that welled up from absolutely nowhere. 'I think that's the nicest thing anyone's ever said to me.'

'It's true,' he said.

'And you're not low-born.'

He stroked her cheek. 'Compared to you, I am. But I don't care about class, and I don't think you do, either.'

'It's who you are that matters, not where you come from,' she said.

'Agreed. Anyway, your team's growing. Me, Mrs Mac, and maybe Finn. We're going to fix Lark Hill. Together.'

The idea made her heart skip a beat. *Together.* She'd expected to have to struggle with Lark Hill on her own. And this definitely hadn't been in her bargain with Dominic.

Just for a moment, the strain across her shoulders eased and it felt less as if she was trying to climb out of a deep well.

'Now, do you need a glass of wine after that, or shall I make you some camomile tea?' he asked.

'Tea would be really lovely,' she said gratefully. 'Thank you.' Before he stood up, she took his hand and pressed a kiss into his palm before folding his fingers over the kiss. 'Dommy. Thank you for having my back.'

He brushed his mouth against hers. 'You're very, very welcome, Trina.'

CHAPTER TEN

'I LIKE HIM, HEN,' Mrs MacFarlane said the next morning, when Catriona came down to the kitchen. 'I suspected you might have married him just to meet that ridiculous clause your grandfather put in his will—but it's the real thing, isn't it?'

Catriona hated lying to someone she'd known for so long, but she didn't exactly have a choice. 'Mmm…' she said.

'You know, I've been thinking about it and I'm sure that's why your grandfather made that clause,' Mrs MacFarlane said. 'Because he was worried about you being on your own. He didn't have a love match with your grandmother, but things changed over the years. I think he wanted you to find someone who'd rub along with you, and then over time you'd learn to love each other.'

'Maybe,' Catriona said.

'He's a good man, your Dominic. He's grounded. And he notices the little things—like your chamomile tea, and the way you drink your coffee,' Mrs MacFarlane said.

'He's a lawyer. He's supposed to pay attention to detail,' Catriona said.

'But he sees *you*, hen,' the housekeeper said. 'Not professional you, not Viscountess you. The real you.'

And that was a seriously scary thought—because Catriona thought Mrs Mac might be right. Last night she'd gone to sleep in Dominic's arms; this morning, the first thing she'd seen when she'd opened her eyes was him. When they made love, she felt like a different person. Cherished, just the way he'd promised on their wedding day. Valued.

She pushed the thought away. That wasn't the deal she had with Dominic, and it wasn't fair to change the terms of their agreement now—no matter how much he tempted her. He had a life in London, with his dream job. She couldn't ask him to change the terms of their deal, give all that up for her and move even further away from the family he adored. She'd just have to be sensible and remember that this was for a week, not for ever.

Dominic charmed the tenants that morning and helped Catriona reassure them that there would be no immediate changes in the estate, and definitely no changes to the rent; though she was looking to make the estate pay for itself and she was interested in any ideas they had. At lunchtime, she showed him the path down the cliff to the beach belonging to the castle.

'Is this a private beach?' Dominic asked.

'Technically,' she said, 'but as far back as I can remember we haven't minded the locals walking here. All we ask is that people take their litter home with them.'

'So you could go swimming in the sea every day.'

'You *could*,' she said, smiling. 'But at this time of year the water's about eight degrees centigrade. I don't think I'd even paddle at the edges, let alone swim properly.' She gave him a sidelong look. 'Of course, should you wish to accept a challenge...'

He laughed and kissed her. 'No. My common sense just about outweighs my testosterone.'

Later that afternoon, they took pictures of the gardens and the greenhouses for Finn, and had a chat with the gardener about what kind of practical experience Finn could get at Lark Hill and how it would work with an apprenticeship. She sent the photographs to Finn, who emailed her a business plan in return.

She read through it swiftly. 'It's pretty good for a first attempt,' she said, passing it to Dominic.

'He's taken what you said on board.' He looked approving. 'We've got time to review it and give him feedback, but then you need to go and change.'

'Change? Why?'

'I'm taking you out,' he said.

'Where?'

'I know you hate surprises,' he said, 'and so do I, but I promise you'll like this one.'

Taking her out. And this felt like a real date, so her stomach was filled with butterflies. He made her feel like a nerdy teenager being asked out by the hottest boy in school. 'What's the dress code?' she asked.

'Smart casual. We're having dinner, afterwards. Oh, but I think layers might be a good idea.'

Once they'd come up with a joint critique for Finn, she changed into black trousers and a pretty, long-sleeved top, wearing the pendant Dominic had bought her. He drove them into Edinburgh, with a bit of help from her satnav; she still didn't have a clue what he'd planned until he walked with her to St Mary's Cathedral. There was a candlelit piano recital, covering everything from Beethoven's 'Moonlight Sonata', Chopin and Rachmaninov through to Einaudi.

She held his hand throughout the performance, and this time it had nothing to do with looking comfortable with him and everything to do with the fact she wanted to do it.

Dinner afterwards was fabulous, too, in a Georgian townhouse restaurant that specialised in seasonal Scottish food, and she enjoyed teasing him into trying haggis. They walked back through the streets to the Christmas markets; there were twinkling Christmas lights everywhere, the scents of orange and cinnamon and whisky floated in the air, and the street entertainers were singing Christmas pop songs—in some cases, accompanied by bagpipes.

Dominic nudged her. 'Hey. I knew I'd get my bagpipes fix.'

She laughed, and they paused to watch people at the ice rink.

'Do you want to have a go?' he asked, gesturing to the rink.

She shook her head ruefully. 'I'm afraid skating's not in my skillset. Don't tell me, you can do all the flashy jumps and spins?'

He laughed and kissed her. 'Skating's not in my skill-set, either. It's probably not going to be helpful if one of us ends up in plaster, is it?'

'Let's just explore the Christmas market,' she said.

'Sounds good to me,' he said. 'And I could do with getting some stocking-fillers for my family.'

It was perfect, wandering through the market with their arms round each other. Catriona was surprised and thrilled to discover that she actually felt like a newlywed—as if their honeymoon was real, particularly when Dominic stopped to kiss her under some mistletoe.

With some helpful suggestions from Catriona, Dominic bought some Scots cream liqueur for his mum and aunts and single malt for his uncles, wrist-warmers for his sisters, and he couldn't resist a soft toy shaped like a highland cow for his nephew Aiden.

He wanted to buy something for Catriona, but what did you buy a viscountess—let alone one who was trying to balance the family estate's books and whose home and office were so clutter-free that it was obvious she didn't like knick-knacks? He gleefully bought tartan wrapping paper. 'See. Told you, tartan's what the tourists look for up here,' he said.

She rolled her eyes. 'Next thing, you'll be wanting bag-pipes lessons.'

'So I can serenade my sweetheart? Actually, hold that thought. And my shopping.' He left her with a bag for a second while he had a quiet word with one of the street bands to explain he wanted something special for his new wife, and gave a decent cash donation to their charity box. A few moments later, he returned. 'Right, wifey. Come with me.'

'Wifey?' she asked in mock outrage.

'That's my ring on your finger,' he said. 'Which makes you *ma noo wee wifey.*'

He deliberately hammed up the Scottish accent, and was rewarded with her laughing. 'That's terrible,' she said.

'You need some proper Gaelic lessons, laddie,' the piper of the band said, overhearing them. 'Is your lassie Scots?'

'She is,' Dominic confirmed.

'Right. Now, tell her *tha gaol agam ort.*'

'What does it mean?' Dominic asked. 'If I'm insulting her, I'm in trouble.'

'She'll know what it means, lad,' the piper said with a grin.

'*Ha geul ak-ham orsht,*' Dominic said, stumbling slightly over the pronunciation and needing a tiny bit of prompting from the piper.

Catriona went even pinker.

'And now you ask her,' the piper said, '*thoir pòg dhomh?*'

Dominic still wasn't sure if his leg was being pulled, but dutifully repeated, '*Hod pok goh?*'

'Go on, lassie,' the piper said. 'He asked you nicely.'

Catriona reached up on tiptoe and gave him a kiss.

Dominic grinned at the piper. 'Thank you. I'll remember that one.'

'You want to leave your shopping here?' the piper asked. 'Because your new husband's asked for something special.' As soon as Catriona placed the bag by his feet, he winked at Dominic. 'Take it away, laddie.'

He began playing 'All I Want For Christmas Is You' on the bagpipes, and Dominic swept Catriona into his arms, dancing with her on the street and singing along to the song.

At first, she looked slightly panicky—and then, to his delight, she sang with him, relaxed into the dancing, and at the end of the song she kissed him.

'Merry Christmas,' the piper said when they collected their shopping.

'*Tapadh leat*,' Catriona replied with a smile.

'Thank you,' Dominic added.

The piper grinned. 'Your lassie's already said thanks. You have a nice night.'

'I had no idea you spoke Gaelic,' Dominic said to Catriona.

She shrugged. 'You never asked.'

'How many languages do you speak?'

'Including English and Gaelic?' She wrinkled her nose. 'Five. My German's a bit rusty, though.'

He should've guessed. Catriona was an over-achiever all the way—though she didn't boast about it. 'My only other language is French,' he said, 'and that's seriously rusty. Still, I'll make a start on Gaelic. *"Hod pok goh"* is "kiss me", right? What was the rest?'

'Later,' she said, turning an even deeper shade of pink.

'I think,' he said, 'I'm going to enjoy Gaelic lessons. *Thoir pòg dhomh.*'

'You're getting very uppity, Mr Ferrars.' She grinned. 'Just wait until I make you spell it.'

'Then I'll need extra…' He paused. 'Which bit's "kiss"?'

'*Pòg*,' she said.

'Extra *pògs*,' he said, 'to encourage my diligence in studying and to reward my attempts at spelling a language that I'm guessing looks nothing like it sounds.'

She laughed, and kissed him.

And, as they walked through the streets of the city together, all felt very right in Dominic's world. He loved the vibrancy of the city; but, more than that, he loved the way the woman by his side continually managed to surprise him.

This wasn't meant to be a real honeymoon at the start of a real marriage; they'd agreed it was a temporary thing.

But what if it wasn't?

The closer Catriona allowed him to get to her, the more he found himself enjoying her company. A walk hand in hand by the sea, tasting the salt on her lips when he kissed her. A cosy dinner by the fire in the local pub. Sitting in her turret and watching the stars, seeing a meteor streaking past in the clear night sky.

'What did you wish for?' he asked.

'Can't tell you, or it won't come true,' she said with a smile. 'Which is why I'm not going to ask you, either.'

He was shocked to realise what he wished for: that their convenient marriage would become real. He'd never expected to do all the cosy couple stuff with her, and it was a revelation to him that not only did he enjoy it, he wanted to do a lot more of it.

But how did she feel about him? If he tried to woo her, particularly from a distance when he went back to London, would she push him away? Or would she try to find a compromise so they could be together?

He'd ask her…but he'd need to find the right moment.

* * *

Monday was dank and miserable, full of the kind of fine drizzle that had you soaked before you knew it. And it suited Catriona's mood. Today was the end of their honeymoon. Day seven of their marriage. She had to be honest with herself: it was also the end, because Dominic was flying back to London.

This near-week had been stolen out of their lives, and it wasn't to be repeated—no matter how much she wished things could be different.

She'd booked a meeting with her grandfather's solicitor so she wouldn't have to stay and watch Dominic walk away from her. Though she was tempted to cancel it when he enveloped her in a bear hug. She didn't want to move out of his arms, ever again.

Though that wasn't the deal.

'I'll message you when I'm back in London,' he said.

'Safe journey,' she said, forcing herself to smile and hoping that she looked inscrutable rather than near to crying. 'I'm not very good at goodbyes. And I've got a meeting in the city centre.'

'OK. But before I go...' He leaned forward and kissed her. A kiss so sweet and yearning that it made tears glint in her eyes. But Dominic wasn't really hers. He was borrowed, and she had to let him go now.

'You'd better check in,' she said.

As soon as he'd taken his case out of her car and closed the boot, she raised a hand in acknowledgement and drove away.

Having to drive, even if it was only for half an hour or so, meant she couldn't indulge in tears; besides, she didn't want to turn up to a meeting with her eyes red and puffy. It would be unprofessional, and Catriona Findlay had the word *professional* practically stamped through her, like a stick of seaside rock.

She felt as brittle as a stick of seaside rock, too.

At least having all the paperwork to sort out meant that she could fill her time completely—and pretend she wasn't missing him.

She knew she'd been right not to give in to temptation when Dominic sent her an anodyne message to say that he'd arrived safely. Of course he wasn't going to tell her he loved her. He'd only said the words to her in Gaelic because the piper had coached him through it, and he hadn't known what he was saying. And of course he wouldn't miss her. He had a busy schedule and his promotion would be announced before Christmas.

Glad you had a good flight. CF, she replied.

She told herself she didn't miss him when she went to bed alone, that night.

She told herself she didn't miss him when she lay awake at three a.m., remembering how his touch had made her body feel as if it was singing.

She told herself she didn't miss him when she checked her phone for the umpteenth time to find no messages from him.

This was crazy, Dominic thought. Catriona had never spent the night in his flat. So why did his bed feel too wide?

A punishing workout in the gym at ridiculous o'clock before work didn't help. The endorphins weren't enough to make up for her absence. And work felt as if he'd never been away: except he was keenly aware of the empty desk in the open-plan room.

How was he going to woo his wife from a distance?

Catriona wasn't like other women. A big, sweeping romantic gesture would be met with a raised eyebrow and a caustic remark. A small gesture, on the other hand—something with a bit of thought behind it—might produce a different result. He could still remember the delight on her face when he'd given her the pendant; she'd loved the fact that he'd had it made to match her grandmother's ring.

In his morning break, he went out for 'fresh air' and called an Edinburgh florist.

A little later on, Mrs MacFarlane came into the study with a mug of coffee and a beautifully gift-wrapped bouquet. 'Delivery from Edinburgh for you,' she said.

'Flowers?' Who would send her flowers? Nobody had ever sent her flowers, even Luke in the day when he'd tried to impress her.

The second she saw the flowers, she knew exactly who they were from. Gerbera—like the ones her wedding bouquet, except these were all bright, hot colours. Scarlet, in-your-face pink, yellow.

Only one person could've sent her these. The person who'd turned her world from monochrome to unexpected bright, hot colours.

'Thank you, Mrs Mac,' she said.

'From your young man, I'll guess,' Mrs MacFarlane said.

'Probably. They're lovely and bright.'

All part of the show, she told herself. He hadn't meant it. Though the message took her breath away.

Fifi—hod pok goh—Fergus.

A tear spilled over her cheek, and she brushed it away. Ridiculous. She couldn't afford to be sentimental. Couldn't let herself hope that he meant any of it.

But she duly typed a message to him.

Thank you for flowers. A+ for colour and form. E-for spelling.

Unexpectedly, she had an immediate response.

Glad you liked them. How's it spelled, then?

No kisses. No sentimentality. Then again, she wasn't sentimental.

She messaged back.

Thoir pòg dhomh.

No WAY. How the hell was I supposed to get that? DH = G? Where does the M come in? And that D is in the wrong place. Huh. From Severely Sulking of London.

She typed back, grinning.

Attention to detail, my dear Fergus.

He was the only man she'd ever met who could make her laugh like this.

And you have no excuse for not checking the internet. You have good Wi-Fi in London.

He didn't reply, and it left her feeling flat.

Then again, she knew he was busy at work. Her own days in the office had been full. They were full here, too—but weirdly they felt empty without him.

The only other message she had that day was from her mother.

Congratulations on getting hitched. Will try to come over in summer to meet him.

Right, Catriona thought. It had taken Victoria nearly a week to reply to her message about the wedding, and they both knew that, even if her mother did make a firm arrangement to meet up, it would be cancelled at the last minute.

Catriona typed back That would be lovely, knowing perfectly well that it wouldn't happen. And she was so used to her mother that it didn't upset her any more.

On Wednesday morning, a package arrived with the label of a Borough Market stall. It was a piece of wrapped cheese, with a note in Dominic's distinctive handwriting.

Why is this package dangerous? Fergus

She thought about it for a good ten minutes before giving up.

All right. I'll bite. Why is the package dangerous?

He made her wait until lunchtime for the answer.

Because, my dear Fifi, it's a sharp cheddar.

She groaned, but the pun had amused her.

It's very delicious, actually. Eating it with some of Mrs Mac's chutney and good bread. PS Any pun you can do, I can do feta.

And she followed up with a little internet shopping, sending him a pair of socks decorated with bagpipes.

He didn't respond to her implied challenge, and she

guessed he was in a meeting; she damped down the disappointment.

But she was surprised by emails later that afternoon from both Tom and Lachy. Lachy apologised for being snippy with her and offered to sort out a website if she was opening Lark Hill to the public or running events; and Tom suggested holding murder mystery weekends, adding that he'd be happy to act as a tour guide, because there was a good surfing beach just down the road and it might be fun to surf in Scotland instead of Cornwall.

Catriona thanked them both, and forwarded their messages, as well as her mother's, to Dominic.

He didn't reply until later that evening—which she guessed was after his usual family video call.

Glad Tom and Lachy are coming good. My mother and sisters send love. Saying nothing re your mother on grounds of least said, the better.

Just how she felt, too.

Dominic loved Catriona's cheesy puns.

Actually, if he was honest with himself, he loved her.

He wasn't quite sure when he'd fallen for her—before the wedding when she was trying to be brave, on the day of the wedding when she'd danced with him and watched the stars, or the day after the wedding when they'd both been so tired that their barriers had fallen apart and they'd taken comfort in each other.

He couldn't woo her with emails and texts. It wasn't enough. He wanted to be with her. Properly. As her legally wedded husband.

But.

He raked a hand through his hair. He'd always put his

family first. Falling for Catriona meant there was someone else he'd have to consider. Someone else he'd need to put first.

Or maybe not. Because they'd all taken to her, and considered her to be part of them. He'd had messages from every single one of them telling him so—including from the ones who knew the truth about the wedding deal he'd made with his rival.

The only barrier to him telling her how he felt was Catriona herself. Because, if he'd got this wrong, she'd back away. She'd put an extra layer of metaphorical barbed wire under those painted hoardings to make him back off.

It was a risk.

A huge, huge risk.

Then again, not telling her would be worse. If he kept silent and simply gave her the divorce they'd agreed to in a year's time, he'd always wonder: what if he'd been brave enough to tell her how he felt and ask her to make their marriage a real one?

Not being with her because she didn't love him back would be hard. But it wouldn't be as hard as not being with her because he hadn't had the courage to challenge her.

This wasn't something he was going to do by text. He needed to see her eyes when he told her. There was nothing in his diary that couldn't be moved, and he had annual leave that needed taking. He'd sort it out in the morning—and then he'd book a flight to Edinburgh.

It was late the following evening when Catriona had a response to the socks.

Wonderful socks. Thx. I was thinking of having a tattoo, but worried you might complain about all the bagpipers.

She got the pun immediately.

Very good, Fergus.

Worth a *pòg*?

Definitely. And if only it could be in person. But that wasn't their deal.

A+ for spelling this time.

Trying to keep standards up. Cough. Where is my *pòg*?

X

Hmm. B-for effort.

<3 X <3

Improving. Still only B+. Try harder.

She could just see the teasing expression on his face as he typed, and longing flooded through her. But how could she tell him how she felt, when she knew they didn't have a future?

He didn't contact her on Friday or Saturday. But on Sunday afternoon, there was a knock on her study door, and a deep voice announced, *'Ma-tin va.'*

'Good morning', in Gaelic. In an utterly terrible accent, but he was clearly trying.

'Dominic?' Oh, and her voice *would* have to squeak. 'What are you doing here?'

'Come to claim my *pòg* in person.' He smiled. 'It seems

I have a bit of time in lieu, so I thought I'd come and save you from drowning in paperwork.'

He'd taken some of his annual leave to help her? She'd never seen this kind of support in any of her parents' marriages, and she was at a bit of a loss how to react. She wanted to run to him, to throw her arms round him and kiss him until he was stupid; but another part of her remembered all the misery she'd seen in relationships. Her parents' constant divorces and remarriages, her own failed engagement. What was to say she'd manage to get this to work? The only marriage she'd seen working in her family was that of her grandparents—and they'd always felt emotionally reserved. So maybe that was just how things were for her family: the only way it could work was if you kept yourself aloof.

He coughed. 'Um... I even learned how to say "good morning" in Gaelic, just for you. *And* I can spell it.'

'I'll be the judge of that,' she said primly.

He came over to her and spun her round on her office chair. 'Oh, will you, Your Ladyship?'

And then *he* kissed *her* stupid.

'I missed you,' he whispered.

She'd missed him, too. Seeing him here again showed her just how much having him here with her made it feel as if the sun had pushed its way through the rain clouds and was making everything sparkle. She wanted to tell him that, but fear held her back. How could she trust him with her heart govern her feelings, when she knew love didn't last? Keeping him at arm's length was the only way to protect herself from the misery of it all going wrong.

He scooped her off her chair, took her place and settled her on his lap. 'So how's the paperwork?'

'Under control. How's the office?'

'Pretty much how you left it. Apparently your temporary replacement is joining us after Christmas.'

'And your promotion?'

'Announced,' he said. 'Last week.'

And he hadn't told her.

As if he'd guessed her feelings, he said, 'I didn't tell you because it still feels like rubbing your nose in it.'

'We had a deal,' she said. 'I have the castle. It would have been nice to know I held up my end of the bargain.'

He stroked her face. 'I apologise. I should've told you. And said thank you.'

'No need. It's what we agreed. Anyway, I had no idea you were going to come here today,' she said. 'I would've met you at the airport, if I'd known.'

'I got a cab,' he said. 'I wanted to surprise you.'

'You certainly did that,' she said, smiling because, for the first time all week, she was genuinely happy.

The world felt back in kilter for Catriona, with Dominic back in the castle. Having someone to bounce ideas off, someone to encourage her in the good ideas and suggest alternatives for the ideas that didn't work. But, most of all, just him being there. Waking up with him in the morning, falling asleep in his arms at night, and even one evening spent on the roof, watching the stars and being thrilled to spot a meteorite.

'Wish on a falling star,' he said, 'but don't tell me or it won't come true.'

Even though she knew it was just a superstition and it wouldn't come true, she wished he could be hers for real. Except then she'd need a second wish to make sure it all worked out, rather than ending in disappointment.

But a couple of days before Christmas, he asked, 'What are your plans for Christmas?'

She shrugged. 'I always used to come here for a couple of days, so Gramps wouldn't be on his own. But he's not here, now. Mrs Mac went to her sister's yesterday. I guess I'd planned to treat Christmas like any other day and work through it.'

'What about Finn, Lachy, Tom and your mum? Aren't you planning to see them?'

'They're all doing their own things. I've sent cards and presents.'

'You could come and spend Christmas with my family,' he suggested.

A real family Christmas.

Dominic had already described it to her: how everyone got together in one place, bringing a dish to share. Crackers and paper hats, Uncle Bill leading the singalongs, games of charades, everyone noisy and laughing and together.

The sort of Christmas she'd never had.

The sort of Christmas that could capture her heart completely—then it would really hurt when she and Dominic divorced in a year's time, as planned. She realised then that if she let herself fall for him and his family, the divorce would leave her shattered. She needed to keep them all at arm's length, to protect herself.

'No, I couldn't,' she said.

'Why not?' he asked.

'I have things to do here.' She tried for a lightness she didn't really feel.

'On your own?' He raised an eyebrow. 'You're not going to be able to hold meetings on a bank holiday.'

'I can do other things. Prep work.'

'Is my family the problem?'

Yes, but not in the way he meant. 'No, of course not.'

'I don't get it. Talk to me, Catriona.'

That was just the thing. She couldn't. How could she even begin to explain all the mixed-up stuff in her head?

He blew out a breath. 'OK. I know you're twitchy about marriage and I know our deal's for a year. But I think things have changed between us over the last few weeks. So I'm going to take a risk and tell you how I feel. I've fallen in love with you, Catriona. I want this to be a real marriage. Obviously we've got things to sort out, with me being in London and you being here, but I think we can find some sort of compromise and make it work.'

He loved her.

He wanted a real marriage.

He was prepared to compromise.

But.

She'd tried before, with Luke, and it hadn't worked out. Her parents had never managed to make a marriage work. What was to say that she could make it work with Dominic? If she let him in and it all went wrong, she knew that this time she'd never recover.

'No,' she said lying through her teeth. 'That isn't what I want.' It was everything she wanted—but she was too scared to take that risk.

'Are you telling me you don't feel the same?' he asked.

She dug her fingernails into her palm and lied again. 'Yes.'

'OK,' he said. 'No problem. I'll catch a flight and get out of your hair.'

She said nothing—and he left the room, closing the door very quietly behind him.

She knew he was going to pack. And then he'd be gone. Leaving her on her own, the way she'd always been.

It was her own fault. She'd pushed him away. He'd offered her his heart, and she'd been too scared to accept it for the precious gift it was.

She ought to go after him. Explain. Tell him she wanted him all the way back, but she was scared. And, every time she tried to find the right words to tell him, her mind froze.

And then it was too late.

He'd gone.

CHAPTER ELEVEN

How HAD HE got this so wrong? Dominic wondered. They'd got closer since their honeymoon. He'd missed her horribly in London—and he'd thought from her messaged that she'd missed him, too.

What an idiot he'd been. The one woman he'd actually discovered he wanted to be with…and it turned out that she didn't feel the same about him. He'd made a deal with her, and she wanted to stick with it. No changes and no compromises—because she didn't love him. Didn't want him.

Her silence when he'd offered to get out of her hair had made him feel as if he'd just dropped down to the bottom of a deep well. The sunlight he'd felt around her had been sucked into a black hole.

It was the first time he'd ever offered his heart to someone—and, instead of accepting it or behaving as if it was something special—she'd thrown it back at him. Smashing it into tiny pieces; every shard had lodged in his skin, stinging and burning.

The cab driver gave up trying to make conversation with him, and Dominic remained sunk in misery all the way to the airport. He didn't want to go back to London, either. He wanted to be with people who loved him. The place he knew he'd be accepted, and where they'd made him talk until all the hurt came out and he could heal.

Though he wasn't sure his heart would ever heal. It was in too many pieces.

Thankfully he managed to get a flight which meant he wouldn't have to hang around the airport for hours, seeing the kind of joyful reunions he'd hoped for and hadn't got. He used noise-cancelling headphones on the plane to make sure nobody talked to him, and again in the taxi once he'd given the address to the driver.

And then he rang his mother's doorbell.

'You look terrible, Dommy,' Ginny said. 'And why didn't you say you were coming? Where's your car?'

'I didn't drive,' Dominic said. 'I flew.'

'From London? Surely the train's easier?'

'From Edinburgh,' he admitted.

She frowned. 'Then where's Catriona?'

'I...' He blew out a breath. 'Mum, it's such a mess.' He filled her in on the honeymoon that had turned his convenient marriage into a real one. 'I fell in love with her, Mum. I thought we had a future. But she doesn't love me back.'

'Are you sure about that?' Ginny asked.

'Yes. I told her how I felt. She said she didn't feel the same.'

Ginny frowned. 'Maybe she wasn't telling you the truth. Take another look at your wedding photos. What I see is a bride in love with her new husband.'

He flicked through the pictures. His bride walking down the aisle to him. The shyness on her face. Confetti. The glint in her eye when she'd thrown the bouquet straight to Lou. Cutting the cake. Dancing with him.

'We were playing a part,' Dominic said. 'It was all part of our wedding deal. It wasn't real.' He shook his head. 'At least, it wasn't supposed to be. Maybe I ought to go back to London and work through Christmas rather than ruin it here for everyone.'

'We'll all be worrying about you even more if you do that,' Ginny said. 'Stay. We can't fix this for you, but we're your family and we love you.'

'Love you, too,' Dominic said. He just wished that Catriona had been able to love him as well.

Pride wasn't a good substitute for the man you'd fallen in love with and pushed away, Catriona thought, wide awake at ridiculous o'clock in the morning.

Maybe she'd been wrong.

Maybe this whole thing with Dominic could have worked out. Hadn't she chosen him as her temporary groom in the first place because he had integrity? Her relationship with him wouldn't have ended up the same way as her parents, split after split after split, because he wasn't like them.

But she hadn't given them the chance. She'd pushed him away.

As she was the one who'd called a halt, it stood to reason that she was going to have to be the one to go after him. Be honest with him.

But first she had to find him.

Catriona threw the covers back and dashed round the room, getting dressed.

Had he gone back to London, or to Birmingham?

In the bathroom, she splashed her face with water. Now wasn't the time to give in to stupid emotions. She needed to think about this logically. It was Saturday. Christmas Eve was tomorrow. So the odds were that he'd chosen Birmingham—or, if he hadn't, he'd be there tomorrow.

She waited until it was a reasonable time of the morning, and texted Ginny.

Sorry to message you so early, but is Dominic with you?

To her relief, the reply came straight away.

Yes.

Please can you keep him there? I need to talk to him, but it has to be in person.

Of course.

And please don't tell him I'm coming.

She checked flights on her laptop. Thankfully there was still a seat on the plane. She booked it, and a cab to get her to the airport, then packed an overnight bag that wouldn't need to go in the hold. If she couldn't fix things with Dominic, she'd find a hotel for the night, or just hire a car and drive back to Lark Hill.

She couldn't settle to anything before the taxi arrived. Every time she glanced at her watch, convinced that minute must've passed, she was shocked to see it was a handful of seconds. But finally she was at the airport.

Her nerves felt as if they were screwing more and more tightly in her stomach, the nearer they got to Birmingham. She was nearly sick when the plane landed, and barely managed to mumble the right address to the cabbie.

And then she was there. Outside the front door.

This was it.

Make or break.

When Dominic would reject her—or maybe not.

Swallowing hard, she rang the doorbell.

And her knees went weak when he opened the door.

* * *

Dominic's breath caught. 'Catriona. What are…?' He stopped. She looked uncharacteristically nervous, and as if she wanted to run away. Asking questions might make her do just that, and he didn't want to take that risk. Not if there was a chance that they could have the conversation they should've had in Scotland. 'I didn't expect to see you,' he said instead. 'Would you like to come in?'

She looked as if the words had frozen in her head and she couldn't answer.

'On second thoughts, let me grab a coat and we'll go to the park, so we can have a private conversation,' he said. 'Leave your bag here.'

She nodded, still saying nothing, and he took her bag. He left it neatly in the hallway and grabbed his coat. 'Just going out for a bit, Mum,' he called, not waiting for the answer.

He led her over to the park; it was half an hour before sunset, so it was almost deserted and it was easy to find an empty bench.

'I'm sorry,' she said. 'I… I'm not good at this sort of thing. I messed up. Badly. And I'm sorry I hurt you.'

'Yes, you hurt me,' he said. 'I'm not in the habit of declaring myself.'

'The words got stuck,' she said. 'I wanted to say yes.' She took a deep breath. 'I want to spend Christmas with you, Dominic. I don't care whether it's here, or London, or Lark Hill—as long as I'm with you. Remember that night we saw the falling star?'

He nodded. Now she was talking, he didn't want to interrupt and give her the chance to clam up again.

'I wished our marriage was a real one. Not like my parents, getting bored and moving on all the time, but a real one—a forever marriage.'

'Me, too,' he said. 'I wished it was real.'

Her eyes were shining with a mixture of delight and disbelief.

'That night in Edinburgh, when the piper made you say things to me in Gaelic: I'm going to be brave and say it to you now. *Tha gaol agam ort.*'

'What does it mean?' he asked, even though he was pretty sure he'd worked it out for himself.

'I love you,' she said simply. 'I don't know how or when or where it happened, but I do. I love you. Dominic—and I really don't know what to do about it. I grew up not knowing what love looked like—I mean, I know my grandparents grew to love each other, but they were from a different generation. I don't know how to deal with this. What to do. What to say.'

The searing honesty made him want to weep for her.

'Just as well I know what to do about it,' he said. '*Tha gaol agam ort*, Catriona. If I'd known what I was saying that night, I would've told you again in English so you knew I meant it. Because I love you, too. I can't remember when I fell for you, either, but it feels like it's always been you. That you were the one I was waiting for.'

'That's how I feel about you,' she said. 'I want our marriage to be real. So much. But...' She shook her head. 'How are we possibly going to make it work? Lark Hill's hundreds of miles away from your job. As the newest partner, you'll hardly be able to do remote working.'

'About that,' he said.

Her eyes narrowed. 'What?'

'I told Lewis I think they have room for two new partners. One who's good at strategy, and one who's good at details. Dream team. You and me.'

Her eyes went wide. 'What did he say?'

'He agreed. When you're back from sabbatical, they'll ask you.'

'Oh, Dommy,' she said.

He grinned. 'I love it when you call me that. When you lose the starch. When your voice goes that little bit breathy.' At the thought of the last time she'd called him that, his pulse started racing. 'You make me hot all over.'

Her face went pink. 'You make *me* hot all over.'

'We fit,' he said softly. 'And, yes, we'll have to work at it, but we'll make everything work out because we're a team. We can do this: together.'

She lifted her chin. 'I can sell Lark Hill. Let someone else look after it.'

He shook his head, knowing that wasn't what she really wanted. She loved the place. 'It's your family heritage. I can't let you do that.'

'How else can we make it work?' she asked.

'We can spend half the time in London, half the time at Lark Hill.'

'Not half and half. We need time here, too,' she said. 'I want to be part of your family. Even though I'm not good at family stuff.'

'We'll teach you,' he said. 'And then you can teach your brothers how to be a family.'

'Ha—' She stopped herself mid-correction. 'My brothers,' she confirmed. 'I can get to know them and make a family with them. Trust them to help me make Lark Hill work.'

'We can have it all,' he said. 'And maybe, if we're lucky, we'll add to our family. I always thought I never wanted children, because I had responsibilities at a very early age— but being with you has changed my mind.'

'What if I'm a terrible mother?' she asked.

'You won't be,' he said. 'You'll be the kind of mother you wanted to have, not the one who let you down. Remember, your grannie loved you. I gather she was a bit reserved, but you knew deep down she loved you.'

She thought about it. 'You're right. And Mrs Mac thinks that's why Gramps put that clause in his will. Because he didn't marry Grannie for love, but they learned to love each other. So if he made me find someone I could work with as a team, over time we'd learn to love each other.'

'Over time,' he said.

She nodded. 'And I have. Just...quicker than I thought it would happen.'

He stroked her face. 'Me, too. You're my heart,' he said.

'*Mo cridhe*,' she said.

'*Mo credi-eh*,' he repeated. 'Which is?'

She smiled. 'What you said.'

He grinned. 'Well, now. My third Gaelic phrase, and I said it correctly.'

She grinned back. 'I have a feeling I know what my husband's going to say next.'

'Couldn't be anything else, could it?' he agreed, his smile broadening. '*Thoir pòg dhomh.*'

And she did.

EPILOGUE

Two years later

'IF YOU'D TOLD me two years ago that we'd be spending Christmas and New Year at Lark Hill with our entire families, I would've scoffed,' Catriona said. 'Yours, maybe—but not mine.'

The ballroom was decked out for Christmas and New Year, with a huge fir tree covered in pretty baubles. Lachie had set up a sound system playing music that would appeal to everyone from Finn to Mrs Mac, and everyone was dancing. Including the tenants and their families, her brothers' mothers and their new partners. Catriona's own mother wasn't there, but it didn't matter any more. There were more than enough people who wanted to be here with her. The family she'd always longed for—even her sort-of stepmothers.

'If you'd told me two years ago that Mum would finally marry Ray, I would've scoffed,' Dominic said. 'But she said we inspired her to be brave.'

'They look so happy together,' Catriona said. 'And the boys have all come good.'

'Because you gave them the chance to run with their own ideas,' Dominic said. Finn was doing his apprenticeship as a gardener, and had got their grandmother's flower garden back to its original gorgeous design. Lachie was in charge of finance, and had set up the barns to start production of

Lark Hill oat-based toiletries, as well as Finn's chili sauce, with the help of the tenants. The castle's tearoom showcased local artists, and everything in the gift shop was produced locally. Tom still surfed for fun—but he'd really come into his own, managing the staff and the visitors. The new biomass boiler had been installed and worked well, the leaky roof was fixed, and the whole summer was booked up with weddings.

'I'm just glad that they see Lark Hill for what it is,' she said. 'And I think Gramps and Grannie would've really approved.'

'Would they have approved of me?' Dominic asked.

'Oh, yes. And Grannie would've wanted you to do exactly what you're going to do in—' she glanced at her watch '—actually, right now. Go and walk round the gardens for five minutes.'

'It'd be nicer if my wife walked with me. So I could kiss her in the snow,' Dominic said.

'Not for first-footing,' she said. 'It's hugely unlucky for a woman to be the first-footer.'

He grinned. 'You could start a new tradition.'

'Nope. We need a tall, dark-haired man. That's you. *Go.*' When he made no move, she rolled her eyes. 'You can kiss me as much as you like in the snow afterwards.'

He drew her closer, and whispered in her ear, 'I'm so holding you to that. Lots and lots of *pògs*, Fifi.'

She grinned. 'Lots and lots. Now, off you go. You know the rules—you have to leave the house before the first strike of midnight. And everything's ready on the kitchen table.'

Of course it would be ready. Catriona would never leave a detail off her list.

When Dominic walked into the kitchen, on the table there was a coin, bread, a small jar of salt, a lump of coal, and a miniature bottle of whisky, to represent all the things they could wish for in the new year: prosperity, food, flavour, warmth and good cheer.

But the bit that Dominic was looking forward to most was claiming his kiss from the viscountess. No, not the viscountess—*his* viscountess.

He shrugged on a coat, gathered up the first-footer gifts, and strolled around the castle until the windows opened— another Scottish new year tradition—and he could hear the countdown to new year.

Once the chimes of midnight had finished, he knocked on the front door.

Catriona opened it, and he could hear everyone singing 'Auld Lang Syne' very loudly.

'Welcome,' she said.

'May this house always be warm,' he said, handing over the coal. 'May there always be food on the table.' He gave her the bread and the salt. 'May the family of this house and all visitors be blessed with good health and prosperity.' He handed over the coin and the whisky and smiled. 'And now I claim my kiss…'

* * * * *

COMING SOON!

We really hope you enjoyed reading this book.
If you're looking for more romance
be sure to head to the shops when
new books are available on

Thursday 4th January

To see which titles are coming soon, please visit

millsandboon.co.uk/nextmonth

MILLS & BOON

Introducing our newest series, Afterglow.

From showing up to glowing up, Afterglow characters are on the path to leading their best lives and finding romance along the way – with a dash of sizzling spice!

Follow characters from all walks of life as they chase their dreams and find that true love is only the beginning...

Two stories published every month. Launching January 2024

millsandboon.co.uk

MILLS & BOON®

Coming next month

PART OF HIS ROYAL WORLD
Nina Singh

'My name is Eriko Rafael Suarez. I'm the man you rescued from nearly drowning the other day.'

Her hand flew to her mouth. 'Oh! I didn't recognize you! You're so…'

He nodded. 'Yes, I imagine I looked quite different. For one, I'm a bit less unconscious now.'

As far as jokes went, it was a rather bad one. Still, the corners of her mouth lifted ever so slightly. His attention fell to her lips, full and rose pink. Her hair was a shade of red he'd be hard-pressed to describe. Arielle Stanton was a looker by half. Riko didn't know what he'd been expecting, but he hadn't been prepared for the jolt of awareness coursing through his core that hadn't relented since she'd opened her door.

'So, I don't mean to be rude. But why are you here?'

'I'm here to personally thank you. For myself and also on behalf of the king and queen.'

She gave her head a shake. 'The king and queen?'

'Of the kingdom of Versuvia. It's a small island nation a few nautical miles from Majorca to the east and the Spanish coast to the west. We're known as the Monaco of the Spanish world.'

Her brows furrowed once more. Again, she eyed him up and down. 'Right.' She dragged out the word pronouncing it as if it were three syllables. 'Listen, I don't know how to break this to you, but I think you might have suffered some type of head injury during your accident. Probably wanna get that checked out.' She began to shut the door.

'Please wait. I know it might be hard to believe, but it's the truth. I'm Eriko Rafael Suarez, heir to the Versuvian throne. Firstborn son of King Guillermo and Queen Raina. My friends call me Riko.'

She stuck her hand out. 'Pleased to meet you. I'm Arielle Trina Stanton, the duchess of Schaumburgia. Daughter of King Alfred III and Queen Tammi, MD.'

He simply stared at her, completely at a loss for words.

For the life of him, he couldn't figure out why he was still standing there. He'd felt obliged to thank her in person, and he'd done so. But something kept him planted in place where he stood, unable to walk away just yet.

Continue reading
PART OF HIS ROYAL WORLD
Nina Singh

Available next month
millsandboon.co.uk

MILLS & BOON

THE HEART OF ROMANCE

A ROMANCE FOR EVERY READER

MODERN — Prepare to be swept off your feet by sophisticated, sexy and seductive heroes, in some of the world's most glamourous and romantic locations, where power and passion collide.

HISTORICAL — Escape with historical heroes from time gone by. Whether your passion is for wicked Regency Rakes, muscled Vikings or rugged Highlanders, awaken the romance of the past.

MEDICAL — Set your pulse racing with dedicated, delectable doctors in the high-pressure world of medicine, where emotions run high and passion, comfort and love are the best medicine.

True Love — Celebrate true love with tender stories of heartfelt romance, from the rush of falling in love to the joy a new baby can bring, and a focus on the emotional heart of a relationship.

Desire — Indulge in secrets and scandal, intense drama and sizzling hot action with heroes who have it all: wealth, status, good looks... everything but the right woman.

HEROES — The excitement of a gripping thriller, with intense romance at its heart. Resourceful, true-to-life women and strong, fearless men face danger and desire - a killer combination!

To see which titles are coming soon, please visit

millsandboon.co.uk/nextmonth